BAD ALPHA

A Sweetverse Novel

KATHRYN MOON

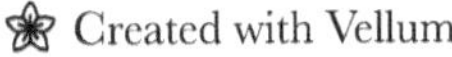 Created with Vellum

If this book inspires you to try something new
just make sure to remember:
Use lube.
Lots.

A Note on this Omegaverse

There are no shifters in this book.

Aside from the unusual human biology, this Omegaverse is not a paranormal romance. These alphas, betas, and omegas are *not* shifters. This is an alternate universe to ours, with an alternate human biology that includes animalistic traits adapted to a romance premise. There are fancy sexy bits, mating instincts, pheromones, bonding marks, growls, purrs, and whines, as well as a slight hierarchal social construct. At the most basic, alphas are considered powerful and prone to leadership and they form family packs, omegas as the precious and sexual glue that holds those packs together, and betas are the average and normal.

This book contains graphic depictions of violence, and deals lightly with themes of past trauma.

ONE

Eve

This city came with a curse, crusted in sand and perfumed with the scent of freezer-burned shrimp cocktail. It was a timeless sort of place, an ancient labyrinth without windows and clocks. We all arrived and walked willingly into the maze, volunteering ourselves for the trap. It made my skin itch. I might've been the predator inside this city, chasing blood, but I was still caught in the web like everyone else. So I chose high ground, watching the mice weave their way in circles around the flashing lights and the bait laid out to distract them.

I leaned on the railing overlooking the main floor of the Lucky Dog Lounge, my eyes tracking the patrons and employees. My mark was here, or would be soon, but I was in no rush.

Adam Robins, twenty-six, beta according to the file I'd been given, hacker. Thorn in my client's side and responsible for a cargo ship going down in the ocean with all the staff onboard now lost. His face was already in my mind, pale with a bold bone structure that refused to compromise. I traced over the cheekbones like daggers in my memory and hunted for them on the floor. I wasn't the first of my kind who'd been sent after him. He was slippery.

I shifted, twisting toward the bar, the sequined dress wrapped around me catching the golden light of the dusty chandeliers hanging halfheartedly over the casino.

I wasn't the judge and there was no jury in this world. My role was simple.

Kill Adam Robins.

Except that I did my own research for my work, and there was no cargo ship, no lost crew. And Adam Robins wasn't a beta.

The bar wasn't crowded. In fact, the entire casino had a slightly haunted quality to it, gamblers wandering with their buckets from one slot machine to another. A few stalwarts hunched by the blackjack table. It was an odd choice for Adam, too old a crowd and too faded. He would stand out here. So would I, not that it mattered.

Except when I finally found him, I realized my eyes had passed over him twice already. He was at the bar, dressed in an ill-fitting suit jacket, hair combed forward to fall into his eyes. He also had a very eager companion with him, a tall man with greased-back black hair grinning down at the young man's head, crooked teeth shifting in his smile eagerly.

I slid away from the balcony and headed for the stairs. I needed to scare this card shark off Adam now while it would be simple, or I'd have twice the mess to clean up later.

The scents were thicker on the floor, a potent and queasy blend. Fuck, management was really slacking on cleaning. This was months of pheromones and residue. Sweaty bodies streaking their marks on machines and tables and seats.

I caught the whiff of the other alpha first and swallowed my growl, savoring the sting in my throat. Sticky pancake syrup, not maple, but the kind that came in the matronly bottle. So the man chatting up my mark was an alpha. Big, ugly, too confident as he leaned in closer to Adam, a heavy arm draped over the back of the bar chair.

Adam's hand—long-fingered, elegant—reached up and ruffled through his brown strands, and my steps faltered. Sweetness filled the air, a little grassy and bitter, but not enough to stop my mouth from watering.

My eyes widened. Adam's scent was coming through strong—stronger than it should've been if he'd still been disguising himself as a beta. He was powdered sugar and vanilla and butter, his omega perfume slightly tarnished but undeniably present. I wanted to lick the flavor right off of him, like frosting off the back of a spoon. Tonight was suddenly looking like a lot more fun. If Adam wanted to attract an alpha, then he was about to hit the jackpot.

Don't play with your food, Eve, a cool voice warned, and I promptly ignored it.

The other alpha looked up as I approached, sensing my threat already. His eyes narrowed, shoulders rustling in his tacky, too tight button-down, booze gut sucking in as he straightened. *Stay away*, his body suggested.

I was all too familiar with what other alphas saw when they looked at me. A woman, pretty, slender. Seductive, yes, but easily squashed if I got any funny ideas. They were always so surprised to realize the truth. The reason I glittered was because I was formed under extreme pressure. I was a diamond and equally unbreakable.

The alpha's chest puffed as I neared, but I saw the moment Adam sensed me, goosebumps rising on the back of his neck. A rare purr, unpracticed and rough, rattled up from my throat, and the fluffy sweetness doubled in the air, overwhelming almost, as Adam twisted in his seat and caught sight of me.

Such a pretty little omega.

So had my client lied or been misled? This wasn't a beta wearing an omega's perfume. This was the real fucking deal. A male omega. A male omega alone. Without a mark on his throat—and there would be one, if he were claimed. No one would let a throat that pretty go unmarked. Unclaimed. He was approaching heat, if I were guessing based on the amount of perfume flooding the air.

My mark. My kill.

My hands tensed, eager to form fists.

Beta or not, Adam's designation didn't alter my goal for the evening, although it raised my curiosity. Why kill a male omega? I was the animal I'd been shaped into, but this lie would change what I planned to do after I was finished for the night. I refused to be manipulated, and the client would have penance to pay for trying to pull this trick.

Adam was warm at my side as I leaned against the bar, letting my hip touch his thigh where he sat. The bartender, a middle-aged beta male, glanced warily between myself and the other alpha, waiting for the tussle for the real unclaimed omega to start.

"Three doubles of vodka," I said softly to the bartender before turning a bright smile to the two men to my left.

The alpha's eyes were narrowed, but Adam's pupils were dilated as he gazed back at me. His jaw was tense, lips parted—probably to try and avoid breathing so much of our scents in—and cheeks flushed.

"For me and my new friends," I said, tipping my head slightly, dark hair sliding over my shoulder. Adam's eyes tracked the movement, his breaths growing rapid in his chest.

"I don't share, sweetheart," the alpha snarled. He had sweaty temples and had already failed to keep holding his gut in. Up close, the syrup scent had a powdery, stale quality. Adam was leaning in his direction, glancing rapidly between us.

I'd been told before my scent was uncomfortable, the warning of danger nearby, oppressive. I'd met few omegas since my childhood, but invariably they shied away, even as their perfumes bloomed. The simple truth of the matter was that an omega didn't have to like an alpha's mark in order to feel the urge to offer themselves up as a sacrifice to our hunger. Adam didn't like my scent, but his hips were sliding forward on the chair, knees spreading to make room for his arousal.

Three short glasses arrived on the sticky counter of the bar, and I passed one to each man. If this alpha didn't share, that meant he didn't have a pack to back him up.

"I think you're…kind of interrupting," Adam rasped, his throat flexing with a heavy swallow as he met my eyes. A soft shade of green, almost gray, full of the black of an omega who was about to beg.

"Oh, sugar, I am definitely interrupting," I purred, arching away from the bar toward him, grinning at the pink that darkened on his cheeks. I glanced at the alpha, my grin sharpening. "And I don't share either. The double shot is a consolation prize."

"Listen—" Adam gasped out.

"Bitch, you better—" the alpha started, a growl rising and making our mutual prey flinch.

"Shoo."

Adam jumped in his seat at my simple bark, and I settled him with a hand on his thigh, sliding it up and breathing in the fresh cloud of perfume from him as I stopped just short of his crotch.

It was the other alpha's turn to flinch. He tried to puff up, make himself larger, but we both knew the truth now. It didn't matter how big he was. If he needed me to prove to him physically that I could bring him to heel, I would, but his reaction to my bark said enough.

Very few knew what created dominance in an alpha. I had learned, one bruise, one fight, and one victory at a time. Confidence, a disregard for fear, familiarity with challenge, with winning, with setting your teeth into an opponent and proving to them that you could *kill* and they could not.

Primitive, certainly, but that was biology for you.

"If you want to argue, feel free," I said, shrugging.

Adam's loyalty was already shifting, just as his hips were scooting closer to my hand, pleading for *touch*, for my claim. I had never *fucked* a mark before finishing a job before, but it would be an absolute waste not to enjoy a male omega when I had the chance.

"I was here first," the alpha growled through gritted teeth.

"And now you're leaving." I used my bark again, the words heavy and sharp, just to remind him that whether he liked it or not, his entire body knew that it feared me.

The alpha glared down at Adam, who was staring steadfastly at the bar top, his lips folded between his teeth and the corner of his jaw ticking. The older man snarled and reached for my parting gift of vodka, slugging it back and slamming it down on the wood before turning tail and leaving.

I stroked the tense muscle of Adam's inner thigh, and then patted it, turning to my own drink. "There. Relax, sugar."

"Fuck," Adam panted, his hips lifting briefly to chase

my touch before he surged forward, grabbing up the glass and slinging back the alcohol.

So easy.

He gasped, shoulders sagging and eyes wide, turning to stare at me in shock.

"You didn't really want his knot up your ass tonight, did you?" I asked, smirking.

Adam paled a little and shook his head. "Whatever he had planned, no, I didn't want it."

"You need this one too?" I asked, inching the second glass to him.

He eyed both me and the glass warily, a slight tension appearing in his brow. "Probably," he admitted softly.

"My treat," I said, leaving a bill on the bar to cover the drinks. Out of the corner of my eye, I watched Adam drink the second glass, this time slower. "I'm assuming you're looking for company, because otherwise, you've made a very grave error in coming here tonight."

"What if it's the latter?"

His voice was light, young. He wasn't a big man, male omegas usually weren't, but I'd noted the muscle under my hand when I touched him. He was fit, not much taller than me, and probably shorter if he stood now while I was wearing heels. Handsome, certainly, but almost shy too.

"Then I would ask if you were having second thoughts and needed an escape route," I said.

"Escorted by…you? An alpha?"

I shrugged. "A female alpha."

He let out a whoosh of breath, laughter mixed with panic. "Sure. A female alpha. You scared off Tony with little effort."

"Ugh, he looked like a Tony," I said with a slight snarl.

Adam's expression brightened, and so did his scent. "Ha, yeah, he did."

I could lie to this omega, tell him he was safe with me, that I would walk him back to his hotel room and leave him at the door. That I understood what it was like trying to move through this world and not get crushed by alphas like Tony. That I was, to him, harmless.

"Would you like the truth?" I asked him.

His eyes narrowed. He was right to be suspicious. Omegas were meant to be protected, but here was one alone and unclaimed. Late in the game, if the file had at least been right about his age. He'd certainly been taught his fair share of lessons in life already. And he'd pissed off the wrong people in one way or another. Maybe he owed them money. Maybe he'd broken a rule. It wasn't my job to care. He wasn't innocent.

Adam nodded slowly, and I mimicked him, sliding closer, offering myself the spot between his legs. He didn't pull away from me this time; he'd already grown used to my oppressive scent, even if he didn't notice it happen.

"I'm going to follow you back to your hotel room," I said, and his eyes widened. "I'm going to fuck you. Lock you inside of me. Make you come until you can't think or speak or do anything but whine for more. I'm going to ride you until you can't even move, and then I'm going to keep going because I want to." Adam was panting now, perfuming, catching the attention of faces across the dismal dingy casino. He'd slid forward in his bar seat and was pressing to my hips, starting to squirm for friction.

"What if I—"

"You won't say no. You'll beg and you'll whine and you'll make the bed so wet, they'll have to flip the mattress before anyone can use the room again," I said, smiling at the thought and at the way Adam gasped, genuinely a little shocked. "But here is the thing, sugar. Here's why you'll say yes. I promise you, I won't bite."

Adam's mouth hung open a little, his eyes scanning my face, down my body. I was slim, but I was strong, muscular, and I caught him eyeing my arms. He rocked into me and let out a little whimper, eyes slamming shut briefly.

"Yes," he said.

———

THE MOTEL WAS around the corner, a shitty little building with cardboard walls and water stains and security cameras that had a layer of dust so thick on their lenses that I didn't have to worry about that loose end.

"I've been…a little low on cash recently," Adam fumbled out, hand shaking as he fit the key—an actual key—into the lock of his room.

"This is a good city to lose the last of what you do have," I said, and his shoulders sagged.

"True," he muttered out.

His scent had gone bitter again, the corrupted air of the city at night clearing his head enough for him to start second-guessing the wisdom of letting an alpha in this rat trap of his.

I scowled at the room as he opened the door.

I was not an ideal alpha. Adam was not a perfect omega. But this…this was an absolute shithole of a nest. Not unlike the casino, this motel room stank of other scents, Adam's creamy sugar almost entirely missing. The floor was dirty, the lighting was harsh and uneven, and the sound of the couple next door arguing was louder from inside than it was out.

Any omega could've done better for themselves. Picked a classier bar to hover by, and they would've had their pick of alphas tripping over each other to rent a penthouse nest or take them right home to a pack.

It was on the tip of my tongue to ask what was stopping him, curiosity burning through me, but then I turned and watched as he lit a slightly less harsh bedside lamp. I turned the overhead lighting off with a flick of my finger, and his shoulders softened.

"You hate it in here," I noted.

"I hate it everywhere," Adam muttered and then blushed.

His baggy jacket came off, and there was a soft, threadbare T-shirt on underneath, one that licked over the definition of well-maintained muscles. One of the back pockets of his jeans was ripped away, leaving a few tears—genuine wear, rather than stylish artifice. The heel of his boot flapped away from the leather. He was beautiful, disguising himself as shabby.

"Tear those blankets back and put them on the other side of the room," I said.

Adam stiffened and stared at me briefly before giving in, grimacing as he yanked the top layers of bedding off and tossed them into the corner. There, better. The mattress was a mess and the sheets were stained, but they were *clean*.

"Take off your shirt," I said, grinning as Adam's shoulders squared and his jaw ground.

He wanted to defy me, it was so obvious, trembling as he resisted the impulse, the exhale of relief as he followed my order instead. Why? Because he wanted to be fucked? Or because he was afraid of pissing me off? Neither answer felt entirely true.

"Lie down."

Adam swallowed and pressed his lips into a flat line, falling back onto the bed, his arms spread and his stare fixed up at the ceiling in annoyance.

"Good boy," I cooed, and that gaze flashed to me,

blazing and then widening as I joined him, straddling him on the bed.

I bent, and Adam stiffened, vibrating with anticipation, holding himself still in the presence of a predator. I set my hand on the bed on either side of his chest and then bent slowly. He shivered as my hair kissed his skin, slid and tickled over his ribs.

"You don't like my scent," I said, continuing when he made a sound to interrupt me, "so let's get that perfume working again."

I licked a line up his chest, bare and smooth, just a surprising happy trail around his belly button and teasing south. Adam gasped as my tongue sharpened to a point, drawing over his skin. He sighed as I moved up to his collarbone, finally going soft, perfume sweetening.

I sucked softly over his chest. That sharp grassy flavor was there on his skin, contrasting with the typical omega edible quality.

"Aren't I already a guaranteed lay?" Adam breathed. His hands slid over the coarse sheets toward my knees, cupping loosely, testing what I would allow.

"A guaranteed lay isn't necessarily a good lay." My mouth moved over to a flat nipple, and I resisted the urge to taunt him with my teeth. I wouldn't bite, of course, but it would've been funny to freak him out.

Adam groaned and arched beneath me, hands growing braver, sliding up my thighs. I laughed as they stalled, one finding an unexpected impediment. I sucked a little more as Adam felt his way around the thigh holster, freezing as his brain translated what he'd found.

I shifted up and savored the genuine terror on his face. He tried to squirm back, and I sat firmly down on him, rocking slightly and grinning as his eyes rolled back at the pressure and friction on his cock.

"Why do you—why do you have—" Adam moaned as I scratched softly over his chest, his own hand wrapped around the handle of my knife.

"Why do you think?"

His brow tensed, eyes opening again, still frightened even as he bucked his hips into mine from below. He shook his head slightly, refusing to guess.

"Take it off. You can throw it in the corner too, hmm?" It didn't matter. I didn't need a knife to kill Adam. Better it was out of his reach anyway.

"What?" Adam breathed, eyes wide and pupils dilated.

My lips twitched, teeth strangely aching in my smile, and I drew the hem of my dress up my hip. Adam's eyes flashed over my thighs, back and forth between the two, hand creeping slowly to the straps of the holster. I let out an uneven rasp of a purr as his fingertips traced the leather until he found the clasp.

It'd been a long time since I'd needed to be this close to one of my jobs. In truth, I didn't. I could've been done and on my way the moment we stepped into the motel room, if not sooner.

A male omega was a treat. One I'd never had the chance to enjoy before. It would be a shame to waste him.

His fingers fumbled, a tart edge to his scent rising between us. Another reason I didn't play with my kills— fear was an aphrodisiac to an alpha.

"Have you ever had a lock?" I asked as Adam finally took the holster off, tossing it eagerly into the corner.

I reached behind me, carefully drawing down the zipper and quietly unlatching my gun holster as well. That one I would keep a secret.

"No. Have you ever...?" Adam trailed off and swallowed hard, watching with parted lips as I pulled the dress off over my head, gun hidden in the fabric.

"I rutted an omega through her heat once," I said, arching and dropping the dress silently onto the floor at the foot of the bed. Adam was propped on his elbows, studying my body, my old scars, a new calculation in his gaze. I leaned forward, forcing him down into the sheets. "But no. We're rare aren't we, sugar?"

"You're rare," he rasped, bucking up to rub himself against me, the friction of his pants against the thin lace of my underwear drawing out another broken purr. "I'm hunted."

He was trying to burrow into the mattress at the same time his hips lifted against mine, body equally torn between escaping me and pleading for touch.

"And how do you feel about being caught?" I nipped at that pretty, cut jawline of his and pressed our skin together.

Adam whined, taut beneath me, and released a shuddering sigh. "That…depends."

I'd never been as omega-obsessed as most alphas. Adam was right—they were hunted, and that was a state I was a little too familiar with. An eager-to-please beta was plenty satisfying for fucking in my experience. But tonight was…

No. Adam was special. Not in the way alphas usually thought of omegas. He wasn't precious to me. I could lock a beta. He didn't represent a lifetime of sexual satisfaction and a soft place to land.

Adam was special because I now owned him. Every breath, I granted him. He craved and feared me, and in this moment, only I was capable of satisfying or destroying him. We both knew it. I knew it perhaps a little better than him, but he wasn't unaware of the threat I posed to his life. I could just as easily take his liberty away with an uninvited bite as I could take his life away with my gun.

"P-please," he gasped out as my nails scratched over

flat nipples, sharpened with need. I was breathing him in deeply, my mouth over his pulse, nose just below his ear. Sweat and that sugary perfume and a slightly bitter note beneath. Suppressants. Adam had come off suppressants recently—medication designed to disguise his omega designation and prevent him from going into heat.

I licked at the sweat as Adam's hands mapped my sides and then grew impatient, dipping between us to fumble with the front of his pants. Either he'd been labeled as a beta in my file because my clients were unaware of his designation, or because they assumed he'd remain on the suppressants. And if the latter—

"You're a lot more patient than I expected," Adam huffed out, shimmying beneath me.

He had nice arms, strong, and a lightly planed chest. I traced my finger over the lines of muscle on his stomach, watching them flex and jump.

A male omega. A female alpha.

Was it too convenient?

His Adonis belt leading down to his hips was beautiful, a little too pronounced. Attractive, but a sign he was underfed.

"What's your name?" he asked.

Dark curls peeked out from the parted flaps of his pants, the root of his cock just visible, red and swollen and trying to rise out of the cage of fabric.

If Adam was a trap set for me, he was poorly considered. Too nervous, not as buffed and shined as an omega ought to be, probably not perfuming as strongly as he could be. More likely, he'd just recently run out of suppressants.

"Just call me alpha when I make you come," I answered, fixing a smile back on my lips and sliding backwards, gripping the hips of his pants and pulling them with me.

Adam grunted and kicked his way out, legs parting just long enough to make room for me. I dove down, spreading his thighs apart, taking a long study of him as he squirmed. A nice thick cock, not exceptionally long, but full and swollen, already starting to drip arousal over the tip. I reached out and cupped his balls, ignoring his cock entirely. They were incredibly heavy and sensitive, and Adam bellowed as I squeezed them a little, letting out a laugh as his cock released another dribble of pre-cum as if he were a pastry bag of cream.

"Long time?" I teased.

"You have no idea," he gasped out, chest heaving and eyes fixed up at the water-stained ceiling tiles.

Omegas and alphas had similarly heightened libidos. It was part of why it was rare to find one unbonded at Adam's age. Omegas needed sex, they needed knots and locks when they were in heat, and it was hard to get that without getting the bite from the alpha along with it.

I took pity on him and helped myself to his cock, taking the fat and dripping head between my lips without warning. Adam shouted again, hips kicking, and I held still, tongue teasing with little whip licks back and forth along the bottom of his length as he fucked my mouth in short and desperate thrusts. My hand squeezed his sac again, and Adam came with a strangled whine and a rush of sticky, slippery sugar on my tongue. I sucked it down with a growl.

Well, that was an upgrade. Betas never tasted like dessert to me. I planted my hand on Adam's jumping stomach and set a slow pace on his cock. My cunt throbbed, aware that I was denying it a new treasure. But there was so much time. I hadn't lied to Adam about my plans, only failed to mention what I would do after we were done.

"Oh fuck, oh fuck, I-I-Alpha," he settled on finally in a long and beleaguered groan as I swallowed him down to his base and sucked hard for more of that sugar cookie flavor.

His hands in my hair were tentative, sliding and combing through my strands, and I was surprised not to mind the touch. He was clearly wary of being too demanding, and the first of his orgasms had taken enough of the tension out of him for him to let me hold control. My pace was slower than his, with long pauses for me to catch my breath and to clean up the overflow of cum with the tip of my tongue.

"I want your lock," he gasped out at one point, as I lifted his balls to kiss and nibble on them for a break, until he was dripping like a melting ice cream cone again. "Please, alpha. Fuck me."

My lock wanted to satisfy him, my cunt already clenching on nothing, demanding I allow both Adam and me to take what our bodies promised one another.

I ignored the demand and made him come again, this time just with my fingers looped around his width—both hands—watching as he let out quick cries, hands fisted in a pillow above his head. He painted his own stomach in splashes of that creamy sweet fluid, and I grinned. Pretty. Tense abs heaving, thighs trembling, cock still twitching and searching for my cunt.

"I think I…might be close to—" Adam's voice garbled as I started to lick his mess off his skin. Sweet and salty. His stomach flexed, and he was quiet, watching me.

"Your heat," I said, pressing my cheek briefly to his skin. He was running too hot. Feverish. And while I wasn't super familiar with male omegas, I could tell the unflagging determination of his dick to get fucked was at least a little unusual.

"Yeah," Adam said. I found his eyes on my breasts as I pushed up on my hands, his tongue flicking out to wet his lips as he stared.

I didn't usually seek much touch during sex. Just relief. I sat up on my knees and tugged my underwear down, shifting carefully out of them. Adams eyes moved eagerly between my legs, another whine falling loose, his cheeks blushing.

"I can avoid the rut."

Adam's eyes finally made it back up to my face. "What? Oh. Sure, I—Or…if you wanted…"

If I wanted, I could partner him through his heat. Give into days of sexual frenzy with a male omega. My biologically ideal fuck.

Except I couldn't. Because Adam needed to be dead by morning.

"Let's just see how tonight goes, sugar."

And to keep any more questions from falling from those lips, I set my hands on Adam's shoulders, swinging one leg over his hip and settling my sex against his cock. We were both wet, sliding easily together, and the sight of Adam's throat as his body arched, head thrown back, created a strange pang in my jaw again.

The alpha urge to bite. To claim an omega and tie them permanently to us.

Was he a trap?

"I want you," Adam gasped out, shivering beneath me, hips shifting and cock searching for a place to bury itself. "I want what you promised at the bar. Fuck me, alpha, until I can't think or—"

I pressed a hand over his lips and took his cock with the other, lining it up at my entrance and seating myself on him in one swift twist of my hips. His groan vibrated against my palm, but my own sounded loud in the room, a shocked and unfamiliar cry of relief. Adam swelled farther inside of me, kissing every sensitive nerve as I started to tighten on him.

I released his mouth only to settle my hand on his throat, the other over his heart, pinning him down and reminding him what I was. Alpha. Control.

Except this didn't feel like control. My body was rocking, riding, urgent and automatic on his length.

He came inside of me, making the movement slick, making my cunt warm and tender. His voice was thin with the pressure of my hand on his throat, rapid pleading words for more falling from his mouth. They were useless. I was giving him more. Or taking it, taking what I'd promised, but without a choice for either of us.

With every slap of our skin together, my lock started to tighten and swell around him, biting into that plush omega cock of his. He was coming in quick succession, filling me and building pressure in my core. Adam's fingers found my clit between us, clumsy but direct.

"Fuck, so good. So good, alpha. Fuck me. Lock me."

Omega begging was heady. Adam's twisted tormented expression was divine. The desperate thrash of him beneath me, trying to meet me faster, rougher, was power in itself. His scent rose up around me until my throat arched high, as if I could escape drowning in him.

A cold, cautious part of me sounded a warning in my mind but it was buried under the rhythm, the pressure, the sweetness I was dragging into me with every lungful, warm and decadent.

Adam's work on my clit succeeded at last, and I came with a snarl. I released his throat, and he let out a bright gasp as he came with me. My lock clenched, preventing any more glide and thrust, and we were tied together, Adam howling and me growling as the orgasm extended.

My fingers clawed into his shoulder, drawing him off the bed and into my chest, pulling his mouth to my breasts and guiding them to kiss and suck and bite as I rocked on his lap, drawing out the locking, the pleasure. It burst, warm and bright and sweet, over and over, rising higher in me with every strike, up into my chest, my throat, clouding my head.

"Yes, alpha, fuck me. Please. Please. Bite me, alpha," Adam gasped.

I snarled and fisted a hand in his hair, yanking his head back to nip and suck on his throat. It was normal for an omega in heat to blindly beg for a bite.

"Bite me. Please, fuck, bite me. Bite me, alpha."

I growled at the offer and tackled Adam back down into the sheets, which had started to bunch and pull away from the corners. My movements were animal, graceless, thrusting and grinding myself into him, into the flares of heat that exploded where we were joined. In spite of my lock, our release was starting to splash between us, running out of room inside of me.

"Bite me."

I ignored the words. I fucked Adam until he was limp, his throat and jaw and chest red from my teeth and lips and tongue.

"Bite me."

My body was sore but mindless, there was still more to take with him tied inside of me.

"Bite me."

Every breath was sweet. Adam's pulse pounded loud in my own head. His blood was high on his throat, drawn out from brutal kisses, so near to the surface I could almost taste it, the metal a sharp relief from the constant sugar.

Adam's hands were weak and trembling in my hair, holding me to his neck. "Bite. Please, bite."

His pulse was hard on my tongue.

His skin was thin under my teeth.

His blood was hot in my throat as I swallowed it down, satisfied at last, exhausted even. He flexed against my lips as he sighed.

Exhaustion and wary relief lured us into darkness.

TWO

Adam

I t was like getting hit by a truck if a truck left a funny tingle in your toes and a satisfying jello sensation in your legs and a burning in your throat and an oddly sharp and metallic scent at the end of your nose.

Wait.

My eyes opened, and I stiffened at the sight of a cool black muzzle of a pistol pointed in my face.

Oh, that was what she smelled like. I hadn't been able to place it the night before, but it was the scent of a freshly fired gun, mixed with enough smoke to make me want to cough.

I swallowed and winced, the bite on my throat throbbing with the motion. On the other side of the gun, the alpha—my alpha, I thought wryly—glared at my bite mark. Her bite mark. Our bondmark.

A bond which was suspiciously…quiet. Had it not worked? I wasn't sure if I was relieved or terrified at the thought.

"I wasn't sure it was you," I said. My voice was ragged from begging the night before. What felt like hours of asking for the bite, of staying conscious, only to plead in the hope I might catch her teeth in the frenzy. The bite throbbed and stung and burnt on my neck, a not entirely welcome victory.

"If what was…" Her lips shut, and she studied me with those incredible cat eyes of hers. "You knew they sent someone after you."

I nodded slowly, the tip of my nose barely grazing the mouth of the gun. She was even more stunning by daylight with that black sheet of hair gleaming, features that only gave away hints—light brown skin, a hint of freckles over her almost hawkish nose, full lips that had wrapped beautifully around my cock now hardened to a firm line. And those eyes, warm and dark in color and as cold as the end of her gun in mood.

"Don't tell me you thought it was Tony," she said. There was the first, faint whisper of a foreign emotion in me, but it was so…cryptic and muffled, I couldn't decipher it. At least it meant there was a bond.

Best case worst case scenario achieved—I was bonded to the alpha hired to kill me. Bonded, but maybe not safe?

"I…" I was too busy analyzing the new connection to know how to answer. And a little too distracted by the gun in my face. I'd been ogling this alpha's arms the night before, and they were every bit as strong as they appeared. She didn't waver even a little. "Are you going to finish the job?"

"I haven't even started the job."

I swallowed again, nodded, though I didn't know why.

"It won't take long when I do," she said, and my heart stopped, sank. So that was it. Last chance, failed. "If I do."

A wild sudden storm swept through me, laughter or sobbing rising up in my throat and strangling me.

"Anything I can do to…help the decision-making process?"

I was naked, sore, and satisfied like never before, freshly bitten and bonded, staring down the muzzle of a gun at one of the most beautiful people I'd ever seen. I wasn't dead yet. There was still hope.

"Is your heat really starting?"

"I ran out of suppressants," I said, mentally adding, *intentionally*. "Unless I can find some, my heat's coming in hard."

She pressed her lips together. Lips that had swallowed my cock down like there was a prize at the base. That had ignored the impulse of biting until I was hoarse with begging.

"Was this really your best plan?" she asked, head tipping.

"I'm not stupid. I can't keep slipping out of these traps. This was my last plan," I admitted. She didn't seem like the kind of person I could pull a full con on. I'd seen her considering the position the night before, I'd nearly lost then and there. "I have one good tool, and I used it."

Helpless omega, begging for an alpha to take care of them. Except…I wasn't begging, was I? Maybe I should've been. Pride had been an issue for me for…a long time. Too long.

My alpha, whose name I didn't even know, remained silent. It was still dark outside of the curtains, although a little brighter than it'd been when we arrived. Dawn was coming. The motel was quiet. A shot would be loud, but I had no doubt this woman would get away fine. The same would not be said for me.

I tried to dig for her in the bond, impatient to know my fate, but what I found reminded me strangely of a ticking clock, a sort of steady and mechanical pattern tapping back at me.

Tony, for all his grease and grabby hands and sour breath, would've been a better mark. I bet it wouldn't have taken nearly as long to convince him to bite me either. Maybe not even the whole two syllables. Instead, I had just barely secured myself an alpha whose mind resembled a machine.

"Dress."

It took me a moment of just staring at the space in front of my nose, now visible without the gun, to process the order.

She was up off the bed, naked except for the knife holster on her thigh and a gun holster around her ribs. She'd put her weapons on but not her clothes. She moved with a total lack of vulnerability.

"Dress or I shoot you on my way out," she said.

I jerked up, ignoring the way all my limbs now resembled the structural integrity of cooked noodles, and scrambled for my clothes.

Not dead yet. Surprisingly, not dead.

"Yes, alpha," I gasped out, my voice choking at the sudden and brief slam of anger in the bond.

"Eve."

I blinked, my T-shirt on over my unbitten side, my pants halfway up my legs.

"Eve," I repeated, and she only stared at me, the reflection of her back in the mirror, fingers zipping up her dress, hiding the gun holster under sequins.

Eve. Oh no.

Eve.

Adam and...Eve. A nervous bark of laughter burst from me.

"You have less than a minute to finish dressing and

grab what you need. No cell phone. No laptop… No electronics," she said, moving toward the door.

I didn't answer, just finished scrambling into my clothes and diving toward the closet. The only electronic I had was a burner phone running out of minutes anyway. I'd been doing my best to hide already.

I grabbed my bag, a beat-up old denim army sack that was starting to split along the seam, and met Eve by the door. She smelled like me. Hell, I probably smelled like her too.

I'd scented alpha cards years ago, before my younger sister Faith had come into her perfume too, and preferred the milder tones. But this alpha, with her sharp edges and heat and nose-burning smoke? I never would've chosen her out of a binder.

My new bondmark throbbed as I shrugged on my jacket, and Eve ripped my bag out of my hand, rifling through it, expression blank.

"I don't have anything," I assured her, but she kept digging. "Look, I don't want them to find me either."

She stopped at last, although it probably had more to do with her being satisfied I wasn't hiding anything other than my promise.

"Stay here by the door. I'll find us a car."

"You don't have one?" I asked, an unexpected tremor of panic shooting through me as she reached for the door handle.

"I had one. I had a hotel room too. More guns. Tech." She glared at me out of the corner of her eye, and I stiffened at a new drumbeat of anger from her. "They're useless now, sugar."

I took a breath, but she was out the door before I could think of what to say.

Good work, Adam. You've secured an alpha who terrifies you and pissed her off in the process.

But I wasn't dead yet. That was the miracle. And if I could just keep being not dead…

The door swung open again, nearly hitting me in the face.

"Move," Eve ordered, grabbing me by the wrist and dragging me out of the motel room.

There was an old, unremarkable, brown Chrysler idling at the curb, and Eve urged me toward the passenger side before sliding into the driver's seat. I looked farther down the row of cars, spotting a sports car that looked less like it was a pothole away from something falling out of the engine, and the passenger door hit me roughly against my hip.

"If you want to have the police tailing you in under an hour, be my guest. This car wouldn't start and was left here two days ago."

"If it's broken how are we—"

"It was just a wet distributor. I fixed it. Get in, Adam," she barked.

My bite throbbed again, and I all but dove into the passenger seat, throwing my bag over the bench and into the back. Eve pulled the car out of the spot before I'd finished closing the door.

"Where are we going?" I asked.

Silence.

"Do we…have a plan?" I tried again.

Eve looked strange in the driver's seat. Like a high fashion model in some kind of incongruous photoshoot. Her scent was sharp and filling the car quickly, less of the rough smoke and more of the metal warning.

"Why did you decide not to—"

Her hand reached out, and I flinched, but she only moved it to the dials of the radio, turning it on blindly.

To static.

We were at the south end of the city and she was driving us north into the heart when I was sure we should've been getting the hell out. But considering she'd chosen loud, abrasive static on the radio over my questions, I decided it was time for a little more preservation and a little less talking.

The car smelled stale, but mild, like a beta. I wished I'd thought to grab the sheets off the bed. I wished I'd conned an alpha to bite me who would've thought of it. The car was small, but it was getting bright out and I hadn't lied to Eve. Without my suppressants, my heat was coming on fast. Her locking me had helped, but it was probably only a matter of hours before I needed it all over again.

Against my better sense, I found myself speaking again. "We don't have long."

Eve's jaw ticked, and her eyes flicked to my neck. To her bite.

"I know. Pick music."

I let out a small sigh. It was the tiniest, weakest consolation prize, but it was something. I turned the dials slowly until I found the first notes of a Sam Cooke song and then sank back into my seat and watched the city grow taller around me.

———

I DREAMT OF HER LOCK, the incredible squeeze and swelling of her on my cock, rubbing against the most sensitive nerves on my length—the magic combination of female alpha and male omega. Of sweat sticking our skin together and our scents clashing. Of Eve spreading me out under the high sun and riding me in full view of a crowd of alphas, ones waiting for their own turn.

I woke with her hand around my cock and let out a thin moan.

"Quiet," she said in a soft bark, and I bit down hard on my lips, my eyes flicking rapidly.

We were in the desert, parked at the far end of a rest stop, the sun blazing through the windshield to beat down on us both as Eve jerked me off, my cum pooling over her twisting and stroking fist.

"Fuck," I gasped out as she squeezed the tip. "Fuck, what are—Unngh!"

I came, and her hand paused, eyes narrowing on me. "Another?"

There were people out, walking in and out of the rest stop, but they weren't looking our way and we were far from any other cars. And my cock was throbbing. My bite too. My heart pounding.

"Another," I rasped, eyes slamming shut as Eve's hand began to move again, stroking up and down, squeezing roughly. Demanding my next orgasm.

"No lock."

I nodded rapidly. No, she couldn't lock me here.

"You were whining," she said. Her voice was so clinical in contrast to the determined and possessive stroke of her hand. I wished she'd put her mouth on me. Anywhere.

"My bite hurts," I whispered.

For a moment, there was no answer, and I peeked out a glance to find her gazing warily around the parking lot. It was weird, wrong, abrupt, but in a way, she was doing what she could for me.

"Twist toward me."

My hips bucked eagerly into her fist, and I twisted. Eve arched into me, and with the first graze of her lips over my mark, I came again.

"Another," I whined immediately. "Please, please, I'll be fast."

Eve's mouth latched onto her bite, tongue soothing rapidly over the swollen, stinging mark, and I nearly reached for her without thinking, determined to get back inside of her where my body wholeheartedly believed it belonged in the moment.

She didn't lick gently the way an alpha was supposed to, and a couple times her teeth actually grazed as if she were about to bite again, but still, there was relief, less burning after so many hours untended.

I came faster than I wanted. Her hand was tight and efficient, and her tongue on my mark was aggressively thorough. I opened my lips to beg again but she was already pulling away, and my mouth went dry at the sight of her hand absolutely dripping with my cum. She licked a line up the back of it and started pulling the car out of the parking lot, humming and going back for more.

She'd sucked me practically empty the night before. Well, no, but it'd certainly felt like it at the time.

"We left the city," I said.

"You fell asleep."

"Which…which way are we going?" Silence again. I held back my sigh. "We don't have any food."

"We'll have to wait until we stop. I can pull over if you need to piss, but the fewer faces we meet, the better."

I nodded and thought I caught the slightest fraction of her face relaxing at my acceptance.

Suddenly, words struck me. Ones I probably should've said hours ago.

"Thank you."

The tension returned to her expression, and she offered no answer.

THREE

Eve

"Where are we going?"

I swallowed my growl and then thought better of it and released the sound, watching with the smallest amount of satisfaction as the omega in the backseat flinched. Adam had retreated there when I'd refused to stop for sex again, and if he thought it was bad to be trapped in the car during his heat, I would've loved for him to try being an alpha listening to an omega in heat whine and moan and fill the tiny space with the scent of his release.

My omega, I thought, head tipping in consideration of the concept.

I wasn't quite sold on the idea. Every minute that I kept him, kept driving, kept not killing Adam, was adding the potential risk to myself.

"Look, I can tell you don't know, okay?" Adam snapped, and I glanced back up to the rearview mirror. "We were going east, then north, now south again. Are we being followed?"

"Maybe," I said, and Adam paled. He'd taken his shirt

off, and his pants were still unbuttoned. He'd been making obscene—obscenely tempting—sounds behind me for over an hour.

"Really?"

"No one who hires multiple hitmen to take someone out is going to give up just because one of them runs off with the mark," I said, shrugging.

"So we're just driving?" Adam asked, sinking back against the leather bench seat in the back, pushing sweaty strands of hair out of his face. "You're almost out of cash for gas. We haven't eaten. And I dunno if you can tell, but my heat—"

"I can tell."

It was getting dark. Unfortunately, Adam was right—I didn't know where I was going. What he hadn't appeared to realize yet was that I hadn't totally made my mind up on whether or not I was going to keep him safe.

I was stalling. It was…annoying.

"Eve—"

"Why don't we go back to the part where you were saying thank you," I snapped.

Adam's jaw shut with an audible click, and I admired the tic of muscle flexing in the mirror. He didn't repeat the sentiment, which was fine. He was quiet again, and I was driving.

"If we stop at a gas station, I can do a quick-change scam. Get us another couple twenties," Adam said.

"You reek of sex. Of omega," I reminded him. "You have a fresh bite mark on your throat."

He huffed and rolled his eyes up for a moment, thinking. "Fine, so…so you come in with me. We're new bondmates on our way home from the city? We'll fluster the beta clerk. Get some food, some gas, and enough money for somewhere to sleep tonight."

I could just as easily walk in, knock the clerk unconscious, take the entire till and whatever Adam wanted to eat, and leave again.

But his version was less likely to involve a review of the security footage.

"I will position us carefully to avoid faces on the camera," I said.

Adam filled the bond with relief and even excitement, and I steeled my expression. This was, by far, the worst part of the bond. Constant assault of overwhelming emotion—fear, anger, shame, lust for hours until I couldn't think straight, satisfaction. On repeat. At least this new glimmer of anticipation, triumph, was original.

"You're a con artist," I said, nodding. "I should've realized. I did, actually, I just…"

"Underestimated me because I'm an omega," Adam said, leaning forward, his bare arms crossed over the back of the bench, chin propped there. He was warm and stressed, but still rich with sweetness.

"I underestimated you because you were frightened. Shabby," I added. A pinch of offense reached me and I was perversely pleased to have injured him. "Oh, I'm sorry. Did I offend you? The omega who used perfume and whines to lure me into a lifelong commitment."

Shock. More of that sharp hurt. Shame.

"Am I meant to feel grateful, Adam? How lucky of me, the rare female alpha, to find an omega willing to stoop to my bite. And to put me in the uncomfortable position of pissing off my clients at the same time. Fool's gold lottery."

Adam slid to the far corner of the backseat in silence, a queasy mix of emotions in his quiet that it was easier to block out than sort through.

"We'll find a gas station in the next ten minutes. Explain the con to me," I said.

Adam stared out the window as I drove, licking his wounds. Or considering mine for what they were worth, I didn't care. Eventually, he answered.

"We confuse them. It'll be better if they seem young or new. Night shift often are. We make a small purchase and pay with a large bill, then offer to correct ourselves by paying with a smaller bill, then tell them that we overpaid, we give another small bill and ask for them to correct our change. You have a hundred so we should get forty bucks out of it, maybe sixty. Adding the gas into the mix might help the confusion."

"You handle the cash," I said, nodding.

"And you overwhelm the cashier," Adam agreed quietly, eyeing me carefully. "Make it seem like you're about to rut me at the counter, and I'll do my best to milk out the twenties."

"Smart."

As fast as his anger and shame had risen, pride came next.

"I'm good at what I do," he said blithely.

"Oh, I know," I answered in a growl.

———

"BABY, NOT HERE," Adam gasped out, hips bucking into my palm, my fingers wrapped around the base of his cock as the young cashier—new to the register, lucky us—stared on in a near panic.

I licked a stripe over Adam's bite and winked at the red-faced cashier while Adam panted.

"Oh! Uh, um, I think. I think I accidentally overpaid you," Adam gritted out, sighing as I stilled my touch in his pants but not my mouth on his bite.

"Uh, sure, um—"

"Here's another three dollars and if you, mmmm, fuck, Ee—baby," Adam corrected, bucking into my hand again, coming in his jeans. I chuckled against his bite. That was mostly an accident.

"You owe us sixty," I said, drawing my hand free and licking it while holding eye contact with the cashier. "Not including the thirty we paid you in gas."

Three twenties slapped down on the counter, and Adam gathered up our snacks in his arms, rushing for the door.

"Have a nice night," I cooed at the cashier, before following my omega out.

"Sixty, plus gas? If he thinks that through, at *all*—" Adam hissed at me as I joined him at the car.

I pointed toward the station where the attendant was hurrying toward the restrooms. "The only thing he's going to be thinking about for the next few minutes are us and his fist."

Adam blushed and ducked into the backseat as I went to fill the tank. The driver side window rolled down with a squeak, and his head peeked out. "And the cameras?"

"We're fine."

He'd forgotten about being mad at me, I could tell. He was all bubbly in the bond again. He'd been like that after I'd gotten him off at the parking lot too, although not when he'd managed himself in the backseat.

Because you're his alpha, I told myself. Maybe it was my tending the bite more than the orgasm? It was starting to heal a little.

"And we'll find somewhere to sleep tonight?" he asked. "Or just drive?"

"I'm locking you tonight unless you object," I said. The gas stopped pumping at twenty dollars, but that was fine. We'd flustered that cashier enough, I wasn't surprised.

I tried to tamp down my smile as Adam filled the bond with a ridiculous, giddy thrill. He did not object.

"I can't do another day of driving with you creaming the cushions," I said.

And instead of shame, Adam just laughed. "I dunno. At least it's starting to smell like a nest in here. It'd be better if you got off too though."

It certainly fucking would. And yet…

I shut down my mind for a moment, closed my end of the bond, stilled everything inside of me until the cool, steady center returned to my head. Adam was clever, but messy. Emotional. Incredible amounts of trouble.

I would lock him tonight for relief, and in the hopes that tomorrow's travels would be less tense and distracting. I was not making him a nest, I was not caring for his heat, I was not being this omega's bondmate, bite or not. Lock or not.

"Orange or apple?" Adam asked, shaking the two bottles of juice I'd grabbed.

"Orange," I said, shooing him away from the door. I'd had enough of temptation.

"I love apple, so it works out perfectly."

I rolled my eyes at him, ignoring his grin, and started the car.

———

ADAM'S FINGER traced a circle over my rib, and I considered batting his hand away. My lock was fastened securely around his cock, but it would loosen soon and let us drift apart unless I decided I wanted more. Or he got too annoying and I needed to shut him up.

"Is this place yours? It doesn't smell like you. It doesn't smell like anyone."

"It belongs to someone I trust," I lied. It was a property of mine, a small cabin in the south, off the grid and out of cell service. There was no nest, but Adam seemed content with the bedroom, which was really only big enough for the full bed and the closet anyway.

Adam hummed and arched his throat, hissing with the stretch. "Can't believe you bit me again. You know you only need to do it once?"

I did know that, reasonably, but my hindbrain liked the way Adam's skin looked freshly bleeding from my teeth. And he deserved it. Little shit wanted my bite so bad, he'd fucking get it.

I licked the mark, so close to the first one it overlapped slightly, and Adam softened and stretched even further for me, his arms looping around my back loosely. It was confining, but only gently so, and I ignored the irritation as Adam started to rock a little beneath me.

"Can we stay here tomorrow?" Adam asked on a sigh.

There was food in the kitchen. The cabin was listed under an alias. The only thing we could be traced by was the car, which really wasn't up to another day of driving anyway.

"We could just fuck all day long." Adam groaned, starting to thrust as I continued to lap and mouth at my bites. "Have I mentioned I'm really good at eating pussy?"

I blinked. He had not.

"You're such a trap," I growled, riding with him, pushing up on my hands to glare down at him.

"I know." Adam's cheeks were flushed, just a darker shade of gray blue in the room, only moonlight to see by. "I am, but I promise to be a well-laid trap." He waggled his eyebrows and stopped moving at the joke.

I barked out a laugh and ignored the triumph and humor in the bond from him. "The well-laid part is up to me," I said, rising up into my seat on his cock, fucking him properly and watching him writhe.

"Please, Eve," he gasped out. "One day. One day, two nights, and then we can drive circles around the country again if you want."

I did not want. I wasn't sure what I did want, but the temporary solution he was offering was certainly appealing. Rutting the young female omega years ago had been fun but exhausting and nothing compared to the perfect indulgence of locking Adam.

"We're at least sleeping in," I decided, planting my hands on Adam's sweaty chest and grinding harder. He wasn't listening, just panting and bucking and whining with pleasure. "I'll decide the rest tomorrow. After you make good on the pussy eating."

"Unnghh, fuck yes!"

I closed my eyes and chased my next release, ignoring the man with his hips kicking up between my thighs.

———

ADAM ALMOST GOT HIS WISH.

We spent most of the next day locked—that was, when I wasn't taking Adam up on his offer to eat me out like an omega possessed with satisfying his alpha. It was almost offensive how good he was at eating pussy. Skilled. Practiced. *"Only on betas,"* he'd promised me with a shy grin. Was that grin a con too?

I closed my eyes at the next flare of lust in the bond and stood straight, whipping my wet hair over my shoulder to glare at Adam behind me.

He raised his hands at his sides, cheeks red. "I can't help it."

I'd been bent over, rinsing myself off with the garden

hose, because the cabin's shower was an outdoor one and the tank was full of pollen and bugs at the moment. I turned the hose on Adam, and he yelped as the cold spray hit him square in the crotch.

"Mercy!"

"Just testing to see what kills an omega libido," I said, trying not to laugh as he danced in place. His body was beautiful. Lithe and muscular, with a perky ass I was sure I'd end up biting if we spent another minute in bed together.

"Basically nothing." Adam grinned at me as he backed out of the water's reach. "Not during a heat at least."

Adam's good mood was burrowing through me but sitting uncomfortably, too much sugar in burnt black coffee.

He stretched, and I turned away from the sight, finishing my wash in peace and without the buffet of lean muscle taunting me.

"How long can we stay?" he asked.

I opened my mouth to tell him we'd spend another night—maybe more, although my instincts told me to keep running until a better answer arrived—when a soft beeping sounded from inside the cabin.

I dropped the hose, water rushing through leaves and underbrush, and reached out to grip my hand around Adam's upper arm.

"What's that?"

"An alarm. Get inside."

Adam stumbled as I shoved him toward the narrow screen door at the back of the cabin, following close at his heels.

"Is it your friend?" Adam asked, the first hint of suspicion in the bond as he twisted out of my grip to look back at me. "The one who owns this place?"

"Would you like to find out while we're both naked?" I asked, seizing his arm again and dragging him inside with me.

Since there was no friend, I knew the real answer to his question. Perhaps Adam did too.

"How could they find us, Eve?"

"Nothing is untraceable." An unfortunate truth. I made it hard enough for potential clients to track me down, but I wasn't going to lie to myself and pretend I was a ghost. The best way of staying out of trouble was to do the jobs I was hired for, not bring them home with me like a cat with a mouse in its mouth.

I spared Adam one glance, enough to see him hunting for his clothes on the bedroom floor, before digging for a spare outfit of my own. Sequin club dresses weren't really the thing in the middle of nowhere. Adam's back was turned to me, making it easy to pull the small stash of weapons out of a cabinet, pulling them on in their holsters as if they were just another garment.

I positioned myself by one of the small cabin windows, keeping an eye on Adam and watching the long dirt road through the woods. At the first glimpse of a black SUV moving through the trees, my lips flattened. But by the time I saw the third vehicle, I'd locked everything down, including my expression.

"Spare one for me?" Adam's voice was soft, his eyes on the gun holster now fastened to my hips, another pistol in my hand.

Tires sounded over gravel, our visitors growing closer.

"If I'm dead, you're certainly dead," I said, tightening my grip around the handle of the gun, wondering if Adam was determined enough to challenge me for a weapon. "Stay inside, and let me deal with them."

Adam's gaze flicked to the windows, eyes widening briefly and feet stepping back toward the bedroom.

"Adam," I soothed, drawing his gaze again, lowering the walls in the bond to share my confidence with him, my determination.

He didn't relax, but hope rose in him, thick and bright and sugary sweet. He swallowed hard, throat flexing, and nodded.

A car door sounded outside, and I turned and crossed the small room with two steps before the men in the vehicles could surround the cabin.

"Stay away from the backdoor," I called to Adam gently.

"Be careful," he answered.

Outside, dappled by sunlight through the leaves of the woods and leaning against the hood of the stolen Chrysler, was Cedric Wicks. I'd never met him, although he'd hired me on behalf of the Epsilon Shipping figureheads. These men did their research on me, and I did mine on them.

Cedric Wicks was a forty-six-year-old beta, fond of tanning, sexually assaulting strippers, and beta on omega porn, specifically ones where the omegas were begging for a knot and being left unsatisfied. He had an offshore account whose contents fluctuated regularly and two ex-packs he'd been excused from.

He was a prick, basically.

"I thought you'd be taller," he called.

I eyed the cars. They'd come with four men per vehicle and an arsenal in each, no doubt. If they were going to let me pick them off one by one, we wouldn't have an issue, but even if I took care of Cedric straight away, eleven armed men was a stretch for me.

"You gave me the wrong information," I answered back.

Cedric scoffed, but his gaze kept flicking toward the car closest to him, like he was waiting for backup or to make sure he had a clear shot if he needed to run from me.

"Are you sentimental? Didn't seem the type. Why should the designation make a difference?"

"Everything makes a difference, that's why I ask for briefs."

Cedric nodded at the car, his eyes fixed to me, and I expected the men to step out, but instead the windows only rolled down, music pouring out of all three cars at a moderate volume.

Disguising our conversation from Adam's ears.

I walked slowly forward, away from the cabin and toward Cedric.

"I assume he's inside," Cedric said, turned in profile, perhaps to hide his words from Adam that way too. I only blinked, and Cedric huffed out a laugh. He was trying to look ten years younger with that tan and those bleached tips, and instead only managing the opposite. "Come on, killer," he said in a tone that set my teeth on edge. "You really want a little omega at home? I mean, if you promised to keep him out of our hair, we might be able to work something out, but…I think we both know the truth. You'd get bored of that kid faster than it would take him to find an upgrade."

I arched an eyebrow. An upgrade on a female alpha in her prime was unlikely. But Cedric was right about one thing—I didn't want a bondmate. I didn't trust this pretty creature who lied to stay alive and needed constant attention. Even if I did trust him, I wouldn't want Adam in the wings as I worked jobs. He was bubbling over with feelings constantly, and while omega heats only came every three months, it was still a disruption, although a fun one.

"We're prepared to see this out, no matter what you

answer," Cedric said, sliding on a pair of sunglasses. Probably a cue to prepare the men in the cars. "But you have an option. You let us take the omega, you get fifty percent of your agreed asking price. You did the hard part of catching him, after all. We'll let the issue of who carried the job out go this time."

Absurd. That was an idiotic offer. Those men should've been storming out of those cars, shooting me down, and taking Adam at no cost. I would kill some of them in that scenario, certainly. Cedric absolutely.

Adam might get away. He had so far.

They wanted him *badly* to offer this.

They wanted him.

And I…didn't.

"Sounds like he's yours," I said, catching the way Cedric's face froze at my announcement. "I'll walk around to the back, you can take the front. Good?"

There must've been a million questions on Cedric's tongue with how he twitched. Was I really just going to hand over an omega to these alphas? After I'd taken the trouble of leaving town with him when I was meant to kill him?

"G-good," Cedric managed.

I nodded, heading for the cabin, moving around the side to head for the backdoor. My gun was out in my hands, held steady in front of me.

Adam was there on the other side of the screen, lips parted and eyes wide, head turning back and forth over his shoulder.

"What happened? What do we do? Eve?"

I stared up at him, wondering what had possessed me to take him in the first place, and if I would be disappointed at his loss. Was it the taste of his blood on my tongue? His cock fastened inside of me, swelling and nuzzling against every nerve? His flushed cheeks and furrowed brow as he begged?

The front door opened, and Adam's face fell in horror at the echo of boots on hardwood floors.

"No," he breathed to me. "But you…saved me?"

"I borrowed you," I corrected, blinking at him, watching the massive shadows of the suited thugs crowding his back. "Sorry, sugar."

FOUR

Adam

I t was so stupid, but…I kept searching for some glimpse of her in the bond.

"Can't believe she fuckin' bit him and handed him over."

"She's crazy," the leader said, shrugging. He twisted in the passenger seat and grinned at me. "Isn't she crazy? Bet she fucked you good though. Consider it like a last meal, except it's a lay."

He waited for me to answer some way, but my mouth was sealed with duct tape, and anyway he was a prick, so I just stared down at my bound hands and ankles.

Had she tricked them? Tricked me too, to keep from alerting them that she had a plan? Except we'd left the dirt road a few miles back, and every passing second made it seem less and less likely that Eve had any intention of rescuing me. And yet…I kept trying to find a hint of her, as if there might be a clue about her intentions, when she'd barely given me any sliver of her emotions before now.

Face it, I told myself, eerily calm. *She took you for a ride, just like she said she would.*

Usually, I was the one running the con. Maybe this was karma.

Maybe this was *all* karma.

I'd been trying to do some good in the world for people like me, but I'd taunted predators bigger than me and pulled their focus in my own direction. And what had I actually accomplished?

I'd fucked up a few shipments of omegas for Omikron, and now my head was on the chopping block. And Faith… I tried not to think about what would happen to Faith, if it hadn't already.

"Guess he doesn't think it's funny," the burly beta at my side declared.

The orange boss in the front grunted and turned to face the road. At least they'd put me in a car with only betas. Or maybe it would've been better if I were surrounded by alphas. I had Eve's bites throbbing on my neck, and to some extent, I must've smelled like her too now, but still, I was an omega in heat. I should've been able to turn a few alpha heads.

Not that it had lasted long with Eve.

Her face on the other end of a gun for the second time in as many days, staring at me with that hard, examining look, beautiful and impenetrable. She said 'sorry' like she'd just accidentally bumped into me on the sidewalk, not like she knew she was handing me over to my death.

Unless they'd made new plans for me.

"Boss, we've got someone coming up fast on our—"

Bang!

I twisted in the seat at the same time all the other men did, seeing nothing but the car behind us for a long moment until…

Smoke in the air, and mechanical parts scattered over the road. It was a narrow little thing, littered with potholes and barren of any landmarks or homes, only wide enough for—

A motor revved, and the brakes of the SUV behind us screeched as a small motorbike rushed toward us, ridden by a slim figure dressed head to toe in black. The muzzle of a gun appeared out of one car window but the biker was faster, one shot fired back before they whizzed around the back of the vehicle and headed over to the driver's side.

"Pull over!" the beta in charge of our car barked.

It was the wrong move. The biker shot through the window to the driver of the second SUV and then tossed something inside. I threw myself down on the floor between the seats as the men around me bellowed and tires screeched. A heartbeat later—one with my cheeks stretched beneath the tape in a grin, with my chest throbbing with excitement, swelling with hope—another explosion sounded, throwing our car forward and up off its back tires.

I'd just barely fit myself under the long backseat, only enough to keep from pitching me around the car like the others, although every bit of me banged and smacked against the seats and the floor. A gun fired inside the vehicle, men shouting orders to one another, and another fell loose from a holster, sliding below my hands.

I didn't know if we were still moving. I didn't know where Eve was—it had to be her, even without so much as a fucking hint in our new bond—but I fumbled for the gun with my bound hands. An automatic with a familiar structure and not impossible to manage, tied as I was. I fired at the nearest body, one of my beta guards, and then again, a bullet skidding off the ceiling when my arms jumped with the kickback.

Other gunshots cracked until everything was a roar of sound and my ears rang like sirens.

"Hold!"

An alpha bark, seizing my muscles with the order.

There was a yelp from the front of the car and then two shots. The driver scrambled out of the window, and I held my breath at the grunts, the boots scuffing over pavement. My back was sweating…or was it bleeding? My neck was burning, and the SUV was growing hot. Were we on fire?!

Bang! Bang!

It took me a moment of bright, high-pitched nothing, to realize that the two betas in the backseat were dead. One by my gunshot, the other by the strange angle of his neck as he hung upside down from his seatbelt.

Bang!

I jumped at the noise and flinched from the sudden blaze of fire coming from the half opened trunk behind me.

"Get out quickly, Adam."

Eve stood, ignoring the inferno from the two SUVs positioned at odd angles on the tiny country road. She had the visor of her helmet up, eyes tracking the surrounding area, and it took me a moment of simply staring.

She'd come.

"Did you break anything?" she asked, blinking at me and then leaning forward.

I shook my head and flinched as she pulled a knife from her pocket, but she used it on tape around my ankles. My entire body could've been shattered, and I wasn't sure my brain would've been able to translate the pain in that moment.

A hand, gloved in black leather with a smear of blood over the bare knuckles, reached into the trunk and grabbed onto my wrists, yanking me out of the back of the car. Another ripped the tape off my face.

"Did you know you'd come for me?" I asked, my voice hoarse and the world sitting at some unexplainable angle.

"No," Eve said, pulling me away from the fires, from the bodies, the whole scene. Her bike was lying on the side of the road, but it didn't look damaged. Just resting. Waiting for us. "I didn't. But you did."

"I hoped," I corrected. I shouldn't have been so relieved to hear her tell me the truth, that she had every intention of handing me over and leaving it that way.

Eve stared over my shoulder and I considered looking back, but I was almost afraid of seeing what she'd done, alone on a bike with a gun. What she was capable of.

"Mm. Hope feels funny," she said, raising the hand not holding my wrists up to rest on her chest for a beat. She blinked and turned back to me, cutting my hands free before taking off the helmet and passing it to me. "Let's go. We have a long ride."

There was blood splattered on her face, her throat. There probably was on mine too, and she looked no more moved by the sight of me before her now than she did pointing a gun at my head. A part of me was screaming in my head to *run*, that any option would be better than this alpha.

We had biology and a bite connecting us. Nothing else.

And then her words turned over in my head.

"You have a plan," I said.

"I do."

I pulled the helmet on and twisted to show Eve my back. "Am I bleeding?"

"Not badly. It can wait."

I would have to take her word for it. She lifted the motorcycle up from the side of the road and shared a little of her impatience in the bond to urge me on. She was slim between my thighs but steady as she folded my hands over her stomach.

Today is just one more day you're not dead, I reminded myself. It was a small reassurance, but it would have to do.

———

EVE DROVE us to a garage on the shitty end of a halfway sizeable city after a painfully long stretch on the bike. We sat outside for a moment in full view of a security camera until I started to twitch with nerves.

The man who finally raised the garage door was ancient, bent over a cane and looking spectacularly unsteady as he wobbled away from the open door to make room for Eve to walk the bike inside. She turned the engine off and tossed him the keys.

"Hot?" he asked.

I was stiff, stuck in place on the seat, but Eve climbed off as if we'd only been joyriding, combing her fingers through the stray hairs that had escaped her long braid.

"No, but people will be looking for it. I'm not sure it's worth the hassle, so I brought you presents instead." She turned and rolled her eyes at me, helping drag me off the seat so she could dig inside.

I couldn't tell what everything was. Money. A bottle of whiskey that I was sure was rare, and something that resembled playing cards.

The old man chuckled and slapped his knee, plaid suspenders almost sliding off one bony shoulder. "Fuck it. What do you want?"

"The red Charger, if you have it," she answered.

It took me a moment to place what was happening inside of me, the kind of spiky and almost playful sensation, a kitten's claws as it pricked over your lap in pleasure.

So this was what Eve felt like when she actually *liked* someone.

I stretched my sore muscles and ignored the offended burn in my chest to know I'd never so much as neared that warmth with her. She flashed a glare over her shoulder in response.

"Oh, she's here. I knew you'd ask for her one day, but… are you sure it's time?" the old man asked.

I wanted to decipher all the little meanings of the words, but I didn't know enough about Eve. Hell, I didn't know enough about cars, for that matter.

"It might be the last time I can ask," Eve said.

Guilt. That was new too. She definitely hadn't been feeling that when she'd handed me over…temporarily.

The old man just chuckled. "If you say so, kiddo."

Eve avoided my gaze completely, even as I pushed my curiosity through the bond to her. I'd always been too inquisitive. It usually got me into trouble, increasingly dangerous as I grew older. And now here I was, bonded to an alpha that kept changing her mind on whether or not she wanted to keep me.

"Do you have anything in his size?" Eve asked the old man, nodding in my direction.

The old man's head tilted, and he studied me head to toe as I tried to hold my tongue and keep the questions from pouring out. Who was he to Eve? Why was the car important to her?

"I expect so," the old man said with a slow nod. "Check the lockers, yours is in the usual."

Eve reached back without looking, snagging a finger into my bloodstained sleeve and leading me through the garage to a small doorway. It led to a backroom lined with rusted lockers, a few hanging open and stuffed with shabby suitcases and duffle bags.

"There's a shower just back there," Eve said, nudging me toward a dark corner behind a brick wall. "I'll find some clothes for you. We can't stay too long."

"What is this place, and who is he?" I whispered, glancing toward the open door. I could just make out the figure of the man puttering around in the garage.

"He's retired," Eve said, going to a locker and spinning the dial on the lock to open it, drawing out a bag so stuffed, she had to wrestle it out of the locker.

"From…what you do?"

Eve ignored the question. "Take a shower."

"Take it with me?" I tried. Not that sex had successfully endeared my alpha to me yet, but I'd been itchy for the last hour of the drive anyway, the unresolved heat still coursing through me.

"No time. Do what you need to."

My jaw ground briefly, frustration and exhaustion rising hot in my veins with the need of the heat. A low growl sounded softly in the dim room, and I shivered, backing a few inches away from Eve at the warning sound.

"I'll explain more in the car," she said, eyeing me out of the corner of her narrowed gaze. "But we aren't doing my friend any favors by lingering."

The shower was nicer than it looked, steaming hot and good water pressure. I bit my lip as I jerked myself off, biting down the whines in my throat that wanted to call to my alpha. It was perfunctory and made me feel even filthier than before, blood and cum rinsing down the drain together.

I shivered under the warm water, and then the shiver grew strong, my shoulders shaking and hands clenching against the tiled wall, chest heaving as I gasped for air.

Oh, I was crying. And as soon as I realized that, the sobs came faster, hard, swallowed and bitten behind sealed lips. I'd been crying a lot lately, panic attacks sneaking up on me in the slow moments. I tensed, scratching my nails against the tile, clenching my whole body down on the trembling, the teary hiccups, burying the feeling.

It wasn't over. I wasn't done, which meant I wasn't allowed to crash yet. Weeks of running, hiding as a beta, out of communication with anyone, had resulted in one last-ditch effort to stay alive. Go off suppressants for the first time in almost a decade. Hook an alpha.

"Alphas can't all be bad, right?" Faith whispered, bundled up in the window seat of the bus. It was the dead of night, and most of the other passengers were either asleep or trying to be. We had to keep our voices extra low for privacy.

I glanced over my shoulder, but there wasn't an alpha on board with us. I'd made sure there wouldn't be before we boarded. I was just paranoid.

"No, and when you're ready, you're gonna end up landing the sweetest, most protective, most ridiculously wealthy, most caring pack around," I answered back, wrapping an arm over Faith's shoulder.

"What about you, though?" Faith asked, looking up at me, dark eyes clear on mine, probably seeing more than I wanted her to. As usual.

I wrinkled my nose and flinched, shrugging one shoulder. "Maybe I'll just stay like this," I whispered. "If you've got a pack and I have one too, we won't see each other as much. Maybe I'm just your beta brother, hm?"

"Maybe we both stay like this," Faith suggested. "Maybe I won't ever hit heat."

I squeezed my eyes shut hard and lifted my face into the drum of the water, letting it bruise my tender eyes, wash away tears, as I struggled to get control of my breathing again. I had an alpha now, one who'd decided *not* to let me die, at least for a little while longer. Which meant I still had time to find Faith.

And if it's too late?

I pushed the thought down with the memories of my younger sister. Faith was alive. I would find her. I would keep her safe.

The pieces *had* to fit. And until they did, I had to keep my shit together.

When I finally made it out of the shower, Eve was gone with my clothes, and a new pile waited for me on top of a filing cabinet. Baggy gray sweatpants, a black tank, and a dark red hoodie that was worn soft and smelled of Eve.

Eve's friend was missing, but there was a blood and wine vintage sports car purring in the open doorway, and I could just make out the shadow of my alpha in the driver's side. The car was glossy and powerful, with an aggressive front end and sleek back. I winced as Eve flashed the orangey headlights at me and hurried for the passenger door. Our bags were in the backseat, piled together, and it looked like there were some extra cases. Maybe some of the tech and guns Eve had left behind.

"What happened to being discreet?" I asked, lowering myself into the front seat.

"This isn't stolen, and it can't be traced back to me," Eve answered with a shrug. "So flash is fine. Anyway, we might need it for later. Buckle up."

The interior was updated, all black and chrome, and I sighed as I buckled my seatbelt and sank back into the seat. "We're not saying goodbye to your friend?"

"I did already," Eve murmured, pulling out of the garage. "You don't need to worry about him. He won't tell anyone we were here."

I opened my mouth and found myself about to say the strangest thing. *I trust you.* But that wasn't actually true, so I shut it again.

FIVE

Adam

"**Y**ou're not asking questions."

I was trembling in my seat, the high of my last orgasm rushing through me, my cock exposed to cool night air flowing in from the crack of the car window. I blinked, gasping for breath, and Eve sat up from where she'd been bent over my lap, wiping the corner of her mouth with the tip of her finger and then sucking on it. My cock jumped at the sight, and I raised a shaking hand to stuff myself back into my sweatpants before I could beg Eve for more.

"How do you expect me to even think when you do that?" I asked, smiling a little. My delight when Eve's lips curled up too was absurd. I didn't even really like her. Stupid heat and hindbrain making me crave her approval. Stupid need for survival requiring that I need her at all.

"You've been quiet since we left the garage," she said, delivering one of her arch looks out of the corners of her eyes. How she could express so much without even looking directly at me was beyond me.

"I didn't really think you liked it when I asked a lot of questions," I admitted.

She smirked again, turning the key in the ignition and studying the mirrors before pulling the car out of the overlook and back onto the road. It was the dead of night, and we were traveling slowly through the mountains, beautiful scenery fashioned into ominous and towering shadows around the car, flashes of eyes in the night and glimpses of a milky moon through the clouds.

The steady thrum of the engine reminded me of an alpha's purr, a proper one, and the vibration of the car around me left me on edge for most of the drive so far, but it was also comforting. Serene almost. Enough so that if I just kept my eyes watching the road, watching Eve, I could forget about how my day had started.

"That's true," Eve said eventually. "I'll trade you an answer for an answer."

My palms began to sweat with nerves. I might be curious, but I guarded my own secrets like treasure.

"Why is there a target on your back?"

"You don't ask the people who hire you why they want someone killed?"

"Sometimes. Sometimes I do my research, sometimes I ask. Sometimes a client makes it clear that it's my job to stay out of things. I know when to push...usually," she said with a frown. The lights of the dash glowed silver on her skin, and I scooted nearer across the bench seat. She had a hand on the gearshift and one on the steering wheel, and I wasn't sure if I was disappointed she couldn't touch me or relieved.

Eve was patient as I thought, weighing my answers. I could give dozens of reasons, all true. Would one be enough, or would I have to spill the entire story?

Eventually, if you want her help.

"Who hired you?" I asked.

Eve snorted. "Does that question mean there might be *multiple* parties who want you dead?" I just stared at her. "Fine, but you owe me an extra answer. An alpha named Warwick Booth."

I swallowed hard. Warwick certainly had it out for me, since I'd stolen the omega he'd paid for out from under his nose. But he was barely a third of the way up the chain.

"In your research, did you find anything called Omikron?" I asked.

Eve's hand flexed on the wheel as she turned us around a tight corner on a mountain road, the car coasting downhill. "An investment company."

"Something like that. Omikron does invest under dozens of LLCs. They also provide benefits to those who work with them." Eve's head tilted in my direction as I spoke. She was calm in the bond, which made it slightly easier to tell her these facts. I wished she were more open, giving me something to trust, but I'd used vulnerability to spin cons in the past and I knew that openness was no guarantee of honesty. "The majority of Omikron's money comes from an omega trafficking system. Usually over international borders."

"How do you know this?"

Did you know this? Do you care? I wondered. "My sister and I went into the foster system as teenagers, and we ended up low on Omikron's food chain. Omegas have to be put into omega only homes, and not all of them are run by well-intentioned people. Some are connected to Omikron."

Eve nodded. "I know of…versions of this," she said carefully.

I bit my tongue before I could ask her for more. "Before I came of age, I ran away with Faith. The beta woman running the house kept taking pictures of us in swimsuits. I broke into her computer and found the emails she sent with those photos. It was like we were an item in a catalog."

Eve's expression was flat, and if it weren't for the edgy tension in the bond, I would've assumed she didn't care.

"So I figured out how to buy suppressants off the record and we ran, and...I should've let it lie, just get us to safety."

"The Omega Center?"

"The Omega Center just wants us to bond alphas, find our way into little pack families," I spat, and then stalled at the note of humor coming from Eve. "Wha—Oh, well, you were... I mean, I..."

"I was your last resort," Eve finished for me, without any feeling to the words.

"Faith's heat hasn't hit yet. It's late, she's only a few years younger than me. I don't know if it's because we've been running since she was fifteen, if she felt more stress than she let on. Or the suppressants, maybe. I thought we could stay on them until she was ready. I wanted to make sure she was safe, and she...she wanted to help the others."

"Others deserve the same chance as us. We have to do something, Adam." Faith eyes wide on mine, hands squeezing so tight, it hurt my fingers. "I'm not ready to stop fighting."

"Others?"

I shook myself and turned back to Eve. "The omegas, the ones Omikron was trafficking. We interrupted a few of their shipments. They actually ship us like animals in crates, drugged to sleep. That's literally what we are to these fuckers!" Eve's expression was impassive, and I cleared my throat. "Anyway. One night, we followed a lead to another shipment, but it wasn't omegas and there was security where there wasn't supposed to be and—" My tongue tangled, and my lungs seized, refusing to let another word out.

Eve drove to a stop sign and the car idled for a moment before her hand settled on my thigh. "They have your sister."

It wasn't a question, and for a moment I thought Eve had already known. She was staring out into the dark, at the shadow of a deer passing through the trees across the road.

"They set up a trap. I thought she was right behind me," I whispered, the picture embedded in my vision. *Faith's hair slipping out from under the beanie, her eyes on the darkness around us as we ran. She was right behind me, running with me, the shouts of men at our back, I had her hand in mine until I was opening a gate, and then—*

And then suddenly, she wasn't there.

"If I'd even seen who grabbed her. Where they'd gone…" The tears I'd buried in the garage's shower rose up again, and I shook my head.

The truth was, sometimes I wondered if I'd given up looking too fast, if that small part of me that would do anything to survive had told me to turn around and keep running.

"I see." Eve turned, and I blinked at the cold absence of her hand leaving my thigh. The car turned onto a new road, and I realized that our exchange, answer for answer, had more or less dissolved. But still, Eve owed me.

"I'm not giving up," I said, turning to stare at my alpha as she drove. "I'm going to find Faith."

Eve nodded, and a thread of calm glowed in its slow travel through me, like a peace offering.

"Where are we going?" I asked, the confessions draining me physically, leaving me sagging in the passenger seat.

Eve blinked and glanced at me briefly. "We're going to cash in a favor. And make a bit of a trade. And…Adam, I didn't know about Omikron."

"Good."

Eve smiled slightly at my answer. "They're after us both now."

Which meant it was as much self-preservation for Eve to deal with them as it was protecting me. If that was what she was offering.

"What will we do?" I asked, relieved when she didn't correct the use of us together.

"Find safety. Eliminate the threat," she said. I held my breath, even though I wanted to scream my question at her. I didn't have to. "Find your sister."

A whine whooshed out of me and I twisted on the bench, crowding Eve and pressing my face into her shoulder to let out a groan of relief. She tensed but she didn't shrug me off, and for the first time, there was a note of comfort to her scent. I wasn't sure if it was changing or I was just growing used to it, but I took deep lungfuls of her, letting the bite burn through my stress.

"Settle down, sleep, we have a long drive still," she said, and I let my brain pretend there was a hint of tenderness in her tone, or at least in the words.

"I can drive some if you need a break," I offered.

"I'll manage."

There were dark circles under her eyes, and she hadn't taken a shower at the garage like I had. We'd barely slept at her cabin, and she'd been awake in the motel before I was too.

"I'm used to it," she said, answering the question I didn't ask.

"How did you get into…your line of work?" I tried,

studying the delicate lines of her profile. There was a faint scar around her jawline.

"Go to sleep, Adam," she said.

I was too pleased that she'd agreed to help me find Faith to care that I was cut off from questions again. I scooted back on the bench, but only so I could lie down, finding a spot for my head on Eve's lap without asking. Her scent surrounded me like this, making the heat antsy for relief and the crotch of my sweatpants a little tight. I rubbed over my cock and then flinched at a sharp pinch on my ear.

"Stop that," Eve snapped.

I laughed and closed my eyes, tempted to tease her by jerking off like this, but I didn't have a death wish.

Quite the opposite. I knew I was always a little too desperate to survive.

———

I WOKE with Eve's fingers in my hair, the car idling and the sound of traffic surrounding us—honks, exhaust, engines rumbling. My neck and shoulders ached from the shitty position. I was sweaty, and my cock was throbbing. Eve's scent had grown overpowering, but so had mine and we were basically amplifying one another's arousal at this point.

I rolled carefully to face the back of the seat, burrowing my face into Eve's lap for a moment, moaning at the heady flavor of her just *nearly* on my tongue. The fingers in my hair tightened and drew me back, and I bucked my hips into nothing, panting up at my alpha.

We were in some kind of tunnel, and Eve pulled the car a few feet forward before stopping again and glaring down at me.

"Please," I whined, even though I knew it was a useless request. We were surrounded. She needed both hands and a foot to drive us safely.

"Sugar," Eve growled, fingers twisting my strands and making me hiss with the strange pleasure-pain of the sting. "Be. Good."

"I wanna be anything but good when you say that," I admitted, laughing and squirming until Eve let me roll over again and sit up. "Where are we?"

"On our way into the city."

I blinked as the first glimpse of the familiar skyline appeared out of the tunnel mouth as we pulled forward again. We'd made it all the way across the country. Downtown rose up in spiky towers and glittering glass windows ahead of us.

"Are you sure it's safe *here*?" I asked. "There are definitely Omikron members in the city."

"There's anonymity too," Eve answered. "I killed twelve of their people, Adam. I'm not taking you back to their nest."

I let out a thin sigh and nodded. That had to be true. Eve seemed crazy but not stupid.

Maybe not even crazy, I thought, glancing between her and the view ahead of us. Eve was…untamed.

"You don't have a pack, do you?" I asked.

"I like alphas about as much as you do," she said.

So she'd been living on her own. A feral alpha. No wonder I'd been able to talk her into biting me. My hand raised, and I winced as I touched my marks on my throat. They were still tender, yesterday's stress had just put it to the back of my mind. I needed to break my heat properly, and I needed Eve to heal her marks.

"So who's the favor coming from?" I asked.

Eve's eyes rolled. "You'll see. And let's hope they have breakfast."

I agreed. Eve had grabbed a bag of snacks from the garage—what didn't that old man have ready in a go bag—but we'd burned through them during the night and I was a little sick of eating out of plastic bags.

The drive through the city was long, and more than once, I thought we must've reached our destination, only to realize that Eve was taking us on a circuitous route, including finding shortcuts through alleys and parking lots. When we passed the financial district and then ritzy condos and old apartment complexes, until we were passing open greens and vast brick homes, I gawked out the window.

When we pulled up in front of a massive, modern, gated home with great greenery in the enormous reflective windows, I only stared.

"Not what you were expecting?" Eve teased.

"I was thinking another place like the garage," I admitted, unable to tear my eyes off the home.

"Keep your head down as we go to the door. I don't want to be caught by the security tapes," Eve said, her own gaze narrowed on the front door.

"Should I…wait in the car?"

Eve shook her head and then turned the car off and let herself out, already on the sidewalk before I hurried out to follow her. I pulled the hood up and lowered my head as Eve deftly entered a keycode on the front gate and then headed for the steps with me close at her heels. I expected her to open the door with the same confidence she had with the gate, but instead, she stopped and found a simple round bell, pressing it once.

"Are they…not home?" I asked, fidgeting at Eve's back. This had to be like…a mafia home or something, right?

"It's a big house," Eve said lightly, waiting in perfect stillness.

A moment later, there was a soft feminine call from inside. "Coming."

Whatever I'd expected, it wasn't who answered. She was young, close to my age, with streaks of peach in her blonde hair. She was barefoot in a pair of cutoff shorts and a men's dress shirt large enough to slide over her slightly rounded stomach. Her knuckles went white around the door as she took in Eve, grey eyes widening and full lips parting on a gasp.

"You!"

"Hello, Lola," Eve said, grinning like a cat who'd just run into her favorite mouse.

SIX

Eve

L ola Barnes acted as the alarm system, and a moment later, two alphas were charging down the stairs.

"Sweetheart? Who is it, what's—"

Wes Pike, the massive alpha who'd hired me over a year ago to protect his beta from another alpha stalking her, bristled at the sight of me, teeth bared in a snarl. I reached back and wrapped my hand around Adam's wrist before he could hurry back to the safety of the car.

"What the *fuck* do you think you're doing here?" Pike snarled at me.

"I need your help," I said, glancing as the next alpha— older and more refined but with a powerful presence— appeared to draw Lola back to his chest. She went willingly, relaxing into him. Good, I'd always wondered how long they would keep her happy, but she seemed settled.

Adam's hand freed itself only to tangle his fingers with mine, reminding me of my purpose here. I'd thought it would be easy to give Adam up, or at least easier than trying to keep him safe. Instead, I'd discovered that the bond from him was impossible to ignore and, even stranger, Adam had some bizarre and misplaced *belief* in me. No one had expected good from me, for me to be the hero rather than the villain, in a very long time.

"We need your help," I corrected, stepping to the side to reveal my omega.

Lola's eyebrows bounced and the other alpha—Matthieu Segal, the one who'd paid for my services in taking out Lola's piece of shit tormentor—studied Adam, but Pike only snarled at me.

"Get the fuck out of my—"

"Wes," Lola said gently, settling an arm at his elbow.

He seemed to shrink, just a small fraction, but he didn't take his eyes off of me.

"Let them come in," Lola said. "It's not a trap, right?"

She was too sweet, although there was a challenge in her stare as she asked me the question.

"It's not a trap," I said, dipping my head to her.

"Better inside than at the front door," Matthieu said to Wes.

"Go make sure the others stay upstairs," Lola murmured to Matthieu, who suddenly looked disturbed at the suggestion of leaving her. She added in a whisper, "Rake's not going to want another omega near us right now, and I don't think it's a good idea for the whole pack to sit around growling together."

Matthieu and Wes exchanged a long glance before Matthieu nodded and headed for the stairs after a kiss to the crown of his bondmate's head.

"You're not an omega," Adam blurted out as Wes moved aside just enough for us to step in, rumbling under his breath in warning at me.

Lola raised a hand unconsciously to her throat, touching on the bite marks shining on her skin as she stared at Adam's. "No. Those look like they hurt. I can get you…something."

"Lola," Wes huffed.

I twisted to stare at Adam, his own hand trying to hide the irritated marks I'd left on him.

"I'm fine," Adam said with a skittish glance in my direction.

The marks needed care. Adam needed care. He was an omega, and care was…not my strong suit. But that was why I was here, wasn't it? I'd given into that strange pride at his hope, his *need* for me to rescue him, and now I had to make sure we both made it out of this alive. Adam required protection and, for whatever reason, I wanted to…not fail him in this.

"Follow me, we'll use the ground floor nest. Rake never goes in there," Lola murmured, leading the way with a tug on her alpha's hand.

Wes held his ground for a moment, Adam and I left pressed in a corner by the front door, before he finally relented, backing up under Lola's guidance and keeping his eyes on me.

"She's not armed," Adam told him softly.

"Of course I am."

"Of course she is," Wes said at the same moment I spoke.

The ground floor nest was a small room hidden behind a bookshelf that swung out. It was lined with plush, rounded furniture, and had one small high window frosted to allow light in but no view. Adam and I stalled outside of the room as Lola and Wes entered. The omega might not use the room regularly, but traces of his scent lingered, spiking anxiety from Adam in the bond.

I reached up and cupped my hand over his marks, letting my touch do the unconscious work of calming him.

"Get in and tell us what you want so you can leave again," Wes barked.

Adam jumped, and I let out a low snarl, guiding my omega into the cramped space, placing Adam in an armchair between me and the door and helping myself to a seat on the arm.

"We need security. I would've thought that was obvious," I said, my eye on the door. "My omega is halfway in heat and we have…very persistent men in pursuit of us."

"And whose fault is that?" Wes growled. Lola was curled on the couch at his side, leaning into him and keeping him on a short leash of reassurance with her hand passing up and down his arm. It was as obvious to her as it was to me that no matter how much her alpha wanted to leap across the small gap and attack me, he wouldn't let a hair on her head be harmed in the crossfire. Good. She was in good hands after all.

"It's mine, actually," Adam said. There was a nervous little catch in his voice, and he shrank slightly as Matthieu reappeared in the doorway.

My own hackles rose at our exit being blocked, but a moment later the older man joined Lola on the couch.

"Eve saved me," Adam continued, and I fought for control of my own expression. "She was hired to kill me and instead she—"

"Bit you," Wes snapped.

"I asked her to!"

"Enough," I said to Adam, slightly embarrassed by his version of events. He and I both knew I was not his hero on a white horse. I was a reluctant life buoy, if anything. "Your pack owes me."

Matthieu scoffed. "You were compensated!"

I shrugged. "I have expenses like anything else."

Lola's lips twitched. "I don't mean to sound ungrateful,

but you came in at the eleventh hour. Indy was almost in police custody."

"Indy almost attacked your alpha," I countered. "And did you really want him in jail for fifteen years and then out again after nursing the grudge?"

Adam's gaze was bouncing between all of us. In all honesty, I'd only hesitated taking out my mark that day to see what Lola would do when forced to confront him. And she'd been magnificent in her fury.

"The fact remains, we don't *owe* you," Matthieu said in his clipped authoritative tone that set my teeth on edge. He might not be an aggressive alpha, but he was the kind with an ego that allowed him to make decisions outside of his jurisdiction. "If you've dragged your problems to our doorstep, don't think we'll hesitate to—"

"Turn an omega over to the police? One who is being hunted for trying to put an end to omega trafficking?" I asked with a tilt of my head.

"Ah, so you're a saint now?" Matthieu asked with an eye roll.

But Wes Pike leaned forward. "Tell me."

The room was quiet for a moment as Matthieu gaped at Wes, and I tapped Adam's shoulder, lifting my brows briefly to encourage him.

"Are you sure?" Adam whispered.

I wanted to laugh. Wes Pike was the kind of alpha Adam should've gone looking for in the first place, not me. He was irritatingly disciplined and moral. I nodded to Adam, and he let out a slow breath before sharing the same information he'd offered me on our drive.

Matthieu looked appalled, Lola paled, but Wes…he stiffened in an almost predatory manner and soaked up every word that came from Adam.

"What is it?" Lola asked him as Adam finished.

Wes' jaw ticked, and he glared at me, at my omega, before letting out a rush of breath. "Omikron came up briefly when we were digging into Indy and the Hangmen."

Lola's eyes widened, but her shoulders squared too and she held Wes' gaze until he continued. She was strong these days—the best evidence that I'd been right in not interfering with her bonds in this pack.

"It was like a breadcrumb trail that didn't go anywhere. But there was a transaction from them to the Hangmen. I wouldn't have said it was enough for omegas, but…"

"Betas," Lola breathed, eyes falling shut briefly, both her alphas leaning closer to her, passing hands and kisses over her.

Adam showed no signs of shock, but he watched the trio with a curious fascination. Was he surprised to see a beta so adored by alphas, or just attracted to the mix of them?

Wes cleared his throat, an arm over Lola's shoulder, and faced us again. "I have a safe house I can lend you."

"I want men too," I said. And weapons, but I probably couldn't push Wes Pike that far so soon.

"You're… I'm not assigning anyone," Wes said firmly.

"I'll pay."

"You're a hitwoman!"

"I'm aware of my profession, thank you."

"The risk is insane," Wes snapped. "And to be perfectly honest, I don't think I have betas who are qualified at the level you need—"

"Alphas then," I said, hoping it wasn't obvious how easily I was guiding him into the corner I'd planned on the drive.

"Is that wise? You just said your omega is practically in heat," Matthieu said.

Lola's eyes narrowed on me, and I wanted to grin back at her. She was smarter than her alphas. Or understood me better. But she stared at Adam for a long moment and didn't speak up.

"I'll do what is necessary to keep Adam safe." I ignored Adam's obvious surprise in the bond and added to Wes, "And I'm sure you trust your men."

Wes rubbed a palm over his face, sagging back into the couch. "You'll pay them, *if* they agree. I make no guarantees aside from the safe house, okay? And they arrive *after* the heat."

If the alphas didn't agree to the job when Wes offered it to them, I would persuade them myself. But I'd try it the subtle way first.

"Agreed," I said, glancing down as Adam's hand linked with mine and squeezed, that bubbling hope distracting me from my calculations.

"Good. Now *please*, get out."

He followed us out, giving me the address and key code to the apartment in the heart of the city through gritted teeth. The lock on the front door beeped as Adam and I stepped back out into the glare of the day.

"I thought the French one called the police on us. They still might," Adam whispered, hurrying down the steps with me to the car.

"Not that pack. They're do-gooders," I said, wrinkling my nose and glancing back over my shoulder.

Lola was in the staircase window, arms crossed over her chest, Wes at her back.

"I know I was telling the truth, but I couldn't help the feeling that you were playing a con," Adam said as I turned to the road again.

I laughed at that. "The whole thing went surprisingly well. I thought I'd have to throw the car in as a bribe."

"You know, if you are running a con, it's always better to clue in your partner," Adam said, blinking as I opened the passenger door for him.

He slid into the seat, and I leaned down until we were nose to nose. The car smelled like us, and it was a relief after the mix of pack scents in Lola's house.

"What makes you think you're not my mark, sugar?"

Adam huffed and rolled his eyes, and I shut the door, heading for the driver's seat. I closed my eyes briefly as I moved around the back of the car, my fingertips following the line of the body. I'd learned how to organize my head, my body's reactions to stimulus, years and years ago. Adam's bond disrupted my system, but it didn't derail it. I placed him in a new corner, far away from my own emotions, and built up what was between the two.

We had somewhere safe to crash now that couldn't be traced back to me. I had leverage to use Wes Pike as a resource in protecting myself against Omikron. And if everything continued to go according to plan, I'd have a pack to tend my omega.

SEVEN

Adam

____

The safe house was a small midtown apartment in a building with good security and shitty water pressure. There was no nest for an omega, but there was a small bedroom with blackout curtains. The whole place—tiny and efficient as it was—smelled vaguely of stale cigarettes, and I couldn't tell if it was coming through the vents. There was some canned soup and fruit in a cupboard, as well as cheap coffee.

I stood, staring down into the unfamiliar contents of the bag Eve had grabbed for me at the garage, and thought wistfully of the pack house we'd just left. I'd never been an omega who looked forward to shacking up with a pack, but after months of running and taking a chance on small cons to pay for motel rooms, was a good Japanese soaking tub so much to ask for?

"Adam."

I flinched at the sound of her voice, sliding into the bedroom through the cracked door. My moods were swinging wildly too, probably from the heat.

"I could've told that pack you bonded me against my will."

"You could have," Eve agreed, her shadow rising on the wall in front of me.

"They would've arrested you—"

Eve scoffed. "Tried, maybe."

"And sheltered me."

"Mm. For a bit. They have an omega. But I'm sure they would've fed you. Found you somewhere to stay. Taken you to an Omega Center," Eve said. "Why didn't you do that?"

"I didn't think of it," I muttered, yanking my T-shirt off over my head.

It was half the truth. I'd been too busy *defending my alpha*, instinctive and stupid at the growl of another alpha against Eve.

"The tub is finally filled. No glitter bath bombs," Eve quipped, and I shot her a glare over her shoulder, frustrated with the way my arousal spiked at her narrowed eyes and soft smirk. "But I squirted some shampoo and swished it around for bubbles."

And even though I knew it was the barest offering, my hindbrain still preened at the marginally thoughtful gesture.

"Is it hot?" I asked, flushing at the prissy question.

"Scorching," Eve said.

I sighed and nodded. My whole body ached from the car ride and the suppressed heat urges. The bath could melt me like candle wax, and I'd be grateful for it.

"How long will we stay here? When can we find Faith?" I asked, shucking off my sweatpants.

Eve was leaning against the doorframe watching me, and I wanted to scream at her for not sharing so much as a whisper of what she was thinking in the bond. "We need to break your heat before we can do anything else," she said.

My cock appreciated the sentiment, but my reason did not. "Do you even care about that bit, or are we just here so you don't have to deal with Omikron wanting your head on a platter for helping me?"

"I don't particularly care about your sister, no," Eve said, shrugging as my jaw dropped. "I told you we would try to find her and we will, and no, I won't drag that out. But we have no resources right now, so unless you'd like for me to swing by the public library and—"

I rolled my eyes and pushed past Eve, ducking out into the main living room briefly and then into the bathroom. It was clean at least, and small, and Eve *had* put bubbles in the bath water. I hated how much that pleased me.

"But I don't know your sister, and she's not the only omega in danger. So while I am not personally invested in her safety, I respect that you are," Eve continued.

I tried to growl at her as she followed me into the bathroom, but when she shut the door behind her and it was only us in the small and dimly lit space, I relaxed on instinct. And since that was really fucking irritating too, I kept my back to her and splashed my way into the water, hissing as the temperature razed my bare skin.

"I knew omegas were petulant, but I hadn't seen it on you yet," Eve said conversationally, undressing in front of me as I tried and failed not to watch.

I almost wished I'd gone with Tony the alpha in that grubby casino bar after all. Maybe he would've bitten me too, maybe not. But it was easier to be disgusted by him. There was lots to hate about Eve, but physically…

The only despicable thing about her was how fucking hard she made me pretty much anytime she moved. Or made a sound. Or looked at me out of the corner of her eyes like she was doing now while stepping out of her jeans.

"The front desk will order food for us."

"We don't have money." Fuck. I *was* being petulant.

"We do since the garage. Scoot forward."

I gazed up at her for a long moment, at the lean lines of muscle and the curve of her waist, the weight of her breasts, the tip of her eyes as she waited for me to move. I had the chance to rid myself of Eve, and I hadn't taken it. She'd had the chance and changed her mind. We'd chosen each other in a way, maybe in an even more honest way than if I'd picked her scent out of a binder, not that I ever would have.

I bent my knees and slid forward, the water sloshing higher as Eve helped herself to the space behind me. It hadn't even occurred to me to tell her to leave me alone. Not that I would've expected her to listen.

Eve's legs curled around my waist and over my thighs, her hands grasping my shoulders and drawing me back into her chest. I sighed and closed my eyes, just trying to savor the closeness for a small and simple comfort. A moment later, fingers tightened in my hair, making me gasp and open my eyes. Eve's other hand made a perfunctory trip down my abs, finding and claiming my cock as I let out a yelp—some combination of shock and relief.

"Fuck. You don't bother with much foreplay, do you?"

In my imagination, Eve would've asked 'Do you want me to?' but instead, she just said, "No," and then latched her mouth onto the bite marks on my throat, sucking and lashing her tongue over them. My cock grew so hard so quickly as I tensed and whined, I thought it might just give up on me entirely. But no, not while Eve was fisting and pumping me like my life depended on an immediate orgasm.

Do you want to be seduced, or do you want to be fucked within an inch of your sanity? I asked myself, since Eve wouldn't.

It was hard to come up with the answer, not when there was a direct line between Eve's bites pounding all the way down to where she fucked me roughly with her tight grip.

Both would've been nice, but going stupid with orgasms was a good start. I sagged in Eve's embrace, and she purred briefly against my throat, tongue licking at the bites like I was an ice cream cone. I focused on staying relaxed, extending the dizzy chaos of her determination to get me off, my entire body pulsing with pleasure, the rhythms not quite in tune with each other and better off for it.

"I want enough carbs to feed a small army," I rasped, forcing my hips to stay still. Eve didn't need my help, she was doing more than fine on her own, the up-down-twist motion of her hand on my length torturously precise, my balls already starting to tighten in warning. "And a steak so bloody, it could almost get up and walk away."

Eve chuckled at that, and the vibration made my whole body kick in response, a surprise orgasm running through me like a sudden lightning strike. I yelped as my foot lashed out and hit the faucet, but Eve only continued her work and I shuddered through the oversensitivity until I was limp and panting again.

"How many times do you want to come like this before I lock you?" Eve asked, the question bald in contrast to the slow release and squeeze pattern she'd started on the head of my cock.

"I want your lock now," I moaned, turning my face

away from hers, only to discover that the bathroom mirror was tilted down enough for me to see us pictured there.

Eve licked a stripe over my marks. "How many times?"

I whined and rocked into her touch, the head of my cock appearing in the bubbles and then vanishing over and over again.

"Eve, please."

"Omega," Eve cooed, nipping my earlobe.

Fuck this alpha. But mainly, fuck me.

"Three, at least once with your mouth," I gasped out.

"Very good, sugar. Now put your feet up on the ledge. I want to watch you paint your belly."

I moaned at the order but obeyed immediately, the hand in my hair releasing for Eve to wrap her arm around my chest and help me float on the surface. My eyes drifted back to the mirror, and I found Eve's gaze there, her smile amused as my mouth hung open, and I released a long groan.

My cock was red and swollen, cradled in her firm grip. Eve's hair was hanging down from a loose ponytail, the ends floating amongst the bubbles. She scratched her nails lightly over my chest, tweaking a nipple briefly and squeezing firmly at the base of my cock. I gasped and my thighs trembled, but I couldn't tear my eyes off our reflection in the mirror. As strange as my position was, as tense as our connection was, the sight of Eve touching me was undeniably intoxicating.

"You're beautiful," I whispered, a guttural groan following as Eve created a pulsating pressure around my base, close to the excruciating relief of her lock fastening around me.

I was too obsessed with the sensation, the way it seemed to take my entire body in a set of reins, drawing me back from the edge and then letting me hurtle forward to the brink over and over again, and I forgot the compliment I'd paid her before she ever got around to answering.

"Thank you, omega," Eve purred, her lips at the shell of my ear and the husky praise curling my toes on the ledge of the bath. "And you're going to be beautiful as I pin you to the floor and fuck you unconscious."

Eve squeezed, brutal but with the immediate result, and I howled as I splattered my own stomach with cum, splashing down into the water as I lost all strength to the ecstasy. I tried to sag into Eve's embrace, but she only patted at my shoulder and pushed me up to sitting.

"Up. Straddle the ledge," Eve said, firm and infuriatingly even.

"Gimme a minute," I mumbled.

"Up," Eve snapped, forcing me into motion.

I snarled, but it was useless to complain. Water went dripping everywhere as I wobbled up onto weak legs and stared dumbly at the edge of the tub.

"One leg over," Eve said, trying to stifle a grin. "Good, now sit, lean back, and scoot your hips forward, good."

I hissed as Eve sat up in the water and then bowed her head over my lap, licking away the dribbles of my release sticking to my cock and belly. "Can I..." My hands hovered over Eve's head, tempted to take a grip like she would with me, demand the rhythm I craved of her lips around my length.

"No. Hands up." I hesitated, and Eve looked up through thick black lashes. "Hands up, sugar, or I'll dry you off and put you to bed, no lock."

The whine rose without my permission, and my hands lifted to the tiled wall behind me as I glared down at my grinning alpha.

"Don't pout," she said with that smile I wanted to kiss

and bite until we were both bleeding. "You know I'll give you what you want."

That's not the point, I wanted to say, but held it in. This was how it was, wasn't it? Eve was an alpha, which meant she got her way, and all I got was…well-fucked. Maybe some shiny or soft present if I'd ended up with a traditional pack.

Eve licked at me until I started to twitch and jerk, until arousal was slipping out of the slit she lapped at and melting over her fist like an ice cream cone in summer. My fingers squeaked and scratched on the tile until at last, she sucked me in, hollowing her cheeks and working me with that almost businesslike precision of skill.

I was too busy crying out, too lost in the slow ease of my muscles calming again, to really notice as she let me droop down off the ledge and onto the linoleum. The bathmat was half scrunched under my back and the floor was cold against my fevered skin, but all I could focus on was the intent in those hazel cat eyes looming over me.

Eve sank down on my tender cock, and our bodies recognized one another immediately. I arched, a scream frozen in my throat, as her cunt locked on me, pressure that increased until I was crazed with the pounding in my blood, the ache in my balls, the *thump thump thump* of my ass against the floor as I fucked up into her.

My eyes squeezed shut, trying to put the woman on top of me out of my mind, the safe house, the months of running, my missing sister. *Just ride the wave of the heat, just feel good*, I wished.

Heavy palms pressed to my chest, dull nails digging in and cutting through some of the density of the lock's grip. "Look at me, sugar."

My face tightened, trying to hold onto the black emptiness of cock and lock and the cold floor, like I could keep pretending I was alone as I bucked and rocked up into Eve's body.

"Omega," Eve snapped, fingers taking my jaw in a firm pinch. I opened my eyes and glared at my alpha, my lips parting and panting breaths falling free as I kicked and thrusted faster, Eve grinding and rocking on top of me. "You're mine."

I was. I'd leashed myself to her. But I didn't have to admit it.

"Mine," Eve growled, eyes narrowing, waiting for me to answer her.

I wanted to roll us over, to be the one pinning her down, making her gasp and whine and moan, but there was no room between the counter and the tub.

"Mine, omega," Eve repeated.

I tried twisting, pulling my face free from her grip, but it left my throat arched under her view, and I realized my mistake too late.

Eve growled again and then dove down, her teeth burning through my skin like knives through butter. It hurt, and it sent lightning down to my cock, a sudden crashing release rocking me up. Eve's arms circled my back, holding me to her chest, to her mouth, our hips fastened so firmly together we could only rub and grind and rock. One hand cupped the two marks she'd already made, and her jaw held me fast on the other side, claiming me once more.

Hers, I admitted privately. I was entirely hers now. For better or, more likely, worse.

I WOKE up alone on the bathroom floor, a towel draped over me in a way that made it unclear whether or not Eve had tried to cover me up or just dropped her own towel onto me carelessly. I groaned as I sat up, body still running too hot, and now achy and bruised on top of it. Eve had fucked me unconscious as she'd promised and then left me on the floor like…trash.

I wasn't entirely sure whether or not I felt like getting up or just staying here in my undignified privacy.

The door opened, and my teeth gritted automatically.

"Food is on its way up," Eve announced, still naked. "Shower or bed?"

I didn't answer. All I really wanted to do was yell wordlessly back at her, and I wasn't entirely sure why. It had been me who'd begged her to bite me in the first place. I'd saddled myself to this alpha, not the other way around.

Eve frowned and crossed to me, bending and staring hard into my eyes, searching for something. "Bed," she decided out loud. "Come on. I don't think I could carry you out without knocking you into the doorframe."

Which meant she'd considered an alternative to just leaving me on the floor. I sighed and pushed myself up, and Eve was there at my side, holding me up when my legs threatened mutiny.

"I look like I've been claimed by a whole pack of alphas," I snapped, just because I *needed* to be angry with her for something, and another bite mark was as good as anything else.

"Mm."

"You know you're only supposed to do it once." I said again, stumbling along with her out of the bathroom and around the corner into the bedroom. The bed had moved. It was pushed out of the center of the room and over into the corner, away from a window.

"Claiming bites protect omegas," Eve said, leading me toward the bed and waiting for me to slide in close to the wall. "You don't want a pack?"

"I think you're more than enough alpha for me," I said with a scoff.

I startled as a knock sounded on the apartment door and then watched Eve slip on a long T-shirt and grab a handgun from the top of a dresser. I itched to follow her but the bed was surprisingly soft and Eve had apparently hunted down all the throw blankets and pillows in the small apartment and thrown them together on the bed. They didn't smell right, but at least they didn't smell like anyone else.

A minute later, Eve returned to the room with an enormous paper takeout bag in each hand.

"Has the heat broken?" she asked, eyeing me as I started to arrange the pillows in a circle around the edge of the bed. I shook my head, and she nodded, dropping the bags inside my work before climbing in. "Better carb up then."

The bags were heady and fragrant with butter and garlic and cheese and that bloody steak I'd requested. "Aren't you tired?" I asked.

"I have another round in me," Eve said simply. She had dark circles under her eyes and her hands shook a little as she tore into the containers of food.

My back was stiff, my throat ached with all the bites so new still, and my muscles were sore. But I'd been bathed. I'd slept plenty in the car. Eve opened a box, revealing a saucy tangle of noodles and chicken and vegetables, passing it to me immediately. I was being fed. She believed we were safe enough here to wash and fuck and eat.

I dug into the food, my anger from minutes ago fading away with every bite. Eve watched me eat for a moment, waiting until I set down one dish before sampling it herself. She had the right instincts, but it was like they were only half developed.

"Maybe just a sleepy nap fuck," I suggested through a mouthful of ravioli, another bite of steak ready on my fork.

Eve's lips curled slightly, and she shrugged, eyes flicking back and forth between me and the closed bedroom door. Waiting for a threat. Ready for one.

Ready to protect me, I chose to believe.

EIGHT

Garrett

"There you are," Jamie greeted, coming in from the garage covered head to toe in sawdust. He stopped, eyes falling to the bag hanging from my hand, his relaxed expression hardening slightly. "A gig?"

"Just came up from Wes," I said, shouldering my go bag. "Rory's coming too."

For a moment, I debated sharing the nature of the job with my packmate, but Wes had made it pretty clear why it needed to be confidential. Rory and I trusted Jamie absolutely, with our lives and all of our own secrets, but he'd also chosen not to be part of our work and the boundary was for his sake as much as our clients'.

"Man, I suppose that means your chicken cacciatore is suddenly no longer on tonight's menu," Jamie said, relaxing and rolling his eyes at me.

"Don't track splinters through the house." I twisted to find Rory taking up the majority of the kitchen doorway, glaring at Jamie's coveralls.

"I've got everything prepped in the fridge, you just have to do the actual cooking," I told Jamie.

He wrinkled his nose as he unbuttoned the top of the coveralls, sawdust floating down to the tile floor under Rory's stare, and then tied them around his waist. "I mean, I'll do my best. When do you get back?"

I looked back at Rory, although we'd both been on the line when our boss, Wes, called and laid out the job.

"I see," Jamie said, glancing between the two of us, reaching one hand up and dusting out his short black dreads. "Well, be safe. Keep me posted if you're able, yeah?"

"Definitely," I answered, knowing Rory was too dour to offer an assurance.

Sure enough, my massive packmate was standing with his arms crossed over his chest, one dark eyebrow arched like I was supposed to remind Jamie that our job was dangerous and who knew what would happen.

Some days, I wondered if Rory ever got tired of being so damn extreme all the time. He thought he was left carrying the world on his shoulders, when really I was pretty sure it was just the weight of his own worries. And a sizeable alpha ego.

"Shouldn't be a big deal to give you a call," I added, and Rory grunted, although it wasn't clear if he was agreeing with me or not.

"We should go."

I nodded and stepped aside so Rory could pass me and lead the way. Jamie shared an amused smile with me before I followed our unofficial head of pack out the backdoor and into our garage. I threw my bag into the backseat and took the passenger side as Rory started the car.

"I feel like we should've given him a heads-up on this one," I said.

"You heard Pike," Rory answered, dark eyes fixed on the rearview mirror, watching the garage door rise.

"I did. But we've never had a job that might bounce back on him like this."

Rory took a moment to stare at me, jaw ticking, before he focused on pulling out of the garage and our short driveway. Living in the suburbs was a little lackluster after our years in the city, but our pack had settled together in the past year after the three of us had more or less co-existed for a decade. We needed to find an omega, and a crummy loft in the city wasn't going to cut it. We didn't have the money for somewhere nicer until we got ourselves out of the crush and into suburbia, and this neighborhood —full to the brim with a network of ex-armed forces—had made an easy transition.

"Nothing will bounce back if we do our jobs right," Rory said.

We'd met after the army, the three of us, mutual respect slowly growing into a quiet but reliable friendship. Rory had the mind of a soldier, but the heart of one too. Even when he was a stubborn asshole, he was loyal and always focused on doing *good* for someone else. He just tended to be forceful about it.

"But if you have any suspicion, or anything seems to be going sideways, call him," Rory relented.

I relaxed in my seat and nodded. "I can't believe Wes even agreed to this."

Rory smirked at that, glancing at me out of the corner of his eyes, and he turned the car toward the freeway. "Omega in distress? That's kinda his wheelhouse."

Thinking of his beta Lola, it seemed more accurate to say that anyone in distress was Wes' wheelhouse. Rory was right enough. Even with Lola's tormentor in the ground, Wes had still been digging into the threads of the Hangmen's web and the organizations they led to. This omega was as much a lead as he was a job.

"You think we're gonna walk in mid-heat?" I asked.

"It's been three days, shouldn't they be…done by now?"

I huffed a laugh at Rory's constipated expression. "No firsthand experience to answer that with, I'm afraid."

How long did it take for an omega's heat to break? Did it depend on frequency or…satisfaction? I swallowed hard and turned my face toward the window.

"We can scout the rest of the building. Run errands. The safe houses aren't really set up for omega nests so maybe it needs…" Rory trailed off and glanced at me.

Of the three members in our pack, Rory was probably the most nonplussed about the prospect of an omega bond-mate. He wasn't a soft guy, and as far as I could tell, his ability to express affection was more along the line of setting the coffeemaker timer and making sure the cars were always in working order. Jamie and I both wanted a bondmate, but Rory wanted…stability. A pack to provide for in his occasionally overbearing but well-intentioned way.

"Candles, chocolate, body lotions, soft furnishings," I offered, mentally reciting the most primitive 'providing for your omega' list I could think of.

"Yeah, that," Rory said with a nod.

"What do you think a hitwoman thinks is a good courting gift?" I asked. "Is it like a cat? She brings him a dead body?"

"Cats do that 'cause they think you can't hunt," Rory muttered, his forehead tangling to tight lines. "But maybe."

I hummed and turned back to traffic for a moment, waiting for the commute to pass, when Rory spoke up again.

"You know I was the one who told Wes about her?"

I stiffened, eyes widening as I turned on Rory, half expecting to discover he was a completely different person. But there he was, same GI Handsome Rory as usual, cropped army hair with shaved sides, his one concession the short beard he wore, a stripe of gray running down his chin.

"How the hell do you know anything about contacting hired killers?" I squawked.

Rory shrugged. "I don't but...I know someone from old ranks who got into it for a while. They recommended her."

I blinked at that. Killing in cold blood didn't quite fit my personal understanding of Rory's morals. But then again, ignoring an alpha abusing their strength against a young woman didn't either. I had no issue with Wes' choice in hiring this woman to do the work.

"Well...I'm getting more excited to meet her by the minute," I said.

Rory grunted, and we drove the rest of the way in easy quiet.

———

RORY and I stood outside of the apartment door longer than necessary.

"I don't hear sex sounds, do you?" I whispered, grinning back at Rory's glare.

"No, but..."

But the hall smelled like buttercream and smoke and aggressive sex, evidence of the heat that had taken place or was still in progress. Even Rory's own creamy and nutty scent was growing a little stronger.

The keys jingled at the end of Rory's fingers as we both remained staring.

"Do we knock?" I asked, mostly just to tease my friend, who seemed frozen in the face of his own biological response to an omega's perfume. He wasn't alone; I was fully prepared to suffer as I stepped into the apartment, but he was hilarious in his surprise.

Rory cleared his throat and knocked, but there was no answer. He glared at the handle for another long moment before squaring his shoulder and putting the key in the lock.

She was waiting for us.

Rory let out a low growl immediately at the sight of the slender, stunning woman sitting on the window frame with a SIG Sauer and silencer pointed directly at us. My own hand went to my gun holster in reflex and Rory's pistol was already out, but she made no other move.

"He's sleeping," she said, and the flex in my hand loosened. "Finally. I'd hate to wake him with the sound of shots. The heat only broke a couple hours ago."

The bedroom door was shut so there was no way to prove she was telling the truth, that the omega, Adam, was still alive. Considering Rory and I both could've been dead by now, I chose to believe her.

"Would you mind if I searched your bags?"

"Yes," Rory snarled.

"No," I corrected him, setting a gentle hand on his arm and trying to nudge it down to his side. It was no use though, Rory was more or less made of iron. So instead, I stepped between them.

Eve's eyes narrowed at me but she didn't do much else, and Rory grumbled with annoyance. She was fucking beautiful. Pure femme fatale, even in gray leggings and a sweatshirt that was no doubt hiding a whole arsenal of weapons beneath it. She had black hair pulled back into a high ponytail, a tactical error when it came to hand-to-hand combat, but I suspected she'd never give anyone the chance to use it against her.

The door to the bedroom opened while I was too busy admiring the woman with a gun on me.

"Eve, what's going…"

If the scent of heat sex had been bad enough from the hall, it was downright deadly with the door open. My purr rose immediately, and shockingly, Rory's followed right after.

The omega in the doorway was young, early twenties, and pretty in a masculine way. His eyes were wide on the scene, face turning back and forth as Eve's lips pursed with annoyance.

"Adam, to me."

"Why do you have a gun pointed at them? Aren't they our security? They look like the pictures."

I arched an eyebrow at that. She had pictures of us? Where had she gotten them?

"To me," Eve barked, although she did it in a low and velvety tone.

Adam stumbled toward her, and that was when I noticed them—a whole handful of bite marks on his neck and shoulders, mostly fresh. For no understandable reason, all the blood in my body seemed to rush south to my cock at the sight of them. They were all hers, an outrageous claiming display.

"Point the gun at them," Eve said to Adam, standing from the window ledge, holding her gaze on Rory and me.

"What?! But—" Adam's objection cut off as Eve wrapped her arms around him and then positioned his hands around the gun.

"Very good, sugar," she murmured, smirking at me as Adam let out a little whine at the praise. "Just like that."

"This is fucking—"

"Just let her check us out so we can move on," I said over my shoulder to Rory.

"Yes, be good boys for me, please," Eve purred at me.

Ha. Fuck. I was fucked. Adam was pretty, Eve was scorching hot, this tiny apartment smelled like pussy and sugar cookies, and I was fucked.

Eve took my bag from me while I was contemplating my own demise and searched it, quick and thorough, before tossing it aside and moving to pat me down. Her scent was lighter up close, and her hair was wet. Fresh out of the shower.

That seemed odd. If I were an alpha who'd been running my omega through a heat, I probably would've savored the scent marks. Adam was certainly coated head to toe with her.

"You'll do," Eve said, patting my back before moving to a growling Rory. "Come on, big guy, don't make me bring you to heel just yet."

"Fuck off," Rory barked, but I turned to find that he'd put his gun away and was letting Eve dig through his bag as he glared at her. His bark seemed to have no effect on the other alpha, which was unusual. Even Jamie and I tended to hop to when Rory snapped.

Eve was slower with patting Rory down, her hands almost caressing him as he stood vibrating in anger. She winked at me over Rory's shoulder, and I turned to find Adam watching the scene with a glazed and hungry expression.

"Is she usually this much of a troll?" I asked him.

He blinked and smiled cautiously back at me, checking

on Eve again before answering. "That or a stronghold of secrecy."

Both of those behaviors are defense mechanisms, I thought but didn't say. Psychoanalyzing the murderous alpha sex bomb wouldn't do me any favors. I checked on Rory again—his cheeks were flushed, and I had a feeling I'd missed some unnecessary groping—before moving slowly toward Adam, waiting for the moment Eve tried to stop me.

"You doing okay? Need anything?" I asked him. *An escape route from your new bondmate?*

Adam looked to Eve again. Wes had said he'd been pretty defensive of Eve when she'd dragged him along to their house. Was it genuine, or born out of fear?

"Do we have any leftovers?" Adam asked Eve.

"A little, but we should order again."

Adam chewed on the inside of his cheek, hesitating. "Maybe groceries this time?"

"Whatever you want, but I can't cook," Eve warned him, finally handing a glowering Rory his bag back.

"I can," Adam said brightly, passing me and heading into the bedroom again. "I'll order, you pay."

It was hard to tell, but the interaction had more of the awkward newness of a fresh bond than of an unwilling captive tiptoeing around their captor.

"We'll pay," I said.

Eve blinked at me and then shrugged. "Fine. Might as well start acting like a pack now."

"A *what*?!" Rory shouted.

I almost repeated it for him, my mind going blank at the suggestion.

"A pack," Eve said, staring at him. She was kind of small. Small for an alpha, certainly, barely coming up to Rory's shoulder and only half as broad-shouldered as him.

"Eve!" Adam snapped, reappearing in the doorway, a laptop balanced in one arm.

"Adam is an omega, he needs a pack," Eve said plainly.

My laugh burst out of me, unavoidable in my state of shock, but Adam had a pale look of horror that said she was being absolutely serious. Rory dropped his bag onto the floor and crossed his arms over his chest.

"We are here as your security," he said slowly.

Eve scoffed and waved a hand. "Well, it's not like I could ask Pike for packmates outright. But you're unbonded, looking for an omega. There's one right there, congratulations."

"*Eve!*" Adam balked again as she gestured to him. I moved quickly, catching the laptop before it could fall to the floor. "What are you—I don't need—the heat just ended, I don't need—"

"It's not about the heat, although I don't plan on either of us being dead in the next three months, so another will come soon enough. It's about...you know..." Eve trailed off, frowning for a moment before rolling her eyes. "I am what I am and you're stuck with me, but you need a pack. To protect you and...I don't know. Alpha and omega things that aren't just me fucking you unconscious."

I choked on air at the declaration, and Adam blushed in silence as if to confirm the claim. It should not have sounded so appealing.

Since Rory seemed to be in the process of swallowing his own tongue, I tried to bring reason to the conversation. "We are hired security, not, um...volunteer packmates?"

Eve thought for a moment and then offered, "I'll pay you to be pack."

"The *fuck!?*" Rory bellowed.

"But I need to meet your third packmate before I agree," Eve added.

"Before you agree," I repeated, unable to stop laughing, looking for anyone else in the room who found the whole thing half as hilarious as I did. But Adam was stricken, pale and shrinking in on himself, and Rory was about to boil over, and Eve…

Eve was deadly serious.

It was a ludicrous proposition; this was not how packs formed. I glanced at Adam and caught him staring back at me, wide-eyed and…desperate? Hopeful? Pleading? I couldn't tell.

"I don't know what fucking game you think you're playing but—"

"Maybe you should call Jamie," I said, cutting Rory's tirade off. He gaped back at me, open-mouthed and red-faced, and I tried to will my thoughts to him by the force of my stare, but it was no good. Rory wasn't an intuitive type. "Just give him the rundown. If he says no on the phone, that's the end of it," I said to Eve.

Her expression changed in the most infinitesimal ways, and even those I thought she was probably in control of. Her head dipped slightly in acknowledgement, but she didn't really look convinced.

"Garrett—"

"Call Jamie," I repeated to Rory. It would give him time to cool off a little after the ruffle of our arrival, of this sudden demand to just…take on an omega. An omega who already had an alpha. It was like using a wrecking ball as a door knocker—Eve was more likely to obliterate our pack than find a home for her omega in it. With another glance at Adam, still pale and frozen, I added to Rory, "Would you mind if Adam made a list of the groceries he wants too? We can skip the delivery."

Giving Rory orders didn't really work, but the request gave him pause, reminded him of Adam in the room, and he took a slow breath in and out before pulling his phone out of his pocket. "Fine. I'll be in the hall."

I stiffened as Eve passed me, one hand reaching out to trail a fingernail over the back of my wrist before she stepped to Adam and plucked the gun out of his hands, flicking the safety on and setting it aside. The door to the apartment snapped shut behind Rory, a little harder than necessary, and Eve batted thick black lashes at me as she drew Adam in against her, his body sagging with relief or need.

"Not bad. Alphas don't usually like to play peacemaker."

"You'd be surprised," I said, rolling some of the tension out of my shoulders. She'd be even more surprised when she met Jamie.

NINE

Eve
____

Garrett Clark was thirty-four years old—six years out of the army after ten years in—specializing in research in Wes Pike's security firm. He reminded me of a lion, all golden tones and that ridiculously luscious hair down to his shoulders, but he lacked the predatory intent. He also managed to make Adam perfume with his surprisingly mild and fresh alpha scent.

Actually, that scent made my own mouth water too, sweet and juicy, a fruit that begged to be bitten and sucked on.

That was convenient for my purposes. Still, I draped my arms over Adam's chest, stroking his rapid heartbeat, and kept the omega between me and the other alpha. It was more important that Garrett took Adam's bait. It would've been better if they'd arrived during the heat.

"We're very good at what we do," Garrett said, moving to sit on the couch. He stiffened slightly as he did so, realizing the furniture was heavy with Adam's scent. As if I'd set a trap without making sure the honey was thoroughly spread throughout the apartment.

"If you say so," I answered.

"I just mean, you don't need us to be pack to be sure that we protect Adam. And you," he added after a moment. "Although, I assume you'd manage that fine on your own."

"How many omegas do you know with only one alpha?" I asked.

"I don't know many omegas at all," Garrett said with an easy grin. Adam's sweetness thickened a bit.

I should've been shoving Adam at the alpha, letting their biology and good looks take over. Instead, my nails dug into the tender skin of his chest and he arched in my hold, sighing out a whimper.

"Can we—can we sit down?" Adam stammered.

"Here, let me get you some water," Garrett said, jumping up and heading for the small, open kitchen. I clutched Adam closer as Garrett passed us.

"What the fuck are you doing?" Adam hissed under his breath.

"Ensuring our survival," I answered, equally quiet.

Adam struggled in my embrace, and I distracted him by licking a stripe up over the newest marks on his throat, marveling at the immediate sexual hunger that flooded our bond. There was frustration and annoyance too, but also something with a cheerful edge.

I didn't know why I kept biting my omega. It felt good. It was an irresistible impulse when he was panting and whining and begging and coming as I fucked him. I liked how Adam looked, bleeding and satisfied and helpless with my marks on him.

"You don't like alphas! *I* don't like alphas," Adam snapped.

"What's not to like?" Garrett interrupted, still wearing that grin. I studied it, searching for the lie in the smile—

teeth grinding, eyes wincing, nostrils flaring in hunger—but if he wasn't sincere, Garrett excelled at faking honesty. "Just kidding, I get it. I know you have your mind made up, but…I think taking things slowly might be in order."

Taking things slowly was exactly what I didn't want. Adam needed a pack to keep him out of trouble, and this one seemed to have virtually no tarnish on them—they would be perfect.

"Alpha packs court omegas," Garrett said.

He settled back into the couch and rested the glasses on the table in front of him, nodding his head toward the chair that faced him. I bit off my growl at the obvious suggestion and loosened my hold on Adam. If I wanted him in the pack, then I had to make room for that bond to grow, and Garrett would be perfect, easy to assert dominance over later.

"I don't need courting. I don't need a pack," Adam added, his hand linking with mine and leading me to the open chair.

It was short and wide, plenty of room for us to settle in together. I jumped ahead of him and spread my legs, smirking at my blushing omega as he sat down between them. Garrett's eyes watched with keen interest as I locked my limbs around Adam's waist. Trapping my omega, embracing him, cuddling…whatever it was supposed to be called.

"If Omikron is responsible for the bid on you—" Garrett started.

"They are," Adam pressed.

"Then you're in for a long wait. We've only uncovered a tiny tip of an iceberg with them so far. And what you're describing is the kind of pervasive network that infects finance, law enforcement, illegal communities," Garrett continued, leaning forward and resting his elbows on his spread knees. "Dismantling them, putting the right figures —the ones that will topple the organization—into prison and out of the sphere of influence is the kind of project organizations like the FBI would put a lifetime of work into."

"What are you saying?" Adam asked, blinking. "That I'm fucked? That it's useless?"

"No, I'm saying I understand why…Eve is looking at us to be your pack. It's unlikely Omikron will be solved and you'll be safe, so why not find the pack that will keep you safe in spite of them?"

Adam was quiet for a moment, but in the bond a soft tendril of interest curled toward me. I rolled my eyes at Garrett. I needed Adam softened toward him, not me.

"You're talking about legal channels," I said and stopped as Garrett raised a hand, eyes widening.

"I am, and please don't correct me. I don't want to hear anything else that I might be obligated to report to authorities."

I scoffed. As if I'd ever intended to share my plans with these alphas in the first place.

"You don't have confidentiality to your clients?" Adam asked him, a slight tease of playfulness in his tone.

I rewarded him with kisses over his marks, holding Garrett's blue stare with my own as he watched Adam shift and lean into the touch. Sexual interest was a start. The other one, Rory Stevens, seemed about as responsive to Adam as a wooden board, but I only needed one of the pack to be hooked. Preferably two.

"Not when it comes to possible *future* crimes," Garrett said.

Meaning I could admit what acts had already been committed if I chose to.

Adam twisted to look at me, brow furrowed, lips pressed firm. "You really want a pack?"

No. I definitely didn't want a pack. Just like I didn't want an omega. But I had one now, and if I wasn't going to let him be killed, then I had to commit to the idea and do the thing halfway right. Adam needed protection first, and a pack second. These men could be both.

I didn't have to answer. The door to the apartment opened again, the massive soldier of an alpha—an enraged bear to Garrett's gentle lion—reappeared, still glowering.

"He's on his way," Rory bit out.

Garrett just grinned. "Despite your best attempts to dissuade him?"

Rory grunted and glared at me with dark eyes. He would be fun to kick down onto his knees, to prove to him what really made an alpha. In time, after the pack issue was settled.

———

"IF ADAM CAN GET us access to everything he has on Omikron, it could be really useful. Even if he doesn't have proof, just names, it gives us new directions to track," Garrett rattled off, his laptop balanced on one thigh, his other foot propped up on the table.

"I know how this works."

Garrett glanced up over the brim of his glasses, blinking and then huffing out a laugh. He combed his fingers through his hair toward the tangled bun at the top of his head, the dark brown shade sun-streaked with blond through some strands. "Right. Of course you do."

His head tipped, and we continued to stare at one another for a long moment of quiet. Adam was in the shower, Rory was running the grocery errand, and the third alpha had yet to arrive.

"You know…your accent isn't quite right," he said after a moment.

It was close enough. Close enough for most people. It could be perfect when I wanted.

"Kill for hire isn't something you just pick up after college. What was it? Not CIA. Definitely not army."

"Why not army?" I asked. "Plenty end up swapping after phasing out of the ranks."

"Plenty do, but not ones with your reputation. They're careful, they have too much of a record," Garrett said, setting the laptop on the cushions and leaning back. Open, casual. Meant to set me at ease. And yet, once again, he was being natural rather than forced. He was smart.

"You meet your clients publicly. You meet your marks publicly. I got the security footage of you at the casino with Adam and at the motel."

In the shower, Adam was growing curious, which meant I was giving him something in the bond to be curious about. I let my gaze unfocus as I reorganized my own thoughts back into control, into order.

"Which means that you know that there's nothing concrete to turn up. Sure, I bet if someone bothered to do the work, your face would pop up linked in a number of deaths, but nothing else to track you down with."

"That…might not be true," I said, tuning back into the conversation. "Omikron found a house of mine."

Garrett sat up at that and then hurried to snatch up the laptop. I stiffened as he jumped from the couch to the table, passing me the device. "Put everything in. We can erase it. I know it's not worth much now, but just to be safe."

My whole body wanted to press into the back of the

chair at the sudden movement, at the urgency in his tone. Or lash out in his direction. I held still and shook my head slowly.

Be calm, he's only a puppy, I reminded myself. "I took care of it while Adam was sleeping during the heat."

Garrett's eyes were flicking back and forth over my face like I was a page for him to read, and I put even more work into shutting down my expression.

"If we're going to be pack—"

"You're going to be Adam's alpha. We don't need to be anything to one another," I said firmly.

The corner of Garrett's eyes crinkled as he laughed. "That's not really how these things work, Eve." His smile faded after a moment, eyes on mine. "Unless…"

The knock on the door startled Garrett away from his thought, and I relaxed as he jumped and hurried to answer.

"It's me," a low, smooth voice called.

Garrett checked the peephole and then opened the door. I rose and crossed the small space to stand outside the bathroom door. Adam was humming inside, and there was a little drum of arousal in the bond that made me think he was probably jerking off. I was tempted to join him, but distracting myself with a newfound obsession with sex wasn't going to remove the presence of alphas in my territory. Ones I'd invited there, much to my own annoyance.

My hand settled on the bathroom door handle as the new alpha stepped into the apartment. Jamie Ford was handsome and Black, and walked with an easy calm that I suspected came from confidence. His jeans had paint stains and one of the sleeves of his flannel shirt was torn at the elbow, like he'd been in the middle of some kind of work when he'd driven here. He was about the same height as

Garrett, and it irritated me to be so dwarfed by these men. He examined me with the same slow study I did him, a bright sweetness and heady spice rolling slowly in my direction.

Jamie was the pack member I'd found the least information on. He'd been army, like the other two, but there was no record for work in the past four years. Was he unstable? PTSD from his time served, perhaps? Both of those options seemed unlikely as he stood before me, hands sliding into pockets and a faint smile on his lips, totally at ease even in the unfamiliar surroundings.

"So you want a pack?"

My spine straightened and my eyes narrowed, searching his expression for mockery. "My omega needs one."

One side of his smile quirked up. "Hm. I see." He turned and grinned at Garrett. "How bad is Rory freaking out?"

"He's rage shopping now. That or halfway across the country, we'll see," Garrett said with a shrug.

Jamie Ford turned back to me, eyes drifting from my head down to my bare toes. "Nah. He'll be back."

The doorknob I had fisted in my grip wiggled, and I pulled my hand away like it was on fire as Adam opened the door, still bare-chested but now with charmingly flushed cheeks and drenched dark strands. His eyes widened on Jamie.

"Oh. Uh…hi," Adam greeted. I tried not to be so absurdly pleased as he sidled into me, but he was warm and I'd…enjoyed the past couple days in bed with him, a rare and indulgent break from my usual routine.

Not that it was hard to enjoy a rut where I could fasten my lock onto an omega's cock.

"Hey. Jamie, nice to meet you," Jamie offered, nodding

at Adam but not trying to invade our space. But his eyes only spent a second on my omega before focusing back on me. I glared back at him.

I had a history with alphas taking an interest in me, and if this one thought he could take the upper hand, he would be very sorely mistaken. Which left Garrett as my angle to fasten Adam to the pack. It would have to do.

TEN

Jamie

"Well, obviously, the five of us can't stay here," I said, sitting up on the kitchen counter, my eyes on the closed door of the bedroom where Eve had retreated with her omega.

"What do you mean?"

"There's only one bed," I said.

Garrett and Rory glanced at one another with furrowed brows, and I laughed. "Look, I know you two are used to roughing it and staying away for days on a stake-out, but *some* of us have learned how to actually take care of our bodies and that includes sleeping on a Tempurpedic mattress. Besides, I have work that needs to get done at home."

"We're *not* bringing them into the pack," Rory bit out.

Why not? I thought in reflex, except I knew the answer.

Eve was exquisite, but she was definitely feral, and I was pretty sure the same could be said of her omega. Oddly enough, it didn't make me less inclined to claim them as pack.

I'd spent the better part of five years fashioning myself

a level of freedom and ease that I'd lacked in my youth. That woman was sure to set the whole thing on fire, so why was I so tempted to hand her the gasoline and a pack of matches? I was happy with the way things were, wasn't I?

I had a pack, a small one with two friends I trusted and understood. Friends who were equally comfortable being their own person, living their own lives, as I was mine. We had the house, two stories with a nest, and a nice backyard. We were ready to start our dues at the Omega Center... whenever we finally got around to submitting the paperwork. It was better than the army—my schedule and my time and my choices were my own now.

We were following the road map. Maybe it wasn't quite...exciting, but it was easy and I was doing it with friends.

"I don't think we should argue the point with her," Garrett said, drawing me out of my head and back into the conversation.

My eyebrows jumped, and I looked away from the blank door at last. "You want to agree?"

"What?!" Rory barked.

"I'm not telling you to go in there and bite Adam, calm down, man," Garrett said with a laugh, stirring the sizzling meat and vegetables in the skillet. He'd talked Adam out of the kitchen when it was obvious that Eve wouldn't unglue herself from his side, and that putting her and Rory in close proximity was only going to lead to a fight. "I'm just saying we can...fulfill that role without finalizing the matter for a while."

"Play house, you mean," I said, arching an eyebrow.

Rory's arms crossed over his chest, but he didn't argue, just scowled and fell into thought.

"Yeah, I guess so. I mean...are we gonna drop this job?" Garrett asked Rory.

"Those two are in danger, right?" I asked. There was no way Rory was going to drop a job if he thought lives were at risk.

"They are, but I don't think we're talking about a woman who is incapable of protecting herself and her omega," Garrett answered, voice lowering. "Just maybe a matter of how hard she has to fight to make sure they both survive."

I bit down on my own tongue and stared at Garrett, trying to sort out where his head was at. Did he want out of the job? My gut said no, so why give Rory the out?

"She already wired us the money, I don't even fucking know how she got the information, but a month's worth of personal security landed. For all *three* of us," Rory bit out, looking at me.

"Hired pack," Garrett said, hiding his smirk from Rory's glare. "What's your feeling, Jamie? This is your life that's getting the biggest wrench thrown in."

Because I was the one who'd opted not to take the obvious career path after the army, who'd veered left and kept running. I'd left military life and violence far behind, and with that, the confining world of rules I'd grown up in. What would a carpenter have in common with a contract killer?

In my case, probably more than she or I realized.

"This affects us all equally," I said slowly. "I might not be a soldier now, but I understand the risks we're discussing. So I think we should take a vote, majority wins, and then figure out some logistics from there."

"I say no, keep it strictly work and make that clear from the start," Rory said, rushing in before I'd even finished speaking.

Garrett stirred the food in the pan for a moment before clicking off the burner. "I say we treat this as an opportunity. High-stakes omega courting," he said, cracking a grin. "No promises, but that we'll consider. So there you are, you're still the tiebreaker, Jamie."

They both turned to face me, and I was as aware of their stares as I was of the quiet from the bedroom. Was Eve listening in on us? Probably.

"I agree with Garrett," I said.

"What?!" they shouted at the same time.

I laughed and shook my head at Garrett. "Wait, why are *you* surprised?"

Garrett's hands hovered open at his side. "I…I dunno, I guess I thought you'd be on Rory's side. Seriously?"

"Because you two want an omega *that* badly?" Rory hissed.

"It's actually not the omega that I'm interested in," I admitted.

Garrett choked on his laughter and spun quickly back to his cooking as Rory gaped at me, baffled and examining.

"And here I thought you were the least likely one of us to have a death wish," Rory said flatly.

"Aw, Rory, chill, man—"

But Rory was crossing the room with heavy steps, heading for the door, and I waved my hand at Garrett.

"Let it go. He's right. You wanna change your vote now that you know how the majority looks?" I asked Garrett, stifling my annoyance as Rory slammed the apartment door shut behind him.

Garrett lifted the pan off the burner, transferring the stir-fry into a large Tupperware. "No. My vote stands."

One of Rory's questions rang again in my head. "Is it the idea of an omega, or that one in particular?" I asked. Garrett shot me a glare out of the corner of his eyes, and I shrugged. "Hey, this is a pack meeting, we're gonna talk this out, right? No judgment, just honest discussion."

"Maybe a bit of both," Garrett admitted slowly, frowning and checking the bedroom door. "I like him. I'm having some alpha impulse to protect him, but I like him too. And maybe…maybe it's not just the omega."

I grinned at that, and Garrett sighed. "Man, imagine if Rory was in here for that," I said.

Garrett groaned and shook his head. "I don't want to. I wonder sometimes if Rory isn't asexual."

"He isn't," I answered. Garrett's eyebrows bounced, and I laughed. "I don't know that I've seen his interest first-hand, but I shared a wall with him before you moved in." Rory was a headboard banger. Or the women he took to bed were. "It was rare, but when it went down, it sounded like a combat zone next door."

I'd caught rare glimpses of Rory with women, but if what I remembered was correct, Eve was his type. Aside from the homicidal tendencies. As far as I knew.

Garrett stifled his laugh with the back of his hand as the bedroom door opened and Adam appeared, hair rumpled and green eyes searching the room.

"Eve?" he called.

Garrett straightened immediately, spinning around. "What?"

Adam blinked at us as a heavy weight sank slowly inside of me. "Is…is Eve in the bathroom?"

But the bathroom door was hanging open, the light off.

"She was in the bedroom with you," Garrett said, marching toward the omega.

Adam's expression fell first, a brief weary look of mourning, and then flattened. "She's gone."

"How the hell could she be gone?" I asked.

"Fire escape," Adam said.

"It's not supposed to—" Garrett grunted from inside of

the bedroom and then huffed. "Open. Fuck. Where would she go?"

Adam's hand floated up to cup the freshest bite marks left on his throat, head shaking slowly as he stared down at the floor. "I don't know. She's not coming back."

"She's coming ba—" I started, and Adam cut me off, eyes blazing up at mine, glaring.

"She's not."

"No alpha that claims an omega with five marks is going to just—"

"She didn't want me!" Adam shouted.

I slid off the counter in the silence that followed as Garrett walked quietly back to Adam in the doorway. My packmate's hands went to the omega's shoulders, flexing briefly until Adam looked the short distance up at him.

"I used my oncoming heat to make her bite me," Adam confessed. "She almost—she *did* let Omikron catch up to us and take me. She changed her mind and came back for me, but…"

Garrett turned back to the cracked open window. "But you think she was just waiting until she found you other alphas? What's in the bond?"

"Nothing," Adam spat. "She's got a fucking bank safe inside of her."

"You guys had a key to this place, is it gone?" I asked.

Adam stared at me for a moment, frowning, probably thinking I was an idiot for asking, but then Garrett patted him on the shoulder and turned him back to the room. As soon as Adam started looking through his things, Garrett stepped back.

"He's probably right," Garrett whispered.

"Maybe, but like you said, five bites? The first one in the heat of the moment, sure, but the rest?"

"It's not like they make the bond stronger."

"No, but they make a hell of a statement," I hissed back.

Every one of those marks on Adam's neck was a scream of warning to unbonded alphas. *Mine!*

Adam did a quick sweep and then a longer, more methodical one, the tangle on his brow slowly easing. "It's not here. The key isn't here."

Garrett's eyebrows bounced in surprise, and I shrugged. "Sounds like she probably has it."

"Then where the hell did she go?" Garrett asked us both before shaking his head and waving a hand in the air. "No, forget it. We don't know. That's fine, it's… She's not our job, you are. Come on, there's dinner if you're hungry. I want to know every second of what happened from the moment you met Eve, okay?"

Adam blushed and rubbed a hand over his forehead. "If you say so."

"And don't skip the dirty bits," Garrett added with a sly grin. "Those are my favorite."

"Ignore him. He's only good for research and stir-fry," I said.

Adam was watching Garrett walk to the food, gaze fixed to the hair that fell loose and tangled around the nape of his tan neck.

If Eve had left Adam to our pack for safekeeping, I was pretty sure her omega was in the right hands. Rory and I would find our own relationships in time if Garrett bonded Adam.

I just wasn't sure how I felt about Eve being left to her own devices without that same kind of backup.

ELEVEN

Eve

At first, being out of the apartment was a relief. No more of Adam's questions and his sticky clingy scent in my nose, drawing out a part of myself I preferred to let out in careful doses. No alphas crowding my space.

I liked the city. I liked the blank white noise of the beta masses in the streets. The anonymity. I'd grown up in sterile environments, white walls, and utilitarian beds, and the safe house apartment bared a little too much resemblance for my comfort. With the alphas storming in, I'd needed an escape route.

I licked grease from my cheeseburger off the corner of my lips and sucked on the cola in the styrofoam cup in front of me. Pop music blared on speakers overhead, disco balls spinning and twinkle lights blinking in alternating color patterns.

Over the partition, couples and packs of friends danced on rollerskates, round and round in a circle. It was meaningless fun and I took a moment to unbox the little shard of envy in my mind, examining it as I watched the normal little people spinning like tops.

Then a tiny woman with neon blue hair-buns trimmed with tinsel and ultraviolet eyeliner plunked into the seat across from me and stole a french fry.

"Tabby," I greeted.

"Hey there, danger. Long time, no see," she answered. She had her own styrofoam cup, and I knew it was filled with some borderline toxic combination of whatever had the most caffeine in the soda fountain. And probably a splash of tequila. "Glad to have you back in the neighborhood."

I was on the opposite end of the city as the safe house, an area that should've fallen prey to gentrification and developers over a decade ago, but instead remained an unstable mix of artists and drug users and the low-income families trying to keep their rent from suddenly skyrocketing out from under them. Tabby came from the entire combination.

"Any rumors about me?" I asked.

She met my eyes over the lid of her cup, her lips puckered around the straw, and nodded.

I'd met Tabby when she'd hired me under a fake identity and then tried to stiff me on the bill after the rapist alpha she'd marked was dead. I liked her. She was clever and stupid all at once, too brave for her own good. Hiring her seemed like the obvious alternative to killing her.

"I can erase some of the inquiries, but—"

I shook my head. "They're not going to forget."

"They sure as shit aren't," Tabby muttered, watching the people on the rink for a moment with a puzzled amusement. "They'll know you're in the city soon."

"Make it days," I said, and her jaw flexed but she nodded. I waited for her to ask about him, about Adam, my *bondmate*, but she didn't. Either she didn't care, or she knew it was better not to dig and find too much out. Her job was keeping me off the radar, that was all. "You have the option to step down."

Tabby rolled her eyes, turning back to me with a half-smile. "You think I don't know that? I'm here, I'm helping."

"Only a little. Not a trace back to you."

"I *know*," she said. "You have a nice ass, but I still like mine better."

I grinned and nudged the fries to her. I'd considered bonding Tabby in the past, just to keep an eye on her and to discourage any other potential alphas, but I'd resisted for the same reason I now resented Adam. Having someone else in my head was too much. Even now, miles apart, Adam was tugging on the bond, trying to dig his way through to reach me.

"Anything else I need to know?" I asked.

Tabby shook her head. "It's been quiet since last year. I keep waiting for another hot shot to come strutting in, try and piss on the territory and start shit, but nah. The Howlers kinda keep an eye on things."

"Are they an issue?"

"They're boy scouts," Tabby said with a laugh.

"Here's everything you need," I said, passing over a napkin with a carefully scribbled list of numbers written out in ketchup.

Tabby stared at it for several minutes of quiet and then swiped a french fry through the first line. "Got it. You know what you're doing? Like…for real?"

"I'm forming a plan," I said.

"So that's a no. I can make it weeks before—"

"No, I only need days." At least I hoped it would only take days, maybe that was overestimating Adam's effect on the alphas. "One week."

"One week," Tabby confirmed with a nod and another fry through the ketchup. "You know how to find me if anything changes."

I nodded and joined her in the snacking until there was nothing legible on the napkin and no fries to be found. Tabby stood and stared down at me for a moment, her lips moving with unspoken questions, her hand flat on the surface of the table.

She settled on, "Good luck, danger," and then turned and left the roller rink, a locker key on a rubber band resting on the table where her hand had been.

I finished my burger and watched the crowd on the floor for two more songs before heading to the lockers. There was a rainbow backpack inside locker 69—wasn't she funny—and I shrugged it onto my shoulders without peeking inside and then left the rink.

Low Town was lively at night, with bar patios spilling over the sidewalk and buskers every twenty feet. I stole a pair of rose-colored glasses from a kiosk and slid them onto my nose, taking a weaving path through the streets, staying in the public places. The farther north I walked, the more the bars and delis turned into retail spaces, many still open late. Record stores and metaphysical shops and adult stores became patisseries and bookshops and mid-range boutiques.

My feet stopped outside of one called Dapper. It had a small collection of good clothing hanging from industrial racks, but also home goods and body products. A catch-all shop for men, or more likely, a place for their girlfriends to find aspirational gifts for them. My lips twitched and I stepped inside, pleased with the clean pine and the worn leather scents in the air and the meek beta clerks behind the desk.

"Can we help you?"

"Just browsing," I answered easily, admiring a refurbished vintage razor kit. I imagined Adam sitting on the bathroom counter, his legs spread for me to stand between, eyes shut as I stroked the blade gently up his throat and over his jaw, careful of my marks on him.

It was a pretty picture.

———

"WHAT THE FUCK WERE YOU–"

The dark growl, the fingers digging into my forearms, the hard wall against my back—I reacted with an instinct older than my training.

One moment, the big snarling bear of an alpha, Rory, was in my face, teeth bared and eyes glowing. In the next, he was on the floor, my fingernails printing crescents into the beat of his pulse in his throat, one knee ramming into his solar plexus, the other his groin.

"Rory!"

"Eve, stop!"

He was too big for me to keep pinned like this, and we rolled in the small hallway of the apartment entrance. I grunted as my shoulder hit the other wall, and Rory's growl choked to silence, his face going red above me. One of his hands left my arm for my wrist, but if he tore my grip away, I was sure I could take his arteries with me.

"Rory, enough!"

The bark didn't make the alpha on top of me so much as flinch, and I fought my legs into position, ready to slam him to the wall and get back on top, when he went slack. His hands left me and raised at his side, body suspended above me, throat still in my grip.

"Eve." Out of the corner of my eye, a figure crouched on the floor just a couple feet away. "You can render him unconscious if you really want, but he's a heavy mother-fucker and he snores."

Garrett.

"If you *kill* him, we're going to have a problem," Garrett continued, too calm.

It was hard to strangle a man, especially one handed, but Rory had about another minute or two until I managed it. Surely his packmates would step in.

"Eve," Adam murmured.

I sighed and shoved Rory off of me, rising quickly from the floor, and darting past Garrett to find open ground. Adam was at the entrance of the hall, Jamie not far behind him, and I snagged Adam's wrist and dragged him with me to the center of the room. Jamie's expression was grave and flat, staring down at Rory, who sat against the wall and caught his breath with heaves of air and coughing.

"You can't grab people like that, man, you know better," Jamie said.

Rory rolled his eyes but nodded, and Garrett stood slowly, arms crossed over his chest, jaw clenched.

I tried to stifle my surprise. It had been natural to fight back. I hadn't bothered with thinking, but if I had, I wouldn't have expected the other alphas to chastise their packmate before me. Adam's hands gripped my waist, and he crowded my side, his face pressed to my shoulder.

Garrett turned slowly, and he was a different alpha than the one I'd met earlier, gaze knife sharp and pheromones snapping with a hint of ginger. "We are not the enemy."

"I'm not your job," I answered. "I can—"

"You're not, but your omega is. If you plan on keeping him safe, you have to cooperate with us, and that fucking includes not sneaking out!" Garrett yelled.

I bristled, or tried to, but Adam's arms were circling closer and he was so *relieved* it was distracting me.

"You coulda been followed back here," Rory rasped, his fingers rubbing over the imprints of my nails on his throat.

"I wasn't," I said. I shrugged Adam away from me, ignoring the little bruised offense from him as I pulled the backpack off my shoulders and passed it to him. "I brought you presents."

"Eve," Garrett bit out.

"I assumed you left," Adam whispered.

A good alpha would reassure him. A better one probably wouldn't have taken off in the first place.

"I did, and now I'm back," I said with a shrug, unzipping the backpack and pulling the shopping bag out. I'd tucked away most of what Tabby had given me—some untraceable guns, a few hacker's toys, a stash of cash and IDs for Adam and me—and used the backpack to carry my little surprise.

"Jesus, you're really gonna play cute about this?" Garrett scoffed.

Adam took the heavy paper bag with wide eyes, and I opened the little rainbow front pocket next, plucking out a small rubber banana, a little bigger than my thumb, and tossed it at Garrett.

"Present for you too," I said as he caught it in his hands.

He stared at it for a moment, lips flat and brow furrowed, before noticing the lines where the peel split. He pushed them back to reveal the white banana, and then pulled that out, sighing at the sight of a USB flash drive.

"This better be digital gold," Garrett said, glaring at me.

"I haven't looked yet, but I'd imagine so."

Jamie moved to Rory, offering a hand and hauling the man up. I stepped in front of Adam, who was gingerly tugging tissue paper out of the bag like he thought I'd just handed him an explosive.

"Don't touch me again," I said to Rory. "Don't touch Adam without my permission. That goes for all of you."

"I'm not taking orders from a client who is blatantly interested in making my job more difficult," Rory answered back. "You want my respect, you take this fucking seriously."

"I'm a very serious person," I quipped, tipping my head so my ponytail swung playfully.

Rory started to snarl again—the sound rough and interrupted after the abuse on his throat—but Garrett held his hand up.

"If you're going to pull shit like this," Garrett said, waving the banana drive in the air, "just *tell* us. You're right that our work is protecting Adam. We can do that better with your help. And if you want to be our pack, then we deserve the courtesy of communication."

I didn't want to be their pack, I wanted Adam to, but I understood that it wasn't time to lay that out clearly.

"How long does it take you to open a package?" I asked Adam.

"I keep waiting for it to bite me," he answered, grinning and moving to the couch with the bag.

"That privilege is mine," I purred, following him and helping myself to a seat nearly half on his lap.

The men behind us whispered to one another, Jamie checking on Rory, Rory telling Garrett to grab his gear for the flashdrive, but I ignored the lot of them to watch Adam open his presents. I couldn't remember the last time I'd offered anyone a gift.

No, I could. Anne-Marie in the orphanage, the day her

perfume had come in. The day they'd moved me to the alpha house. I'd given her a knife I'd stolen from the kitchens. She would need it to protect herself. I hoped she got the chance to use it.

Adam unwrapped the black cashmere blanket from around the other items, brushing it over his cheek briefly, giddy delight in the bond.

"Needs your scent mark," he said, pushing it in my direction, green eyes meeting mine shyly. I took the blanket and threw it over my shoulders before nodding at him to continue.

The shaving kit was next and Adam swallowed hard at the sight of the beautifully sharp blade. "I don't know how to use one of these," he laughed.

"I do," I said, scratching a fingernail lightly up his throat, careful to skirt the still tender marks.

Adam shivered and blushed and I wondered if he was as aware of the stares on us from the other alphas as I was. Last was a small bottle of warming oil, and Adam let out a little laugh and rolled his eyes. "Like I need to be more sensitive."

I shifted on the couch, straddling his lap and trapping him there with my arms on either side of his head, three pairs of eyes fixed to us. "I like you sensitive," I teased Adam in a near whisper. "Begging," I said, lowering my head as Adam arched to present his throat. I brushed my lips over my bite marks and flicked my eyes up to stare over his shoulder at the pack of alphas watching us. "Whining like a good little omega."

I grinned as Adam whined, Garrett's throat flexing with a hard swallow, Jamie's lips curling in amusement, and Rory's hands forming tight fists. I kissed my omega's pulse, sliding one hand down to rest over his pounding heart, as his future pack watched on.

TWELVE

Adam

This is just temporary insanity, I reassured myself as I buried a cry of relief into the pillow. Above me, Eve took mercy on me, slowing her grinding and rocking to a halt, bending to kiss the marks on my throat as I caught my breath.

"You should be louder," Eve said, nipping my earlobe.

I grimaced, but then she sucked on one of her marks and it was hard to focus on my anger. "You don't get to pick my future pack."

"You aren't really in a position to choose," Eve answered.

I tried to buck her off of me, but instead she just sat up and grinned at me from above, streaks of orange light from the lamps outside glowing on her skin. She was so fucking beautiful, and I was becoming uncomfortably addicted to her presence. I didn't know if it was the marks on my throat, or just that this was the longest I'd spent time in company with an alpha, or if it was just the way she held herself back from me. She had me as a possession, and I had…

I wasn't sure. Possibly nothing.

"They can give you what I can't," Eve said, smile softening but eyes narrowing in calculation.

"You're assuming I want more than good sex and presents," I said, trying for the same casual quality she always had so easily.

"You *need* more than that," she said, one fingertip tracing around one of my nipples and making me grunt. She'd used the warming oil there and on my *ass*, and finger fucked my prostate as I'd tried to quiet myself face-first on the mattress earlier. I was sure it hadn't worked, that the alphas outside of the bedroom were perfectly aware of what we were doing.

And I was sure that had been her intention.

"I have something else for you," she said, flicking my nipple and then rising slowly from my lap.

I watched, fascinated, at the mess that seeped out between us. "Are you on birth control?" I asked in sudden horror.

Eve let out a laugh, a warm and surprised sound, so perfectly genuine it made me sit up grinning. "Wow, you really are out of the heat fog," she said. "I can't get pregnant, Adam." I frowned at that, and she sighed, sliding off my lap and reaching down to the floor to pick up a towel. "Do you want kids?" she asked.

I shook my head. "I don't like the designation lottery." I knew there were plenty of omegas who were glad to be the blessed minority, but for me it had felt like a trap. Being used as an alpha's stud horse was the last thing I wanted.

She nodded and shrugged. "And I am not a mother. I took care of that a long time ago."

"And you don't think the guys out there should be able to make the same choice?" I asked. "On whether or not they have a pack open to children?"

Eve didn't answer—I always pushed her too far—just walked to that absurd rainbow backpack and dug deep into the bottom of it, pulling out a flat, shining black smartphone.

"Jailbroken," she said, tossing it onto the bed by my side. I stared down at it in silent surprise and then back up at her. She cocked a hip, nude and imperious. "I assume you and your sister weren't playing renegade without a single contact. That you had people you were sourcing information or supplies from."

"Not ones I trust now," I said.

"But maybe ones who might know something about Faith."

I swallowed and set my thumb on the screen of the phone, the glare of the generic background sudden and harsh in the bedroom. "You heard what they said. We…we need to cooperate in order for them to keep me safe."

"So tell the pretty one everything," Eve said with a shrug, picking up a T-shirt off the floor and sliding it on over her head. "You're not stupid and you're not helpless and I bet you've been on the inside of this longer than they have. Show him the phone if you want. Play it right, and he'll let you keep it, sugar."

Or keep the phone hidden in case I needed a secret later.

Eve was heading for the door, black hair hanging almost as low as the just barely modest enough hemline of the T-shirt.

"Wait," I called, not sure if she would actually listen or just ignore me the way she did when I asked too many questions.

Eve stopped, turned to face me, and I froze as I realized I had no plan.

"Come here for a second," I said.

Eve's eyes narrowed, but she took slow steps back to the bed and I twisted to sit at the edge.

"Yes?" Her voice was silky, bare knees bumping against my own.

I reached out slowly, and her eyes fell to my hands and then flicked back up to my eyes as I cupped around the back of her thighs, stretching up and lifting my face to hers. Eve stared at me for a long moment before bowing just enough for me to kiss her.

My hands tightened on her legs as I helped myself to slow sips and nibbles from her mouth, waiting for her to soften. The bond had been quiet all night since she returned from her excursion, but it opened now, gentle amusement and…I didn't know the word. Something less than affection and yet more overwhelming, considering the source.

And then Eve's hands smoothed up my chest to hold my jaw, pressing back, licking in. It wasn't a leading kiss, she wasn't pushing me back into the sheets, climbing back onto my lap. Our mouths were thorough, gently hungry for one another. Her nails scratched back into my hair, and my hands slid up and helped themselves to the muscular swell of her ass.

"Thank you," I breathed as we pulled apart for air.

Eve nipped at my bottom lip, teased the nape of my neck with her nails, and her nose stroked against mine for the briefest second. Then she was walking away, back to the door without answering me, smoke and leather and a hint of something airier than I'd caught before curling around me in the wake of her.

I slid back into the bed, drawing my new blanket up and over me with the sheets, and fell asleep to the sound of the shower running.

———

EVE WAS NEVER there when I woke up, which was a shame because I would've liked a nice morning fuck for once.

At least this time, there was the smell of bacon.

The scene outside of the bedroom made me pause. Garrett was on the couch, long legs spread across the cushions and feet propped on the far arm, his laptop open on his lap but the screen blacked out, and one of his arms draped down to the floor in a sleepy flop.

Jamie was at the kitchen bar with a mug of coffee, watching Rory cook a staple of breakfast options—hashbrowns, pancakes, eggs, bacon, and sausage. And Eve, my feral blade of an alpha, sat at the corner of the bar, eyes darting over each of the men. It was almost domestic, the four of them scattered through the tiny apartment in the morning.

I thought of the way Eve had reacted to Rory last night, his sudden grab on her arms and her immediate retaliation, expression like glass as she'd dropped him to the floor.

"Morning."

It was Jamie, who seemed to be the most mellow of the lot and who watched Eve with a soft curiosity through heavy-lidded dark eyes. He toasted me with his mug as Garrett sat up with a start, twisting to blink at me.

The pretty one. That's what Eve had called Garrett the night before, and I hadn't even questioned it. He *was* pretty. He was hot, the kind of masculine beauty that came off as ease and carelessness. He was a little taller than me, broad-shouldered, and obviously strong without looking brutal like Rory. He had thick hair I wanted to touch, maybe twist around my fist, and a scent I wanted to drink by the gallon.

I realized suddenly that I was staring at him, my tongue tracing my lips, and the only person in the room who looked more pleased at this than Garrett—smiling warmly back at me and filling the room with that nectarine sweetness—was Eve.

"Bar's full. Sit with Garrett, and I'll bring you breakfast, sugar," Eve purred.

If Garrett knew what Eve was up to—I wasn't totally sure I even understood her whole plan—he didn't let on, just slid his legs off the couch and patted the cushion in invitation.

"How'd you sleep?" he asked as Rory banged plates down on the counter.

I thought of fucking Eve and the kiss before she left to shower, and shrugged. "Fine. But I've got a bedroom, what about you guys?"

"Like shit," Jamie said, but he smiled at me as I looked at him.

"We're switching safe houses later this week," Garrett said, reaching up to ruffle his fingers through his hair. "Jamie needs to get back home to work in his shop, unless you have objections, boss."

"Why would I—" Rory started.

"What kind of shop?" Eve asked, ignoring Rory's growl of annoyance.

Garrett winked at me, and I realized once again, I'd been caught ogling him, this time for the flex of his arm.

"Woodworking. Mostly custom furniture," Jamie said.

Eve didn't seem to know what to make of that, so instead she watched Rory like a hawk as he slid a plate of food in her direction.

"You can bunk in the bedroom with Adam if you really

need a bed," Eve said to Garrett over her shoulder as Rory glowered at her. "I'll take a turn on the couch."

Garrett barked out a laugh before I could hiss at Eve. She wasn't *wrong* about my interest, I just didn't like her throwing it out for the whole pack. "Seems plenty big enough for three," Garrett answered with a grin.

Eve's spine stiffened and she whirled, her hands braced on the back of the chair so fiercely, I thought she was preparing to swing it through the air and slam it down onto Garrett's pretty face. Anger blazed in the bond, and a thinner sliver of something I recognized too well. Fear. It was tiny, but all the sharper for it. It had been there last night when Rory grabbed her too.

"If you want to find out what happens to alphas who try to pin me, I would be more than happy to demonstrate," Eve growled, sinuous and dark.

The room was quiet, Jamie studying Eve, Rory glaring down at the floor, and Garrett's eyes going wide.

"Sorry, I thought it was kind of obvious I'd be bottom," Garrett mumbled.

I coughed out a laugh and tried to stuff it back into hiding just as fast. Garrett wasn't cowering from Eve, but he was clearly aware of her threat. Her tension loosened, but she held his gaze in silence for another long stretch. I was getting slightly hard, without really understanding why, and it grew so much worse as Garrett tilted his head away from Eve.

Jesus Christ. He was baring his throat. An alpha, a *male* alpha, was baring his throat to another alpha. *My* alpha.

More than anything in that moment, I wanted to watch Eve lunge forward and sink her teeth into the muscle of Garrett's tan throat, as if I could live vicariously through the claiming, see whether or not it was as exquisitely brutal as it felt when she bit me.

There was a purr, uneven, rough, and it died as soon as Eve realized it came from her. She threw herself into the chair, stiff back turned to Garrett, hands snatching up the cutlery from the counter. Garrett's cheeks flushed, and he slouched into the cushions of the couch, probably as surprised by his display as the rest of us were.

It was a strange scene. Rory obviously hated Eve, and maybe even me. Jamie was a comfortable stranger at best. And here I was, as aroused by the prospect of watching Eve dominate Garrett as I was when she tackled me into the bed for sex.

As puzzle pieces, we didn't fit, not for a pack. But I was beginning to wonder if they could.

I was beginning to wonder if I wanted them to.

THIRTEEN

Rory

Adam's hands tossed the deck of cards together with a steady *shht shht shht* sound as he rattled off names, businesses, aliases, and addresses. Garrett was typing at high speed, browser tabs popping up one after another to collect Adam's information.

"You knew some of this?" Adam asked, twisting the cards, sliding them together again. A nervous habit but also a deft skill that I suspected came from a practice of cheating at cards.

"Not enough of it," Garrett muttered, catching up with the last dump of information from Adam. He stopped typing and smiled at the omega. "Thank you. This is going to make serious headway, and it fills in some gaps for us."

Adam nodded, fumbling the cards in his hands and blushing.

"You remember a lot of details," I pointed out, a touch suspicious of the young man who'd already admitted to being an amateur con artist.

"Details are important," Adam said with a shrug. "A lot

of the time, we had to use those details to name drop our way into a club or a warehouse, or to chat up the right security guard at a bar to get the shift schedule. You mess up a little detail, and you immediately ruin your own credibility."

"You like that part of it? Manipulating someone into giving you what you need?" I asked.

"Jesus, *Rory*," Garrett growled.

Adam's chin lifted slightly, his eyes meeting mine with just the slightest wince of shame. "What I like is the moment where I open the back of a freight truck and the five omegas inside realize they're *not* going to get sold to some alpha that will lock them in a basement. I like seeing the panic on all the peoples' faces, the ones who're in charge of keeping those omegas quiet and hidden, because I know it means their bosses just failed to satisfy Omikron and its clients." His hands tightened until his knuckles were white around the deck of cards. "I'm not a liar for fun. I lie when it can help omegas, and *yeah*, sometimes I am one of those omegas. So, fuck you," he added finally in a mutter.

Garrett's purr burst forth suddenly, his gaze bright on Adam, who glanced up with a whole new blush that went right up into his hairline.

On the windowsill, Eve watched the pair together with a darkly smug smile. Garrett and Adam were attracted to one another. I wasn't surprised, Garrett was likable and inclined to liking others. I wanted to believe that meant Garrett could see through the obvious ploy the bonded pair had concocted—tying the omega to my pack for protection and drawing us into a tornado of shit—but I wondered if it would make a difference either way. Alphas and omegas didn't spend a lot of time together when they weren't courting. Biology would take over. How long did we have before Garrett gave in to the physical impulse to claim the omega?

Adam smelled like a trap to me, one of those sticky strips to attract bugs and hold them. And Eve…

Eve was infinitely more dangerous.

She met my gaze and winked, satisfaction turning hard and cold with a flick of her gaze. I tried and failed to stifle my growl as she rose up from the windowsill, prowling on elegantly sculpted legs toward and then past me. I twisted in my chair, glaring at her back, forcing my gaze to her shoulders, and then startled as I realized where she was headed.

"Where are you going?" I asked, jumping up and running to intercept her before she could reach the door.

"Out."

"No."

"Yes," she hissed, glaring up at me, body tensing and preparing for a fight.

I'd learned my lesson the first time. It wasn't even that she'd laid me on my ass faster than I could blink, it was that taking on an alpha who challenged her was as instinctive to her as breathing. That was probably partly to do with nature—her scent was borderline explosive and our pheromones were meant as a warning—but also habit. She'd been challenged regularly and only had one reaction to threats. Violence. Putting the other alpha down.

I could relate a little. I'd been over six feet tall before I was out of elementary school, a bit of a string bean but still a giant. By the time I reached high school, even before my alpha pheromones hit, the older boys saw me as a challenge. Prove their strength against the giant, haze him, harass him. My options were to be beaten up or be the stronger one. Fueled with the start of hormones, anger won out.

I'd grown out of that need to prove myself in the army. Being stronger didn't mean much when you had to work as a unit, and I'd learned that *not* fighting for status was actually a relief. Eve was still living in that mental space, holding tight to her dominance. Between prey or predator, she'd chosen the latter.

I kept my hands to myself this time but spread myself wide in the hall to prevent her from passing.

"If you need something, I can handle it," I said.

Eve's laugh was bubbly and mocking, forced out as she rolled her eyes. "I doubt that."

"You need to keep a low profile," I tried instead, growling.

"Your packmate came and went. I can guarantee I'm less likely to be noticed than he was if we're being watched."

"Jamie knows how to handle himself, and he's not the one hired killers are looking for," I answered. "Are you seriously this messy on your jobs?"

"I've only failed to fulfill one," she snapped back.

We'd attracted Garrett and Adam's attention from the living room.

"I am leaving. Your broken bones are up to you at this point," Eve warned.

I could subdue her. She was incredible, I wasn't too blind to see that, but then again, so was I and I had at least sixty pounds on her. She might make good on her promise, but still, I could keep her from leaving. But then what? Short of keeping her unconscious, how long would it last? Going back to my own old habits of youth was the last thing I wanted and the most likely way of ruining any possible rapport with Eve.

I looked to Garrett, and he grimaced and shrugged.

"Eve," Adam called.

Eve's smirk slid away, her face locking in annoyance.

"Will you come back tonight, alpha?" Adam continued.

The calculation was obvious, his voice infused with a carefully measured dose of hopefulness and need.

"Of course, sugar," Eve answered, equally false in tone. She arched an eyebrow at me.

I frowned and stepped aside just long enough for her to be inches away before shifting again, our bodies bumping briefly. Eve recoiled and released a soft snarl, too quiet for the others to hear.

I lowered my head and my voice. "I don't care what happens to you. I don't care where you go or when you come back. But if you jeopardize that omega's safety for your ego, we are done. Clear?"

I knew she wouldn't take it well, but I failed to predict her reaction. Eve's body went from stiff and defensive to fluid, swooning closer, our chests brushing, her face tilted up to mine. I was too confused to remember the threat she posed, and her hand was skimming down my chest while I stood frozen. And then she had my cock in her grip, firm and possessive and just tight enough to make me grunt and keep me from pulling away.

"Listen, alpha," Eve purred up at me, my nose burning as her scent enveloped me. "We aren't going to get along. Not for Adam's sake. Not for mine. I will tolerate you, if you behave," Eve murmured, squeezing harder on my cock.

Adam and Garrett were bowed over Garrett's computer, and I was trapped by her hand, my shock, and the sudden and hypnotizing recollection of being touched with intimate aggression.

"I am sure you are very impressive. I can tell, actually." She glanced down, smiling. "And I'm sure there was never a question of who was in charge in your pack. But when I am in the room, I am the alpha. It's not an argument. We can fight, if you like, but I've already won. So focus on what you can control, because it certainly isn't me," she said. She grinned and stroked her hand over me through my shorts, the pair of us equally aware of how hard I'd grown during her speech. "Doesn't seem to be your cock, either."

My teeth were grinding in my jaw, muscles coiled to keep from springing myself at her. I didn't know if I wanted to challenge her, wrestle for that dominance she was stripping me of, or...

I blinked, and she was gone, the apartment door cracking hard into my shoulder as she swung it open and left.

Fuck.

I turned to face the door, just to avoid Garrett seeing the state I was in, and took slow breaths until the brutal throbbing in my cock subsided. I liked conflict in bed, wrestling with strangers. I liked women who were blindly desperate to get fucked, and who took what they wanted without asking or waiting on me to initiate.

That wasn't what was on offer from Eve, pretty much the opposite, but I was having a hard time convincing my dick of that.

Fuck. That woman was my type—fierce, confident, aggressive, sexual.

She also happened to be morally bankrupt, possibly insane, and with a deep loathing of alphas.

"She's probably not kidding about being able to handle herself, but you could follow her if you wanted to," Garrett said, totally misreading my crisis.

"She'd spot me in no time," I said. Stealth wasn't a weakness of mine, but it wasn't a strength either. I was big and notable. "I'm taking a shower."

———

"SHIT."

I sat up with a grunt, wincing in the dark at the glare of Garrett's computer screen. He was sitting on the floor in front of the couch where I slept.

"What?"

Garrett's head whipped in my direction, profile outlined in silver. There was an article up on the screen that I could just barely make out.

"Sorry. Didn't mean to wake you up," Garrett whispered. "But I guess you need to know. I set up search notifications on all the details Adam gave me earlier. This just popped up."

I'd never been a heavy sleeper, but the army had trained me to wake up at a few key phrases and 'shit' was one of them. I took the offered laptop and shifted on the cushions. It was after 3 a.m., and I checked the door of the bedroom. It was still hanging open.

"She hasn't come back yet."

I rubbed my face, ignoring the irritation over Eve still being missing, and focused on the screen again.

'Tech King Murdered, Captive Omegas Found In Investigation.'

I skimmed the article, but Garrett didn't wait for me to finish.

"Hugh Redmond was one of the names Adam mentioned," Garrett said. "Earlier today…"

"In front of Eve," I finished for him, handing back the

computer. "See if you can pick up chatter, get any details on the crime. I'll start coffee."

"What do we do?" Garrett whispered.

What did we do if it was Eve who'd committed the crime? Fuck if I knew, at least not in the dead of night with no coffee.

I had more respect for the enemy soldiers I'd fought overseas than men like Hugh Redmond. Whatever he'd accomplished in life, someone else would easily manage in another year.

But killing him? It was reckless, and it wouldn't escape Omikron's attention. She might as well have announced she was in the city, and Adam along with her.

The coffee was bubbling in the pot when the door to the apartment opened.

"Me," Eve called before I'd finished reaching for the gun in the nearby drawer.

Garrett looked up from his seat on the couch, pulling his headphones off one ear as she stepped into the living room.

"You probably just exposed yourself," Garrett said. "They'll know Adam is with you. Richmond's not even a critical role in the organization, he's just a customer."

Eve stood still as Garrett delivered the lecture in a rare, firm tone. Her hair was hanging down her back, still wet from a recent shower. I wondered what kind of killer she was. She'd sniped Indy, but I had a feeling she liked up-close and violent kills as much as she did efficient and distant ones. Was Redmond's death a bloodbath or a carefully calculated shot?

"Moving to a new safe house is risky enough, but doing it now that Omikron knows where to look for you guys?" Garrett continued, voice rising to a hiss. He was trying not to wake Adam, and I wasn't sure he needed to bother. Of all of us, Adam probably had the best chance of getting through to Eve.

"Redmond hired me to take out an overseas competitor three years ago," Eve said as Garrett took a breath.

"So what? You're mad that a bad man hired you to kill someone?" I asked, shaking my head. "I hate to break it to you, but all your clients—"

"Even your boss?" Eve interrupted.

I bit my own tongue. No, Wes wasn't a bad man. He'd made a shitty choice tangling his life up with Eve even for a second—my current situation was proof—but he wasn't a bad person. He was one of the rare good ones, as far as I could tell.

"Marcus Heyman, Samuel Phelpps, Victor Crowe. More of my clients," Eve said.

I'd only been paying half attention when Adam reported to Garrett, but I still recognized the names.

Garrett sat up straighter, eyes drifting aimlessly around the room as he thought.

"You think Omikron's had you on call," I said. "They've been sourcing you out like…"

"They recommend my services the way they hand out omegas like candy to their clients," Eve said, arms folded over her chest.

"That doesn't make Redmond's death productive," I said.

"Tell that to his harem of sex slaves trapped in rooms without windows. Three omegas, seven betas. The only English they spoke to me was 'Please, no.'"

Garrett pushed the computer aside and set his elbows on his knees, dropping his face into his hands. I continued to watch Eve.

She looked tired, the bravado and smug satisfaction of earlier washed away. She was staring out the window, unmoving, and I wanted to dig into her thoughts, unearth what was running through her head.

"You didn't do it for them," I found myself saying.

Eve turned to me slowly, unguarded but empty. "Does it matter?"

I honestly didn't know.

FOURTEEN

Adam

For the first time ever, I woke up and rolled over, bumping into another body. For a split second, before really being aware, I assumed it must've been Garrett taking Eve up on her offer of the bed. Then a whiff of addictive smoke teased me. I reached out, keeping my eyes closed as if to suspend a dream, and found a familiar slim frame.

Eve shifted, an arm sliding under the pillows to wrap around me, and I helped myself to the offering. I pressed my face to her throat, my groin to her hip, and tentatively twined an arm over her waist, reaching up to cup a breast. The hand behind me slid into my hair with that tight warning grip that now made me instantly hard, waiting for her command.

"I'm tired," she breathed out, her other hand coming to caress my ass.

I waited for her to dismiss me, to toss me over her side and out of the bed, or to push me away again.

"Slow and deep," she said instead, guiding me on top of her with a squeeze of my ass and a yank on my hair.

I was on top. I was on top of Eve! The closest I'd gotten to this was when she wanted to be eaten out, and she was always careful to keep her legs over my shoulders, body in charge of me. I'd been fantasizing about fucking Eve like this for days, and now—

"Adam," she purred, and I opened my eyes to find her smiling, amused and relaxed beneath me. Totally naked too, our chests warm and pressed together.

Right. Eve wanted to be fucked, and I was the chosen one. I reached down, pushing my shorts far enough to free my cock, and then settled myself between her parted thighs. Eve's eyes were closed, lips curved, but her hands were still claiming me. I might get to be on top, but I wasn't in charge. I rocked over her slowly, rubbing my cock against the folds of her sex until they grew slightly slippery along my length, mostly my arousal but some of hers too.

"Kiss?" I asked, wondering if I was pushing my luck with this new version of Eve.

Her fingers twisted, the sting in my scalp zipping down to my cock, and then she drew me down to her lips, licking in immediately, fucking my mouth with her tongue. I shifted and started gently nudging my cock inside of her in time with her claiming kiss until I was buried to the hilt, my balls pressed tight to the crease of her ass.

"Fuck," I gasped out as she fluttered a little tighter around my length. I groaned and tucked my face against her throat, slowly drawing out, sinking in, the wet glide and squeeze of her cunt wrapped around my cock a delirious high.

"That's good, sugar," Eve murmured, her body slack beneath me, aside from where she gripped me. "Nice and slow."

Slow was wonderful but challenging. I'd never had the freedom to set the pace before, and I wanted to buck and thrust until the bed was creaking and the sheets were rucking and—

Eve moaned and arched briefly, and it brought me back to the moment, settling me before I could chase my orgasm. She was never soft like this, never mine to touch and watch. I wanted to break the spell with questions as much as I wanted to suspend it endlessly.

I rolled my hips, stroking myself against her front walls, and stared at the pretty bow of her mouth parting on a silent sigh.

"That's so good, Adam."

I whined and stretched, resisting that impulse to race again, and then repeated the motion, rewarded with a flutter of Eve's eyes, her smile.

"Yes, sugar, just like that."

It was just another form of control, but I was greedy for the praise. I held her hips in my hands and rose up on my knees, swiveling with every thrust, gasping as Eve stretched and moaned for me.

"More, Adam. A little harder."

I let out a garbled yelp of relief as our bodies clapped together and Eve's cunt clenched around mine. She was holding off the lock so we could fuck like this, and it was my new favorite form of torture.

"Come inside me, omega," Eve purred. "Make me soaked."

I gasped and collapsed down on Eve, my hips snapping into hers on instinct until I came to a quick and shuddering release, a small whine of frustration escaping me.

Eve just laughed and combed her fingers through my hair. "Good boy. Now back up on your knees and fuck me with that pretty cock like you were."

The skin of my throat ached as I forced myself back

up, regaining the slow dragging pace that made Eve sigh and soften in the sheets.

You're whipped, I thought to myself. There was a whole list of things to worry about, and another even longer one to resent the woman in bed with me, but none of it mattered. I wanted to know how long she would let me have this moment, how many times I would get to come, when she would lock me, when she would give up this game and roll me over and pin me down and fuck me the way I wished I didn't want.

"Look at how pretty you look, that thick cock fucking me just right," Eve said, stretching her arms up over her head, her breasts on mouthwatering display. I wanted to sink my teeth into them as if I could claim her in retaliation.

"Jesus Christ," I whispered, staring down at myself, at the reddened, slick lips of her pussy swallowing me.

"Would you like Garrett's cock in your ass right now?"

My pace stuttered at the suggestion. "The fuck! Eve!"

"He could fuck you into me, make you go so deep," Eve continued, grinning wickedly up at me. "I bet you'd like a knot in your ass as I locked you so hard, it made you see stars."

She was evil and obvious, and I ignored her orders to behave, diving down and stopping her mouth with a hungry kiss, bracing my hands against the bed and fucking her as hard and as fast as I could, just to shut her up and keep that vision out of my head.

I only got a second before I was on my back with Eve pinning me down with a hand on my throat, eyes sharp and a little wild. I held still, aware I'd pushed too far, and waited for her.

"Or you could sit on his cock," Eve said after a moment, one hand reaching behind and then down.

I yelped again as she fingered around my hole, teasing it for a moment before sliding one digit inside.

"I could ride you like this with his cock plugging your ass," she said.

"He did say he wanted to be bottom," I answered.

Eve giggled, actually giggled, and turned her head to the door. "Should I call for him? Hey—"

I wrestled hard against the hand on my throat, managing to shake her off, and sat up. I grabbed her face with my hands and forced her into another kiss, driving my tongue in, ignoring her momentary stiffness. She relented after a moment, arms wrapping around me and hips taking over the rise and fall of our fucking as she answered the rough kiss against my lips.

"You're mine, Adam," she said, pushing my legs apart and bouncing faster, harder.

I was nearing another edge, and I nodded, panting, clinging to her.

"But I know you want that alpha," she continued, yanking on my hair before I could hide my face. "He'll spoil you and protect you and suck your cock and fuck your perfect ass."

In the moment, I didn't know which of those things I really wanted, and they started to meld together into one picture. Garrett was sexy and more sincere than Eve. He would answer my questions when she wouldn't, would cuddle up to me when she was prickly and distant.

"You can do those things," I hissed as Eve tightened around me. I wanted to wait for her lock, but I opened my eyes and found her smiling at me, and it set off a sudden and shocking orgasm that made me cry out, embarrassingly loud and obvious.

"He'll be a good alpha. And you're such a good omega, sugar," Eve growled, locking fully, grinding down onto me, her cunt squeezing rhythmically, milking another sharper release out of me. "Mine."

And like the trained puppy I was turning into, I arched my throat and came again as Eve dug her teeth deep into my shoulder.

———

A WALK of shame was one thing, but walking into the living room after sex with Eve—sex where I'd been explicitly encouraged to imagine getting fucked by the handsome alpha on the couch—was a whole other head trip.

Garrett was sprawled out on the couch again but moved one leg down to the floor, spreading his thighs and offering me a seat by his other foot, with a view of his lap. He smiled over the screen of his laptop, long sun-streaked dark hair draped over his shoulders. Before I could stop myself, I pictured him on top of me, grinding his knot against my cock, that hair hanging around our faces like a curtain.

"Um. Coffee," I managed, heading for the kitchen.

"She sleeping?" Garrett asked, rising from the couch, following me. Rory seemed to be out of the apartment, and Jamie hadn't been back since the first day, which meant…we were more or less alone.

"I think so," I said. She'd held me until her lock loosened, then kissed my lips and rolled over, stealing my spot near the wall. I'd been tempted to curl myself up around her, but it was nearly noon and I had a feeling she wanted to be left alone. "She was out late."

Garrett let out a slight huff, but he didn't meet my eyes when I looked at him. The coffee in the pot was cold and probably stale at this point, so I set to making a fresh one, trying to ignore the presence of the alpha crowding the space with me. Easier said than done. Garrett smelled good in a way that made my skin warm and my body just a little too aware of my own cock.

"I have a serious question for you." Garrett held out two bags of bagels. "Everything, or vanilla cinnamon swirl?"

"Both," I answered, trying to fight my smile.

He nodded and pulled the toaster forward on the counter. "Okay, smart choice. I have another serious question for you. Are you ready?"

I laughed and shrugged. "Sure."

"Do you want to be Eve's omega?"

My smile fell away, eyes flicking over to the bedroom door immediately. It was closed, but that didn't mean she wouldn't hear.

"Adam, look at me," Garrett whispered, stepping closer.

"I am," I said. "I am her omega."

I looked up. Garrett's eyes should've been that sunny day blue of the sky, but they were steely, a stern shade of gray, a reminder that behind the soft hair and easy smiles, there was a serious man watching everything around him.

"Do you want to be?" Garrett asked again.

I'd been ignoring this question in my own mind for over a week now, since I'd begged her to bite me. In a different life, I would never have chosen Eve. She would never have been mine to choose. But in this one…

You're still alive, I reminded myself.

"Yes," I said, looking back at Garrett. "A week ago… no. But today, yes, I do."

Maybe we weren't what an omega and alpha ought to be, but Eve was protecting me, and I believed her when she said she would help me find Faith. There were presents too, and the bedroom was turning into one of the better nests I'd ever had the time to make for myself.

Garrett let out a breath and nodded, leaning back against the counter. "Good. Okay."

I wondered what he would've said if I'd answered no, but at the back of my head, I already knew. *You keep finding opportunities to get free of her and then turning them down.*

"What about you?" I asked.

Garrett's eyebrows bounced at the same moment the bagels popped up from the toaster.

"Butter and cream cheese," I instructed, turning to pour myself coffee. "She wants to wheedle us into your pack. Do you want Eve to be pack?"

Garrett let out a burst of laughter. "Do I want a lawless feral hitwoman alpha to be my packmate?"

"Well, when you put it like that…"

"Rory isn't here, so I'll tell you the truth," Garrett said slowly. "I'm…not completely opposed to the idea." He passed me a large plate with my bagels and then moved closer, reaching over my head for a mug. "There's another half of that question you didn't ask me."

"Is there?" I asked, trying to concentrate on my coffee or the food in front of me, rather than the alpha so close, his warmth was bleeding into me.

"Do I want you to be my omega?" Garrett asked, voice low and quiet.

I stuffed my mouth with a bite of food, considered backing away, but my eyes only traveled up to meet Garrett's gaze as he took a sip of his coffee, one eyebrow arching at me, waiting.

Damnit. I did want the answer, even if I could guess by the focus of his stare. I swallowed and tilted my head. "Hypothetically, if you did, is that why you're not opposed to the idea of Eve?"

Garrett grinned. "It should be. But no, she's…got her own appeal."

I sighed and nodded. The whole thing seemed like a car crash I was watching in slow motion. Eve had set us in these men's path and demanded a bond. For good or bad, I had a feeling she was going to get what she wanted. It would be better if Garrett was open to her too.

"And do you want me to be your omega?" I asked, trying to throw the words casually. I headed for the living room, hoping to break the connection, but Garrett just walked backwards, keeping pace and grinning at me.

"Do you want me to be your alpha?" he asked instead.

I glared up at him for not answering, but Eve's coaching during sex bubbled up in my head, the fantasies she'd infected me with, and my cheeks started to burn. Garrett set his coffee down on the counter and rested his other hand against the wall behind me. I looked to both sides and realized he'd pinned me in. Not too close, not aggressive, and he was still filling the room with that sweet and fresh scent of his.

"Yes, Adam," Garrett said, catching my attention. "Yeah, I think I do."

His face was over mine. I could close the distance or let him do it, or we could just stay here like this, breathing each other in until one of us broke.

Or the front door could open suddenly, and Garrett could jump back from me as Rory stormed into the apartment with bags of groceries in each arm, glaring at us for a moment before grunting and moving to the kitchen.

I hurried for the couch with my coffee and bagels and pretended for a moment that I hadn't just nearly kissed Garrett.

FIFTEEN

Eve

"Please. Please, you don't want to do this. I can make your life—" Blood dribbled down from the wound at his receding hairline into his eye, and his voice gurgled to a muffled yelp as I stuffed his soiled underwear into his mouth.

I reached up to the rope hanging down from the rafters of the four-poster bed, yanking hard, watching his face go red and his voice strangle to silence, then fastened the loose ends to the far posters. He was still erect, body responding to the danger and the fear, ignoring the reality of the situation.

Hugh Redmond would be dead soon.

I turned out of the bedroom and headed for the empty space on the floor plans, hidden behind an indoor water feature. Wealth could afford any number of absurdities, including a secret wing in a penthouse apartment. I swiped the key I'd snatched from the bedroom over the pad, and the water fountain turned suddenly to the left, revealing a short hall.

It was silent. Redmond's security would be unconscious for another hour at least. I would check to make sure Redmond was dead before I left. But first…

The walls of the hall had large glass windows…no. Two-way

mirrors. There were six rooms, all dimly lit, with massive, lavish beds featured centrally and what I suspected were minimalist wash stations tucked behind partial walls. Only two of the beds were visibly occupied, small bundles hidden under the blankets.

I stopped in front of one of the doors and turned the knob, surprised to find it unlocked. Surely only from the outside.

The bundle on the bed sat up with a gasp as the light in the room came on automatically at my entrance.

The girl was tangled in the sheets, with sallow olive skin and rich black hair. Her neck was covered in bruises, the marks of alpha bites that had been somehow dulled—because Redmond wouldn't want these omegas bonded. He wouldn't want to feel what he put them through, of course.

The girl whimpered and scrambled back, heading for the edge of the bed. "Please, no. No. No, please," she cried in heavily-accented English.

I opened my mouth to speak to her, and then shut it again as she cowered out of sight. There was a mirror on the ceiling over the bed and on either wall, my reflection bouncing back at me, hers revealed at the corner against the wall.

"Please, no. No, no, no."

Hugh Redmond had said the same to me as I'd strung him up. I turned and left the room, taking a knife from my pocket and using it to prop the door open. When she was ready, she would leave the room with something to defend herself with.

I WOKE late in the day to the sound of buzzing, surrounded in the bed by Adam's scent, but blissfully alone. The door was closed and there was a steady murmur of voices from the living room, so I shut my eyes and held the moment to myself for another breath.

Killing Hugh Redmond hadn't been entirely planned.

Not when I walked out of the apartment yesterday. I'd left to send intel to Tabby, to check on what I'd hidden away, and I'd seen his name on a newstand.

The other names, the men I'd killed for, rolled through my head, and I turned on the bed, pressing my face into the pillow Adam had used. Instead of blocking out the anger, Adam's scent only seemed to make the fire rise higher.

I didn't give a fuck about omegas. Not in particular. I wasn't more inclined to believe they needed protection than any other designation. Anyone could be hurt, even an alpha.

Trafficking, on the other hand, I took issue with. Discovering I'd been a tool for the hands of Omikron, after where I'd come from, left a burrowing unease sliding through me, like I'd just discovered a leech attached to my back and couldn't shake the sensation that there were more to be found.

The buzzing started up again, and I sat up. That was the phone I'd picked up when we stopped at Eddie's garage. I pushed the blankets out of the way as I slid off the bed, amused and irritated that Adam had clearly tucked me in before leaving. The phone was still in the duffle bag, and I pulled it out along with a fresh shirt, sliding the latter on over my head.

My hair was a tangled mess after my morning in bed with Adam, and I combed my fingers through it and winced as I tapped the phone.

"Hot Opportunity!! 50% off storewide at 29874 Westview Ave! Just use code MIKEQUINCY1935 this Saturday!"

I snorted at the message. It was from a private agency I used for the occasional booking, where jobs were sent in text code. Jobs were pinged to whatever freelancer on the books was closest to the location of the intended hit.

Fifty percent off was fifty thousand dollars, higher than my usual asking price, although not outrageously. Less than I was offered for Adam. Mike Quincy at 7:35 p.m., 29874 Westview Ave on Saturday.

The bedroom door opened, a sudden gust of cinnamon and toasted nuts and a scratch of leather reaching me at the same moment that Rory's shadow loomed.

"What was that sound?" he asked.

I turned and found his eyes on my bare legs, the usual scowl on his face. I lifted the phone to his face and wiggled it, grinning as his eyes crossed. "I got a job offer."

"You have a phone?" Rory snarled as I ducked under his arm that was braced against the doorframe.

Adam and Garrett were together on the couch, their knees touching until Adam twisted to face me.

"Wait, did you just say a—"

"Job offer," I repeated, nodding. "Someone is very unhappy with… Actually, I suppose I'd better not say," I teased, smirking and batting my lashes in Rory's direction over my shoulder.

"You can't take a fucking job!" Rory barked.

"That's got to be Omikron trying to smoke you out, right?" Garrett asked, ever the calm one of the pair.

"You're seriously telling me you got an offer to kill someone, and you haven't even put pants on?" Adam said. "Are you wearing underwear at least?"

"Don't answer that," Rory muttered.

"Of course I can take a job," I said to Rory before turning to Garrett. "Of course it's Omikron trying to smoke me out. And of course I'm not wearing underwear. I just woke up, and I certainly wasn't wearing any when you left, was I?"

Adam turned bright red as I winked at him.

"Eve!" Rory snapped.

"I need a shower."

"Give me the phone."

"Sure, catch," I said, tossing the cell at Rory, heading for the bathroom.

"Wait," Garrett called, a shuffle of movement behind me as I ignored him. "Eve, wait!"

I closed the door to the bathroom and turned the water on, but a moment later, the door opened again and Garrett stepped inside.

"Did you already accept the job?" he asked.

I turned to face him, crossing my arms over my chest. "You're not really following me into my shower, are you?"

"You're being funny and sharp, and I think you do it just to piss Rory off, but you and I both know how serious this is. Did you accept that job?"

"No," I answered, and Garrett sighed. "Now, if you don't mind—"

"I do mind. This is not done."

I rolled my eyes and reached down to the hem of the shirt, lifting it up over my head.

Garrett looked a little flushed, but he held my gaze. "If you think that's going to deter me, you're really misreading the situation. Rory has the phone. How do we turn down the job?"

I took a step closer, just to see what would happen, and Garrett stiffened, eyes falling to my breasts and then down to my hips before quickly rising again.

"Eve," he said lowly. "Please. For Adam's sake, tell me what you're thinking."

"I *just* woke up," I repeated with a huff, heading into the shower. I considered leaving the curtain open, partly to keep teasing Garrett and partly to keep an eye on him, but it would just make a mess of the bathroom. "Why do I have to be thinking anything?"

"Because you don't become an international contract killer by not thinking quickly, by not having a constant supply of plans. You got that text, and I don't believe for a second that you didn't make a decision. It's meant to be a trap. They know if they can take you out of the equation, it will make it that much easier to finish Adam too, and they're *right*, so tell me how you turn the job down."

He was almost desperate. That was good, as long as his concern was for Adam. I lifted my face to the jet of the water and closed my eyes, rubbing my hands over my cheeks and jaw, over my forehead, working out tension.

"I will get in the shower if you don't answer," Garrett said, voice cracking slightly.

The job offer came sooner than I'd expected. I was counting on more time, but then I went and ruined that by taking out Redmond. I sighed and leaned back against the wall, flicking the curtain to the side. Garrett was right there, and this time he didn't bother meeting my eyes as quickly.

"They'd have to think I was completely stupid or completely crazy to take it," I said.

"I'm betting on the latter," Garrett said, finally glancing up before watching another rivulet of water slide down my skin.

My blood was warm with awareness, and I was surprised to find myself comfortable. Garrett didn't feel like a threat, despite being an alpha.

Maybe this wasn't too soon. Maybe it was exactly on time.

"I don't accept or reject the job, I just don't show up," I told him.

He blinked, taking his eyes off the V of my sex and

staring dazedly back at me for a moment while the words sank in. "Oh."

"Yes. Oh. Rory can keep the phone."

"The phone," Garrett repeated, eyes drifting toward my breasts again.

I let him watch the water—me—for another minute, curious to see if he would try and help himself, before clearing my throat. "Are we done now?"

He startled, finally flushing for real, and stumbled away from the tub. "Yeah, sorry, um… Okay, so. The phone, yeah."

The curtain flicked back into place as Garrett headed for the door, and I stepped back under the water. The rush of the shower was loud in my ears, and it took me a moment before I realized he'd spoken again.

"What?"

"You won't go, right?"

My lips pressed into a firm line, and I rolled my eyes. "No, Garrett, I won't go," I lied.

"Good."

I reached for the shampoo, working it into my hair, before I realized the door hadn't ever made a sound.

"He actually likes you, you know," Garrett said.

Adam. I did know. It was clearer every day. Adam was shit at keeping his emotions to himself in the bond.

The door finally clicked shut, and I let out a long sigh. Adam was like an infection, warming me up from the inside like a fever, constantly present in my thoughts. There was no cure for him. At least not one I wanted to take at this point. But Omikron wasn't going to be solved by sitting in the apartment collecting data and looking for the legal routes.

And I was never going to be a good alpha, one who gave him a safe nest and a stable environment.

I finished my shower and let it continue to run as I wrapped myself in a towel and moved to the toilet, lifting the lid to the tank as silently as possible. I reached down to the bottom where I'd duct-taped a waterproof bag with a second phone inside.

Thank fuck for mirroring software.

I turned the phone on, disconnected the cell I'd offered to Rory, and then opened the identical text.

RSVP Request: Alt loc and date, I typed out.

I turned the shower off, pulled a hair dryer out from under the sink, and set about tidying my hair as I waited for the text to come in. I could hide it back in the tank if I needed to, but usually, the staffers were quick.

Halfway through my hair, the screen lit up.

Hot Opportunity!! 60% off storewide at 58734 Smith St! Just use code MIKEQUINCY2245 Next Monday!

I snorted at the raise in offer, money that was undoubtedly never intended to be of any use to me. But I would make sure Adam had access to it, if Garrett was ballsy enough.

RSVP: YES, I typed out.

SEE YOU THERE!!!

I glared at my own reflection in the mirror, brushing and drying my hair methodically, using the order of the motion to organize the boxes in my mind.

Adam needed Garrett's bond, but I was a distraction. I had no doubt the potential was there, and perhaps my leaving would be the necessary push.

It's too late to change your mind, I told myself.

I had until Monday night.

I finished my hair, turned the phone off and dropped it to the bottom of the tank to let it drown with the bag and tape wadded up. Rory or Garrett might discover it eventually, but they wouldn't find the texts.

Rory was glaring and thumb-mashing the cell I'd surrendered, probably trying and failing to find anything useful on it, while Garrett cooked and Adam worked on the laptop. My omega sat up as I entered the room, a smile stretching over his lips to match the mischievously pleased feeling in the bond.

"They let me pick out our next safe house. We have to wait a few extra days, but it has a jacuzzi."

I blinked at that and looked to Garrett, who was watching Adam with a satisfied smile on his face. *There* was a good alpha. One who took pleasure in doting on and spoiling an omega.

I was still wrapped up in the towel, and all three men watched as I crossed the room, kneeling down at Adam's side. I scowled at the picture of the two-story simple home.

"The suburbs?" I scoffed.

"It's discreet," Garrett said.

"It's mundane."

"Eve, I'll be able to go outside. There's a privacy fence," Adam said, reaching out and stroking a hand absently over my bare back. He turned and grinned at me, cheeks rosy and eyes bright. Garrett was already doing the job better. Good.

"Fine. When do we leave?" I asked, rising and letting Adam's touch fall away.

"Monday," Rory answered.

I nodded. Perfect. "Monday then."

SIXTEEN

Eve

"You two all packed?" Garrett asked, popping his head into the bedroom.

"Yeah, more or less," Adam said.

"Go ahead and grab anything from the apartment that you like so you can set up your nest at the house," Garrett said, smiling at him. "You good too, Eve?"

I'd itched all through the weekend, staying in the safe house like a good little tamed alpha. Rory watched me like a hawk until Saturday night passed, waiting at every second for me to dash to the door. It was dull and confining, with one or the other of the alphas awake at all hours, working on their computers, researching and networking and digging for more leads. I'd spent the majority of the time in the bedroom, but it was like being imprisoned. The only positive was that I had Adam to fuck through my frustrations. He had two more bites that I'd done my best to heal before we left the safe house.

"I have some things to grab on my way, but yes," I said to Garrett, putting the last of my clothes in my bag to ignore his stare.

"Um…we're not making stops."

I turned to face him, finding Adam near the door, almost leaning into Garrett's chest. "You're not. I am."

Adam's brow furrowed, and Garrett's eyes narrowed.

"I have the Charger. I can't leave it here," I said, looking to Adam, whose expression relaxed. "And I set measures in place to keep under the radar in the city. I need to take care of that. I'll meet you at the house tonight."

"No way," Garrett said, laughing and shaking his head, backing away from the door. "No, we travel together."

"We don't," I answered, following him out, Adam torn between us, head turning back and forth.

"What's the issue?" Rory asked, his own bag sliding onto his shoulders. He scowled as Garrett repeated my claim. "No."

"This isn't a discussion."

"You're not traveling alone. Garrett will take Adam to the next location, and I'll ride with you," Rory said.

I let out a bark of laughter, genuinely surprised by the suggestion, my mind running at high speed to shoot it down. "Not a chance."

"Not a discussion," Rory answered, mimicking my tone from a moment ago with a twitch of a smile.

"Adam is *your* job. You protect him. And there's not a fucking chance I'm letting you anywhere near my contacts," I said, body tensing for a physical fight on reflex. "If you rub two brain cells together, I think you'll agree that isn't information you want to know."

"You don't know where the—"

"Of course I do," I said, cutting Garrett off with a roll of my eyes. "You really think I haven't been mapping out the area since the moment you showed me the picture?

The street address was on the front door. It wasn't hard to find."

I'd arranged for Tabby to do the work for me, but it was still true. I knew where they were taking Adam next. I just didn't plan on meeting them there.

Rory let out a soft growl and rolled his shoulders, turning for the door. "Fuck it. Let her go. But you're not there by 11 p.m. tonight, and we move Adam again. No arguments. No secret little missions."

I bristled at the order but forced my mouth to smile. "I'll be home by dinnertime, honey."

Garrett appeared to be unconvinced, but Adam stepped up to me with a smile, his nose just in front of mine.

"Pick me up a swimsuit for the jacuzzi?" he asked.

Rory huffed behind him, and I stifled the aching answer in my chest, leaning in and grazing my lips over Adam's in a tease. "No. We'll use it naked."

Adam laughed, kissed me—simple and almost automatic, strangely effortless—before stepping back and turning away. "Fine. Don't scratch the Charger. I wanna joyride in it someday."

I scoffed at the notion that I would ever let the car get damaged and followed the men to the door, biting down on the possessive growl that tried to escape as Rory rested a hand on Adam's shoulder to guide him out.

There was an uneasy turning in my stomach, a harder than normal pound of my pulse, and it seemed to grow worse with every attempt to ignore. I pulled it out and examined the feeling. My eyes flicked up from the floor, landing on Adam's back, and this time it was a stabbing sensation in my chest.

Adam. I didn't want to leave him. He was mine, in a simple and biological claim but…more than that. I liked him. He was clever and easygoing, especially for an omega, and he accepted me as an alpha. As his alpha.

I hadn't been prepared to regret this decision, but I sat with it now, calculating the odds in my head. How likely was Adam to survive in my company? How likely was I to be able to make him happy?

The odds were terrible, and the certainty was the weight of a boulder coming down on me.

My steps were dragging slightly as I sorted through my head, Adam and the alphas far ahead of me in the hall, but he stopped suddenly and turned to me with worry in his eyes.

"Eve?"

I'd let something through in the bond, just enough to alert him to my crisis. I shut it down now, pushing every little scrap of irritating regret and disappointment away until I was empty again. They were near the elevators, but the stair door was just to my left.

"I'll see you tonight, sugar," I said.

Adam frowned, and I escaped to the stairwell.

———

"FOCUS ON HIM NOW?" Tabby asked over the phone.

"Yes," I said, adjusting the gun harness around my hips.

There was a garden level apartment on the east side of Downtown that served as my base when I was in the city. It was meant to be untraceable, but I'd avoided it thus far with Adam, just in case.

I found and disabled three minor explosives, and destroyed half a dozen listening devices upon my arrival. It would alert Omikron to my presence, but I didn't think they'd jump me here. We had a date, after all, in a location of their choosing, where they were sure to have the advantage.

"The others too," I added to Tabby. "Keep the pack off their radar as well."

Tabby sighed. "One of them has a Facebook account, danger."

I let out a little laugh, turning to the mirror. Head-to-toe black tactical gear wasn't my wardrobe of choice—it reminded me too much of being an agent—but in spite of the utter lunacy of taking the bait, I did actually want to survive the night. An unlikely outcome, but I'd give it my best effort.

"Do what you can," I purred. "They're not *entirely* helpless."

"High praise coming from you," Tabby answered.

I fastened the buckle over my throat, bristling at the contact of the fabric on my skin and ignoring the irritation. Rory made my hackles rise, but I could stand to admit that he was good at his job. I wouldn't have left Adam in his care if I had any doubts of that.

"You have everything you need?"

I had body armor, an arsenal of weapons, the layout of the building where I was supposedly taking the job.

"If you want backup, I know a few—"

"No," I said immediately, glancing at the phone. "I'm all set, Tabby, thank you."

"Right. Well… Good luck, danger."

I ended the call and then braided my hair back, close and tight, tucking the long tail under the collar of my jacket.

It was almost time to leave, and I scanned the small studio apartment. Omikron would probably come and wipe it after tonight, regardless of the outcome. I'd already arranged for Adam's new ID to reach him, as well as the

information to an offshore account with half of my earn-
ings. If the pack had any sense, they'd get Adam out of the
country, help him start over with their protection. They
were the kind of men who would sacrifice their own lives
for someone in need.

It was all a little melodramatic for my tastes.

I grabbed my black bag from the floor and turned off
the lights as I headed for the door. The taxi Tabby had
ordered for me waited at the end of the block, exhaust
turning the red brake lights hazy. I slid into the backseat
and recited the address, ignoring the driver's attempts to
make conversation as I pictured the blueprint of the
building.

It was an apartment complex in renovation, supposedly
owned by this Mike Quincy, according to the paperwork.
Which meant the entire place was a massive playground
for whomever Omikron rounded up to deal with me. I
traced the halls in my mind, the positions in the lobby
where a sniper would be best concealed, the service shafts I
might be able to use if they weren't booby-trapped.

Suicide missions were never really my thing and part of
the reason why I'd gladly left agency life behind.

A new, entirely random address was on the tip of my
tongue. I could just disappear. Tabby was sure the only
lead Omikron had was on me, not Adam and the pack.

But one wrong move on their part, and that won't be the case, I
reminded myself.

And then the taxi stopped at a quiet corner in an
industrial neighborhood.

Time to move.

———

THE CELLAR of the building Omikron had chosen had once connected to another building's around the corner. I found the door two levels below ground, rusted and warped, with an easily broken lock. I moved through in silence, hearing the rare scuffle of boots above me. They hadn't known about this old entrance—thank you, Tabby, for the historical records—and I took my time in the empty quiet.

There were at least three men in the basement, probably stationed near the ground level stairwells and elevator just in case I managed to clear the first floor. They would be listening for activity above them, not expecting the attack from below, which made my first moves easy.

But there were still five levels above ground. They would concentrate men on the first floor and the roof, the two most accessible places for my entrance. There was still another ten minutes before I was scheduled, and I snuck quietly to a stairwell, listening to the radio from the hip of the man above me.

"Alpha floor, no sign yet."

"Zeta, same. Every apartment covered."

There were ten apartments on the top floor, so at least ten men there?

I held my breath, counted the clicks of the radio, the voices reporting the status in low murmurs.

Dozens of men in one building. I'd never make it above the ground floor once they knew I was inside, not without having to deal with each and every one of them. That much gunfire, and we'd attract the entire city's police department.

I needed to get to whomever was giving orders, presuming they were in the building. There was a security office taking up the majority of the back of the first floor. It was the smartest place to set up and probably the most dangerous part for me to try to get into.

Is it worth coming here if you don't find anything useful? I asked myself.

"Basement A clear," the voice above me said into the radio.

I raised my gun, rushing up the stairs in silence, and fired at close range into the back of the man's head. I caught my arm around his waist as he dropped, lowering him slowly, the radio echoing three more calls from the basement level.

In for a penny, in for the pounding of a lifetime. I took the radio from the dead man's hip and raised it to my lips.

"Hey, boys."

There was a moment of silence, the entire building seeming to take a single breath in unison.

"Basement A," the voice from Alpha floor suddenly called over the radio.

A flurry of boots from the halls around me and the ceiling above stormed in my direction. So the radio communications were all connected to someone on that main floor. Good to know.

I ran to the right, heading directly toward two of the men rushing to find me. Another approached from the stairwell behind me, and I pressed myself to the wall, a gun in each hand, waiting for the first glimpse.

A hand appeared from the stairwell first, and I fired, their gun clattering to the floor and letting off a stray shot. The man in the stairwell cried out, and I held my breath.

A woman from the basement level entered next from my right, skidding from around the corner and firing at me. It hit my Kevlar first, winding me, and I retaliated just as quickly, shooting her firing arm and then her skull as she snarled and flinched.

A shot from the left barely missed me and I fired back, luckier than the young man who'd failed to hit me. I still couldn't breathe after the shot to my chest, but it would come, and staying still to wait for the entire building to come down on me in these narrow halls was a death sentence.

I forced myself forward, listening behind me and firing toward the stairwell so the men there would keep cover.

"She's got three down," someone shouted on the radio. "One wounded."

"Do not let up, aim for the head. This is kill, not capture."

I took down the last of the basement level killers before he'd finished coming around the corner and then paused. The stairwell behind me was going to rush into the hall any second, and the one just ahead of me was sure to be crowded. I holstered one gun and pounded my fist against my ribcage, trying to reawaken my body beneath the Kevlar until I could breathe almost fully again.

There was someone else's blood on my lip and at the tip of my eyelashes.

I dropped to the floor as boots charged over the hall behind me, pulling my second gun back out and running at a crouch, firing up as I headed for the stairs. Their first shots were aimed well above me, hitting the cement wall at my back, little shards of stone scattering against the floor.

I threw myself into the body of one soldier, tossing him toward another who was firing at me. Taking one as hostage would be useless. I had no doubt these men and women had been ordered to take me down at all costs, so instead, I shot one dead and then hauled them onto my back as a shield.

"Jesus fucking Christ, she—"

"No chatter! What's the fucking holdup, people!?"

An arm reached for me, hauling me up, and I fired into the face before I could even make out the features.

Once upon a time, I'd wondered about the people I killed, who they were out of their uniforms, behind their safe doors. It made the work unpalatable, and I'd learned to lock those questions away. They were the same as me now. It wasn't personal, and I didn't relish the kills. We were just two bodies on opposing sides of death. Either they would kill me, or I would kill them.

So far, it remained the latter.

I put the pieces of myself away as I worked my way out of the stairwell. The pain of a knife in the meat of my back thigh? That was for later. The sound of a gurgling scream in my ear as I'd turned that knife onto someone else? Muted.

Third door on the right hall behind the lobby desk.

I caught the back of one black jacket in my hand and yanked the man over my head like an umbrella, his boots screeching on tile. Shots rained down from the balcony, until he was too heavy and needed to be tossed away.

Another bullet striking the Kevlar against my spine left my legs nearly numb and tingling as I ran for the door. I fired out at the growing crowd as I reached the door, kicking once just below the knob and barely keeping my balance.

My ears were ringing from the gunfire. I'd turned my own awareness of my body down low, trying to muffle the pain. I was bleeding from my head, but since I was still standing, I assumed it was just a graze. I needed a reprieve before the reality caught up.

The door opened before my second kick, and I fired quickly into the body in front of me until it collapsed, then I stormed inside, slamming the door shut.

There, at a desk with his arms raised, was a diminutive young man with bright blonde hair and thick glasses.

"Don't shoot!"

"Order them at ease," I snapped. There was blood in my mouth too, and it took me a moment before I realized it was my own. I'd bitten into my tongue to distract myself from my other wounds.

"At ease. Stop. Give us a minute!" the young man barked into his headpiece.

I scanned the large office-like room. No one else. There was a door on the far side of the room, but according to what I knew of the building, it was meant to be a closet.

"Please don't shoot," he whispered again, drawing my focus back. He was poorly protected, presumably collateral. Either they didn't expect me to make it this far, or they didn't care what happened to him if I did.

Don't take your eyes off him. I knew better than to think that because he was small, he was unarmed or incapable of firing a gun at me.

Everything was too loud in my head. The alarms going off in my body—it'd been a long time since I'd been in a position to get this badly injured, and I'd forgotten how much it fucking sucked—the hyperawareness of being under attack, even the sudden stillness of the room, of facing one opponent, was overwhelming.

"You're the field operator," I said.

"Paul—"

"I don't give a shit. Put me on the line with your superior. Don't touch that," I said, lifting my hand and firing just shy of his foot as he tried to reach under his desk.

Paul screamed and startled, his hands raising high again. "I don't know how to—"

"Yes you do. Call them. I'm honestly not in the mood, and I eat betas like you for breakfast," I said.

Paul's expression hardened, so at least he wasn't completely spineless. I charged forward and caught him by the throat, dragging him up out of his seat. My reflection was visible in his glasses, face freckled with dark stains, one thick stream of blood running down my temple.

"Call them, or I will walk out of this room and we will see if those men outside are more interested in listening to your orders or delivering me to whoever you report to—"

"Fine, fine, yes, yes, I'll call them!" Paul panted out, his toes barely reaching the floor.

I dropped him and found the gun strapped beneath the desk, taking it for myself as Paul whimpered and scrambled around the surface, pulling up an outdated flip phone.

I watched over his shoulder, memorizing the numbers on the recent call list before he dialed.

"Speaker," I instructed, and he hit the button.

The call rang five times before a low voice answered. "Finished already?"

"No, not quite," I said.

Quiet followed, and Paul sat down in his chair, my fingernails digging into his shoulder, my gun pointed toward the door.

"Evelyn."

I blinked. I hadn't heard that name in a long time.

"Have you figured it out yet?" The accent was American, the voice distorted, warped beneath some kind of computer program.

But they knew more about me than anyone had a right to know.

"Omikron owned the orphanages," I said. It had been a guess. This confirmed that.

"Very good."

It was, in fact, very bad.

"I was always optimistic about you. I assumed you would play well with us."

"I rarely play well with others," I said, taking a little bit of the rage trying to fight its way through me out on Paul's shoulder until he let out a whimper.

"He isn't dead yet?" the voice on the line asked, obviously surprised.

"Please," Paul whispered.

Omikron. How long had I been a convenient number to call on the books of this organization?

Since the beginning, I thought. Since I'd been born and then shortly abandoned. Since I'd fallen into their hands, helpless and alone. And underestimated.

"Your mind is just spinning, isn't it, Evelyn?"

"My mind is surprisingly clear," I answered.

There were at least twenty dead outside this office already, but that had to be less than half.

"You will be a great loss. You were one of our best assets."

I blinked at the open phone and then smiled.

"I will be your greatest regret," I promised.

There was a rattle from overhead, and my smile vanished as a canister of dark gas came *thunk-thunking* into the office building.

I held my breath and jumped back into motion.

SEVENTEEN

Garrett

The heel of my boot was jiggling against the floor as Adam sat cross-legged on the living room couch at my side, his eyes fixed to the clock above the fireplace.

"We're not really going to leave at 11, are we?" Adam asked.

Rory was out of the room. Probably pacing the driveway and growling under his breath about uncooperative alphas. *Come on, Eve. Don't seriously do this to him.*

"Are you...getting anything from her?" I asked, checking the clock again.

10:58.

Adam shook his head, shifting on the couch to face me while I avoided his stare like a coward. "She keeps me locked out."

I frowned at that. "If she ran into any trouble..." It would be her own damn fault for not coming here with us.

"Garrett, are we going to leave at 11?"

Adam was solemn, and I sagged back into the cushions of the couch, twisting until my knee bumped against his. "I could probably talk Rory off the ledge. Do you want to wait?"

Adam frowned at that and looked at the clock.

10:59.

"You think she's not coming. That she left me with you guys and…" Adam trailed off for a moment, watching the second hand ticking away around the face of the clock. "What happens to me if my alpha doesn't come back?"

"We're not going to let Omikron get to you, regardless of whether it's a job or just…our duty as halfway decent people," I assured him, reaching out to cup his shoulder. He leaned into the touch but continued to stare at the clock.

"I mean, what happens to me…as an omega. Without my bondmate."

I took in a deep breath. I couldn't say for sure whose fault that first bite was. Adam blamed himself, claimed he'd forced Eve into it in the heat of the moment. I'd never been in rut, and everything I'd been taught, warned, promised I'd be more or less mindless in the moment. But Adam had a half dozen other bites on his skin from Eve when she was entirely sensible of what she was doing. She'd made a choice with him by the end.

But what if that choice was just putting him into our care?

"11 o'clock," Adam said, letting out a long sigh and sliding into the couch, my hand somehow finding its way around his shoulders, drawing him into my side. His head fell back, throat exposed and shining with Eve's bites, mocking me. Daring me to claim the omega in front of me now that he'd been abandoned by his alpha, an outright unheard of act.

I *would* claim him too. If it was what he wanted. In time, when he felt safe.

The door from the garage banged open and shut,

heavy boots hitting the tile of the kitchen and then doing their best to be as loud as possible over the living room carpet. Rory in a rage, coming to demand our departure.

He made it as far as the arm of the couch, expression blazing with temper, before Adam let out a sudden howl, spasming at my side.

"Fuck!" Adam shouted, eyes wide and body contracting in on itself. He let out a wounded groan as Rory and I reached for him.

"What is it? What's happened to her?" Rory rushed out.

Adam only whined, and I searched him for injuries I knew perfectly well weren't there, passing my hands over his arms and torso.

Adam's throat flexed as he fought for air, and his hands flashed out in front of him, gripping my wrist like a vise, seizing Rory's shoulder. "NO!" he cried out suddenly with a gasp, jumping up from the couch, eyes searching the room wildly. "She shut me out again—I—Fuck, what do I —Garrett—"

I stood too, wrapping my arms around Adam, trying to absorb his tremors.

"God, she's fucking… *Everything* hurt."

"She's…?" Rory gaped up at us from the floor. "Is she alive?"

"I think so," Adam murmured, his head against my chest as my arms passed over his back slowly. "I don't think she meant for me to…feel that."

Which meant she'd let whatever guard she had up slip in the middle of—

"Shit. She fucking took that job. That trap!" I snapped at Rory. "She literally fucking *rescheduled* with Omikron so they could—" I ground my jaw shut. Was she trying to get killed?

Did she have *anyone* looking out for her tonight? And if so, who the fuck were they, and why weren't they doing a better job?

Adam gasped again, falling back into the couch with another open-mouthed expression of excruciating pain at the same moment my phone rang. I tossed it to Rory without thinking, joining Adam on the cushions.

"Just breathe. Deep as you can. Fuck, you've barely gotten used to the bond with the way she's been using it," I muttered.

"Jamie, it's not a good—" Rory paused on the phone as I coached Adam.

"Good. Another deep breath. If she can put space between you guys in the bond, so can you," I told Adam. I should've been asking where she was injured or if he had any idea where she might be, but I was more concerned for him than her. Eve had made her bed, kicked the rest of us out of it, and now she could lie there broken for all I cared.

"I think—ughhn—" Adam's hand found mine as his eyes squeezed shut, and his grip was strong and desperate.

"Okay. Okay. Look, this is up to you, but I don't think we can stay here," Rory said over the phone. "I can make arrangements or—You sure?"

I glanced between Adam and Rory, stamping down my worry for Eve that she wasn't shutting the bond as fast this time.

"I think she's winning, but it feels like hell," Adam squeezed out, eyes blinking briefly up at the ceiling. "Fuck, this is insane. We can't leave, she—"

"She had a package delivered to the security firm," Rory announced. "They sent it to our place."

I startled, staring up at him, my phone clenched in his hand as he stared grimly down at Adam. "A package."

Rory nodded. "Whole new identity for Adam. Bank account numbers. Everything."

Adam's grip on my hand relaxed, and I turned back to him. A little sweat had broken out on his forehead, and he was breathing heavily. If he weren't so pale, I would've said he looked—

Focus, Garrett.

"Bank accounts," Adam repeated.

"Passport. Driver's license. Social security number. Everything," Rory said. "We have to get out of here."

"What? Why? We can't. Eve is—"

"Eve is compromised," Rory said to Adam.

"Look, we can take a minute," I said.

Rory arched an eyebrow at me. "She knows this address. She could give it up—"

"She wouldn't!" Adam said, sitting up and snarling at Rory, a decent imitation of an alpha, if not for the fact that compared to Rory, he looked like a kitten glaring at a bear.

"You don't know what she would do. You don't know what anyone would do in that kind of situation," Rory warned Adam, his arms crossing.

Adam turned to me for support, and I hesitated, my gaze bouncing between them.

"She's injured. She's going to come here and—"

"And potentially lead Omikron to you," I said, but I was meeting Rory's eyes, our thoughts rolling slowly together in the same direction. "They know the two of you are connected. If she gets away, they can still use her to track you down."

"The safe houses are untraceable. They won't get linked back to the firm. Eve was seen out in the city by herself. There's nothing that currently links us to you," Rory said to Adam. "Nothing they can find."

"What are you saying?" Adam asked him.

"If Eve does come back to this house, which…I'll be honest, I don't think is her plan, you can't be here. And if she gives up the address to them under extreme duress, she'll be counting on you not being here," Rory said.

I looked at the clock again. 11:05.

"We don't have another safe house lined up," I said to Rory.

Rory's jaw ticked as he nodded. "I think we need to take Adam to our place."

"Home?"

"What?"

"Jamie agrees. It's better if the pack is together—"

"I'm not your pack!" Adam shouted.

"—if we have to leave suddenly. In the meantime, I would be more comfortable defending our own territory on the off chance that Omikron is able to figure out where Adam is," Rory said.

"Eve could just as easily give up his new identity as the safe house."

Rory shrugged. "Then we get him a new one. We don't have to use what she gave us, we just need to get him out of here. Now. Before they know where to look."

I knew what Rory wasn't saying. Eve had forced our hand. Gift wrapped Adam and then left him on our doorstep. As far as omegas went…Adam was a stick of dynamite with a short fuse.

But that wasn't his fault. And he needed our help.

"What about Eve? She's…" Adam's head shook slowly. "She's injured. She's…fighting Omikron for *me*. She…" His voice died, and he swallowed hard, making one attempt to speak again and then giving up with a soft groan and a full body wince as the wall in the bond between him and Eve faltered again.

"We'll…make a decision after we've got you moved somewhere safe," Rory said, raising his eyebrows at me and nodding toward Adam.

"She's smart. She can track you down," I said, leaving off what we were probably all thinking. *If she wants to.* I wrapped an arm around him and guided him up from the couch. "Rory is right—we need to move out of here before we do anything else."

Adam stared up at us, face hard and wary. I didn't know Adam well, but I knew he'd survived a long time without Eve. He was probably considering running again. I turned him to face me fully, and his chin jutted up in defiance, drawing a small twitching smile to my lips that I quickly put away.

"We want to help you. We want to shut down Omikron for good. We want to bring your sister back to safety, I promise you," I said. Adam's shoulders sank into my touch, but his gaze remained narrowed. "We can be your security or your friends or your pack. Whatever you decide. We will listen to you and trust you. Trust us too."

By some miracle, Rory chose not to contradict me. Maybe he was on the same page anyway. Adam's eyes searched my face, back and forth, reading me, and I wished there was such a thing as a temporary bond, just so he would know I was serious.

But he didn't need me to bite him, to tie him to me permanently. Adam nodded once. "Fine. I'll trust you guys."

"Good. Grab the bags and meet me at the car," Rory said, tossing me my phone. "Text Jamie and tell him we're on our way."

———

IT WAS after midnight when we finally pulled into the garage and Rory turned the key off in the ignition, going still in the driver's seat for a moment. We'd been away from home for over a week, and it was almost…unsettling to be back.

Adam was staring out the backseat window like he had been for most of the long drive to our house.

"Tired?" I asked, and then turned away to roll my eyes at myself. Rory snorted at me and then let himself out of the car, heading for the trunk to grab our things.

"I can't tell if she's dead or just…shut down," Adam said softly from the backseat.

"The latter," I said, pushing open my door and moving to open his too. "Which is…" *A dick move.* "…A good sign, right?"

Adam's head tilted, his eyes narrowed at me, dubious and uninterested in playing along.

"Want to see the nest?" I asked.

He startled at that, all but falling out of the car. "Nest? You have a nest here?"

I nodded and shrugged. "It's kind of common for pack houses, right? Obviously, ours isn't in use, but it's nice…I think." Why did I mention the nest? Did omegas usually only want it during their heat, or would it comfort Adam now?

"You probably shouldn't offer it to me until, um, we all decide," Adam said, shouldering his bag. "Another omega wouldn't appreciate it."

If we ended up bonding an omega that wasn't Adam. The thought alone made me uncomfortable, which quickly spiralled because it wasn't my right to just *assume* that Adam was our omega now just because Eve had all but shoved him at us.

Jamie opened the door from the garage, dressed in a T-shirt and sweatpants, and waved his arm back into the house. "Welcome. Any word from your alpha?" he asked Adam.

Rory, Adam, and I all winced, and Jamie's eyebrows rose.

"Shit. I see. Drinks or food or bed?"

"Drink," Rory said.

"Bed," Adam answered.

"You fill Jamie in, I'll take Adam to the guest room," I said to Rory.

My arm fell around Adam's shoulder again, and I tried not to take too much pride in the fact that he always leaned in. He was in crisis. Omegas naturally found comfort in alphas' presence, and it was important that I didn't confuse the lines between us.

I tried to see the house through Adam's eyes. It was an old Tudor revival—Jamie's request—in a quiet neighborhood with houses from the forties and fifties. The ceilings were tall—Rory's request—and most of the walls had built-in shelves. But we were three ex-army guys living together. Jamie's work meant we had a few beautiful pieces of furniture around, and then it was somehow paired with beaten-up leather armchairs and couches. The walls were bare, none of us especially clear on our taste in art, and we were missing a lot of soft furnishings.

"It's… We haven't been living here that long," I said. Adam blinked at me, and I realized that he didn't actually give a fuck. He was thinking about Eve. A spark of jealousy rose up in me, and with it, anger. She'd *left* her omega. And maybe she was right, maybe we were safer for Adam. Better for him. But right now, he was busy being worried about her and she was…

The anger sputtered out like a match.

Eve was probably in serious danger, if not dying. Why

hadn't she just spoken to Rory and I for more than two minutes about her plan? *Because it would've put us in danger too, and with us, Adam.* I pushed away the tangle of thoughts and reminded myself of the task at hand. Get Adam somewhere to sleep. Try and make him comfortable.

"Come on, I'll show you upstairs."

He followed me in silence, and at one point when his steps paused, I turned to find himself braced against the wrought iron handrail to the stairs, grimacing and breathing through clenched teeth.

"Fuuuck," he gasped out as the spell ended, and he stood straight again, shaking his head.

"She's… What's happening?"

"I don't think she's fighting anymore. It's like it's…not as sharp, but somehow it hurts worse?"

That meant adrenaline was wearing off and shock would set in soon. "Any sense of if she feels safe or not?" I asked. I wanted to strangle Eve for putting Adam through this. And me too, a little bit. Worrying over her. Feeling helpless in the situation and unwanted.

Adam shook his head. "It's just the pain coming through. Like it gets too much for her to keep the bond closed. And then when she has it under control again, *blip* goes the connection. I'm fine now."

He wasn't. Maybe physically, but this was putting him through the wringer. I held my hand out without thinking, and the coil of stress in my stomach unwound just a fraction as Adam's fingers locked with mine.

"You're right here," I said, frowning at the guest bedroom door.

"What's wrong?" Adam asked.

"I just…don't like having you right at the stairs?"

"Think I'm going to escape?" Adam laughed.

I shook my head. "It's just not as secure. The nest is…" At the end of the hall. If someone broke in, they'd have to make it past me, Rory, and Jamie to get there. I fidgeted in place. "The guest room is kind of barren. Just a bed and an empty dresser at this point. Do you… Would you rather use my room? We'd share the adjoined bath, but it's at the end of the hall and—"

Adam stared at me, amused and suspicious.

"I'll sleep here," I said, pointing to the guest room, some alpha authority appearing. "It's better that way. Safer for you."

And Adam would be surrounded by my scent, my things. He'd be in my bed.

Sounds so reasonable when you look at it that way, I hissed to myself.

"I have all the stuff from the apartment," he said, patting his bag at his side. The blankets and sheets he and Eve had used.

"Good, use them," I said, nodding. "In my room."

I tried not to think about how unbothered I was at the idea of Eve's scent marks all over my space too.

"Come on," I said, grabbing Adam's arm and leading him down the hall before Rory or Jamie could come up and wonder what the hell I was thinking.

My walls were painted a dark ash blue, and the room was tidy with a military precision. My bed was a simple oak sleigh bed, and a king, central and obvious in front of us as we stepped into the room. The door to the bathroom was open, and I flipped on the light switch, moving around with an almost frantic energy.

It wasn't a big deal that I was putting Adam in my bedroom. It wasn't a hindbrain thing. It was for…security. Obviously.

If Eve actually was planning on coming back for

Adam, she would probably snap my dick off for the presumption.

"The rooms are bigger than I expected," Adam said.

I turned out of the bathroom to find him standing by the corner of the bed, eyeing it speculatively.

"I can change the sheets," I offered.

He shook his head. "I'm fine, honestly. I like your scent."

My purr erupted, sudden and loud, in answer to that declaration, and Adam's eyes widened, his cheeks going pink.

Be cool, not weird. Cool, not weird.

"I like yours too. Make yourself comfortable. We'll probably be in the kitchen. You know how to find your way back?" I needed to leave Adam here. In my bedroom. Leave, not tackle him to the bed and rub my scent all over him like he was an unclaimed omega waiting for my bite.

But he kind of is, a wicked voice offered.

"Yep, I'm good."

I did not run for the door to the hall, but it was safe to say I made excellent time as I bolted downstairs to find the others.

Rory was sitting with Jamie at the kitchen table, a glass of ice drained of alcohol in one hand and a hard drive in the other.

"He good?" Jamie asked.

I nodded and bit down the urge to shout that he was staying in my room while he was here.

"Is she alive?" Rory asked.

"Seems like it, like she might've gotten away."

Rory held out the hard drive to me. "I duplicated her laptop while she was out last time. Seemed pretty skeletal, but I'd like you to look through it."

"Look for what?" I asked, still thinking of Adam

upstairs, imagining him in my sheets, Eve's scent mingling with mine.

"Anything to give us a lead on where to find her," Rory said.

The picture of Adam popped. "Find her," I repeated.

Rory frowned at me. "Yeah."

"You want to find Eve?"

"She's injured."

"Badly," I supplied, based on what Adam had said.

"Then her best chance of survival is us, and Adam's best chance of survival is her and us," Rory said, shaking the hard drive in my direction. "There has to be something on here. Just a bread crumb to start us off."

"What if she doesn't want Adam? Or us?" I asked. And since when the hell did Rory care?

He let out a short growl, more of a grunt in terms of Rory's expressions. "Look, this isn't my first choice, but Adam needs her. And alphas need other alphas too. She's been on her own too long. She wanted a pack so bad, she's going to get one."

He slammed the words out, mostly directing them to the surface of the table. I glanced at Jamie, who shrugged and fought a smile. Rory wanted to rescue Eve? The hitwoman he'd been growling at for over a week?

I took the hard drive, and Rory brought the glass up to his lips again, scowling when he found only ice water.

EIGHTEEN

Eve

The alarm clock blared, and I wrapped my teeth around my lips to swallow my growl, reaching out to click it off before pushing myself up from the mattress with agonizing slowness. My arm trembled beneath me, a concerning numbness in my legs and around my lower back.

Time to move. Time to move. Time to move again, my head chanted.

Not a fucking chance, my body answered.

There was sunlight scratching through the cracks in the newspaper pasted over the windows. I'd managed two hours of sleep, as much as I could safely spare, but I needed to switch locations.

I closed my eyes for a moment, but dizziness struck alongside the memory of the night before. There were survivors, but not ones who could follow me out. The carnage in my head drew bile up to my throat, burning and scratching to be released. I put the night into a box and sealed it shut, shuffling it into the corners. I breathed through my teeth, trying to ignore the flavor of mildew and dust in the air, and then opened my eyes again when I knew I wouldn't be sick. My body couldn't take the effort of heaving right now.

I forced my legs to the floor, with a little encouragement from my swollen and bruised hands, and ignored the piercing shot of pain that ran up my spine.

The basement I was in was quiet, cool, and carefully stocked. The med kit I'd used the night before was still out, bloodied cotton scattered on the floor, the needle that had stitched me up now dirtied from the cement. I reached for the bottle of pills—antibiotics, slightly expired—and swallowed another one down, grimacing as it scratched against my throat. My wounds were all swollen, especially the one at the back of my thigh where I'd been stabbed, and there was blood crusted on my face, pulling at the strands of my hair.

I needed pain meds, a blood test to check for diseases, and better antibiotics. I needed somewhere safe to rest.

I needed to get out of the basement and to the next flop station I'd set up. Out of the city as soon as I could.

There was a jug of water at the edge of the bed, just out of reach, and I stifled my scream as I dragged it toward me, one numb hand cupping at my bruised ribs.

You were one of our best assets.

The words kept popping up, no matter how many times I tried to bury them.

I'd been in Omikron's pocket since I'd been dropped off at the orphanage. I'd been shaped into a killer by these people, and then landed myself into working for them. Which meant I'd earned the right to tear them down.

And I couldn't do that while squatting in a basement. My body was nearly broken, but not quite. I would just have to rely on momentum to keep me going for a little bit.

I reached out to a pipe running up the wall and grabbed on to drag myself to standing.

Blood rushed to my head, and the basement went black, my body swaying. In the darkness, Adam found me, scrabbling panic and sudden relief reaching out as if he could haul me across miles just through the bond. He was still safe with the others. I squeezed my fingers around the pipe, and the grinding ache of my hand settled me back in the basement. I gasped for air as my vision cleared, winced against the stab of my ribs, and shut the bond closed again.

Adam would be fine. I had to keep moving.

————

I BLENDED in with the homeless people of the city, sleeping under newspapers on park benches, scrounging up meals from grocery store dumpsters. I was sweating through thin layers of clothing stolen off hangers in Salvation Armys. Tearing my stitches climbing over wire fences to sleep in the hollows under bridges.

I shivered in a Low Town alleyway, watching the front door of the apartment building across the road, a hood hiding my features from the spotty street lamps. It was late, after last call in all the bars around the corner from here, and traffic had trickled down to only the occasional set of legs marching quickly past me.

The wound in my thigh was infected. My ribs were more likely broken than bruised, and poorly wrapped by swollen and trembling hands.

My plan, as it turned out, was shit. I hadn't learned anything useful from Omikron. If anything, things were much worse than I'd realized, and I'd been tangled in the mess from the start. The only thing I'd accomplished was getting myself beat to hell.

My eyelids were heavy and my vision blurred, but I recognized the glitter of light-up boots stomping down the sidewalk right away. The whine of a wounded animal crawled up my throat, every nerve, muscle, and bone protesting as I dragged myself to standing and stepped out of the shadow of the alley. The figure at the end of the block stiffened at the sight of me, dodging toward the street, and I swept the hood back from my face briefly.

Tabby paused and then hurried forward as I pulled the hood back up and ducked back into the alley.

I'd been resisting coming to her, too aware that I'd risk her safety if I accidentally drew eyes to her, but I didn't have any choice now. My old stash of antibiotics had failed to save my ass, and now I needed…*help*.

"Jesus, danger, where have you been?" Tabby hissed, chasing after me.

"Tabs, I'm sorry to come here——"

"You look like hell," she said.

I felt like it too. "I need you to get some stuff for me," I said, holding out a napkin with a list of medications scribbled and scratched on.

Tabby's lips pressed firmly together, her eyes flicking over her shoulder to the quiet neighborhood. "You should come inside."

"No."

"Eve, you need to shower and you need——"

"I need what's on that list. It was bad enough that I came here," I said.

Tabby searched my face, the mischievous light in her eyes already faded after a long night of dancing at the club she worked for. "Maybe…maybe you should call that pack. One of them reached out——"

"Tabs," I snapped, grabbing for the paper, but I was too slow and the alley was starting to spin.

She lifted it up out of my reach, lips twitching as I raised my arm and grunted in pain. I gave up trying to steal it back, falling back to lean against the alley wall. She arched an eyebrow and then pulled the list down to read it, that brief smile sinking.

"This is… I'm not sure I have a connection to get all of this."

"Please," I wheezed.

She looked back and forth between me and the napkin before nodding once. "You think you can make it…three days?"

Maybe. Maybe not. "Of course," I said, flinching as I attempted a casual shrug.

"I could maybe make it two—" Tabby said, biting at her electric pink lip.

"Three. In the park, gazebo by the pond," I said, lifting my chin.

Tabby took one long look up and down, her nose wrinkling slightly—probably deciding whether she thought I would survive that long—and then nodded once. "Good luck, danger."

For once, I really needed that luck. I turned toward the dark end of the alley, trying to keep my steps steady until I finally heard Tabby's retreat.

I wasn't sure how far I could make it tonight before finding a place to rest and hide, but the park was halfway across the city, and it would probably take me all three days to get there.

If I make it there, I admitted to myself.

I made to an abandoned mattress by a dumpster on the far end of Low Town before sinking down to rest. I waited, my eyes open on the dark and blurry city around me.

Sure enough, Adam slipped in as I was falling asleep, right at the last moment before I fell unconscious. Every night, he was less relieved and more resigned, not pleading but observing. He was moving on. Just as I'd planned for him.

I was surprised to find that stung.

NINETEEN

Adam

"What about that one?" I asked, grinning and pointing to the large brick ranch style house with the blue and purple Christmas tree taking up the majority of the front window.

Faith hummed, hand reaching up absently to rub the pink tip of her nose. "Four alphas, no omega, but at least one of them has a beta girlfriend who spends all her time cleaning up after them and decorating the place for the season."

I snorted at that, snow crunching under my sneakers.

"Your turn," Faith said, nodding at the little white cape style house with its windows and gutters trimmed in silver icicle lights.

"Older beta couple, retired," I said, shrugging.

"Come on, put some imagination into it," Faith said with a laugh, stomping her feet as we walked.

Both our shoes were too thin for this time of year. Our coats too. But we were staying with a friend who wouldn't be back to their apartment until late, and this was a better way of passing the time than risking being chatted up at a bar.

"Umm…okay," I hemmed. "Okay. The wife is a dominatrix.

She makes him change the decorations every week and then she hogties him with the string lights in the bedroom when he's done."

Faith let out a stream of giggles, bright and giddy, and I grinned as those giggles hiccuped into snorts.

"Your turn. What about this one?" I asked, pointing to the pretty, pale blue Victorian with its wraparound porch and thin gold string lights twining around every post, window, and door frame.

"Oh." Faith's steps slowed as she stared up at the old house. "Oh, I think…I think this one has a pack."

I nodded. "Certainly big enough for one."

Faith pointed up at the rounded corner tower, the windows an ornate floral stained glass pattern and dimly lit from inside. "That's the nest."

"They have an omega?" I asked.

"Not yet," Faith said shyly. "No, but they've met one. They're courting her. And… And they're going to have her come for dinner on Christmas so they're making everything nice inside for her. They're… one of the good packs."

I stared at my sister, bile churning in my stomach as she gazed wistfully up at the house, obvious longing in her gaze. This was what she wanted—a house like this, a fantasy pack just waiting for her arrival, preparing her nest and courting her slowly. And she would find them.

And then my place in her life would be…moot.

Faith's smile hitched. "But one of them has a foot fetish."

I huffed out a half-hearted laugh at that, and we started walking again, past the dream house, back into our reality with cold feet and noses, biding our time until we could make our next move against Omikron.

I stroked my hand over the polished wood shelves in the living room, absently pulling open a drawer to find odds and ends inside—batteries and dice and rubber bands and a deck of cards.

I should've taken her to the nearest Omega Center that night, I thought, frowning. I should've found Faith that perfect pack and perfect house, and then I should've carried on without her. But I hadn't. I'd pretended to believe her when she said she wanted to keep fighting them with me. Because I wanted it to be true.

Selfish.

"Hey."

I startled and spun to find Jamie studying me from the doorway of the dining room.

"Hi, sorry, I was just...snooping," I admitted with a fragile smile.

Jamie shrugged. "Snoop away. Garrett's busy?"

I nodded. "Doing some research for his boss."

Jamie looked around the room, and I realized he'd come in from his shop, his short dark dreds and close beard flecked with sawdust. "You look like you could use something to do," Jamie said, eyes wrinkling at the corners with a smile.

I let out a rush of breath and nodded eagerly. "Please. I'm...kinda stir-crazy."

"Any news from that wayward alpha of yours?" Jamie asked carefully, turning and waving his hand for me to follow.

I grimaced and shook my head. "No, she's... I can feel her sometimes but it's like...I get dizzy and the room gets blurry and I'm really tired and then she's gone. I'm getting her symptoms, not *her*."

Jamie frowned at that, pausing in the kitchen to fill up two large water bottles. "Those sound like pretty serious symptoms."

Which was true, and not at all what I wanted to hear at the moment.

"Sorry, you must be..." He paused for a moment and

then shook his head. "No, actually, you don't have to be anything. How *are* you?"

"Angry," I said immediately, my hands clenching at my side. Jamie just nodded. "And also…worried. And hurt. I think she's a psychopath, you know, but I started to like her and I kinda thought she liked me too."

"Maybe she does," Jamie said with a shrug. "I mean, I can see her argument for leaving you with us."

I opened my mouth to argue and then shut it again. *Like I should've taken Faith to the Omega Center to keep her out of danger.*

"She would be safer here too," I said slowly.

Jamie nodded. "She would. I missed a lot having to come back here. What was it about her that you liked?"

He turned away as I flushed, and I found myself following him out of the house, through the garage and into the yard. The first thing about Eve that came to mind was the sex, which wasn't really something I wanted to bring up to the pack member I knew the least about.

"Um, well…it's not that I didn't think of her as an alpha," I said.

"Kind of impossible not to," Jamie said, grinning over his shoulder.

"Yeah. But she was different, maybe because she so obviously wanted to be alone. And so did I. I thought if I just had her…I wouldn't have to do the whole pack thing. Um, no offense."

"None taken," Jamie said, and there was just something so easy about it him that he made it sound absolutely true. He opened the door to his shop and waved me inside. "I just have some hand sanding to do, you're welcome to help or just fiddle around with whatever."

The shop was tidy and open, and had a warm, fresh quality to it, not unlike Jamie's scent that reminded me a little of cilantro and some kind sweetly spiced cocktail. I helped myself to a seat on a stool, accepting the bottle of water he passed me, and watched him work.

"We aren't the same, but Eve and I…complement each other," I said before rolling my neck on my shoulders. "Or at least I thought so."

"She was feral, right?" Jamie asked, even though the answer was kind of obvious. "I did a little research on that after I got back home from the safe house. It can be hard to transition out of that for an alpha. Being around stability can feel like a threat to a feral alpha's identity. So we can guess she thought you would be safer here with us. And maybe she thought she would be safer away from us."

"That's the thing though—I don't want Eve to be… tame. I like her feral," I said, grinning briefly.

Jamie nodded and glanced up from where he was smoothing the seat of a chair with slow, circular motions. "Sure. But where would *you* rather be right now? Here at this house? Or wherever Eve is, in the shape she's in?"

I opened my mouth and then shut it again, reaching into the bond. I had to grasp onto the table in front of me as the dizziness swept in. This time, it brought with it a cold sweat breaking out over my skin and a sharp pain running through my bones.

Did I want to be with Eve right now? Or was I just a little more like Faith than I realized? Would I pass up this house and the politely patient pack and…*Garrett*, to be withering away with my alpha somewhere?

Selfish.

"It's okay to want to be safe, Adam," Jamie said.

"She said she would keep me safe. That she would help me find my sister," I said, holding in my whine.

Jamie frowned with me, the pair of us staring at one

another. Maybe Eve had thought these men would do a better job in helping me. Or maybe she'd just lied.

"You know we're going to do everything we can to follow through on those promises, right?" Jamie said.

It wasn't the same as when Garrett said something along those lines. I didn't have the impulse to crawl into Jamie's arms. But there was something calming and familiar about the man in front of me, in spite of how little I knew him. He was friendly and straightforward. And maybe a little bit magic at drawing information out of me.

"How did your pack meet?" I asked, hoping to turn the focus away from my problems.

Jamie went along with the pivot of topic easily. "Believe it or not, Rory is the lynchpin for us. Being in the army is kind of like an automatic pack sometimes. A lot of units with alphas phase out together and stay that way. I left mine a little early, and Rory was leaving at the same time as me. We didn't…click the way most packs describe doing, but he and I got an apartment in the city together and it felt pretty natural from that point on."

"And Garrett?"

"Garrett looked up Rory after he left too, since they'd crossed paths in service a couple times. Rory got him the job with Wes Pike and…" Jamie shrugged with a crooked smile. "Honestly, it wasn't really a bromance. We all got along, but partly because we're all busy doing our own things. Garrett's lease went up around the same time as ours, and so we found a slightly bigger place. It was about two years down from that before we really called each other a pack."

"So I'm really throwing a wrench in the works, huh?" I asked, attempting a laugh.

Jamie just smiled. "You're making things interesting. We probably were overdue for shaking it up a bit."

The door to the shop opened before I could say anything else, revealing Rory with his shoulders almost up to his ears. He spotted me, and they dropped immediately.

"There you are. I, uh—have something to show you."

Jamie's eyebrows kicked up at that, along with mine, and I slid off the stool.

"It's in the house," Rory clarified.

"Can I come?" Jamie asked.

Rory grunted, probably a neutral answer, and the three of us left the shop together. Jamie's explanation of the pack cleared things up a bit. When it wasn't about work or what was for dinner, I didn't really see the guys in many discussions. They were just shy of being only roommates, and I didn't know what that meant for me as their potential omega.

Garrett was coming down from working upstairs as we entered the living room. I stopped short, my eyebrows bouncing up. Rory had rearranged the furniture—somewhat haphazardly—to make room for a round table and four chairs in the corner. It had a familiar green felt on the top and a small drawer in the table at each seat. A poker table. Rory had gotten me a poker table.

"Are you a card shark as well as a con artist?" Rory asked.

If it weren't for the slightly nervous quirk of his lips, I would've taken the snarl of his voice the wrong way.

"I could've made this," Jamie said, with slight offense.

"So make a new one," Rory said, shrugging and glaring back at him.

"Are you prepared to find out?" I asked Rory, cutting through their bickering.

Garrett laughed. "Who cares if he is? We each put fifty dollars in the pot and see who comes out the winner."

"Garrett fleeced a lot of his unit back in the day," Jamie said, low in my ear.

"I'd love to play for money, but I...kinda don't have access to any," I said, widening my eyes and exaggerating the shrug of my shoulders.

"I'll spot you," Rory said quickly, crossing his arms over his chest and raising an eyebrow at me.

Which meant if I won, I'd have to pay him back. But I'd still have one hundred fifty dollars. And something to think about besides Eve for an hour or so.

"Deal," I said.

TWENTY

Eve

"No! No! Stop it!"

I watched the little girl running, the beaming grin on her face as the man chased after her, slowing his steps to allow her the lead.

"I'm gonna get you!"

"No!"

He dove for her, scooping her up off her feet as she screamed and laughed.

"Got you!"

The view over the gazebo ledge was serene, the city gleaming over the tops of the trees in the park, the water of the pond shimmering under the sun. I flinched as it glittered too brightly and turned my head on a stiff neck to search for Tabby's arrival. My entire body ached, right down into my bones. I'd had to stop to catch my breath five times on my walk to the park.

Sepsis was setting in, the antibiotics failing to fight the extent of infection running through me from my wounds. It had been over a week since I'd made it out of the building, and all I'd been doing was faltering in my attempt to survive.

Except it wasn't Tabby approaching the gazebo.

I stiffened, my breath catching in my lungs as I tried to sound a warning growl at the sight of the massive alpha taking slow steps closer. My ribs refused the noise, and it became a muffled whimper. Rory's gaze bounced between me and the civilians in the park around us.

I started to stand and hissed when my legs trembled. I looked too weak. Better to stand—sit—my ground on the bench and convince him to leave.

Rory stopped just in front of the steps. There was no one nearby. A couple had considered coming into the gazebo but left at the first sight of me.

"Your friend didn't know where you were staying," Rory said.

My hands were too swollen and weak to tighten around the bench but they formed weak claws. Rory was huge, and he wasn't half dead. I didn't stand a chance against him physically. I probably didn't even have it in me to scratch him. I'd give it a decent effort.

"You're in better shape than I expected," he said.

"Fuck you," I spat, my voice rasping.

His hands raised, and fisted in one was a paper pharmacy bag. "Hey. Not being funny. There were like fifty plus in there with you from what we gathered."

I glared at him, but my eyes kept sliding to the bag.

"You should've taken one of us with you," Rory said, dark eyebrows drawing together as he scanned me.

I was dressed in layers and still shivering, sweating, on a perfect sunny day in the city.

"You never would've agreed to come," I answered.

He was quiet, but he watched me carefully as he stepped slowly up the wooden stairs and into the shadow of the gazebo. "You're probably right. It was a fucking stupid move."

I groaned as I laughed, sagging back against the wall and trying not to pass out.

"Okay," Rory said. "I lied, you look like shit scraped off the side of a boot."

"Fuck you," I said again, but with less feeling this time. I eyed the bag. "Is that for me?"

Rory nodded but he didn't approach.

"Is it conditional?" I bit out.

"No. Well. A bit. You just have to listen to me for a minute or two."

"Forget it," I said, and Rory's eyes widened, a growl rising up his throat.

"The fuck, Eve, you're *dying*. You cannot be that fucking stubb—" He blinked at me as I shook and let out a strangled groan with another hiccup of laughter. He rolled his eyes and huffed. "You're joking."

"And you're a genius."

He snarled but charged forward, only pausing as I flinched. "I'm not gonna grab you," he muttered, slamming down into the closest bench, but still feet away. "Adam is making himself sick worrying about you."

"He'll be fine as soon as—"

"Look, I get it. Garrett's gonna bond Adam, and then you think that absolves you of the duty or whatever, but guess what? It doesn't," Rory barked out, finally losing the patience he'd been feigning. "That's your omega. I dunno if he made you bite him, or if you thought you could bond an omega and then kill him. The two of you are...fucking messes, as far as I can tell."

"Charming pitch," I said, my eyelids growing heavy.

"But you are messes that are involved with my pack. You wanted a pack for Adam? That means you have a pack too. If Garrett bites Adam, that's not going to cut your connection, it's going to add Garrett into it. And he comes with me and Jamie," Rory said firmly, glaring at me.

"How much more of this do you have to say?" I asked, my words slurring. "If Tab—my friend were here, she would've given me the shot by now. Where is she? How did you—"

I startled and snarled as suddenly, Rory was just inches away from me, gaze tracing my features.

"Calm down, you're right. Shit."

There was a ripping sound and then hot hands were pushing the sleeve of my sweatshirt up my arm. I looked down and scowled at the size of Rory's fingers. I was not weak just because he was big.

Well, I was weak. At the moment.

"Garrett found just barely enough info to track her down, but only because I had access to your hardware," Rory muttered, prepping the shot with those careful, over-sized fingers. "She's safe, about as uncooperative as you. But she couldn't get her hands on this stuff on her own, so I bargained."

I didn't flinch as he injected me with the antibiotics.

"I've got good pain meds for you too, but I wasn't sure how you'd feel about them," Rory said. "So that's up to you."

"What do you want?" I asked, trying to glare at him, but mostly wanting to curl up on the bench and sleep. He was a strange mixture of broad, harsh features and a certain amount of dark elegance. I usually found his scent oppressively strong, too sweet, but at the moment, it made me hungry, all warm and sugary, totally the opposite of the man's personality.

I wanted to bite him.

I was getting delirious.

Rory's chin lifted as he drew the needle out of my vein, dark eyes landing on mine. "I want you to come with me. You need rest and medication and probably some PT. I want you to take responsibility for your omega instead of trying to leave him in our hands like a coward. And look, we will be there too. With you."

"You don't want me to be pack," I said, shaking my head. "I'm a killer."

Rory's frown deepened, so severe on his face, I wanted to flick him on the nose. Oh, whoops.

My fingernail made a little *thwap!* sound against his nose, his eyes crossing to stare at the spot briefly, a giggle rising from my throat.

"It's not ideal," he said, and I'd already half forgotten what we were talking about. "But we'll figure it out."

"I'm in charge," I growled at him.

His full lips pressed flat, and his eyes glinted sharply. "Being head of pack is not about absolute rule," he snarled back. "You're spoiled, is what you are."

"Spoiled!"

"You've been having your own way for your whole life—"

"You know shit-all about my life."

"And you think that you can bully everyone into doing what you want."

"Fuck off. Now."

Rory bristled and sat up straight. He was twice as broad as me and a head taller. And he wasn't beaten up and fighting infection. He was, however, spinning weirdly. The whole park was.

"No," he said, glaring down at me.

"You said—"

"Fuck what I said. Eve, you are coming home with me,

to your pack. You look like shit. You smell like shit. Try and tell me you don't feel like shit."

"If you think I'm going to let you—" I mumbled, trying to sit up but only sinking further into my seat, my body protesting every tiny shift.

"Let me what? Pick you up and carry you out of the park to the car? Stop me. There was a sedative in the antibiotic," Rory snapped.

I growled, but the sound was pathetic, kittenish.

Rory sighed, and I closed my eyes to my swimming vision of him wavering. "I'm sorry. Not my proudest moment. I fully expect you to beat the shit out of me for it. When you're feeling better."

I slapped out a hand in his direction, a worthless effort of protest, but the best I could do now that my mouth was gummy and my eyes refused to open again. Rory caught my wrist gently, and a moment later the world tipped precariously as I was lifted off my bench. I was unconscious before I had to suffer further indignity.

TWENTY-ONE

Adam

"Why do you keep checking your phone?" I asked Garrett, stretching a leg down to nudge my foot against his hip.

"Um," he stalled, tucking the phone back into his pocket and blinking rapidly as he stared straight ahead of him.

I sat up, frowning. Garrett was the exact opposite of Eve. He was open, playful in a way that felt sincere rather than guarded, and…

Nurturing. I'd been trying not to think too hard about the way we'd been circling one another for the past week, but the truth kept staring me in the face. Garrett was a perfect alpha. He was constantly bringing me a snack or a blanket or pillow. He did it like a reflex. Even better, he included me in every piece of research on Omikron, not just using me to build his web but showing me how the threads connected, including me.

"It's…uh—" Garrett's eyes widened as I sat up suddenly, sliding over the cushions and then settling myself on his lap, my knees bracketing his hips.

Jamie was out in the shop working on an order. Rory had been at his job in the city the past couple days. Garrett and I were alone in the house together. We'd been friendly all week, maybe a little more flirtatious and touchy than friendship warranted. But Garrett was being his perfect, respectful self and leaving the rest up to me.

"You keeping secrets all of a sudden?" I asked, arching an eyebrow and bracing my hands on the back of the couch behind his head, digging for information in the easiest way between an alpha and omega.

I grinned as Garrett's cheeks flushed. He was so transparent. "Maybe. Yes. One."

He would've been an easy mark, I thought. Garrett probably wouldn't have even taken any con. He was the kind of alpha that you only had to ask for what you wanted. Maybe give him a good reason to help.

I scooted closer, gratified by the kick of Garrett's hips up against my own. He wasn't too much bigger than me, so sitting up on his lap like this gave me the advantage of height.

I tested my theory, bowing my head so it hovered just over his. "Tell me your secret."

Garrett's eyes fell to my mouth, his own tongue flicking out to wet his bottom lip. It was a nice lip.

Eve was an entirely unique creature, but she was an alpha, and sexual, and I'd been treated to a lot of physical attention while with her. I was missing that connection. Missing touch. And Garrett's scent was gentler, mouthwatering, rather than overwhelming like Eve's. It would be different with him, and I was growing curious as to the specifics. We could just fool around a little, couldn't we? He wouldn't push.

I dipped my head, focused on that shining bottom lip,

and then found myself halted by his hand over my mouth, his body suddenly stiff beneath mine.

"Wait, I—" Garrett gasped out. I reared back and he sat up with me, the hand on my mouth moving to cup my throat before flinching away. He stared up at me, eyes wide and forehead creased with worry. "Rory has Eve. He's bringing her back here."

Like a reflex, I reached out in the bond. I'd had glimpses of her all week, ones that made me queasy and stressed, but she'd always pushed me away again, until slowly those glimpses were less brief sources of relief to know she was alive, and more infuriating proof that she was choosing to avoid me.

"What?" I asked, my voice flat.

"We tracked down a contact of hers. It took some convincing, but I... Rory says Eve is really sick. She needed medication."

"We?"

Garrett paled and swallowed. "*I* tracked down the contact. Rory reached out. It...was his idea. No, fuck, sorry. It was, but I should've told you what I was doing, I just—"

"Didn't know if you'd actually find her," I finished for him, and Garrett sighed and nodded. I looked down to my legs spread over his, remembered the way his hand had pulled back from my throat like it was burnt. From Eve's marks. I slid off his lap and back onto the couch at his side.

"I'm sorry for not warning you," Garrett said softly.

"So she needs our help. She's coming back 'cause she's hurt?"

Garrett stared at me for a moment and then sighed, digging into his pocket and pulling it out again. "She's coming back because Rory drugged her unconscious. But yes, she needs our help."

I took the cell from him. He'd opened it to a text conversation with Rory.

Almost home. I don't know how much longer she would've survived.

My hand clenched around the phone, my heart stuttering in my chest. I couldn't make sense of my own emotions, so I pushed them away like I was shutting down the bond.

"She's going to be pissed when she wakes up," I said.

Garrett took a deep breath, lips pursing and head nodding. "Yeah. But I think she's pretty beat up—"

"She won't want to be in any of the bedrooms. They smell like you guys. We should put her in the nest," I said.

Garrett's mouth was parted, eyes blinking for a moment. I'd been ignoring the nest all week, perfectly content in Garrett's room, surrounded by his safe scent. I didn't think Eve would feel the same, and I wasn't sure I wanted her in there with me.

"Nest it is," Garrett said. "I need to go give Jamie the heads-up and see if we can get some more meds. Probably some fluids too."

I dug my fingers into my hair, trying to imagine Eve's reaction when she woke and realized Rory had more or less kidnapped her. I winced as the door from the garage banged open, heavy boots hitting the tile.

"Shit," Garrett breathed, jogging for the kitchen and then stopping, frozen in place in the doorway. "*Shit.*"

My arms folded over my chest, shoulders shrinking as I listened to every step, until Garrett was falling back and Rory was revealed. He looked as grim and irritated as ever, but I only spared him a glance before my stare was fixed to the bundle in his arms. Eve looked impossibly small against him, swamped in dark, stained clothing. Her head was propped against his shoulders at an odd angle, and I had a ridiculous impulse to take a picture, as if to tease her later with the evidence of being cradled by Rory.

My throat throbbed, my bondmarks calling to their maker. I shook myself and stumbled backwards to launching forward and colliding into her. "We're putting her in the nest," I said, as if I had a right to order Rory around in his own house.

He only nodded and turned for the stairs. "It's got the best bath. Smart," he said. "She needs to be undressed, you better come with me. Garrett—"

"Meds and Jamie. On it," Garrett said, staring at the limp sway of Eve's feet dangling.

It took me a moment, and Rory looking over the stair railing at me with an arched eyebrow, to remember to move. I hurried after him and finally saw Eve's hand hanging, knuckles swollen and bruised purple and green.

"She's weak, but I think I've committed enough crimes against her already. You should be the one to undress her. The sepsis is pretty bad, and she's a little delirious already," Rory said, his low voice almost a murmur as he walked to the end of the hall. "You'll have to be careful. I don't know all of her injuries."

"You saved her life," I said.

Rory's steps paused, but only for a beat. "She wanted to finish off Omikron for you. Just making sure they don't get the privilege of finishing her."

I wasn't sure if I liked Rory. I didn't think he liked me. As far as I could tell, he and Eve hated each other. But I was beginning to understand why his scent reminded me of cinnamon buns. He was just a slightly burnt one, extra crispy around the edges.

"Can you get the door?"

"Oh!" I hurried ahead of him and opened the door without thinking.

A nest. I'd been in a couple, but not ones meant for me. *This nest* isn't *meant for you*, I reminded myself quickly. But it hadn't been claimed.

The room was small, with a low ceiling that Rory nearly scraped his head against, and on the far end a frosted skylight revealed a thin line of muted sunlight overhead. There was a short entrance way, hutches built into the walls, shelves lined with pillows and blankets, and a door on my right opened to reveal the bathroom. Rory moved ahead of me, kicking off his boots and stepping down into the pit of the mattress with Eve still in his arms. They were a fairly small pack with only three alphas, and the nest wouldn't accommodate much more than the three of them and…and their chosen omega.

It was a modest nest, but it struck me as…safe. Clean. Comfortable. I'd only really used nests in hotels and the Omega Center, and no amount of sanitation really removed that feeling of it being a shared space. I wanted to dive down into the mattress, where Rory was lowering a stirring Eve, and rub my scent over every inch.

A soft, ragged growl sounded from below, and I remembered why I was here. Not to claim a nest, and a pack with it. For Eve.

"Can you get me a warm, wet washcloth?" I asked Rory. "She's probably not ready to be moved to the bath." And I didn't want her griming up this sacred space with the smells of the city streets. It was too perfect.

He hesitated a moment, towering over the tangle of Eve with deep lines of a frown in his forehead. Maybe the hate I'd been sniffing between those two was more one-sided than I'd realized. I stepped down to the mattress, and Rory squared his shoulders, heading for the bathroom.

If Eve stayed in here while she was healing, and then later it *was* my nest, that wouldn't be so—

She growled again, a weak grip clamping around my wrist but with her ragged fingernails digging into my skin.

"Hey, hey, it's just me," I said. I bent over her, and Eve hissed as she lurched up, eyes unfocused but face pressing immediately to my throat. She was pungent, her scent smothered in filth, and her hair was greasy. Her fingers trembled around my wrist and her teeth only rested against my pulse. I expected her to bite again, but instead her breath rushed over me in fragile pants. I relaxed, rubbing my cheek against the crown of her head. "It's me. You're safe."

Her tongue swiped the outline of one of my bites, and the whine rose in my chest in spite of my best efforts to stifle it. I thought of Garrett, his face open and struck as I hovered above him, and then of Eve riding on top of me, sweaty and focused as I begged for more.

Eve sagged down into the cushions with a huff, her eyes fluttering shut and her fingers rubbing gently on my wrist before dropping.

She had a dark bruise spider-webbing out from her hairline, and her lips were pale. I reached for the zipper of the hoodie she was wearing, waiting for her to bat me away, but she only blinked and frowned up at the ceiling.

"I'm gonna get you cleaned up," I said.

"The fuck are we?" Eve muttered, shifting and then freezing, face twisted in pain.

"At their house," I said, slowly peeling the shoulders of the hoodie down.

"Stupid," Eve said, dragging one hand out a sleeve.

"It's nice, actually."

She opened one eye to glare at me and then bared her teeth in a snarl as Rory reappeared with the washcloth I'd asked for. Actually, he'd brought a whole stack and a pretty porcelain bowl with steaming water. He ignored her and then set it on the ledge.

"I'll be in the hall. Call if you need any help."

Eve and I were quiet until the door clicked shut behind him. I'd only managed to get the hoodie off of her, and already I was starting to see the extent of damage. Her ear was clipped and scabbed over. She had hand-shaped bruise marks around her throat and all over her wrists.

"How bad is it gonna be?" I asked, staring down at her.

She growled and shook, pushing herself up on weak arms. I wrapped my own around her shoulders and helped her, listening to the catch and hiccup of her breath.

"Bad," she said.

IT WAS AWFUL.

All the little scratches and bruises were upsetting enough, a wild map of marks on her skin. But the massive bruise at the base of her spine, rising up her back and down over her ass, had made me shout for help. Garrett said it was a miracle she was walking around, and it had taken the both of us to wrestle her face-down long enough for him to give her a shot for swelling and pain.

Then we found the stab wound at the back of her thigh, and I'd nearly thrown up.

The injection Garrett had administered left Eve weak enough for us to give another antibiotic shot directly to the wound, cleaned and cut the old stitches away—although she'd howled promises of our untimely demise at her hands the whole time.

She was milder now. Downright docile.

"You're mad at me."

Her hands were wrapped and a few fingers splinted, but her arms were draped over my shoulders as we stood together in the shower. I held her up, her body heavy against me, reassuring. I was careful not to touch her back, just in case, so instead I ended up cupping her ass, the injured leg propped up on the ledge of the large bath. I needed to wash her hair, but I hadn't quite sorted out how to go about the process when she was barely standing on her own.

"Adam," she mumbled, drawing me back.

"I'm not… I am mad at you," I said flatly, annoyed that she'd figured it out before I had.

"It's for your own good," she said.

"You getting killed?" I snapped.

"Me out of your life."

I gritted my jaw and let go of Eve, reaching for the shampoo. There was a petty enjoyment as she tightened her hold around me to keep from falling, her leg shaking in place as I reached up and dug my fingers mercilessly into her hair.

"Why don't you ever just try having a conversation with me? Especially where it fucking concerns me," I said.

"I'm your alpha," she bit out, a little breathless as I yanked on a handful of her hair.

"You're my alpha when it suits you. You're not my alpha when you throw me at a pack and then disappear on me," I said, taking mercy on her and steadying her with the grip of one hand while the other lathered the shampoo into her long hair.

"I'm not trying to be noble or sweet or loving," Eve said, sounding weary. I tried not to flinch at the last bit. "That's not who I am. You stand a higher chance of survival with these men."

"With the way things are looking, so do you," I

muttered. I pushed forward, forcing Eve to arch, and she glared at me as the water ran into her hair. "I never asked you to change. I asked you to *talk* to me."

I don't know why I was surprised when she remained silent. Or why it hurt so much.

TWENTY-TWO

Eve

I woke to the sound of cement walls shattering, bullet casings clattering on tile, boots running toward me, and sat up with a shout.

Above me, rain peppered the dark frosted glass of the nest ceiling, the memory dulling as my racing heart slowed and the blood pounding in my head subsided. My fingers dug loosely into the cushion of the mattress beneath me, the gesture pulling on my taped wrist, an IV pumping fluids back into my system. I sat up, easing into the padded wall, and stiffened as footsteps approached the door.

I was dressed in some of Adam's clothing, surrounded by clean blankets and pillows. It was as if *I* were the omega, and the notion made me want to tear the nest apart and launch myself at the door.

It opened, and I narrowed my eyes against the glare of the hall light.

"Hey, I've got some bone broth for you."

The voice was smooth, deep, calm, and it took me a moment to place him.

Of course. The third alpha, Jamie.

"Door open or closed?" he asked.

"Open," I answered immediately.

He nodded and walked slowly inside, an enormous mug cupped in his hands. He didn't move to the stairs but off to his left, leaving me a clear path out the door. He smelled clean, freshly washed and not heavy with his pheromones, and he was dressed in loose gray sweatpants and a threadbare blue T-shirt. Disarming. Jamie had done his best to appear non-threatening, which as far as I was concerned, was even more of a warning. But he sat down on the ledge of the nest and stretched out one arm to me.

"If you're cool with it, I'd like to check the knife wound and the bruise from the shot," he said. "But drink some of that first?"

"Because it has a sedative in it?"

He huffed and shook his head. It was hard to make out his features with the hall behind him and the room dark, but I remembered how handsome he was. Quiet. Steady.

"No drugs, no meds. Just the magic of broth," he said.

I took one tiny sip and immediately licked my lips. No bitterness, no chemical tang. Just broth indeed.

I wasn't sure if it would've stopped me if he had put anything in. I was starving, and I'd trusted these men with Adam for a reason. I was safe here, even if it rankled to be dragged in by Rory.

"You know the longer I stay here, the greater the chance your entire peaceful life is going to implode, right?" I asked before taking a deep gulp of the broth, savoring the salty burn of it running down my throat and warming me from the inside out.

"You know that's probably true of Adam too, right?" Jamie replied.

"I gave him the means to—"

"Accidents happen. You can give him the means, and it

can still go sideways. He could still pass the wrong person on the street," Jamie said. "There could be a loose thread you didn't plan for that connects him."

"So why agree to have him in your home then?" I snapped.

"Because the two of you need help, and from what I've already learned from the others, Omikron needs to be shut down," Jamie said with a shrug.

"You left the army for a reason."

"Yeah, sure. And I opted out of similar work for another reason. I like carpentry," he said, grinning as I glared at him. "What? It's the truth—I like making stuff."

I grunted in acknowledgement and then rose up on my knees, shuffling until my back was to him. My whole body prickled in awareness, goosebumps rising on my skin, waiting for the strike from behind.

"Mm, gimme a sec. Turning on the lights."

My heartbeat was loud in my ears as I waited for Jamie. His bare feet slapped lightly against the floor, soft lights rose around the room, and then the nest rustled as he joined me.

"Lifting up the back of the shirt," he said.

The touch was gentle. He was doing his best to not actually make contact, leave a scent mark, just carefully raising the fabric up enough to reveal the bruise.

"Woof. Could you feel your legs after that shot?" he asked.

I blinked at the question and shook my head. "Barely. Enough to keep moving."

"Mm. I just wanna check on the nerves, so I'm gonna press real lightly, if that's okay."

I stayed silent, and it took me a moment to realize he was actually waiting for my answer. "Fine."

"'Kay, I'll count, and if there's a number where you

don't feel anything, let me know."

I nodded and held my breath as Jamie counted to eleven. The presses were mostly dull and aching, reminders that I wasn't healed, but...

"Five and eight," I said after a moment of silence.

"Good news. Those were just to see if you were lying. No loss of feeling," Jamie said brightly.

I snarled, but he just laughed through it, settling deeper into the nest behind me. "What do you want to do about this wound? The wrappings need changed. You wanna do it yourself or let me?"

"Can it be stitched again?" I asked.

"I very much doubt it at this point," he said. "But we can check."

I growled, mostly for the sake of it, and then passed him my mug of broth before settling down on my belly. Jamie was clear out of the corner of my eyes, a pair of dark-rimmed glasses resting on the bridge of his nose as he stretched backwards to place the mug on the ledge.

"How's the fever feeling?" he asked. "Garrett said you were almost boiling."

"Better. Less clammy. You were a medic?"

"No, but I did some EMT training before opting to be self-employed."

His scent was growing clearer, herbal and tangy-sweet, masculine without being abrasive. He was equally as careful unwrapping the wound on my leg as he had been lifting the shirt, and I tried to imagine him with my omega.

"How is Adam?" I asked, clenching my jaw as it took a little coaxing to pull the bandage away from the ragged, barely healing skin.

"You don't use the bond to find out?" he asked.

"It's... He's learning how to keep it closed."

"And you would have to share yourself with him in

order to find out more," Jamie continued, a note of amusement gentling the observation. He released a slow breath, fingers gently testing the muscle around the wound. "This is going to take physical therapy to get back to normal. Adam is fine, I think."

So he wasn't reaching out to Adam.

"He and Garrett are growing close," he continued.

I nodded at that. "Good."

"It's good as long as you're not expecting Garrett to replace you. The fever is definitely down around here. Antibiotics are working. You should stay on fluids through tomorrow, just in case."

I scowled as he jerked the conversation back to me. "And who will you be to Adam?"

"Also not your replacement. Hopefully his friend. His packmate, maybe, if that's what he wants."

But not his bondmate. A bubble of relief rose up in my chest to hear those words missing, and I stamped it down.

Jamie remained quiet as he rewrapped my thigh, and I pulled myself up and out of his reach as soon as he was done, twisting to face him. A wry smile spread over his full lips, and he sat up on his knees, standing and heading immediately for the stairs.

"I'll bring you some more food. You're okay to move around in here?" he asked with a politely oblique nod to the bathroom.

"I'm fine."

"Grab some more sleep if you can," Jamie said, walking toward the door. "It's good to have you here."

I opened my mouth to correct him because whether they insisted on it or not, I knew I wasn't a houseguest who was *good* to have around, but he'd already flicked off the light and shut the door behind him.

I sat in the dark nest, rain drumming on the thick glass

above me. I was weak, defenseless without any armor or weapons, and for all I knew, locked in this room. I certainly wasn't getting very far with an IV bag to tote around. I was trapped in a house with three alphas.

Alphas who hadn't threatened me. Who'd taken significant measures to find me and bring me to…safety. I was safe here.

The knowledge only left me uneasy, aware of my own vulnerability, and I shuffled myself slowly into the corner, dragging the little IV stand along with me, and a blanket. I sat there, huddled, eyelids drooping as I tried to watch the door, until my stomach growled like an alpha's roar, startling me awake again.

The soup mug of broth was waiting on the ledge, still lightly steaming. I snarled, snatching it to my lips and gulping it down.

I WOKE with the flavor of juicy nectarines on my stale tongue and sat up with a snarl, ignoring the protest of my body in favor of lunging toward where Garrett watched me from the nest steps.

"Calm down!" he barked in a rare use of his alpha tone. "You'll rip your IV out."

"The fuck are you doing in here, watching me sleep?" I tried to make my fall back into the mattress look intentional rather than the defeat of my sleep-loose muscles.

Garrett's gaze flicked away, a hint of guilt, before turning back to me narrowed and fierce.

"I spent all night working out what I wanted to say to you. Something you couldn't just bullshit your way out of, or try and be cute and clever about."

I pursed my lips and arched an eyebrow. I was too

fucking exhausted for all these petty little lectures. As far as being taken advantage of by alphas went, forced moral conversations was working its way up my list of least favorite methods.

"Biting Adam does not mean you get to move him around like a chess piece," Garrett growled. His hands were tense on his knees, knuckles going white. He was holding himself back, trying to direct his aggressive energy, and it made the hair on the back of my neck stand on end. "Being alpha is not about playing god."

"You will be better for him," I said.

"Because you don't want to be! You don't want to change, or grow the hell up, or even try—"

"I've changed—"

"You were fucking dying on the street, and you *still* spent energy on keeping Adam locked out of the bond," Garrett tossed back. "And the fact that you realized Adam was not only innocent, but a victim, isn't growth either. You don't get maturity points for not killing a person, Eve."

Maybe it was better, or it would be faster, to just let him vomit his opinions at me.

"Don't," he hissed, pointing a finger at me. "Do not fucking lock up and just stare at me right now."

"Oh, for fuck's sake, what do you want?"

Garrett leapt up, but took one look at me—my shoulders rising and my fingers clawing into the mattress—and sat down again with a huff. "I want you to accept that you have an omega who, against all odds, actually *likes* having you as an alpha. You are *bonded*, and that's permanent. If you'd been killed, it would've hurt him."

I grit my teeth and forced myself to remain staring at Garrett, refusing to shrink away as much as I wanted to. "If I accept that, it doesn't change me."

"Are you sure about that?" Garrett asked.

I considered admitting to Garrett that I actually liked Adam, but even I knew that the only person who deserved hearing that admission was Adam himself. "You want Adam."

Garrett froze for a moment, and then let out a slow and controlled sigh, his shoulders dropping. "I do. And because I care about Adam, I care about what matters to him. Which includes you."

I let out a groan and sagged back into the wall. "Give me a break."

"Fuck you!" Garrett barked. "Fine, okay. You know what? I actually...I—ugh! I like you too. Fuck if I know why, because you are the worst kind of alpha and a complete asshole. It's *true!*" he roared as I snarled at him. "You're aggressive, controlling, emotionally unavailable. You make choices for your omega without consideration to how they will feel about it. You're constantly jockeying for dominance."

"Well, gosh, I sound awful."

"You are awful, and you know it, and you use it as a fucking excuse," Garrett snapped.

I flinched at that, and Garrett deflated, chest heaving.

"You are also protective, commanding, seductive, and thoughtful when it suits you," Garrett said, rumbling the words out. "Adam is not asking you to change. And honestly, I'm not either. Just to give up trying to walk out on your omega."

"Is it so impossible to believe that his safety is a priority to me?" I asked. "That I had...good intentions in—"

"In taking on dozens of Omikron agents on your own without a word of explanation to the rest of us? Or to Adam? Don't tell me you don't think he would've kept that secret from us. We both know he's loyal to you," Garrett said.

Adam's loyalty was a sore spot, pinching a nerve near my heart.

"He…complicates things," I admitted slowly. He complicated my life. My priorities. My fucking thoughts.

"And you're such a simple girl," Garrett scoffed, but he stared at me, trying to read past the bruises and the jut of my jaw. "I think you're still angry at him for tricking you into the bond."

Yes, where was Adam's lecture on that topic? Why was I the one stuck here being chastised like a child?

"If you're going to run for good, tell him so," Garrett said softly, pushing up on the ledge and readying to leave. "Because I don't think he would give up on you unless you really forced him to believe it. But for the record, I think you should stay. I want to bond Adam, be his alpha. And I'd like for you to be here too."

I turned my face away as Garrett turned to try and catch my eye again.

"Not all of his complications are that bad, right?" he asked.

I released a puff of breath and rolled my eyes. I did not *dislike* Adam. Or even being his alpha.

Maybe I was still angry about being tricked. Maybe I needed the predictable rhythm of my previous life to keep my head in order, uncertain if the compartments I'd arranged in my mind might topple and create a chaos I couldn't find my way out of.

"Do I have to stay in here?" I asked.

"One of us can show you around when you're up for it," Garrett said. "Can we trust you not to jack one of the cars and take off?"

"For this week," I said, trying to sound bright, teasing, but it came out as hollow as Garrett's stare, and he left the room without rising to the bait.

TWENTY-THREE

Adam

"There's a chat server I can log onto to get in touch. A few of the others said they'd keep an eye out for Faith before…before I was in Las Vegas," I said. Before Eve showed up and I caught myself in a bond with an alpha that didn't want me.

"You're better off—we all are—out of touch with those people," Rory said immediately, arms crossed over his chest.

I sat between him and Garrett at the kitchen table. Jamie was upstairs, apparently checking on Eve, and I itched to go up and join him.

Which was insane. Faith was missing, and I'd let myself get completely distracted by running, by Eve, for too long. I needed to focus on what was important. My sister had been there for me, had followed me into this hellish mess, and I'd repaid her by letting her be kidnapped by the men we were trying to destroy.

"The server's untraceable; they won't be able to figure out where I am, and if anyone has discovered anything, I need—"

"You need to keep your head down, or you risk losing it," Rory said, tone firm and just shy of a bark.

"What have *you* found out?" I challenged, straightening in my seat. "I gave you everything—"

"Everything you knew, half of which we knew already—"

"And I haven't heard of shit getting done yet! My *sister* needs my help. She is the only person I have! And I fucked up and—"

"And if you fuck up again, she may be out of your reach for good," Rory growled.

"Okay, pause!" Garrett called, a hand settling high on my back and the other reaching out between Rory and me, waving away our glaring contest. "Rory, we can fill him in. And I can check out the server. Adam is probably right about it being secure, and that's a possible resource for our research too. We have to work *together*."

Rory glared over my shoulder at Garrett, dark eyes flicking between us. "No communications outside of anywhere we aren't one hundred percent confident in. No matter what they offer on the hook."

"I'm not clueless. Someone on that server is probably responsible for Faith going missing," I said at the same time a bitter voice sounded from the back of my head, *You're responsible for Faith going missing*. "But a lot of them are trying to stop alph—organizations like Omikron. They'll help."

Rory's lips flattened, but he nodded slowly, tipping his head to Garrett in an unspoken permission.

"The FBI isn't the easiest organization to work with, but we've got a friend inside that's made things a little more cooperative," Garrett said.

Electricity shot up my spine, and my fingers scratched against the surface of the table. "You went to the FBI? Do they know about Eve?"

"No," Garrett and Rory said, equally sharp, and I let out a sigh.

"And you would be smart to leave her out of any mentions on the server," Rory said. "There's a chance Omikron might assume the two of you have already parted ways and the less information—"

"I'm not going to make the same mistake twice," I snapped.

Garrett's hand at the base of my neck gripped a little tighter, but it was a massage rather than a warning, and I relaxed slowly under the touch. My hands slid to my knees and my fingers dug in, resisting the impulse to whine, my hindbrain needy for Garrett's comforting purr.

"The FBI isn't big into sharing information, but we're turning over everything we know won't blow back on you or Eve, and we're getting the assurance that the case is building."

My eyes flicked up, thinking of Eve in the nest upstairs.

"We can't only do things her way," Garrett said softly. "It isn't safe for you. For any of us. Hell, she was nearly killed, and what did she really accomplish? Taking out hired goons? Omikron will find more."

"There has to be strong evidence that will put these men—these alphas—into prison, that will break their control of the organization," Rory said with a firm nod.

Garrett might've been right about Eve's solo job being useless and nearly getting her killed, but I wasn't totally convinced that a slow legal battle would save the day either. It wouldn't save Faith.

"Go ahead," Rory said with a heavy sigh, pushing back from the table only to stand, looming over us. He crossed his arms over his broad chest and shrugged at me. "Be careful, and see what you can find out. Your sister is a personal issue, I get that. We'll deal with it outside of help from the FBI if we have to."

I sighed and found myself nodding up at the intimidating alpha, sagging into Garrett's side, some of that juicy and sweet fragrance enveloping me. "Thank you."

Rory jerked, his face twisting with awkward discomfort. "I'm gonna give Wes a call. Let him have the update, see if he needs an extra hand this week."

Garrett's arm was heavy around my shoulder as Rory left the kitchen. As eager as I was to get back to work, something about the weight of his touch, or the alpha pheromones clouding my lungs with their syrup, made my head sluggish and satisfied, like I had nowhere else to be.

"So I think now is a good time to tell you that I got you something," Garrett said.

"You got me…like a—" *Shut up, Adam, shut up.* "Like a…present?"

Garrett grinned, a little hint of dimples flashing beneath the dark stubble of his short beard. "Uh. Yeah, actually. Guess so."

A courting present? I wondered, but was too disturbed by the giddy bubbling sensation in my chest to ask. Since when did I want courting presents?

Maybe since the night that Eve brought me a razorblade and then made me sit on the counter as she ran it up my throat. Or maybe just because it was from Garrett. Did I want an alpha now because Eve was pulling away, or did I want the man in front of me specifically?

"Do you want to see it?" Garrett asked, his smile tight and nervous.

"Yes! I do, yeah."

"Cool, it's upstairs, actually. I can, um…bring it down here, or—"

"No, I'll come with you."

It's not sexual tension, you're just awkward, I told myself. Except then Garrett took my hand as I stood, all thick calloused fingers and strong grip, and I realized it was definitely sexual tension. Days ago I'd climbed onto his lap, ready to offer him pretty much anything he was in the mood for, possibly even a bond just to spite Eve.

Garrett led us upstairs and paused at the guest bedroom door. "Um, meet me in my—your room?"

I rushed there on my own, pausing at the sight of the cracked door to the nest. It was dark inside, and silent. Who knew, maybe Eve had snuck out of the house and none of us were the wiser. Or maybe she was sleeping, healing. I turned on my heel and marched into the room I'd commandeered from Garrett. It still smelled strongly of the alpha, but it was becoming more and more comfortable every day, my perfume almost complementary to his pheromones. I'd put up a spare set of dark blue sheets for a curtain over the window, and it made the room feel close and quiet.

I settled on the bed up against the headboard and waited for Garrett to appear. When he did, he had a long, flat box tucked under his arm. My eyes widened at the sight, a familiar shape and size.

"I didn't wrap it," Garrett said with a half grin, drawing out the box from under his arm and tossing it to the bed.

I scrambled forward to catch it in my hands. "Holy shit. This is—you got me a laptop?"

"Yeah, I knew Rory was probably going to be a dick about it, but I can't imagine being cut off like that. I wanted you to know that I trust you," Garrett said, striding toward me on long legs and then climbing onto the bed at the opposite end.

"This is… This is a good laptop," I said, staring down

at the sleek and familiar logo, my fingernails already scratching at the plastic wrap.

"Good for hacking. Good for gaming. I personally enjoy both," Garrett said, and the pair of us exchanged equally dopey smiles. "Go on. Break the seal."

I dug in, peeling back the plastic, tossing the lid of the box aside, grinning at the little alien head staring up at me. I was pulling it out of the styrofoam, rifling for the charger, ready to crack open my new toy, when I paused and glanced up at Garrett. He was leaning back against the end of the bed, watching me with a relaxed curve to his lips.

"Is this a courting gift?" I blurted out.

Garrett blinked, his expression freezing as he took in a sudden breath and lifted his gaze to mine. "Do you…want it to be?"

The non-answer was too much like Eve, and my excitement slipped, my eyes falling back to the computer, prepared to let the moment pass.

"Yes," he said, simple and firm, catching my attention again. "I mean, no, I got it for you because you—because I thought it would make you happy. But, yes. I want to court you and if I can, um, sort of slide this over into that as a starter, that would be—"

I pushed the computer aside—carefully and only momentarily—before leaping forward, catching Garrett by the collar of his T-shirt and dragging him closer. His mouth was open on a gasp as I kissed him, our eyes both wide and crossed before I slammed mine shut and leaned in. Garrett's hands grasped my face as I twisted the cotton of his shirt in my fist and dove into the open-mouthed press, searching for a taste of him. Sweet, just a little sharp, with a secret layer of slightly bitter spice that lingered on my tongue. He licked back and groaned, one hand falling from my cheek to wrap around my waist.

The kiss was messy and a bit uncoordinated with our eagerness, and I found myself smiling into the touch, and then Garrett was too and our teeth were knocking. He nipped at my top lip, and I pressed my hips into his, grinding there for a minute, soaking up the vibration of Garrett's purr against my chest, the heat and steadiness of him. His mouth softened over mine, finally transforming into that gentle first kiss, sipping and pressing.

I swallowed hard and just breathed him in, and Garrett rolled his hips back in retaliation, a tempting bulge nuzzling against my own slightly erect cock.

"It's a good gift," I murmured. "Omega-approved."

Garrett huffed, pressed one more simple kiss to my mouth and then slowly pushed us apart. He looked unexpectedly solemn, almost frowning, but his eyes were too soft on mine. "Adam-approved, I'll take."

It was comforting and unsettling at the same time. I'd always hated being an omega, the knowledge that at some point I would be claimed, give way to the demand of biology and pheromones. Something had shifted since Eve bit me, and I was embarrassed to realize I was starting to like being an alpha's omega. As packs went, the one I was in was still a broken puzzle, and yet I was craving bonds, gifts, alphas' attention.

I slid back to the headboard, retrieving the laptop under Garrett's watchful stare.

"I can use the server on this?" I asked him.

"Of course. Do you mind if I grab mine? I can start taking notes as you go."

It was a safe space to retreat to, and I nodded eagerly.

You have to think about Faith, I reminded myself. About all the omegas Omikron had its claws in. It was time to get back to work.

Garrett returned with his own computer and watched me work in silence until the server screen was popping up. It was intentionally rough in appearance, reminiscent of chats from the early nineties, but I immediately showed Garrett the backdoor.

"Shit. Is it... Does any of this even ping to US servers?" he asked.

"Every once in a while. Never anywhere we're actually located in," I said. "We used to be less careful about what we said inside, but even before Faith and I were caught, I could tell some of the regulars were getting cagey," I said. "Like, here, HuntedBiTheWolf, she's a first gen omega—"

"First gen?" Garrett asked, brow furrowing.

I stared back at him for a moment before my eyes slid back to the screen, tracking the light conversation. It wasn't business at the moment, at least not clearly so. "Uh, yeah. Like, she's the first in her family that she knows of."

"I didn't know there were terms for it," Garrett admitted with a shrug.

"Well, an eighth gen is like guaranteed to produce omega children, right? A first gen is less likely."

"Why does it make a difference?"

Okay, so Garrett really was that clueless. Were all alphas, or just the ones who were— *Sweet. Interested in the person rather than the genes*, I reminded myself.

"Umm, so if Omikron wants to produce more omegas, they would grab a higher gen omega and use them for breeding. Bigger investment, but bigger payout to sell all those future omega children to buyers. First gen would be less valuable, but could be sold immediately," I explained.

Garrett grew pale, glancing between me and the

screen, lines carving into his forehead. "Adam, what are—what are you and Faith?"

"Second," I said, shrugging. "Not likely to get snatched for breeding, but I don't *know* what Omikron wants with her. And they might keep her close like that just to make it harder for me to get her back."

Garrett covered his mouth with a tight grip and nodded.

"Yeah, and—Oh, hey, BetaThinkTwice is on. She's an omega who presents as a beta by staying on suppressants. I mean, a lot of us do that. But she's married to a beta, I think, and has, like, a whole identity to back it up," I said.

"Isn't long-term use of suppressants really dangerous?" Garrett asked.

"Yeah, but so is…" I trailed off, face flushing. Being an omega. Being claimed by an alpha you don't want.

Garrett stared at me and said nothing, his eyes reading me, face falling. "Do they know you're in there?"

I shook my head. "Ready? It's gonna be a lot of questions."

Garrett sat up a little straighter, and when I shifted closer to his side, he nudged back, relaxing enough to offer a smile. "Let's dive in."

Don'tGiveADam is typing…

●

"WE GOT FUCKING NOTHING FROM THAT," I said, huffing and pushing the computer away. I'd fielded questions for an hour, did my best to dig for another two hours, until it seemed like most of the server was logging off to avoid me.

"Look, I think there was information there, we just

need to sort through it. And hey, you've been off for how long?"

"Over a month," I said, flopping back onto the mattress, propping my feet up at the top of the headboard and waiting for Garrett to chastise me.

Which, of course, he didn't. "So can you blame them? Some of them probably don't even believe that was really you. I thought SubnBreed69 was especially pushy."

"They usually are," I said with a wave of my hand.

Garrett arched an eyebrow at me. "Okay. Well, my fresh eyes say that was suspicious. On the other end, Beta-ThinkTwice was online for that whole three hours but only really chimed in on a surface level."

"Pushy is bad, but so is surface level?"

Garrett shrugged. "Maybe. She was definitely watching the chat. How many of these people have you met in real life?"

"Hunted and Jabroni," I said.

"And you trust them?"

I nodded, and then thought longer. "I definitely trust Hunted," I said, carefully avoiding her real name. "Jabroni is…kinda intense. Like, I guess we're all sort of conspiracy theorists on there, or we were to start with when there was no evidence against Omikron. But Jabroni is extra suspicious. But I… Yeah, I trust him."

"Then we work our way backwards from there," Garrett said, nodding and typing furiously on his own computer.

I watched him for a minute, thinking over the conversation with the others on the server, my mood growing more sour by the second. "We're not any closer to tracking down Faith."

Garrett paused and looked over the top of his screen, eyes flicking over to my feet beside his head. "We're not.

I'm sorry," he said. "I'm not going to stop helping you look for her, using every resource I have to look for her myself, but…"

But. But Omikron was a network, not a single person who could be tracked. But she might already be gone.

"If this isn't enough, if you want to get out on the road and—I dunno, just chase after every Omikron asshole we've got on the list—" Garrett continued, "—just, you know, don't leave without me. Or honestly, without Eve," he said with a grimace. "She's gonna be off that IV soon, and even sick, she's still probably a total badass."

A single, simple laugh fell out of me at the idea of Garrett and me getting back in Eve's backseat while she drove day and night. Actually…it sounded halfway nice.

"I don't want to get killed," I whispered, my eyes filling up. "I—I could be *with* Faith right now if I hadn't been so—"

"Hey," Garrett sighed, shifting his work to the bedside table and scooting closer, a warm hand settling on the center of my chest. He winced and shook his head. "I know everyone wants to be that hero, the one who saves the rest of the world before themselves, but the truth is most of us would run, Adam. Survival is instinct. *That* is every bit as much our biology as our designation."

"Especially for an omega," I hissed, turning my face away.

Garrett sighed, his fingertips drumming in time with my heartbeat. "You know they wouldn't have kept the two of you together. You're stronger with the people you love. That's why they grabbed her in the first place. Separating you two would've been their first goal. So you're safe, and that means you can do the work to bring her back, okay?"

I turned back to him and shook my head. "It's not okay, you know that."

Garrett's head dropped, some of that long lion's mane of his falling forward as he nodded. "You're right—it's not. I'm sorry."

And even though it was the exact opposite of what would help Faith, that selfish, impulsive, survival-driven omega inside of me wanted one thing in the moment. The only thing that would convince my hindbrain everything *would* be fine.

The sheets on the bed whispered as I moved, shifting closer to Garrett. I lifted one foot from the headboard and swung it over his head as he looked up from his hunched posture, and then down again at my spread legs, the jeans tight around my thighs in this position. He met my gaze, a little worry furrowing on his brow, and I shifted my other foot to press against his back, nudging him toward me.

The worry deepened, even as his smile quirked.

"Do you want me, or do you want a distraction?" he asked, his hands settling into the mattress on either side of my hips.

"Both." Garrett's eyes narrowed at that, and I rethought. "I want you. You…you and Eve both make this whole situation feel like it could still turn out okay. Because she'll shoot everyone who stands in her way, and because you…you will make sure I am…" I winced and rubbed a hand over my face. "That sounds really presumptuous, actually. I don't know when I turned into such a—"

Garrett pulled my hand away from my face, suddenly hovering over me, balanced by one beautifully muscled and taut arm. "I'm a good shot too, if it comes down to it, but you're right," he said. "I'm in it to make sure you're okay. Which is why we're not gonna rush this."

I opened my mouth to answer that compared to Eve and the two hours it had taken us to be bonded, Garrett and I were at a snail's pace, but I didn't get the chance to speak. Garrett's body lowered, heavy and broad, and I was only distracted from rocking up into the weight of him by the sudden press of his lips on mine. The kiss was slower than the one I'd claimed earlier, furthering his promise of not rushing, but it was deep and languid.

I whined, and Garrett soothed the sound immediately with his purr. His hands framed my face, pinning me to the mattress beneath him. The pressure alone sent my blood straight to my cock, and I grimaced into the kiss with the first bite of my jeans zipper against my hardening length. Garrett's tongue drove in, fucking my mouth, his hips barely rising as I wrestled my pants open between us, reaching for his too.

"No," he rasped, lifting up slightly and glaring down at me. "I said slow."

"Fuck slow," I hissed, arching up and rubbing myself against him. He was hard too, but the denim of his own jeans was too rough, and I fell back with another whine.

Garrett's glare vanished with a low laugh and he leaned back, pulling his hips out of reach as his head bent to my throat. "But we already agreed I'm courting you," Garrett said, words dark with his running purr. His lips grazed wetly over my pulse, and I shuddered. "And courting means it's about *you*."

His hands moved to my waistband, and I let out an involuntary gasp as they slid beneath my T-shirt, pushing it up my chest. He shifted lower, and his next kiss landed on my stomach.

"I'm not going to bond you without talking to Eve," Garrett said, words solemn in contrast to the gentle pressing kisses he left up one side and then down the other.

I ripped my T-shirt off over my head and fell back on the bed with a huff. "She's all but put your teeth to my throat. I don't think it's going to be an issue."

"You said you want us both," Garrett reminded me, looking up from his teasing. He was stupidly pretty, hand-some, and his long hair was falling over one shoulder, sun-bleached ends tickling at my belly button. "I want to make sure she's going to stick around and not slit my throat at the same time. But I agree, I think it will be fine. I'm still going to be sure."

He stretched up, and I dug my hands into his hair to try and keep him in place as he kissed me. A large hand slid between us, cupping over my crotch, gripping around my erection through my boxers, and I moaned loudly into Garrett's mouth.

"In the meantime…" he said, rising and grinning at me.

"You're going to spoil me like an omega?" I asked, arching a brow and trying not to sound so excited by the prospect.

"Something like that," Garrett purred, and then his lips trailed to my jaw, nipping at the corner and down my throat to suck a mark in the hollow where it met my chest, one of the rare spots not ragged from Eve's marks.

His hand rubbed and circled over my swollen cock, and I released a groan. I'd spent a lot of my teenage years and early adulthood mastering my natural omega arousal, not allowing it to control me, to make demands of me and my body. The suppressants had helped in that, but they had only worked so far.

Going off of them, bonding with Eve, it was like the dam had broken.

The boxers were already growing wet with pre-cum as Garrett kissed and nipped and sucked his way down my chest. His tongue sharpened to a point and circled my nipples with the same slow deliberation that his thumb rubbed at the head of my cock, stroking around my wetness, rubbing it into me and into the fabric of the boxers.

"Please," I whined, bucking my hips into his hand, ignoring the irritation of the fabric for the sake of the friction of fucking. It wasn't enough though. His grip was too loose, and I was already craving the brutal fix of Eve's lock.

I'd almost forgotten about the bond, so used to it being shut, as if it didn't even exist. Even now, the awareness came on slowly, like a curtain being opened a sliver, enough for the person behind to peer out but not for me to see in.

Garrett's kiss was on my hipbone, his hands not quite stroking my length, my boxers sodden around my cock. And Eve, who'd dropped me into this man's lap and then tried to walk out on me, was more or less spying on us. I moaned again, as if she could hear me, and whimpered as Garrett scratched his teeth over my hip briefly. My focus was split between them, the heat gathering in my blood from Garrett's teasing, and the prickle of awareness in my head of Eve observing my pleasure.

I lifted my hips blindly with Garrett's gentle urging, not realizing what would come next until my boxers and jeans were around my thighs and Garrett's hair was tickling my hipbones, and his lips were closing in a sucking kiss around the head of my cock, tongue lapping over my slit.

I came with a dissatisfied shout and whine, barely touched, and Garrett mouthed and swallowed and lapped at every drop until I was shivering.

The curtain parted fully, and for a moment I was hollow, carved open and exposed to the bond, to *her*.

"You taste like fucking frosting," Garrett praised with a chuckle, and my eyes squeezed shut as he dove down again, taking me deep, right to the back of his throat.

I gasped in approval, the immediate and demanding

suction of his lips drawing me back to the edge I'd fallen too quickly from. My approval, for his mouth, his care, his *need* of me.

And her approval. For my pleasure, for giving in to the attraction to Garrett. Eve was *pleased* with me, and it was like a brand new bite on my neck, claiming me even in a moment with the other alpha. I had done what she wanted, and the rush was sudden and explosive. Garrett purred and laughed as I came again, swallowing me to my hilt without stopping, nose nuzzling my skin.

She owned me, even in this, and her satisfaction clouded in with mine. I was her omega. I was being good. She was pleased. It was as powerful and potent as her lock around my cock.

Garrett purred and I let out a yelp as his teeth teased the base of my cock, squeezing gently, drawing me back to him, with Eve cheering on the high of ecstasy through the bond.

"More," I pleaded, starting to thrust. "Fuck, I want more."

I wanted them both.

TWENTY-FOUR

Eve

My hand clenched around the doorframe of the nest at the same moment that Jamie appeared out of his bedroom, dressed in a stained and weathered blue jumpsuit, the sleeves rolled up to his elbow.

"How does it feel?" he asked, adding to my blank stare, "To be up?"

"Worse than when I was a mess."

"Probably to do with your body coming out of shock. Are you taking the pain meds?" I shook my head and frowned at the simple smile he wore in answer. "Are you hungry?"

"I'm going insane in that room," I snapped.

"Gotcha," Jamie replied with his usual nonchalance. "Well, I'm headed down to my shop if you want a change of scenery. I'm just doing some final touches, so nothing too exciting."

It wasn't the most promising offer.

Jamie tilted his head and continued, "Rory is down in the gym, and Garrett is working with Adam, I think, so—"

"I'll join you," I said.

I didn't want to interrupt Garrett and Adam, not after their progress from the day before. And I sure as fuck didn't want to spend time with Rory in the basement.

"But I don't have anything else to wear," I added, frowning down at the pajama set someone had brought me, along with a ridiculous amount of clean but plain underwear.

"None of us were brave enough to pick out more clothes for you," Jamie said, almost laughing. "I'll grab you something."

I followed him to the door of his bedroom, watching as he rifled through an impressively chic dresser. His room was tidy and simple, but he'd obviously built the furniture for himself. The bed was a unpretentious but large platform, with a tall headboard. The dresser was designed with a herringbone pattern to the wood, stained in two dark tones, the lighter of which matched the bed.

"Here's a shirt," he said, and I caught it without looking, a soft blue button-down with a tear in one elbow.

I unbuttoned the pajama top and slid on the shirt, waiting for my hackles to rise at Jamie's pheromones. His scent was obscure and deep, not too sweet and not too harsh, and I was surprised to find it didn't bother me.

I realized too late that Jamie was watching me sniff at his collar, his eyes fixed to the same spot as his hand held out a pair of cargo pants.

"These are old and they've got a drawstring. Best chance of fitting you, I think."

We remained staring at one another as I shimmied out of the pajamas and into the pants. The shirt he'd lent me was long enough to hit me mid-thigh, and he took a moment to run his glance over my bare legs before sliding it right back up to my gaze.

"Do you do that kind of thing to be seductive, or because you're testing me?"

I had one leg in the borrowed pants, and I narrowed my eyes at Jamie.

He raised his hand and shook his head. "Look, I think I've made it pretty obvious that the last thing I want is to be confrontational with you. If you want to make me uncomfortable, I'm kind of hard to ruffle. And I have no interest in making you uncomfortable."

"Testing you," I said.

Jamie nodded and then shrugged. "Fine. I don't play around with ambiguous signals."

"What does that mean?"

"It means I don't assume a woman is interested in anything from me unless she tells me so. Explicitly," he added with a slight grin.

"Haven't you heard? Alphas take what they want," I said, tying the knot of the drawstring.

"You're confusing alphas with predators," Jamie said.

"We're the same, in my experience."

"Not in this pack."

I looked up at the sharp command in his tone. His body was relaxed, arms loose at his side, and there was very little tension in his expression, but his gaze was hard on mine. The words were part promise and part warning.

"The boots you were wearing should be good for the shop. Need socks?"

I nodded, and the subject was dropped. Jamie was possibly the most dangerous of the three alphas, or at least the most disarming.

He's the most tempting, a voice reminiscent of Adam's warned.

A handful of minutes later, I was regretting taking Jamie up on his offer, or at least regretting not taking any of the pain meds. The stairs had been a rough battle with my healing leg and weakened muscles. I made it as far as the dining room table—the view of the backyard and large woodshop clear through the window—before I was sweating lightly.

Jamie dawdled in the kitchen, allowing me to catch my breath while he poured us both bottles of water.

"We can just sit on the back porch," he offered.

It was more tempting than a confined space with him, but I shook my head. "I'm tired and it hurts like a mother-fucker, but I'll be bored again in five minutes just sitting."

"If you want a hand, ask for it," he said, gentle and stern at the same time.

I didn't ask for his hand, and we made it out the back-door into the garage and then out to the backyard a few minutes later. I paused on the cement patio, struck with the breeze of fresh air. It was cool and clean, and while there were shouts of children somewhere farther off in the neighborhood, it was a far cry from the crush and oppression of the city. I mourned my cabin retreat for a moment before following Jamie to the shop, trying to walk lightly on my injured leg.

Jamie's shop was a simple steel pole barn, with a large sliding garage door facing the house and an entrance on the side. It was clean inside, and smelled more like varnish and sawdust than the alpha who occupied the space.

Jamie hurried over to a desk, pulling out a beautiful wooden rolling chair with a dense cushion and pushing it over to me.

"Don't be stoic," he said firmly.

I wouldn't even have considered refusing the chair if he hadn't said anything, but thankfully my stubbornness didn't outweigh my need for a comfortable seat, and I settled into it gratefully.

"It's okay on the back of your thigh?" he asked.

"I'm fine," I said, just a bit too sharp.

Jamie just let out a brief laugh and left me there, moving over to a shelf to turn on a bluetooth speaker, lo-fi hip hop flowing out at a low volume.

"So…a Black carpenter," I said as Jamie settled into what was obviously a comfortable work routine.

He snorted and glanced at me out of the corner of his eyes as he pulled down a craftsman style side table. "So. Adam and Eve. We're getting biblical around here."

I let out a grunt and nodded my head in acknowledgement. "Not an entirely conscious decision on my part."

"Yeah, Adam filled the others in, and I got the telephone version of the story. Do you resent him for conning you into the bite?"

"He didn't," I said.

Jamie was pulling sanding paper out of a meticulously labeled set of drawers, and he paused to glance at me. "He was going into heat and put you in rut."

"I remember. I remember him begging and I remember refusing. And I remember deciding that I could bite him and still kill him," I said, shrugging. "It's not his fault that I was wrong. And while I don't expect an alpha of the year award for it, I'm aware I made the right choice."

"You should tell Adam that," Jamie suggested.

I rolled my eyes and he let it go, settling into his work of hand sanding the table. I took the opportunity of quiet to study the rest of the large open room. There was a set of six chairs hanging from hooks on a wall, beautifully stained and unvarnished, and a few pieces I suspected were table legs. On a high shelf was a series of vintage wooden framed clocks, all different styles, that must've been a collection rather than Jamie's work.

"What's that?" I asked, pointing to a familiar and almost feminine form resting up against the wall.

"I'm trying to make my own guitar," Jamie said.

"You play guitar?"

"A little. Not well. I just…I think the instrument interested me because of the craftsmanship involved in making one? But to make one well, you have to understand the acoustics of the music too," Jamie said with a shrug.

"You want to make guitars to sell?"

"No. I mean, maybe. I just like to learn new things sometimes," Jamie said.

I answered with silence, pushing up from the chair and testing my weight on my leg. He looked at me every so often, as if he were checking on me, but seemed content to let me exist in his space.

"Do you have a hobby?" he asked, something almost teasing in his tone.

"There was a piano at the orphanage where I was as a little girl," I said, testing the words slowly, waiting for the tiny confession of my past to bite me. "No one taught us any lessons, but I liked to sit and…make sounds. Play. Not songs, just notes."

"The resonance is relaxing," Jamie said with a nod. "How long were you in an orphanage?"

I shook my head. "I don't know."

The soft scratch of the sandpaper paused.

"We didn't celebrate birthdays," I explained.

"So you don't know your birthday?"

I shook my head again. "They just said it was time for me to leave one day. I assumed I was eighteen, but I might've been a little younger."

I kept the rest to myself. The move from one house to the other. The agent in the office, recruiting me on the day I no longer had a home or anywhere else to go.

"How old are you? Roughly?"

"Between thirty-five and forty, I think," I answered, wobbling a hand and then using it for balance against one of the counters, rolling the ankle of my injured leg and ignoring Jamie's stare. "The birthdates on my IDs always move around. It gets a little confusing. I don't really care."

"Around the same age as the rest of us," Jamie said, meaning himself and the other two alphas. "So you don't have your birth certificate."

"No." I'd been given a birth certificate when I joined the agency, but I'd known even then it wasn't really mine. Evelyn the orphan had become Grace the agent. Grace eventually became Hannah, my first moment of independence. On and on for a few years, until I'd grown better at hiding my own tracks. Or at least until I thought I was. All the former versions of myself were quietly packed away and hidden in my own mind.

"I haven't decided on a stain for this piece yet. There's a basket of chips right by you, would you bring it over?"

It was a release from the conversation, but also a reminder of whom I was with. I'd revealed more to Jamie in a handful of minutes than I'd offered to Adam in weeks. Disarming indeed. Dangerous.

And yet somehow a relief, like I'd just loosened a grip that'd been bruising me for years.

I picked up the basket, rifling through the colors and drawing my favorites up to the top before passing it to Jamie.

ADAM ANNOUNCED himself long before he appeared in the nest, tendrils of curiosity reaching through the bond, searching for me. It was the dead of the night, and my bones were throbbing with a pulse of pain after pushing myself. The door cracked open, a pair of scents tangled together wafting in, equally sweet but sharply distinctive. Adam had been spending all of his time with Garrett, and even if they hadn't bonded, the scent marks were growing sticky, attached to one another.

And yet here Adam is, I thought as he tiptoed down the stairs and slid through the blankets to find me.

"What do you want?" I asked, trying to gentle the question. I was too tired and too sore for fucking.

"Nothing," Adam answered, slipping closer, making space for himself against me.

The aching pound in my bones lessened. Adam turned on his side, and one of my bites on his throat taunted me, shining in the darkness. I curled around my omega's back, his warmth seeping into sore muscles, and lowered my lips to that bite, grazing over the spot, licking lightly. That fragile, just-about-to-shatter sensation that'd been threatening my edges seemed to heal.

The bond.

"Better?" Adam whispered.

Alphas weren't meant to reject their bonded omegas. Omegas weren't meant to give their alphas the cold shoulder. It was going to cost me too much to stay away from Adam. It was just one more irritating trap set by that single bite.

I sighed and wrapped an arm around Adam's chest, wrapping myself around him as tightly as I could stand, as if I could pretend it was a punishment to him for avoiding me.

"Yes. Thank you."

Adam's relief was soft, brushing through me, soothing the frustration that had risen.

The bond was already in place. There was no slipping the noose now.

"Do you like your nest?" I asked.

Adam huffed a small laugh, a tentative hand finding and covering mine on his chest. "I do, actually. I like this… this pack. I want us to stay."

Us.

I closed my eyes and settled my head on the pillow with Adam's, my nose tucked to the back of his neck to breathe in his perfume.

TWENTY-FIVE

Rory

"Stevens."

I winced and paused in the hallway before taking two steps back to pause in front of Wes Pike's office door.

He had his thumb and forefinger pinched over the bridge of his nose where his glasses bothered him, and he waved me in with his free hand.

"What's up?"

"Close the door," Wes said before rolling back his shoulders. "Nothing serious, I just want to check in without the whole office listening."

"You do love to hire gossips," I said, shutting the door behind me but staying close.

Wes was a not-quite middle-aged alpha and, much to our competitors' shock, exceedingly good at running his own business, despite appearing more like one of his bulky and reliable employees than the brains behind the operation. I appreciated the plainness of his behavior as much as the forthrightness with which he ran the company.

"Well?" he asked.

"It hasn't been…smooth," I admitted. Garrett and I hadn't told Wes about leaving the second safe house to take Adam to our own house. Or about Eve taking off… multiple times. Or about why she'd chosen us in the first place.

To be pack.

Mostly because we didn't want Wes to know how stupid we were being in going along with it all.

"I wouldn't expect it, not with her," Wes said with a grimace. "But you're okay. And the omega—"

"Adam."

"—is safe?"

I nodded slowly, staring out the window of Wes' office to the buildings across the street, the city warped and reflected on the windows. "Garrett's picked up lots of evidence of them being searched for, but so far, it only helps grow the picture of who exactly is looking. No…no incidents," I said.

Unless you count Eve running headfirst into a building with fifty plus mercenaries waiting for her with a kill order, I thought. That would've been a lot harder to hide from Wes if it weren't for Omikron already doing their best to clean it up.

"I got a weird vibe from them," Wes said slowly, frowning at his computer screen and then glancing up at me. "Do you still feel confident with the goal?"

I frowned and stuffed my hands into my pockets. The goal being: keep both Adam *and* Eve safe. Together. Alive and bonded. Because we'd considered the idea of turning Eve in when Wes first brought us the job.

"I do. They're not…conventional. But she's sincere about his safety, and he is genuinely loyal to her," I said.

Wes shrugged and nodded. "Who am I to disapprove of unconventionality? Fine. Be careful and be safe."

"How are you managing without Garrett and me in-house?" I asked.

Wes grimaced but offered me a half grin. "Surviving. Garrett's still been running his side cases smoothly, and you trained the others to fill your shoes well. I consider the cause against Omikron pretty well worth losing you guys in the office."

Which was why I liked working for Wes. His bottom line wasn't the profit of private security, but the duty of keeping others safe.

"Just…keep your guard up with her," Wes said.

I stiffened and stared back at Wes, who was thankfully staring at his computer screen—where his gaze always drifted while he was thinking, conveniently to the desktop picture of him with his bonded beta, Lola.

"Eve?" I asked unnecessarily, bringing her name into the conversation out loud for the first time.

Wes gave me another one of his sideways smiles, brow furrowed, puzzled by the question, but he let it go and nodded slowly. "I got a funny feeling when she asked for you and Garrett, like she'd already picked the two of you out."

For our pack. For Adam, not for herself.

"Either way," he continued with a wave of his hand. "You can't say she's not dangerous."

She was significantly less dangerous recently, wandering around the house in hand-me-downs that drowned her in fabric while sporting a feline scowl on her face. She hadn't been at all dangerous when I'd carried her back to my car, unconscious and battered. But I had a feeling I'd pay for that sooner or later.

I nodded to Wes. "We're not likely to forget, no."

———

EVE WAS STANDING in the garage when I made it back to the house, glaring directly into the headlights of my SUV as I slammed on the brakes before I accidentally mowed her down.

"The fuck," I snapped, but the windows were rolled up and I was alone in the car with no one to bear the brunt of the anger.

She was dressed in one of Jamie's old button-downs and seemingly nothing else, her arms crossed over her chest, and she remained still for a moment, just glaring at me. Then she stepped aside, bare thigh flashing beneath the curve of the shirt hem as she made room for me to slowly pull inside.

"What are you doing out here?" I barked, opening the car door before I finished shifting into park.

"I want out."

"Not a fucking chance."

Can't you try having an actual conversation with her? I wondered.

"I didn't say I want to flee the state, I said I want *out*," Eve bit out slowly, as if she too was trying to resist the impulse to just lunge for my jugular. "Out of the house. The yard. Maybe the cul-de-sac."

"We don't live in a cul-de-sac," I muttered, digging my fingers into my beard and tugging briefly before looking out the open garage and then back at Eve.

"I also want my car."

I blew a long breath out of pursed lips and tried to drag that mule kick response of temper back under control. I wouldn't want to be stuck in the house for weeks on end, and it was my house.

"How's your leg?" I asked, turning off the SUV and grabbing my bag before sliding out.

"Better." Eve bounced back on her toes away from me, keeping a bubble of space between us.

"We can start with a walk," I said, staring down at her. "But you're gonna need something else to wear."

I opened the door to the backseat and pulled out a collection of bags, holding them in her direction while I pretended to search the car.

"What is this?"

"Clothes?"

There was nothing left to look at in the car, and I had to either face her or pull a complete coward's move by just climbing into the trunk and locking myself inside. Eve was gingerly peeling back a bit of tissue paper from one bag as if she were waiting for it to explode.

"Adam gave me your sizes. I got him a couple things too." I opened my mouth to add that I hadn't gotten her anything personal but then shut it again.

Her eyes were narrowed in their usual suspicion when directed at me. I'd found her mid-conversation with Jamie recently, and she'd looked halfway relaxed until she'd caught a whiff of me. But Jamie was a relaxing alpha to be around. So was Garrett.

She and I were a different breed of animal. Predators. Or maybe that was just her.

"A walk?"

"Around the block, if you're up for it," I said, sliding in the challenge.

"Very trusting of you," she sneered.

"Oh, I'm going to be with you," I answered, squaring my shoulders before the first rumble of her snarl. "I like our neighborhood, but the locals all know each other. I don't put it past you to hotwire a car and go joyriding for the hell of it, but we'd have a lot of questions to answer when you get back. So yeah, if you want to get out, we'll start with a walk."

"Supervised."

I nodded. "Supervised."

Eve eyed the bags of clothing again, checking the brands on the side. I was glad I'd thought to order from some of the nicer places rather than just a big box store. If I was going to be heavy-handed, I might as well prove I had decent taste.

"Where's the lingerie?" Eve purred, laced with poison.

"Earn it," I answered on impulse, and then immediately steeled my expression before I could choke on my own tongue. I hoped it was dark enough in here to hide the heat rushing up my throat.

Shockingly, all I got in answer was a brief snort of amusement and the simple reply of, "I'll go change now."

I debated going inside to see the others but went to wait outside instead. Garrett would want to discuss Wes, Jamie would have some kind of intuitive reaction to Eve and all those bags, and Adam…Adam would look nervous around me, something I hadn't learned to fix yet.

Eve was quick, and she walked out the front door a handful of minutes later looking…

Downright suburban.

Chic, but domestic. Her hair was in a high and intentionally disheveled bun, and she'd chosen a pair of slim blue jeans and the black running shoes I'd picked out for her. She was still wearing Jamie's button-down though, and I swallowed against the itching in my throat. She looked like she belonged in our little corner of the world, calling back inside to one of the pack as she shut the door behind her.

It was terrifyingly easy to twist the picture into a story as she walked toward me. The pair of us going on a walk together. Or maybe a morning run, a routine for just the two of us. Enjoying silence and probably the competition of the race, the others waiting to start dinner or breakfast until we got back.

I forced myself to remember the real woman, the one who'd pinned me to the floor, or to the wall with her hand on my reluctant erection.

Actually, that didn't help at all. I was attracted to that woman. And imagining her in my day-to-day…

"Are we walking or—"

"Walking," I said, drawing myself out of the not-quite fantasy and marching for the sidewalk.

Eve followed but not at my pace, and it took me a moment to remember that she was injured and she'd looked winded by a walk to Jamie's shop and back just a few days ago. I slowed and waited for her to catch up. She walked just behind and to the right of me, almost in my blind spot, and I found myself repeatedly turning my head to say something, only to change my mind.

"I want my car. It's still in the city," Eve said.

"I'm not sure that's—"

"They don't know about it."

"You don't know that."

"It's important to me."

I frowned and found I didn't have an argument to that. "Why?"

She was quiet and slowing down again, and I made myself keep pace with her. "I don't get to keep things. Everything always has been turned over, dropped off, traded in. I wanted that to be the last car I picked up."

"Why that car?"

Eve huffed. "Because it was fucking pretty, okay? I liked it. It's going to be dragged off to an impound lot if I don't pick it back up, and it's a 1968 black cherry Dodge Charger. Practically mint."

I was not a car guy. Wes would've understood, and I wondered if I could risk mentioning it to him.

"I will do something stupid to get it back, if I have—"

I spun, and Eve bumped into me. She'd been glaring daggers at the back of my head, and she continued doing so as I hunched until we were eye to eye.

"I don't know what your problem is. Or the collective accumulation of them. But if you're determined to get your head on a chopping block, then why fight so hard to get out of the office building? You could've let them finish you off there. You are risking Adam—"

"Rory, that you?"

My tirade was cut short, and Eve and I both turned to stare at the interruption.

"Oscar," I said, holding in a groan.

"Hey, buddy!" Oscar was our two-hundred-and-sixty-pound alpha ex-marine neighbor, currently out with his mastiff. He was originally from Hawaii, smelled like bubblegum, and had a similarly cheerful disposition. I also knew he was about as deadly as the woman at my side. He and Dobby, the enormous dog, slowed in their approach on the sidewalk, and I was surprised and relieved by the way Eve slid behind me slightly.

"Never see you out here," Oscar said, smiling. And the bastard had a whole inch on me, rarely achieved, so he was helping himself to peeking over my shoulder at Eve.

"Yeah, I…" I, what? "It's a nice night and, um…"

My mouth remained hanging open like an idiot as a slim arm wrapped around my waist.

"Hi. Eve."

Oscar stared at Eve's hand outstretched before

grasping it in his enormous paw, grinning between us both and arching an eyebrow at me.

I should've realized then how much shit I was in, but instead I remained staring blankly back at my neighbor.

"New packmate," Eve continued, in this new sweet and syrupy tone she'd turned out.

My jaw gritted as her hand on my waist slid down and helped itself to my pocket. Somehow, even her scent went sweeter, warmer. *Fine*, I thought. *If you want to play pretend…* I curled my arm over Eve's shoulder, waiting for her to take my wrist and twist it until the joint snapped. Instead, she rested her head on my chest as I rubbed a scent mark on her throat and then relaxed, stroking my hand over her bicep briefly.

"No fuckin' shit," Oscar breathed out, face momentarily slack before a monstrously massive smile stretched across. "You sneaky bastards. A new packmate, and the neighborhood hears shit about it?"

"Two, actually," Eve said. She was all curled and tender against me, wearing Jamie's shirt, and I was starting to wonder if I weren't hallucinating. "I kinda came as a package deal with—"

"Alex," I blurted out.

Inside my pocket, Eve's fingers pinched my hip.

Oscar's eyes were huge on my face. "An… Shit, did you guys find your omega?!"

Bitch, I thought at Eve. Except I admired her for it too. With one tiny accidental run-in, Eve had planted herself and Adam into our pack, at least in terms of local chatter. Oscar might not look like a gossipy housewife—he looked like a cheerful wall of muscle with a wild mane of dark hair—but the military crowd was just a giant game of telephone. And our neighborhood was nearly eighty percent ex-armed forces.

"It's all still getting settled," I said, trying to find us a loophole for later.

Isn't this the truth, though? I thought. Eve had demanded a pack for Adam, and at the park I'd more or less told her she was getting one, for herself included. Aside from giving Adam a fake name for his protection, we kind of *were* in the process of settling things.

Oscar gave me a skeptical look as Eve twisted against me, her breasts pressed up against my side, hips leaning hard into me, looking about as settled as two alphas would together. More than.

"Well, fuck, this is going to make the barbecue way more interesting," Oscar said, grinning.

Fuck, indeed.

"Barbecue?" Eve chirped brightly.

"Aw, did big man not tell you? Yeah, we're having a barbecue this weekend. You're coming."

"We absolutely are," Eve agreed.

I looked down to glare at her and suddenly found the cause for Eve's insistent cuddling. Dobby was tugging on his leash, sniffing curiously at her side. Was Eve—big, bad, killer-queen alpha Eve—afraid of dogs?

I turned, pulling Eve with me, to reach out and pet the mastiff, encouraging him closer and grinning to myself as Eve all but climbed my hip, refusing to give up the facade of our closeness.

"We'll make sure Alex and the others are up for it," I told Oscar.

He snorted and shook his head. "You'll just stir up more interest if you wait to introduce everyone. Have people peeping in your windows and bringing over casseroles," Oscar teased.

Dobby gave up on Eve and me, and I found myself stroking Eve's back as she relaxed slightly.

"I know how to talk him into things, I'll take care of it," Eve answered Oscar with a broad grin.

And because it was permanently seared into my memory, taunting me hourly, I thought of her pinning me to the wall, hand on my cock, snarl pointed up at my face.

"She is persuasive," I said, with a slight grimace.

Oscar barked out a laugh. "Good to know. Maybe a little change of management coming for your pack, eh?"

"Ooh, I like him. He's *very* smart," Eve said. And for a moment, with her smiling up at me, eyes laughing, I almost fell for the illusion.

"Then we'll see you all Saturday. Can't wait. Anticipation will be *high*!" Oscar said. "Come on, Dobby, let's get back and spread the word. See you, Stevens. Eve."

Eve waved cheerily as Oscar and Dobby retreated, until I turned us roughly.

"You just lost walking privileges," I growled, keeping my arm tight around her shoulder.

"But I won social barbecue privileges," Eve answered brightly, her own arm remaining comfortably around my waist. "So I think I can safely call the victory in my favor."

"We'll see what the others say." But I had a feeling I already knew the answer, and Eve was right. She'd won. Even if Adam and Garrett didn't want to go to the barbecue, the neighborhood would just find reasons to start showing up at our door.

"Feeling outgunned, *big man*?" Eve purred.

We hadn't made it far from the house on the short walk, and the trip back was propelled by me all but carrying Eve back. Instead of heading back to the front door, I ushered Eve into the garage, hitting the button for the door to roll down before caging her in against the wall.

Eve chuckled and squared her shoulders, chin lifting in defiance. "You *are* ruffled, aren't you?"

"If you wanted to play house in front of the neighbor-hood, all you had to do was ask," I answered. I stepped in closer, and Eve's eyes narrowed, her smile freezing as our chests brushed. I knew soon enough Eve would be healed and I would have to answer for drugging her and dragging her here unconscious. Why not add this to my sins? "And if you think I'm not willing to act like you've got me wrapped around your finger just because I'm an alpha, you've been reading me all wrong."

Eve snorted. "Oh, have I?"

Either she was willfully misunderstanding me, or she didn't want to know. I would make her face it. I reached between us, grasping gently around her wrist, ignoring her tug of resistance and lifting her hand up to my throat. Her fingers rested open, thumb over one drumming pulse, finger-tips on the other. I relaxed until my weight was against her, fixing her to the wall, the control mine in the moment, but only because Eve was watching, waiting, expecting a trap.

"Liar," she hissed.

I arched an eyebrow at her and then dipped my face closer, grazing my cheek against hers, grunting as her hand finally squeezed in reflex. "Tighter," I growled in her ear.

Eve was quiet, still for a moment, and I wondered if I'd played my hand too early or if she really only wanted me out of her way, a pack member in name only. Then her hand tightened, my heartbeat alive against her fingers and my breath all but strangled.

My purr burst from my chest, muted by her chokehold, but eager. I rocked against her, and Eve let out a soft laugh as my growing erection pleaded against her stomach. She pushed my face back so she could glare into my gaze.

"Beg," she said.

I couldn't speak, not with the grip on my throat, and I

knew that wasn't what she meant. My hands stroked her side, careful and respectful, skirting the edges of her breast, her ass, wanting to grab and claim. I ground my hips into her as she watched me, clinical and curious. Her free hand slid down from my chest over my crotch, gripping and squeezing my length, and my eyes fell shut, mouth open on a pant, the purr scratching up from my strangled throat as I bucked and kicked into her hand.

"Kinky," Eve said, a soft laugh brushing my jaw.

"I'm—" She loosened her grip, and I gasped a breath before speaking again. "I'm not saying I won't fight."

"You'd better," she answered softly, the first hint that maybe, just *maybe*, she wanted this battle between us as much as I did.

Her body arched forward, and I groaned, eyes opening again. But we were at the wrong angle, not fitting together. Risking her anger, my hands took hold of the back of her thighs, hauling her up against me, my mouth falling to hers.

The kiss was a bite, rough and demanding, exactly like I'd imagined. I snarled into her, but the sound that answered me was ragged and pained.

Her thigh.

I dropped her, steadying her at the last second, and jumped backwards. Her nails scratched against my throat as I ripped myself out of her grip, my jaw fell open in shock as our actions caught up with my brain.

Eve's lips were pressed shut, a wince in her gaze as she stared silently up at me, leaning on her good leg. Those hands that had possessed me bodily lowered to her sides as she shrunk back, her eyes wary.

She was still injured, still healing, and I…

Whatever we were to each other—enemies, pack, hate-fuck in the waiting—it wasn't settled yet. I'd jumped the gun.

"I want my car back," Eve said.

I blinked in confusion at the sudden left turn in the moment, a cold splash of water on my overheated brain.

"I'm not going to let it go."

I shook my head and covered my eyes before she could see them roll. "If you want the car, you're going to have to trust me to bring it back to you."

Eve straightened, masking any pain behind her brutally beautiful and smooth features. "Fine. I'd threaten to scratch you if you so much as nick the paint job, but apparently, you might be into that?"

I huffed and looked away. "I might."

Eve's hand reached out and snagged me by my waistband, yanking me closer and catching my jaw in a bruising grip. "Then be good, bring me my fucking car, and I will kick your ass right to the floor, no matter how hard a fight you put up."

My lips quirked, and Eve's eyes lightened.

"We'll see," I said, pulling away and trying to bite down my grin as I strutted inside, Eve's glare clawing at my back.

TWENTY-SIX

Eve

"How's that feel?" Jamie asked me.

I grimaced, my foot hooked in the handle of the weight, slowly lifting the weights on the chain by forcing my foot to the ground behind me. My thigh burned, screamed, threatened to split all over again. But no, that was just muscle rebuilding.

"Like hell," I panted out, my leg trembling as I held the weights up. There was sweat on my temple, but this was the mark in my physical therapy I'd been waiting for.

"Now for the hard part—lower it back down *slowly*," Jamie said. "Want a hand to hold steady?"

I shook my head immediately, testing myself by lifting my heel off the floor. My leg protested but obeyed, and slowly I lifted my foot.

"Good. It'll be nasty tomorrow, and don't think I won't hover and make sure you take it easy. But this is great," Jamie said.

I rolled my eyes at the threat, but I knew better than to think he wouldn't keep to his word. Jamie had put himself in charge of my recovery, and it was…not the worst.

Slowly but surely, I was getting used to the idea that Jamie wasn't calm and steady as a way of getting me to lower my guard, he just *was* that way. Patient, observant, difficult to rile—I'd tried.

I would've doubted his designation, except I'd realized in our sessions that there was *bite* to this alpha. He just chose to dull his teeth. If I wanted to push myself too far too fast, he warned me once, and then barked the second time. A bark that drew me to a sudden stop.

Bastard.

"Fantastic," he said as the weights clinked gently down. He stepped in closer, catching my arm in a steadying grip and offering balance as my healing leg went all but limp. "Relieved?"

I glanced into the mirrors across from us. Rory had outfitted the finished basement into a decent gym, including a full wall of mirrors. Jamie was reflected there, holding my arm, staring firmly at me, waiting patiently for my answer.

I'd thought any possible attraction I might've had for men who were alphas had been beaten out of me growing up, but…

This pack was fucking with my head. Garrett with his casual and playful fluidity. Jamie with his unthreatening command.

Ugh. Even Rory. Ever since he'd made the suggestion, I'd been itching to tackle him, unsure if I really wanted passion or just to prove my dominance.

"Eve?" Jamie prompted.

"I suppose," I said, nodding, barely remembering the question.

Jamie frowned and tilted his head in confusion, and I scrambled to remember. Right. Was I relieved?

"I'm still not one hundred percent," I admitted grudgingly.

"Are you saying you're not deadly?" Jamie teased.

I sniffed. "I've always been deadly…give or take the sepsis."

Jamie grinned and did me the courtesy of not correcting me. He stepped back and grabbed a water bottle from the floor, offering it to me at the same moment the basement door opened and Adam jogged halfway down the stairs.

"Dinner's ready."

"Perfect timing," Jamie said with a nod, checking on me once more. "Good?"

"I'm fine," I said with a short nod as Adam bounced impatiently in the bond, wanting my attention. "Up in a minute."

Jamie only had to glance between us once before nodding and heading for the stairs. "See you there."

He patted Adam's shoulder absently on his way up, comfortable but not close. There still didn't seem to be anything brewing between them—I'd more or less occupied Jamie's attention when he wasn't working—and I was still irritatingly pleased by the fact.

I lowered my wall in the bond, just enough for Adam to know I was paying attention, and was rewarded with a grin.

"Hey."

I arched an eyebrow at him. "Hey?"

His smile grew wider and he laughed, hurrying down the stairs and over to me as I walked gingerly over to where I'd left a fresh shirt folded to the side. Adam watched as I stripped out of my sweaty workout clothes, biting his bottom lip.

"I know Garrett hasn't been leaving you that unsatisfied," I purred roughly, sliding into a pair of drawstring pants from Rory. They were black silk, and I was unsettled by how well he'd judged my tastes, the fabric a cool relief on my fevered skin.

Adam's cheeks flushed, and he glanced away. "You'd be surprised. And he's not you."

"You mean he can't lock you," I said, laughing and pulling on a shirt.

Adam caught me by the elbow, frowning and tugging me closer. "You are not interchangeable to me, and it isn't about your lock or his knot. You're my alpha."

I opened my mouth to answer that Garrett could be too, but Adam must've known what I would say because he lunged forward and caught me in a brazen kiss, holding my face to his just long enough for me to give in, digging my teeth gently into his bottom lip. Truth be told, I was missing having Adam in my bed. He snuck in at night sometimes, fresh with Garrett's gentle marks and kisses, but we hadn't had sex since before we'd left the old safe house apartment.

"But I do want to talk to the others about…about becoming pack," Adam murmured, pulling away slightly.

I blinked. "What's to talk about?"

Adam's smile was crooked and a little weary. "Well, some of it you and I have already talked about. But they should know too. That I…don't want kids. Don't want to be *just* the omega. They might want a family, you know."

Obviously, there were ways around the fact that I couldn't have kids, but Adam was right. Neither he nor I *wanted* to be parents. And as much as I didn't want a new kink in the plan of getting Adam a safe and protective pack of alphas, perhaps he was right.

What if Jamie was expecting children?

I tucked my tongue between my teeth to keep from

grinding my jaw and nodded at Adam. "Fair enough." Adam sighed and turned for the stairs, and I stopped him with a hand on his chest, sliding it up to his sharp jaw and turning his face back to mine. "Do *you* want them?"

Adam blinked at me for a moment before glancing up at the ceiling. "Oh, you mean the pack?"

I nodded.

Adam smiled and wrapped his arms around my waist, crowding closer and nuzzling at my jaw. "Late to the party, but thank you for asking. I'm still getting to know Jamie and Rory but…I want Garrett, and…I dunno, there is something about the whole idea that's growing on me."

It was called biology. Adam's omega hindbrain senses knew that surrounded by us, his alphas, he was safe. He would be provided for. Cared for. I scratched my nails over his back, and he shivered and sighed against me happily.

I was…glad that he'd come around to the idea of the men. I'd chosen them for him, and now it was a relief to know I'd made the right choice.

I opened my mouth to tell Adam as much and then shut it again. It was too late for apologies, he'd made his decision in the end.

"We should go up," I said, and I managed to graze a kiss over his temple as he nodded and pulled away. His cheeks were pink and his eyes were bright, all tickled and happy by stray affection. "How is it going with your server friends?"

He groaned at that, leading me to the stairs. "Not very fruitful. It's hard to exchange information with anyone when I'm not actually allowed to tell them anything. I look more suspicious than they do, you know? But Garrett's been able to prove everything we have learned so far. No closer to figuring out who the liar is."

"They don't have to be a liar to have betrayed you. You

need to figure out what their prices would've been. Their own safety? Someone else's? More information? Money? And then we figure out what Omikron had the power to pay."

Adam's hand squeezed around mine, and he looked over his shoulder as we entered the dining room. "Garrett and I could probably use you for a day, if you're up for it."

Garrett had mainly avoided me since he'd delivered his lecture that first day of my arrival. He was defensive of Adam, which was the role I wanted him in, but he glanced at our joined hands now and offered me a smile, and I found myself relieved to see it.

I shrugged. "Of course."

Garrett pushed a chair back for Adam, and Jamie pulled the other one open for me. Rory sat across from us. The family table was round, no figurehead seat, and obviously made by Jamie. It was sturdy and simple, not unlike this pack.

Garrett was already filling up his own and Adam's plate, and Jamie caught my eye, glancing at the pair in amusement. Adam was fidgeting nervously, fingernail picking at the label of the beer Rory had passed him.

"Do the three of you want kids?" I asked.

Silverware scraped at porcelain, and Adam choked on his drink as four sets of eyes turned to me.

"No," Rory answered, apparently surprising Garrett and Jamie, whose stares swiveled in his direction. "What? Kids are weird. They make me uncomfortable."

"What is—Why are you—" Garrett stuttered, carefully setting the dish of chicken back onto the table.

Adam groaned and covered his face with his hands, head shaking. "It's me, it's my fault. I said we should talk about it and she—you—"

"Subtlety is just a stalling tactic," I said, shrugging. "I can't get pregnant, and I don't want to."

Jamie's whole body jerked, and then a sharp and abbreviated laugh rose from his lips. He tried to cover the sound, but his cheeks were full of a grin. "Sorry. Just had a...weird mental image of—"

"Me as a mother?" I finished for him, my lips quirking as I helped myself to the salad bowl. "No, thank you."

"And I don't want kids. I know I'm supposed to, but..." Adam shook his head slowly.

"You're not supposed to anything." Adam's eyes lifted from his lap to stare wide-eyed across the table at Rory, who stiffened with discomfort and then shook it off to continue, "No one is holding you to any role just because of your designation."

Not the speech I expected from the consummate alpha. I held my glass out to Jamie when he offered wine and watched as Adam dipped his head to Rory.

"I think...I think we assumed we might fill the role of parents when...if our pack found an omega, but..." Jamie spoke slowly, and I suspected he was waiting for the final voice of the group to chime in.

Garrett had gone quiet, watchful, since the announcement. I had known no example of what a father might be, but I suspected Garrett would've been suited to the role.

"We're having this discussion because you want to stay?" Garrett asked, reaching out to Adam and resting a hand on his thigh.

Adam swallowed hard and nodded. "I know what omegas are for and—"

Garrett shook his head. "You're not *for* anything. Not to us, I promise. I want a partner, a bondmate."

"But—"

"Having a pack does not have to include children," Garrett said.

"But did you want it to?" I pressed. Garrett was important. Adam needed another bonded alpha, one who would fill in the gaps of what I couldn't offer. As much as I wanted to force the two of them together…Adam's happiness was significant to me. If this raised doubts for Garrett, their bond would suffer.

Garrett was quiet, thoughtful, but he kept hold of Adam. "Like Jamie said, I think I assumed it would. But that was in a hypothetical future."

"The one you're looking at now is dangerous," I said, this time to all of them. "It may not even be in this home. Not if Omikron finds us before this is over. I stand by the decision that this pack is what's good for my omega, but…"

"But maybe they need to choose if I'm what's good for this pack," Adam said, shoulders slumping.

At the sight of his worry, I opened my mouth with a threat ready on my tongue, but then forced it shut again. *This can't be forced*, I realized. Not if it was really going to work. Not if Adam was going to be happy, safe. If they all were.

"It's too late to back out now," Rory bit out, taking up his fork and knife and cutting into his dinner. "You're pack."

I let out a snarl, and Rory cocked an eyebrow at me. "You don't speak for them."

Rory's fork clattered against his plate. "This is what you wanted! It was your idea. You wanted a pack and you got one."

"This is an interesting turnaround," Jamie said to Garrett, but the other alpha's focus was still on Adam.

Garrett and Adam were leaning into one another, words murmured under their breath.

"Are you saying you changed your mind?" Rory barked at Jamie.

My growl rose, but Jamie just laughed and leaned back in his chair, hands raised in surrender. "Not at all, I'm in."

"But your work," I reminded him.

Jamie shrugged and nodded. "I love my work. But I like to travel too. Learn new things. I'll move on if we need to. I don't want my decisions to be defined by what I do for a living."

He tipped his glass to mine, a chiming note of welcome between us before he lifted the wine to his lips. I watched the motion, a curious hunger in my belly to taste the liquid from him rather than the cup.

There was a soft sound from my other side, and I turned in time to catch Garrett pressing a firm and slow kiss to Adam's mouth. Adam was bursting with relief in the bond, something settled between them.

"We're pack," Garrett said simply, the tiniest curve to his lips hinting at the bright light in his eyes. "We will tackle the future together."

"To pack," Jamie said, lifting his glass to the center of the table.

Rory rolled his eyes but held out his beer, Garrett and Adam quick to follow. I watched until I realized they were waiting on me. The reality of what I'd forged sank in, sudden and cold and shocking. A pack. A family. A bond-mate. My hand around my glass tightened, a cage squeezing around my heart.

Run, I thought. Forget about breaking Adam's trust. Forget about Garrett's anger and Rory's resentment and Jamie's passive disappointment. I didn't have to carry their emotions with me. Just get up from the table and get out of the house before it was—

Too late.

I had demanded this, woven the spiderweb around these men, and then found myself encased in my own trap.

I raised the glass slowly, aware of their wary gazes, of my own reluctance.

"To pack," Adam said softly.

———

"YOU LOOKED like you were about to bolt for a minute there."

"I assume you came out to be sure I hadn't," I answered, not glancing behind me.

It was late, the fireflies in the backyard almost done with their ritual of light. I'd escaped the house after dinner, and for the first time, no one asked me where I was going.

Garrett slid into the deck chair next to me, passing me a bowl. Ice cream. I stared at it for a moment before picking the spoon up cautiously and scratching at the scoop.

"It's not drugged or poisoned," Garrett said with a soft huff.

Dark chocolate with some kind of fruity swirl. I helped myself to a larger spoonful.

"I came out to see if you were okay."

"The chicken was a little dry, but it wasn't that bad."

Garrett sighed, hands cupping the arms of the chair, about to push to standing again.

"This was my idea. My solution," I said. "Why wouldn't I be okay?"

"Because you don't like alphas. And I know you want what's best for Adam, but I don't think joining a pack of alphas is what you want for yourself. You don't trust us."

"I trust you fine," I said with a sigh, digging for more of that ribbon of dark cherry jam in the ice cream.

"With Adam. With a plan maybe. With information. But not with *you*. Not as a pack, or…a relationship."

"You're harmless," I bit out.

"I know that, but do you?" Garrett asked. "And I don't mean that you know you could fight me off, or take me out or whatever. I mean, do you know that I would never *try* to hurt you?"

A firefly buzzed closer, lighting up near my knee, and I reached out for it, catching it briefly on the back of my hand before it left again. I stirred my spoon for another bite of ice cream but came up empty and set the bowl on the deck table behind me.

Garrett was waiting in silence at my side, unusually solemn.

"Jamie wouldn't either, and I know you and Rory don't get along, but he—"

"I grew up in a home for presumed omegas," I said, cutting Garrett off before he could offer more reassurances.

"A… Like an orphanage? Just for omegas?"

I shrugged. "Orphaned or abandoned. I'm not sure. Children who had the genetics to turn out alpha or omega. It wasn't a warm place to grow up, but it wasn't harsh either. Like a waiting room of a childhood. But I started presenting signs of being an alpha early. I was overly protective of my friends, aggressive with authority. So they moved me to the alpha house when I was thirteen. I was the only girl."

"I've never heard of this. I mean, I've heard of the Omega Center, but—"

I shook my head and glanced briefly at Garrett before turning back to the yard. "Not here, not in the states. I'm not sure where I was, actually. They taught us English, but...kids arrived speaking other languages."

Garrett went silent in understanding. A house of abandoned omegas in waiting. A stable for alphas in need, outside of a jurisdiction to protect the omegas. Trafficking in the waiting.

"The home for alphas *was* harsh. I thought at first they were just trying to make us burn off aggression, energy, but in retrospect I think we were meant to be kept in shape. We were observed, but not closely monitored. It was like they *wanted* us to fight. Wanted to know who would come out on top." I took a slow breath. "I am fully aware of the nature of alphas. Packs might keep us tame, but a swarm proves what animals we really are."

"A swarm?"

I glanced at him and shrugged. "When there's too many of us. Too many for control, for order, all that's left is the worst of our traits."

Garrett covered his mouth, a growl soft in his throat, head shaking slowly. "I—Look, I..."

"You don't think so?"

"No! It's—I'm not disagreeing. I'm fucking pissed on your behalf."

"Don't be. It took me a little time, but I ended up the one on top," I said, forcing a smirk. It had taken me three years, actually. Three years of hell, of being held down, of being the weakest, the easiest target, slowly sharpening my teeth through every day of torture.

Garrett's eyes narrowed on my lips before flicking up to my eyes. "Yeah. Yeah, I bet. And honestly...good. I won't tell you I would've been your hero if I'd been there—"

"I didn't need one."

Garrett nodded and rubbed his hand over his jaw. "Just...no one in this pack is out to prove dominance. I mean, I guess—" Garrett sighed and looked back at the house, the light from the kitchen casting a glow over his worried features. "Is it Rory? He's a grumpy asshole, but I know he'd respect your limits if—And I'm sure as hell not about to stand in your way," he said. His hand reached out to clasp mine, and he paused, eyes wide on our linked fingers, surprised by his own gesture. "And…and Jamie's not that kind of guy either. We can talk to Rory—"

"Stop." Rory had made his own argument clear in the garage, an interesting temptation.

Garrett stopped with a swallow and looked up, eyes wincing. "I'm sorry you grew up in that. But that is not what pack is. Not with us, I promise."

Our hands were still connected, neither of us gripping onto the other, just frozen in the position, waiting for the other one to pull away.

"I'm still here, aren't I?"

Garrett's lips twitched. "Surprisingly enough."

My own fought an answering smile. "And I know I could bring you all to heel if I had to."

Garrett blushed, and his fingers squeezed around mine briefly. "Only if you have to?"

I huffed a laugh, but Garrett sat still, watching me. I tipped my head and pursed my lips. "Have you fucked my omega yet?"

Garrett cleared his throat and shook his head. "Worked up to it. I've been waiting on you."

"Are you not clear on the mechanics? I don't have to be involved."

"I *want* you involved, Eve. You're staying, right?"

It was mostly settled, but I knew myself too well to be certain. I couldn't very well say I hadn't made up my mind yet, not if I wanted a chance of leaving without one of them catching up to me, so I nodded.

"Then this isn't just about Adam and me. It's about us. If Adam and I share a bond, you're kind of along for the ride. It'll tarnish if you're not on board with it. I know you gave us an out tonight because you want Adam to be happy. I'm giving you an out now for that same reason. Do you really want to share Adam? Because if you don't, this pack won't work."

I pulled my hand from Garrett's and then raised it to his jaw, taking a possessive hold. "I'm resigned to you," I said, softening the words with a smile.

But Garrett's eyes shuttered, and he tried to pull away.

"What? I was teasing! I want you to be Adam's alpha. I accept you," I said. Garrett's jaw flexed under my fingers, and I tightened my grip, glaring back at him. "What do you want me to say?"

His lips parted on a snarl, and the kitchen light inside flicked off, leaving us in the pure blue light of the night. Garrett's breath caught, his hand raising to curve around my wrist, thumb stroking over my pulse.

"I think I was waiting to hear that you wanted me," Garrett whispered.

I frowned at the words, every muscle in me tensing, a reflex to *run* from the interest of male alphas.

"I just realized why that's a lot to ask," Garrett said, his fingers sliding up to cover mine on his jaw, gently pulling away my hand.

I thought of Rory in the garage, holding my hand to his throat and asking me to squeeze. Of Jamie watching me with warm eyes, waiting. Panic rose like talons scratching up my lungs, a drum of wings begging to take flight, and with it the urge to *fight*, to throw Garrett away from me and to the ground, to keep him there by whatever means necessary.

A kiss dropped into the center of my palm, warmth spreading up my arm and distracting my impulses.

"I'm sorry. You're right—I accept you too," Garrett said, releasing my hand at last and pushing up from the chair. "I don't want to rush with Adam, but I won't hold back anymore."

I squeezed my eyes shut. My head was too loud, too many old memories unpacked and clamoring for renewed attention. Garrett's fingers touched my shoulder briefly, drawing away as I flinched, his steps retreating softly and the backdoor creaking.

I sat in the dark, my feet itching to run, my hands fisted against the arms of the chair, and tried to reorganize the safety of my own mind. Sorting through the strange energy of the omega house, my possessive love for the girls around me. The fear of entering the alpha house, of being hunted, cornered, fighting against boys who were practically men, of having my own weakness proven to me.

Put it away, I reminded myself, breathing through the phantom pain in my wrists made worse by my punishing grip on the wicker chair.

Lingering in my blood was the horrible joy of breaking another alpha's arm when he tried to grab me. I pictured Garrett's face instead of the boy's, and the joy sickened.

I didn't want to hurt Garrett. And in spite of what he said and my own knowledge, it was hard to imagine him like them. I couldn't picture him as anything but what he was, disgustingly kind and funny, handsome and sweet, protective.

Good for Adam, I reminded myself weakly, pushing the old memories back into their dark corners.

The house was quiet as I stepped inside, and I locked the doors behind me, checking every window and door, the security system, on my way upstairs. Jamie's door was open, and he stepped closer as I passed.

"I locked up."

He nodded, brow furrowing. "You okay?"

I waved a hand absently and slid past him for the nest. Adam was inside, the light in the bathroom on, and he grinned at me from the pit, hair falling into his eyes and a hand rustling the sheet over his hips.

"Took you long enough to come to bed."

I sighed, surprised by the purr that rattled my chest, and dove down into the nest, pinning my omega to the cushions as he laughed and grinned up at me.

"Looks like we conned our way into a pack," he said.

The pack was the last thing I wanted to think about, but I knew exactly how to distract Adam, covering his mouth with mine and tearing back the sheets.

TWENTY-SEVEN

Jamie

I glanced up at the rearview mirror, singing tunelessly along with the radio, intentionally missing notes and reaching for ones I had no hope of hitting. It had been an entire hour, and I was surprised I'd made it this far, halfway into the city on the errand Rory had requested.

Take the SUV to his office, retrieve and drive the Charger back home. "For Eve," Rory had muttered out at the end, glancing away from me.

Behind me, the backseat remained still and empty, and I sang a little louder, wondering what hiding spot she'd chosen. There was a tire port in the trunk that would be a bitch to fit into, but I didn't put it past her. If that was where she was, she had to be cramping by now.

"So did you tell Adam to distract Garrett, or what?" I called out, impatient with the waiting game.

Nothing but the radio answered me, and my brow furrowed as I drove slowly into the tunnel leading to the city. I reached out and turned the radio off.

She'd somehow managed to dampen her scent, but it

was still lightly present and I was partial to it now, pleased anytime I came across traces of her in the house. A wisp of smoke on the stairwell, the warning kick before she appeared around a corner, the occasional hint of dangerous florals out of the nest, nearly buried under Adam's sweetness.

"Just come out. I'm not turning around now, and I promise not to sound the alarm to the others," I said, raising my voice and hoping it reached her.

Unless she really had stayed home. Somehow, I just couldn't picture—

There was a thump and a huff, a zipper sliding free. My eyebrows raised. Had she hidden in a duffle bag in the back?

"You are a horrible singer." Eve's face, cheeks flushed and hair stuck to her forehead with sweat, appeared over the back of the seats, scowling at me in the mirror.

"I was a soloist in my Baptist choir and the lead in my senior year musical," I answered, grinning. "I just wanted to drive you nuts."

Eve growled, and my cheeks hurt from smiling. I'd heard her put bite into the sound before, and this one was practically a purr by comparison. She climbed over the back of the seats and then the console to slide into the passenger seat. She sat curled up on her side, facing me, with a hood pulled up over her face.

"If they text, I'll have to let them know," I said.

"Adam was only sworn to secrecy until Garrett figured it out on his own," Eve said, and I nodded.

Garrett probably wouldn't be surprised by Eve sneaking out. Rory would be furious, but if the trip to pick up the car went smoothly…maybe he wouldn't have to know anything about it.

"So what am I in for?" I asked.

Eve stared at me for a moment before glancing out the dash window. "You should drop me off well before the office."

I frowned at that. Eve was uncooperative when it came to working with us, no matter what she said about being part of the pack. As much as it drove Rory and Garrett insane, I almost understood her reasoning. She knew how to take care of herself—no one else would've survived at the level she managed after the office building battle with Omikron—but what she didn't trust was *us*. Would we get in her way in a dangerous situation? Would she have to compromise her own skill and safety to protect us?

"You want to grab the Charger by yourself?" I asked.

"I…told Rory that Omikron couldn't possibly know to go looking for it, but I can't say that for certain," Eve admitted slowly, fingertips drumming along the edge of the bucket seat.

It wasn't a straight answer, and I dug into the opening she left for me. "You're not armed now?"

"…I have some steak knives," she said.

I laughed and glanced over in time to see a quick flash of a genuine smile on her lips.

"Look, I know there's only one real way to prove that I can back you up and it's by you allowing me to try. I will drop you off where you tell me, and if you wait for me to leave the SUV for Rory and come back to meet you there—if you *can* wait for me—I would really like to go get the Charger with you."

Eve was quiet in the wake of my offer, and I waited, holding my tongue between my teeth to give her plenty of time to think over the words before I pressed my case again.

"I was part of two black bag ops before I left the military," I added, fingers tightening on the wheel. The guys knew, of course; we'd all been part of a couple classified projects in our time. It was part of how we found one another.

Eve startled at that, studying me more closely. I tried not to puff my chest out or preen under her stare.

"I'm lead," she said.

I nodded, relief and a bit of triumph rushing through me. "Obviously."

"If I…if I don't wait, it's only because it didn't feel safe," she said.

"I understand," I said, although it hurt my teeth to form the words. I could grab a train home, but it would be agony wondering what happened to Eve in the meantime. And the rest of the pack would tear me a new asshole for it.

Eve offered an intersection to stop at, one I was familiar enough with to know it would be busy any time of day and close enough to Rory's office to catch up with her on foot. I wondered if she had the entire city mapped out in her head.

"How do you keep your scent dulled?" I asked, although I thought I probably knew the answer.

Eve blinked at me for a moment, and I wanted to dig into that head of hers, no matter what I might find there. "I just…put everything away. Everything but my senses."

"Do you compartmentalize a lot?" I asked.

"Everything."

I nodded. "That's common for us." For those of us whose living, profession, relied around the death of others by our own making.

"Do you unpack it? Now that you're out?"

The question surprised me, and I tapped my fingers along the steering wheel, finally pulling out of the tunnel and into the streets, buildings rising up rapidly around us.

"Some of it," I said with a nod. "I did some therapy when I got home again; that helped me realize I wanted to take a step back from military and contract work. Figure out who I was outside of that life. But honestly, some things are just better left boxed up."

Eve nodded at that, and my chest ached.

"Is that how you keep the bond closed too?" I asked.

"Adam is a constant assault of emotions. He distracts me, and then…"

"And then all of that organization that you need to function starts to slide out of place," I said, the realization sinking in.

Eve let out the faintest sigh in answer.

"You should—" I'd already told her in the past to talk to Adam, and butting in a second time wouldn't earn me any favors. And yet…she'd agreed to be pack, albeit reluctantly. She wasn't a feral alpha anymore, even if it might take years before she realized what it meant to have us at her side. Even if she was always more predator than protector.

And my dad had always told me I was too quick to stick my nose in where it didn't belong.

"You should tell him that much. He doesn't need to know everything. Hell, I don't think anyone would recommend you attempt to start to unpack all the shit you have sorted safely. If a boundary is what's best for you, he'll respect that."

I wasn't expecting a reply, and Eve seemed to relax into the passenger seat. "I have an idea of how to get the heat off the car, but it won't be painless." I nodded, and she studied me, continuing, "Are you better with close-up combat or long-distance targeting?"

"Close-up," I said immediately, trying not to laugh as her eyes narrowed.

"We won't go back to the pack house immediately. Not until we know we aren't being followed. I have a garage we can drive through, it'll check for tracking, listening, explosives," Eve rattled off. "If I feel like we are in any danger of risking the pack by returning—"

My hand reached to Eve's knee of its own volition, and I had to steel myself, preparing for her growl as her words stopped short.

"I'm following your lead," I said.

"Does it bother you? To step back?" she asked, holding still under my touch.

"It depends on who I'm following," I admitted, wondering if I could just keep pushing my luck, her leg warm and strong under my palm. "It was a mixed bag in the military, but it wasn't about alpha bark. One of my best commanders was a beta. Another was an alpha. My pack dads were equally inconsistent in getting me under control."

"Were you wild?" Eve asked, smirking.

"I tried to be. They put me in military school, but it was kinda a family tradition on my dad's end of the line. I took off for a year after, but it was…kind of like having my roots pulled out. I was only really familiar with one world, and I wasn't ready for the rest," I admitted.

I'd thought I was a rebel, but a year out of the pack house and working on my own, I realized that rebellion had as many trappings as following orders did.

"I went back in, served and then some. When I was ready to get out, Rory was the one who helped me find my sea legs," I said, glancing at Eve, finding those dark eyes on mine already.

"And carpentry?" she asked, frowning.

I shrugged. "I was good in shop class. One of my pack-dads did a lot of building, mostly for fun. It was weird to get into it while living in the city, but our old loft was a mess anyway and the building was full of artists, so no one cared when I had a bandsaw running in the middle of the night."

"And yet you'd be willing to drop everything, everything you've gained, everything you achieved for yourself?" Eve asked.

I couldn't hold her gaze while driving through the crowded surface streets of the city, but it was tangible on my cheek.

"I meant what I said when we settled the pack," I said, nodding once. "I am a good carpenter. I was a good soldier and operative. I can pick up an old hat if I need to. I can find a new one too."

She was silent, and we were running out of time together. I was aware of what I was risking by agreeing to let her out. She could take off, grab the car, leave the city, and get away like she'd meant to all along. But we couldn't keep Eve in a cage and call her our packmate. I had to believe she'd decide to stick around.

"You're worth the risk, and I'm not afraid of change," I said.

I didn't know Eve well, none of us did, but I knew we were making progress. She added possibility to our pack, the unknown seed of what we might grow into, tenuous and tentative as our dynamic still was. Eve was powerful, potent. Maybe she didn't belong in the suburban life we'd started building for ourselves. Maybe we didn't either.

Eve's hand covered mine on her knee, but only for a moment. "Slow down, let the light go red. This is the corner."

My stomach sank slightly, and the sudden refusal to the plan popped onto my tongue. I bit down lightly, holding it in and coasting to the stoplight.

"I will watch for you," Eve said, meeting my eyes, looking…impenetrable as usual, but calm—maybe honest, or was that just wishful thinking on my part?

"I should be about fifteen minutes," I said as she slid out of the passenger side of the SUV, hood up and head down, weaving through the idling cars to the sidewalk.

————

"AND WHAT IF SHE–"

"Garrett, I know. But what if one day we woke up and she wasn't in the house? It's either going to work or it isn't."

"Adam is…"

I covered my free ear to drown out the city, jogging across the intersection, still two blocks away from where I'd dropped Eve off.

"This is my fault, maybe. I pushed her really hard the other night."

I frowned at that and studied the crowd around me as if Eve might just appear out of one of the department stores or narrow pizzerias. "You're assuming the wrong thing. Is Adam worried?"

"No, but he's—I mean, he's the one who went along with her plan in the first place."

"Trust him," I suggested. "I think there's more to their bond than either of them realize."

Optimistic maybe, but our pack probably needed some optimism to hold it together for a while.

Garrett sighed over the line. "I hope you're right. What about Rory?"

I winced, turning sideways to cut through the coming crowd. "Just wait for me to—"

A slim, strong hand slid into mine, gripping tightly, and my words stuttered. I squeezed back, sucking a quick lungful of airy smoke and lick of petal softness. Out of the corner of my eye, Eve's nose peeked out from under a dark hood.

"Jamie?" Garrett called.

"Just tell him we'll be back later," I said, my voice a little more cheerful than warranted.

"Wait, is she—?"

"We're gonna go run errands now," I said, resisting the urge to pull Eve to a stop, to wrap an arm around her and drag her close to my side so I could grab another whiff of her, like a drag from a cigarette.

Garrett huffed. "Okay. Okay, good luck."

I put my cell phone back in my pocket, Eve's steps quick and sliding ahead of mine to cut us a clearer path through city traffic.

"They're at the car," Eve said. "We need to pull them away, and I know somewhere we can pick up some supplies. It's going to be messy."

"You want to draw them in our direction?" I asked. I was a little rusty on my hand-to-hand lately, but I went to the firing range with Rory and Garrett sometimes and I was still a better shot than either of them.

Eve was quiet as we walked, tugging gently on my hand to lead me down a wide alley between a deli and a computer repair storefront.

"That's the plan," she said, glancing at me for the first time. She was watchful, examining, but I realized that the suspicion she always seemed to carry around us, the alphas, was missing now.

"Gonna share any of those steak knives?" I teased.

Eve smirked and led me to the right down a thinner alley, shadowed by the buildings rising sky high around us. I assumed we were traveling some shortcut of hers until we stopped short at a dark utility door. Understanding dawned on me as Eve pulled her hand from mine and flipped up a plastic cover, keying in a code.

"Follow me," she said as the door clicked open slightly.

The stairs led immediately down into a densely shadowed hall with one flickering light barely managing the work of lighting the way. Eve slid past me, jogging down the hall, and I followed quickly, the heavy door slamming behind us. The hallway was filled with more doors, more keypads, and the yellowish green bulb flickering in the middle.

"Is this place intentionally ominous or is it a maintenance issue?" I whispered.

Eve was silent, moving quickly toward the end of the hall, and I held back the rest of my questions. There was no one else in the hall, although I thought I heard some questionable, possibly sexual, pained groans behind one door halfway down the hall. Eve entered another code and took my hand again, pushing the door open.

I'd been expecting some kind of storage unit, a place Eve had stashed away weapons and supplies. Instead, I found myself standing in a brightly lit waiting room, complete with comfortable chairs and a stack of old magazines on a side table. Shit, there was even a watercooler.

On the far wall was a glass window—I suspected bulletproof—with a young woman scrolling her phone on the other side. She looked up at our entrance and smiled brightly.

"Hey there, account number?"

"Delilah," Eve answered, and the young woman nodded, turning to a thin computer screen.

"What can I help you with?"

"Two discrete power packages," Eve said with a glance at me. "Disposable."

This was an arms dealer. I had no doubt we'd be

walking out with untraceable guns. And it just existed here, practically right under Rory's nose. And Eve said she wanted to draw the fire to us...

The girl behind the counter tapped quickly into a keyboard, studying her screen for a moment before nodding. "Not a problem, just give us a few minutes."

Eve pulled me to the set of corner seats, her eyes bouncing between the glass window and the door we'd entered through. Our seats gave us an eyeline of both, and the hair on the back of my neck rose. Eve was on edge, expectant.

"It should be a small crew," she whispered.

"You think they'll come here?" I asked, propping my elbow on the armrest to lean in and keep my voice down, murmuring into her ear.

"The car isn't far," Eve said slowly, nodding.

"And this isn't run by friends?" I asked.

Eve's gaze met mine briefly, a rare hint of worry. "It's not above being influenced. There's a knife in my boot." And then she nudged her foot gently against mine. "I can handle the rest."

Arm myself, but let Eve take on whoever came to find us on her own?

"Please," I scoffed. "Give me a little credit. Don't let me distract you. I'll be my own priority."

Eve was still healing, although she was in solid shape compared to when Rory had brought her back to the pack house. It would be hard enough for me to not leap in front of her at the first goon who came after us, but I wanted her to believe that she could trust me. I trusted her to handle herself. I would show her she could do the same with me.

The tension around her eyes eased slightly as I reached into her boot and tried not to laugh as I found one of our simple handled kitchen knives carefully tucked in a makeshift sheath made out of cereal box cardboard.

There was a knock on the glass window, and Eve's knee nudged mine. "Wait here. Behave."

I huffed a laugh at that—behaving was more Rory or Garrett's speed than mine—and Eve's lips twitched.

I leaned back in the chair, watching the hall door as Eve prowled slowly to the window, her spine straight and shoulders just a little high, like a cat refusing to acknowledge the threat at its back.

The girl behind the desk held two plastic shoebox-sized containers, a glimpse of black peeking over the rim of one. Her eyes were on the door to my right as she slid the window to one side and handed Eve the containers.

"Good luck," the girl said, quickly pushing the window closed behind her and turning her back.

Eve turned to face me, expression tense and withdrawn, and my heart started to drum so heavy, I could hear it in my ears.

Crack!

The door banged open, slamming against the wall at my side. Eve dropped to the floor as I jumped from the chair.

Gunfire railed against the wall and the glass window. I took the chair I'd been seated on and threw it at the man entering through the doorway, catching him off guard and sparing Eve a second. She loaded the cartridge into the gun in one of the buckets with an audible snap, kicking the other bucket toward me as she returned fire. I caught the lip of the container with my shoe, lunged low toward the next man entering, the knife wrapped tight in my grip. I moved with an old muscle memory I'd put away, rising from my crouch, jamming the knife up and under his jaw into his skull.

Shots fired, and a body thumped to the floor on my left. Eve had taken out the man I'd hit with the chair.

"They didn't give them blanks!"

"Jamie, back!" Eve barked.

I jumped back, giving Eve free reign to fire on the doorway clogged with Omikron's hires as I ducked and loaded my own gun, firing up at a stranger with a focus I'd forgotten I possessed, detached and precise.

This was familiar. Not welcome, but not shocking. Easy.

"Pushing for the hall," I called to Eve, barreling low and knocking one man down to the floor as she covered me from standing.

Maybe it was a little exciting too. Time to brush off that old hat.

TWENTY-EIGHT

Eve

Four figures in basic tactical gear barred our exit from the far end of the hall near the alley door, the first party of goons already dispatched on the floor at our feet.

Jamie had a speckling of glittering blood on his cheeks and hands, and his eyes were dilated, but his hands were steady. He stood with his back straight and pressed to the wall by the door, and he was staring at me, waiting.

He'd not only not needed me to manage the situation, he'd actually…made the work significantly easier.

"Wait for them to come to us?" Jamie asked me.

I shook my head. "Too much time for them to call in others."

Jamie didn't argue with me, his eyes scanning the room, ear leaned to the hall and listening for changes. The team would be at the disadvantage if we forced them to come find us in here, and the opposite was true for us if we met them in the hall with only guns and knives on us and no protective gear.

However…

"I ordered the power package," I said, crouching down and picking up the canister Jamie had ignored, and his head tilted, nodding once. "I have another in my pocket."

"Did you hear them mention blanks?" Jamie asked.

I nodded, smirking. "Closing out my account was a bribe to the clerk."

Jamie grinned back. "Thank god you're sexy *and* smart."

I blinked at that, still a little baffled that he and I were here. That I'd brought him with me. That he wasn't useless. Better than that even, he was…

Impressive. Which was even more attractive to me than his handsome features.

"Ready?" Jamie asked me.

Get it the fuck together, I snapped at myself. I tore the hood off my jacket with the help of one of my knives, cutting it down the middle and passing half to Jamie, pressing the other half over my mouth and nose.

Jamie took the gas canister from me, and I moved to the wall across from him, out of sight from the hall but ready to move. He didn't have to ask for directions, just took one look at the device, unlocked it and jumped out the door, tossing it down the hall. My hand was already around his arm, yanking him back inside to the sound of muted gunfire and the dull clatter of the gas can bouncing on tile.

Jamie grinned at me once, bright smile and sullied face, his hand steady and holding his gun, and then he covered his mouth and nose as I had with his other hand.

"Let's go."

We were lucky they weren't already wearing gas masks. We were also lucky our guns weren't holding blanks. But the agents on the other end of the hall were no doubt in Kevlar, and we only had the smoke and gas to our advantage.

Adam's going to be so pissed if I get shot again, I thought absently, dashing at odd and uneven angles down the hall, relying on luck more than anything. I jumped high, knocking a flimsy ceiling tile out of my way and hoisting myself above the gunfire for a beat, my abs aching from the sudden use. There was no use wasting bullets until we knew where our enemy was, and Jamie was staying low behind me, fast and quiet.

The light in the hall went out, either shot out or turned off, maybe even by the clerk behind the desk whom I'd given a small fortune to in the hopes it might see us out of here. Lights off wasn't a big help, but it didn't hurt. I swung myself farther along the hall and then dropped. I collided into another body before I'd even realized how far I'd made it down the hall, immediately gripping and twisting the arm, abandoning my facial covering and holding my breath.

My eyes were watering, but we were blind in here anyway. I needed both hands.

I shot under the chinstrap and dropped the man, wondering if the grunts behind me were Jamie or the enemy. Another arm banded around my ribs, lifting me from the floor, and the texture of the sleeve was rough and synthetic. I threw my legs up and backward in the dark, flipping the man to the floor and then rolling away onto my back. I yanked out the knife from my waistband and lunged forward, finding his throat with a groping hand and plunging it in. Fire scorched down my throat now.

"Jamie—" I rasped.

A shot fired in my direction, missing me, and then

another directed toward the first's source. I stood and moved for the door, finding the stairs closer than I'd expected, rushing up and pushing on the metal door bar hard.

Daylight flooded into the hall and Jamie winced, staring up at me, his hand guarding his mouth and nose with fabric, four bodies dead on the floor behind him. The alley was empty, suspended but for the smoke swirling and settling, but my ears were ringing too hard to know if it was as quiet as it seemed. Jamie jogged after me, and I stopped him on the top stair, keeping my eye outside as I peeled off the ruined hoodie and passed it to him.

He arched an eyebrow at me.

"You're bloody," I said, choking on the words and coughing once. The smoke and gas was starting to dissipate, but it would take me a while to clear my lungs.

Jamie looked down at his white shirt, blinking at the blood spray there. I took the fabric from his hand and used it to wipe off his face as he shrugged on the hoodie, too small for his broad frame really, but doing the job of hiding some of the gore. He glanced behind him for the first time, expression impassive, and then back to me, arching an eyebrow.

"All this for a car, huh?"

I let out a cough in lieu of a laugh. "Wait till you see her."

———

I'D GUESSED CORRECTLY. Omikron had either cleared out the watch duty on the Charger to come after us at the dealer's or decided following us would be more prudent. I cleaned off three trackers from the underbody and a few bugs from the interior before deciding that the garage could take care of the rest.

Jamie was quiet in the seat next to me, but he'd given the Charger an appreciative pet upon first meeting.

"You good?" I asked.

They could still be listening, so we'd said as little as possible. Very little needed saying, probably not even this question. I'd been driving an odd route through the city to avoid a physical trail, and Jamie seemed not only patient but relaxed.

His head rolled on the headrest to look at me, and he nodded. "You?"

I nodded.

Jamie reached out as I turned another corner, taking us slowly out of the city, in the wrong direction of the pack house. His thumb skimmed over the back of my hand, brushing away thin flakes of dried blood.

"Injured?"

I shook my head and glanced down at Jamie's thumb, still stroking, not an outright offering of comfort, but not really cleaning me either. I lifted my hand from the gearshift and turned it over, catching his palm against mine before I could think too long on it. I'd held his hand during physical therapy sometimes, but it'd been perfunctory. I'd taken it on the street earlier, leading him to the dealer through the crowds, grounding myself in my decision to trust him to help me.

But this was just…for the sake of it. I pressed the heel of my hand to his, our wrists brushing briefly, exchanging scent marks, and Jamie's breath hitched. My heart was steady in my chest, a rare kind of ease in the moment between us flowing gently alongside the rush of the fight, of escaping. The fact that we'd escaped, this time without serious injury, just made the high even more intense. The injury, being taken into the pack house, had forced me to accept an uncomfortable vulnerability. Today was a reminder of my own strength and an attractive demonstration of Jamie's.

I wanted to fuck, but it would be hours before we got back to the pack house. Jamie's own scent, cool and sharp, spicy and sweet, was thick in the car, but I'd grown so used to him that instead of being aggravating, I found it supportive.

And just a bit mouthwatering.

I pulled away again, back to the gear shift, slowing to stop at a light, but the sensation remained, swirling gently through my veins. Hunger and triumph, arousal and calm. It was less distracting now than I'd found it in the beginning, Adam having somehow conditioned me to…

To genuine connections with the others? My nose wrinkled and Jamie sent me a questioning smile, but I shook my head in answer, focusing on the adrenaline high and the need to burn it off with a bit of physical friction.

The rest of the drive passed in a tense but comfortable quiet. Jamie moved closer on the seat at some point, his arm spread over the back of the bench, knees splayed so one occasionally bumped against my grip on the gear shift. There was an unspoken offer rising between us, issued mainly by our pheromones, Jamie's growing more succulent by the second, my own warming.

We were craving relief. Craving each other too.

The only question was if I wanted to accept the offer.

I pulled up to the open doorway of an auto shop in the northern suburbs of the city and sighed at the familiar face who stepped out of the office.

"Wait here," I said to Jamie, who nodded, studying the slim young man with his hands stuffed in his coverall pockets.

I stepped out of the car just in time to hear Ricky's appreciative whistle. Ricky was a beta I'd met one night in the city, who'd let me ride him in an empty subway car and somehow managed to steal my gun without me noticing. I'd tracked him down eventually and discovered his intriguing combination of hobbies and total inability to stay out of trouble. He was independent, and one of the rare people in the world who I found trustworthy.

"I might've been followed," I warned him. "So I can get my gas and leave."

Ricky scoffed, flipping his mess of blond hair over to the side and shaking his head.

"You're not getting out of letting me touch that beauty," he answered easily. "It's just me here tonight." He bent and squinted into the window of the car, surprise brightening his baby blue eyes. "But I see you have a friend with you."

"Can we grab showers as you give her a full detail?" I asked, nodding my head at the Charger.

"Showers, beers, bag of popcorn. Hell, I'll close up and you can take a nap for all I care. Just leave me alone with her for a couple hours," Ricky said, grinning.

I tossed Ricky the keys and rounded the front of the car. "Shout if you hear tires."

I needed Ricky working on the car, but I briefly considered the idea of using him to relieve my sexual frustration rather than Jamie. Surprisingly, the idea delivered an immediate bolt of discomfort running through me. Ricky was a friend and a fun former fuck, but he wasn't…

I wanted to say he wasn't an Adam, but the truth was that he wasn't *any* of the pack I'd found myself in.

Jamie stepped out of the passenger seat as Ricky hurried for the driver's side door. I reached for his hand without a word and dragged him into the garage behind me as Ricky revved the engine.

"Work first, then play," I shouted at the car over my shoulder, catching a quick glimpse of Ricky's manic grin through the windshield.

"Is he gonna be okay with us here?" Jamie asked me.

"He's resilient," I said, and Jamie's hand tightened around mine in some kind of warning. I looked at him over my shoulder as I led him to the bathroom behind Ricky's office, fully equipped for quick wash downs after working on cars. "Yes. The garage is set up with some frequency jammers, and Ricky's good at protecting himself. We'll stay close by."

Jamie nodded and relaxed at that.

The bathroom was open and chilly with no curtain for the shower, just a brief wall hiding the toilet from view of the shower. There was a small cabinet in the corner to my left with a stack of towels inside and space for our clothes on top. It was cold and quiet, and my ears seemed to be ringing again, all the rush and chase of the afternoon now settling into an unsteady stagnancy.

I turned around and reached for the zipper of Jamie's hoodie, tugging it down roughly. We would strip and fuck and shower, and that would be the end of it. It was all I needed, and I wasn't sure I'd settle down until it was done.

"Hey."

I frowned as Jamie's hands wrapped around mine, preventing me from undressing him. His thumbs stroked the backs of my hands again, and a soft growl broke free from my throat, my eyes flicking up to glare at him.

"Spell it out for me," he said, calm and focused.

I blinked and remembered his words from before. He didn't want me playing games. I had to tell him that I wanted to be fucked, not leave it up to interpretation.

"It's just to calm down," I said instead, blinking at him. "You know how it goes. It'll be quick."

Jamie frowned for real now, eyes narrowing on me. "You need to center?" he asked.

It sounded so silly in that term. I needed an explosive orgasm to rinse out the jitters of the fight. It was just a coping mechanism.

"Sure," I said with a shrug. Not explicit enough, probably, but—

Jamie stepped forward, his arms wrapping around my stiff shoulders, drawing me into his chest. I froze, and it was a miracle I didn't immediately throw him off, down to the floor with my hand on his throat as I had with Rory. Jamie had worked his brand of magic on me over the past couple weeks. I was used to his touch from his help with healing, used to his scent from proximity.

"It's called a hug, Eve. But it helps if you breathe," he said in my ear, then took a deep and audible breath that brushed our chests together, letting it out noisily and rustling my hair with the force.

I was tight and frozen in his arms, listening to the huff and puff of his breath for a long moment. Jamie was warm. His grip wasn't tight, the noisy rush of his breathing was almost like waves breaking. And the sneaky bastard was so goddamn patient all the time.

It took another minute at least, but I relaxed, my own arms looping around his waist, my cheek resting on his shoulder, irritated by the shockingly fresh and unoppressive scent of him. I softened in the hug and allowed my breathing to mimic his. His weight started to lean into mine, a perfect counterbalance, and I realized he was settling himself as much as me. His hands smoothed up and down my back, and I inched my feet closer, his stance widening to make room for me.

My purr arrived, a sudden and almost startling vibration in my chest, as I felt the outline of his cock, semi-stiff and pressing into my stomach. Jamie's purr followed immediately, softer and more even than mine at first, but growing louder the longer I remained in the embrace.

"Tired?" he asked.

The question puzzled me. I wasn't tired, although I was growing somewhat loose and lethargic the longer we stood like this. I shook my head.

"Centered?"

I was, actually, perhaps more than I had been in months, or maybe some collapsing moment during Adam's heat.

"Yes."

Jamie's hands slid down to my hips, resting and remaining there, the touch expansive but not gripping. "Still want that orgasm?"

His throat bobbed with a swallow in front of my open eyes, like he'd had to force the question out and then brace himself for my answer. It came slower than I expected. The tension I'd wanted to break was already gone, and that made the prospect of the act less impersonal and more exposing. We wouldn't be fucking for anything but the sake of intimacy, of being *together*.

My lips curled up slightly at the corners.

I leaned back, my hands on Jamie's shoulders. I'd never had sex with an alpha—or at least not by my personal choice of accounting. Jamie's designation was undeniable; I was aware that in some ways he was as potent or more so than I was. That he *could* force me, or certainly try, that at the very least our battle for dominance would be incredibly close and challenging.

But force didn't come with questions.

It was one of the rare moments I could read Jamie's

nerves on his face, but they relaxed the longer we stared at one another.

"Yes."

Jamie's dark eyes warmed, lips curving into a slow and *nearly* predatory smile. His hands on my hips slid up, lifting my shirt with them, and I finally was able to push back the hoodie from his broad shoulders, taking a moment to appreciate the width of his biceps and huffing a laugh as he flexed them briefly.

We both took over the work of stripping out of our shirts, and mine barely reached the top of the cabinet before Jamie's arm banded around my waist, drawing me back to his broad, bare chest. I stiffened on reflex, and Jamie's other hand stroked up my ribs slowly, sliding across my back to the fasten of my bra, waiting there. I tried to force myself to relax, but I only tensed further as Jamie leaned in, my jaw dropping to guard my throat.

Full warm lips grazed my cheekbone instead, a heavy breath cascading down and over my bare shoulders as the kiss slid to my ear. I let out an equally full breath and sagged, my hands sliding between us to Jamie's pants.

"I would really really like it if we could get into that shower and I could get on my knees for you and just fuck you with my tongue until you're satisfied," Jamie murmured in my ear.

My purr blended with a growl at the offer, hunger hot in my belly. I yanked roughly on the top snap of Jamie's jeans, thrusting my hand into the waistband of his boxer briefs. His arm squeezed around my back as I found his cock, wrapping it in my fist and pumping lightly. His eyelids grew heavy, a thick groan falling out of plush and parted lips.

"Eve," he gasped out.

I rose up to my toes and bit at the bottom lip on offering, sucking on it, then kissing him properly. He tasted a little soapy but sweet enough to be pleasant, and it was his turn to grow tense against me, holding himself back as he let me test him.

I ignored my fear, refused it, around other alphas, but that was easier to do when my interactions with them were aggressive. Affection, sex, the kind that Jamie was interested in, would require me to put aggression aside temporarily. He didn't want to fight me into fucking, like Rory, didn't want to force me, or be forced.

Jamie was bucking slowly into my fist but with a seductively purposeful pace, a demonstration of long and full strokes I might enjoy at some point.

"Or we can just do this." Jamie chuckled, the sound breaking into another groan as I squeezed him a little tighter. His knot was starting to swell at his base, but I ignored it, shimmying my back against his hand and watching him smile in response.

"Oh, I definitely want you on your knees," I admitted.

Even the idea of it, Jamie staring up at me, mouth around my cunt and eyes dark, had me clenching on nothing. His hand on my back finished the work of opening my bra, and I pulled my own out of his pants, his shoulders dropping as he took a step back, watching me cast aside my bra and then tackle my own pants with a quick shove to the floor.

Jamie tried to stifle his answering purr, but it echoed off the tile around us and I froze again, my blood hot with craving but my muscles tight with an old instinctive warning.

"This doesn't have to happen," Jamie offered, trying to swallow the warm rattle from his chest. "Or just whatever pieces work for you—"

I shook my head, burying the instinct as I passed him

on the way to the shower. The rustle of fabric behind me had me flinching as I reached for the shower handles, cranking on the hot water and stepping out of the way of the initial frigid blast.

Jamie and I stared at one another through the spray, studying one another's bodies, reactions. The pace was too slow. I was used to action, demand, the rush and release of fast fucking. This left too much room for studying my own responses.

Jamie's hips were lean, thighs and calves rounded with muscle, sturdy and reliable. His cock was thick and not too long, knot pronounced at the base and surrounded by dense black curls. He was waiting for me. Patient bastard.

"Come here," I said, now that the water was steaming, stepping beneath the rush and turning my back to him.

There were rivulets of red running down me, a reminder of what we'd escaped, and I closed my eyes. Jamie's warmth appeared at my side, and I blocked him from my front, pushing him to stand against my back, his cock half hard against my ass. I gripped his arms and wrapped them around my waist.

"Don't tell the others," I said.

He was quiet for a moment, arching over my back, dense beard soft against my shoulder. "What happens between us is private, of course."

I shook my head. "I don't mean about us hooking up, I mean…"

I meant that I found it so…so difficult. So tempting and uncomfortable at the same time. So fucking vulnerable it made me want to scream. I sighed and leaned back into him as his hands smoothed down my stomach, over my hips, to cover my sex, fingers just cupping around my core.

"Hooking up?" Jamie asked, a lilt of amusement in his voice.

I growled, and his head turned, sucking with tongue and lips at my bare shoulder, avoiding his teeth entirely.

"What are you going to call it?" I asked.

He shrugged, and then his fingers slipped between my lips, stroking simply, almost toying. "I'm not going to gossip about it, Eve. I just want to touch you, taste you, be with you. Is that good?"

I wasn't sure if he meant his speech or what he was doing with his fingers, so I rose onto my toes and arched my hips into his hand, rubbing myself there. I reached behind me to grasp his shoulder for balance, growing used to the vibration of his purr at my back, of my own rushing in and out in my chest.

"Could be better," I muttered.

Jamie laughed and then moved two fingers to my opening, pressing inside immediately, pumping and pressing around the clench of muscle.

"Do I have to say it?" I whispered.

Jamie hummed and kissed my shoulder again. "No, but I'd really like it if you did."

I sighed and turned my head to bump and nuzzle against his. "Yes. That's good."

He is tempting, and he is dangerous, and he is safe, I decided, turning in his arms, moving my hands to his face and lifting it to mine. I had found a new art to kissing Adam, and I borrowed it now, savoring the feel of Jamie, the smell of him, even the tension of our purrs blending together as our tongues stroked one another.

"Limits?" Jamie rasped, pulling away.

"Teeth," I answered, immediately.

"Who uses teeth in oral? No, no, I got it," Jamie rushed out as I leaned back to glare at him.

"Get yourself off, and don't...don't grip me," I added,

slightly galled to admit to any limits but also relieved to make the demands.

Jamie stole another kiss, fingers still teasing me, thumb just rolling my clit enough to leave me warm. He nodded as he pulled away, lashes trimmed with drops of water from the shower, lids low with hunger.

"What…are your limits?" I asked, words halting. It wasn't a question I was familiar with asking when my partner and I were already naked.

Jamie purred in approval, his eyes hooding. "Just don't try and kill me, yeah?"

I nodded too. "Easy enough. Now down on your knees and make the trip there worth it."

Jamie grinned at the order and then ducked his head, more licks and sucks on my collarbones, skipping my throat entirely. I reached up and tilted the showerhead, stepping back and smiling as Jamie followed immediately, hot mouth kissing up and down, back and forth, over every inch on their way to my breasts.

My back hit the tile wall as his mouth found my nipple, tongue circling as I groaned and arched into him. His purr thrummed into my breast and right down to my cunt, his fingers still petting and stroking gently, keeping me simmering with arousal without delivering satisfaction.

Music was bleeding from the garage into the bathroom, chorusing with our breaths and the thunder of the water echoing in the room. Jamie's back bore the brunt of the water, and I reached to run my palms over his skin, humming as he pressed kisses to the undersides of my breasts. He bent to one knee and brushed his thumbs over my nipples until they pointed and pressed into the touch. His tongue was wet and hot against the muscles of my stomach, pausing to kiss over an old scar.

"Leg up," he said, one hand lowering to pat his shoulder.

I obeyed without thinking, but was too distracted by the sudden plunge of his fingers into my cunt to chastise myself. Even better, Jamie did as I asked, dropping his other hand down to his own cock. My hands tightened on his shoulders, digging into the rich muscle there, riding his hand and watching with a rare patience as he lavished my skin with kisses.

"We'll have a long drive tonight. I want to be careful, so we'll have to run a pretty absurd route back home. Mmmm, good, double back," I murmured, stroking the back of his neck as he sucked on my hipbone and then headed back for my stomach. I laughed and grinned down at him. "No, I meant we'll have to double back while driving."

His eyes flicked up at me, so heavy and black with arousal. He shrugged against my hands and then turned his head and rubbed his cheek over my mound. "Fine. No rush, right?"

I purred and nodded. Jamie blinked lazily up at me for a moment before finally kneeling fully, ass resting on his heels, cock jutting out proudly. His fingers pulled out of me and went immediately into his mouth, the sight of them slicked with my arousal catching me like a punch to the chest. His eyebrows bounced as he tasted me, cheeks darkening slightly.

"Spicy," he said with a grin, and I found myself leaning back against the wall and laughing at the exact moment he made good on his promise of a tongue fucking.

And it wasn't an exaggeration. Jamie wasted no time in enveloping me with his lips and tongue, lapping at every tender fold and sensitive nerve before dipping inside of me. It was easy to tease Adam, to order him around in bed, but there was a raw quality between Jamie and me that tied my tongue in my mouth, and the only sound released was a strangled cry of relief.

Jamie's hand was cupped gently over my ass to help me balance, his eyes fastened up to my face as his lips devoured me. I tested him slowly, pressing into his lips, my moan echoing his answering groan, trying to force that probing tongue deeper inside of me.

And it wasn't enough.

No, that was a lie—it was too good, as hungry and desperate as Adam, but with the force of confidence of an alpha.

"Get up," I gasped out after another glorious minute of him devouring me.

Jamie ignored me, easing up to lick from ass to clit, until I dug my fingers too deep in his shoulder.

"Get up, Jamie," I snapped.

He frowned and rose, opening his mouth, no doubt to ask if I was okay. I wrapped my arms around him, ignoring the fact that it trapped me between the hard tile and an alpha.

Not an alpha. Not *just* an alpha.

"No knot," I breathed before slanting my mouth over his and jumping slightly. He grunted in confusion against my mouth, but his hands caught the back of my thighs, holding me in place against his chest, his hard cock trapped between us.

"What—"

"No knot. But fuck me..." I growled slightly, pulling away to glare at him. "Please."

Jamie blinked once and then glanced down as I reached between us, lining him up at my entrance. He didn't make me ask twice, adjusting his hold on me to perfect the angle, before sinking an inch.

As thick as Adam, harder, and my lock almost immediately tried to clamp down on him, the pair of us gasping.

"Holy shit," Jamie breathed, brow furrowing, staring between us for a moment before looking up again to meet my gaze, thrusting in a little deeper.

It's not about alpha, I reminded myself as I drew in a lungful of his pheromones. I rocked myself onto him and placed a hand on his chest to feel his purr. These were Jamie qualities, not alpha qualities. I liked Jamie. After the fight at the dealer, it wasn't even hard to admit.

He was mellow, sexy, and patient, and he'd held his own without any help from me.

Jamie, not alpha, I chanted to myself as he continued those slow and purposeful thrusts.

"I like your cock," I said, a simple smile on my lips as I fought the urge to let my eyes shut.

Jamie huffed out a laugh that unraveled into a moan as he rocked inside of me, right to the slight swell of his knot, but he didn't press any farther. I couldn't really control the swelling and tightening of my lock any more than he could stop his knot from growing thick and hard. I'd found being knotted explosively uncomfortable, even when my lock wasn't engaging, but I rubbed against him there with a twist of my hips and discovered I didn't mind the heady moan of satisfaction I heard in response. Outside of me, a knot was just a convenient place to grind against.

I gripped his face in my hands and drew it in, licking into his mouth in time with the plunge and grind of his cock and hips. His knot pressed to my clit, a dull and determined pressure for me to work myself against. My nails dug into his jaw, our breaths blending with sounds of need, an almost alcoholic glow of heat building inside of me. Not the threat of explosive ecstasy, but something dark and dense, just on the right side of gentle.

I didn't notice the moment I was pinned between his chest and the wall, didn't care. Jamie grunted in time with his thrusts, deep and hard, never pulling out, never driving his knot in, but using me to stimulate the spot, using it to punish my clit with pleasure.

My toes curled as soft heat became stunning fire, my arms tight around Jamie's shoulders, his body working hard and close against me. My teeth ached and I pulled away from the kiss, burying my face against Jamie's shoulder, baffled by the urge to bite him and ashamed of how curious I was at the idea of receiving the same from him in the moment.

It was easier to shout as I came, relief and shock together until the sound was thread-thin and weak. Jamie's own voice cried out, almost pained as I snapped tight around him, nearly forcing him out as his release rushed inside of me.

I caught one breath, found a sudden urge to growl and fight him again, and then he stepped back with me wrapped around him, giving my back space again as he stepped under the water. I sighed and drooped in his arms as the warm water struck my back.

"That lock is no joke," Jamie wheezed out.

I huffed and lifted my head, glancing at him out of the corner of my eyes. He looked like he was holding his breath, and I squirmed in his arms, laughing at the strangled yelp in his throat.

"It hurts?"

"It feels like I haven't stopped coming yet," he gasped out. We wobbled, and he turned and hit the wall with his back. "I'm good, I'm okay."

"I'll relax in a minute," I assured him.

He swallowed hard and nodded, eyes dazed on my face. I leaned in and pressed my mouth to his once, and he caught a breath and groaned as I rocked again.

"Fuck. It's…strangling, like a vise around my orgasm, but…" His voice was garbled into a moan as he arched and tried rolling his hips into me. "But I kind of love it."

Which was good. Because I already wanted to fuck Jamie again.

TWENTY-NINE

Adam

Garrett's hand rested on my knee, but my foot just kept jiggling nervously as I stared blankly at the television. Some asinine beach dating show was playing on the screen, but my eyes were fixed to the digital clock just below.

Suddenly, a bowl of buttery popcorn and a plate of apple slices—complete with smears of chunky peanut butter—appeared in front of my face.

"You didn't eat enough at dinner," Rory said, shaking the bowl and wafting the butter and salt smell at me.

"Uhhh." I reached up and took the offerings, my brain too busy fixating on my missing alpha and requiring a few detours on its way back to the living room. I looked up at Rory again and almost startled at his intense glare before realizing that he'd just brought me a snack.

"Your stomach is growling," he added.

"Thank you," I said as Garrett shook with silent laughter at my side.

Rory remained standing over me, frowning, and I took the hint, picking up a slice of apple and stuffing it into my mouth under his watchful stare. He 'hmph'ed and nodded, moving to sit in the recliner near the couch.

"You guys don't need to wait up with me," I said, although I knew Garrett wouldn't move an inch until I did. "I know she's okay…I just want to see it myself."

"They're pack. We're worried too," Rory answered me.

I smiled at that and grabbed a handful of popcorn before offering the alphas some as well. Rory wasn't half as much of an asshole as I'd originally thought. I was pretty sure both he and Jamie were more interested in Eve than me, which suited me perfectly. I was growing used to having a pack, but I'd gone from wanting no bonds with alphas to wishing the one I had was stronger and craving a second with Garrett. That was enough change for me.

I'd cleared the plate of apple slices before I'd even realized, and Garrett and I were making good work on the popcorn. A new and equally atrocious reality show had started up when headlights struck the walls of the living room through the front windows.

My heart kickstarted in my chest, running at double-time, and I nearly knocked the bowl to the floor.

"Garage," Garrett snapped, but Rory was already up and running into the kitchen.

The garage doors sounded as I pushed away the empty plate and bowl of popcorn, chasing after my alphas. Rory took up the entire doorway and grunted as I shoved him aside.

"Huh. That is a nice car," Garrett mused over my shoulder.

The Charger looked almost black until it rolled into the garage under the light, that glossy pool of blood red glinting at us. Eve parked the car, and I jolted at the gentle nudge from her in the bond, like a private greeting. She glanced at Jamie in the passenger seat, saying something brief, and he nodded before they both stepped out.

Be calm, I thought, but my body didn't give a shit and I was already hurrying down the stairs and heading for Eve.

She had an arm out, allowing me to crash into her, her cheek rubbing immediately over mine. I froze as I found her scent accompanied by Jamie's, and then sagged and wrapped myself around her, pushing her up against the driver's side door.

"Are you hurt?" I asked.

"Nope."

She didn't just smell like Jamie because of the car ride. Something had definitely happened. An odd flash of jealousy whipped through me, and then an even harder stab of need struck.

"The Charger's had a full sweep and tune-up, as well as a license plate change, but she'll need to lay low for a bit," Eve told the others over my shoulder, her hand rubbing up and down my back, not fighting to push me off of her.

"Can I be on top tonight?" I hissed in her ear.

Eve purred again, too loud for me to hear Rory's greeting to her. "Aren't you tired, sugar?"

I was tired, but—

"How about we go up to the nest, and grab Garrett on our way. Little cuddle pile?"

There was no lilt of teasing to her tone, no seductive growl. She really meant it. Just her, me, and Garrett, snuggling down in the nest for some sleep. The energy that had gripped me now flooded away, leaving me almost limp. It was after three in the morning. I was exhausted, and literally nothing sounded better to me than being the middle spoon between her and Garrett.

"Are you big spoon?" I asked her, leaning back.

Eve grinned. "Always."

Which left Garrett as little. He probably wouldn't even mind.

"That sounds amazing," I said with a nod.

Eve cupped my face in her hands and drew me in for a slow and thorough kiss, sweet and demanding, but simple too. "Missed you today," she said, and my eyes widened. She smirked at me and then nipped the end of my nose. "Come on, sugar. Bedtime."

Eve slipped around me, my hand in hers, heading for the garage door where our three packmates were waiting. Jamie's hand brushed over Eve's shoulder as we reached them, and she didn't growl or flinch at all. Rory backed away from the door, his eyes drinking my alpha up like he was re-memorizing her in personal detail.

"Come on, pretty boy," Eve said to Garrett.

Garrett's eyebrows bounced, and I grabbed his arm with my hand not already holding on to Eve's. "Bedtime," I explained to him.

Garrett's feet tripped as he followed us.

"We've got that barbecue tomorrow—" Eve said.

"No," Rory groaned.

"—and it's been a long day of not being killed," Eve added, drawing out Rory's growl even further.

"It wasn't *that* hard," Jamie said.

"You were *spectacularly* capable," Eve purred to him.

I grinned at that. Figures if Jamie was a badass, it would be what turned Eve on. The jealousy was fading quickly under her teasing and affection, easily replaced with appreciation. Jamie had kept Eve safe, or vice versa.

Rory was busy locking up the house as Eve led me and Garrett up to the nest.

"Do you want to shower?" I asked her.

She shook her head. "Jamie and I grabbed a shower on the way."

Garrett's hand squeezed tight around mine, his eyes wide on Eve's back. I wondered if he smelled his packmate's marks on her skin too.

"Snack? Rory made popcorn?" I asked next.

Eve smiled at me over her shoulder. "I just want to sleep all curled up around you, sugar."

The nest was dark and warm as we arrived, and Eve wasted no time, shedding her leggings and shirt, sliding down into the blankets in nothing but a pair of underwear. I followed her, nearly tripping out of my clothes and then sighing as she made good on the promise, wrapping herself around my back and tucking her face against my throat.

"No licking and sucking," I warned her. "Garrett probably doesn't want my boner up his ass all night."

"Wanna bet?" Eve teased.

Garrett's laugh burst out of him, a little high and nervous, but he shrugged his shirt off as we both watched and then stepped out of his jeans a moment later. "You're really okay?" he asked Eve.

"I'm fine," she said, her voice surprisingly soft and calm.

The bond was flickering in and out, almost like she was trying to share but found it easier to keep closed. And I didn't care, because the glimpses I did get were sweet. Not soft, but teasing and affectionate.

"Sure you don't have any head trauma?" I asked, and then laughed as she nipped my shoulder and pinched my hip in retaliation.

Garrett grabbed more pillows and blankets from the cabinet. I'd wondered if someone had been buying more and filling them up again, because it seemed like the nest was just growing fuller and more padded every day. The obvious guess was Garrett, but after tonight I thought maybe it was Rory who kept an eye on the stock.

"The barbecue is a potluck," Garrett mumbled, sinking down in front of me, taking my hand and drawing my arm around his chest. "Have any trademark recipes, Eve?"

"I have excellent taste in store-bought salads."

I snorted at that and Eve nipped my throat again, and then she and Garrett both started purring. It was the middle of the night. My pack was safe. My alphas surrounded me, their purrs a heady drug.

I was out like a light in minutes.

"SO, Alex, you met the guys through the Omega Center, but what about you and Eve?"

I'd already forgotten most of the names of the people I'd met in the neighborhood, and in my head I was calling the woman in front of me Amber. She seemed like an Amber—a pretty beta with dark hair and a great deal of questions she only half paid attention to the answers of.

"At a bar. She kinda rescued me from an over-interested lone alpha," I said, shrugging and searching the spacious backyard for Eve.

She was close—of course she was—and she offered me one of those new and soft smiles of hers. She was also standing with Jamie, their arms loosely around one another as they chatted up another neighborhood couple. I smiled back and itched to go join her, but at least I had Garrett at my side. And we were meant to mingle. To seem like a real pack—or at least a normal one.

"I'd been avoiding pack life for a long time, but it came pretty naturally after meeting Eve," I said, turning back to Amber just in time to catch her glancing at her phone.

She smiled up at me, automatic. "That's so cute," she cooed.

It was cute, actually, and I was annoyed she hadn't paid closer attention to my refashioned version of the events. Garrett had, at least, his eyes crimped with amusement and his scent sweet and juicy.

"Where's Rory?" Amber asked Garrett.

I'd been briefly introduced to Amber's beta husband, an equally disinterested man who looked about ten or more years older than her and who'd gone to smoke cigars with some of the other locals.

"Around," Garrett said, before turning to me. "Wanna go find him?"

I shrugged and nodded. I didn't mind leaving Amber behind.

"I told you this would be boring," Garrett said in my ear. "But it's fun watching you play omega."

"I *am* an omega," I reminded him, arching a brow.

"Sure. But you don't usually go along with it. 'Oh, Eve saved me at a bar and made me appreciate the strength and stability of an alpha, found me a pack,'" Garrett mimicked, mirroring my expression. "Con artist."

I'd told him as much, just as he'd given me the heads-up on the military population of the neighborhood, and also that some of the beta wives found excuses to do yard work when Rory went for runs in the morning. Rory had ducked into a circle of other burly alphas almost as soon as we arrived, and I wondered if that was his own method of defense.

Eve and Jamie joined us as we wove through the crowd, the familiar presence of the three alphas blocking out some of the discomfort of being surrounded by strangers. There were a few other omegas here at the party, safely ensconced in their own alphas' company. I'd talked briefly to one omega woman, received her congratulations on finding a pack, but it hadn't taken me long for her scent to set my teeth on edge and make me uncomfortably jealous of every glance she sent in Garrett's direction. I was sure she felt the same any time one of her alphas made small talk with me.

People thought alphas were territorial, but they had nothing on us omegas.

Eve's arm slid over my shoulder, and I sighed, arching my neck and relaxing as she pressed a kiss to one of her marks.

"Stressed, sugar?"

"I think I'm missing my suppressants a bit," I admitted. They dulled my own scent, but also my sense of smell in general. It wasn't so bad when I was just around pack I'd grown used to, but there were a lot of alphas in this neighborhood, and I wasn't accustomed to being crowded by so many strangers' pheromones.

Eve and Garrett glanced at each other over my head, Garrett nodding in unspoken agreement.

"We could get you some," Eve said.

"I'm worried about the prolonged use effects, but for stuff like this? If it'll help, then why not?" Garrett said.

"Seriously?" I asked. The suppressants would dull my perfume, which would likely irritate Eve and presumably Garrett too. Alphas wanted their omega's scent flowing, marked as a sign of their success, and they always wanted their own scents clear on their omegas so there was no confusion of claim.

Eve kissed her mark again, a small reminder that there would be little confusion of her claim on me unless I felt like wearing five scarves in summer. "If you want them, then yes."

We reached where Rory was camped out in a circle of lawn chairs with a collection of equally enormous and tatted-up alphas, and Eve leaned into my ear. "Want to watch me make him squirm?"

I laughed. I didn't think it would take much. Rory had been glaring at Eve's tiny jean shorts with their cuffs rolled up almost to her ass as we were leaving the pack house.

Eve slipped away from me and up behind Rory, stroking her hands down his chest and making him jolt. "Hey, lover," she purred in his ear, a few of the other alphas smirking knowingly at one another. "Miss me?"

Rory yanked on one of Eve's arms, and she flounced into his lap, looping her arms around his shoulders. "Always, *baby*," he growled, and then he slapped one massive hand against the back of her thigh, making Eve bounce on top of him. Her teeth flashed in a brief snarl before she forced herself to relax and cuddle closer.

"It's some weird kind of foreplay," Garrett muttered with a shake of his head and a grin in my direction.

"Nah," Jamie whispered. "It makes sense for them. They'll be antagonizing each other every inch of the way."

"What about you?" I asked him, since Eve was distracted learning more new names and taunting Rory with a hand stroking over his chest.

Jamie smiled at me, easy and as unbothered as ever. "I like a smoother ride, personally. Want to be sure everyone's having a good time."

I'd only seen glimpses of him and Eve together so far, and that obtuse answer made me more curious than ever. I had a hard time imagining Eve on a 'smooth ride' with an alpha, but she did seem unusually comfortable around Jamie recently.

"Hey, pretty boy," Eve called to Garrett, to further amusement of the other alphas. "Grab me a lemonade?"

Garrett rolled his eyes but nodded and glanced at me. "Want anything?"

I opened my mouth to refuse and then realized I didn't have to. There were no strings attached to favors from Garrett, or any of the others for that matter.

"Beer and some of that buffalo chicken dip," I answered.

"You got it." And then he leaned in and kissed me, natural and brief.

All I could think of was how incredibly unfair it was that he hadn't knotted and bonded me yet.

"Hey guys, new neighbors are here." Oscar—just another huge alpha in the whole mess of them, and Eve's apparent new best friend—appeared in our circle with a couple.

The man and woman at Oscar's side were a bit older than most of the families at the barbecue, in their early fifties at least, with the faint and almost undetectable scents of betas. The man was tall and lean, with freckled skin and thinning pale red hair. He waved genially at the alphas, shoulders just a touch too tight to really be comfortable. The woman at his side was bottle-tanned, with carefully dyed blonde hair and bright blue eyes. She was small and curvy, in a pretty pink sundress, and she stepped shyly back as the focus landed on her.

"Marc and Hannah Graves," Oscar introduced. "Just in that ranch style around the corner. Not too far from you guys," he added, nodding at me, Jamie, Rory, and Eve. "Eve and Alex are new to the neighborhood too."

"Glad to not be the only one," Hannah said, stepping forward with her husband to shake hands.

It wasn't until she reached me that I caught the first real whiff of synthetic scent, flat and just a tiny bit metallic.

Suppressants. Hannah wasn't a beta, she was an omega on suppressants. Her husband, Marc, smelled just a bit floral, barely there, but I knew the tang of suppressants almost better than my own natural perfume. She was like BetaThinkTwice from my server.

Hell, she could've been the woman on the other end of the chat group for all I knew, although I doubted the deception was *that* uncommon.

I felt a strange moment of kinship with her, whoever she was. It hadn't been such a long time since I was trying to escape alphas' notice, and even now, with a pack, I still felt nervous here at this party surrounded by them. She had to be holding her breath until her lungs burned in a crowd like this.

"It's nice to meet you," I offered. Simple and benign, even as I burned with curiosity.

She shook my hand briefly, in that careful way of touching fingers only to avoid scent marks, her eyes sharp on the bite marks decorating my neck.

"Nice to meet you too, Alex."

We parted, but I watched her move through the party for a little while longer. Oscar said they weren't far from our place. Maybe I could find a way to speak to her. My alphas had to let me out of the house eventually, right?

THIRTY

Eve

Adam's stomach growled against me as I finished rinsing the conditioner out of his hair. We were wrapped around one another in the shower, Adam weak-legged and leaning into me after our time together in the nest. I hadn't invited Garrett to join us after the barbecue, a little too irritated by all the alpha scents in the air, but I might check to see if he'd join us for sleeping. Adam's delight was so adorably obvious when I did.

"You get back into bed, and I'll go get us some water and snacks," I offered, turning the water off and holding Adam a moment longer.

"You don't have to," Adam said, nuzzling into my shoulder. "It's late. We can just sleep."

His stomach growled again, and I pinched a lock of hair between my fingers and tugged it lightly. "No. I'm practicing, you see. Omegas who behave themselves at big parties get fucked cross-eyed. And hungry omegas get fed. I'm learning the rules."

Adam laughed at that and pulled away. "My eyes did *not* cross."

I delivered my best impression of his face after a handful of labored orgasms, and he huffed and climbed out of the large tub, shuffling toward the towels.

"Jerk," he muttered, but he was all bubbles and sugar in the bond.

I dried off and grabbed a shirt I'd essentially stolen from Jamie, ruffling Adam's wet hair on my way out.

I heard the voices on my way downstairs, Rory's low growling rumble and an unfamiliar tenor tone. I skipped the two stairs that creaked and moved silently through the living room, glad I'd just washed and was more or less invisible.

"I've been debating in my head whether or not we should've told the neighborhood," Rory muttered.

"I say protect your people first," the other man answered. "I just wanted to know if I was imagining things. When I gave you her name—"

"Trust me, this was the last thing on my mind when I heard about Eve."

I moved through the dining room and into the kitchen, stopping still in the doorway and squinting at the man. He was tall and lean, a bit older than me and Rory, with light blonde hair streaked with gray, grown out long enough to tuck behind his ears.

"My ears were burning," I said flatly.

Rory sighed. "Eve, this is Nate. He and I were in the same unit with Oscar for a while. He recommended your services to me when Wes was having issues."

Nate nodded briefly at me, studying me head to toe and remaining casually propped against the counter by the backdoor.

"You recognized me?" I asked him sharply. I certainly hadn't recognized him, and I didn't like the idea that there was so much information about me floating around.

He shook his head and then paused. "Well, I recognized the energy of someone pretending to have fun at a party while constantly assessing their surroundings. Not really unusual with this neighborhood, but then your name rang a bell."

"Couldn't have come up with something new, huh?" Rory asked me.

Nate shrugged before I could snarl back. "I'm not here to ask a lot of questions, honestly. Just wanted to be sure and…know whether I needed to have my guard up."

"Not from us," Rory said, glancing at me. "But it's not a bad idea at the moment."

Nate remained watching me, and I let out a sigh. "I'm not looking for a job in the neighborhood, I'm just… protecting my omega," I said, raising my hands at my side, nearly tripping over my own tongue when I nearly said 'pack' instead of 'omega.'

"Do you think the neighborhood should be warned?" Rory asked Nate.

"The neighborhood? Or some of the old crew who are a little bored and with too much time on our hands?" Nate asked, wearing a smirk. "Forewarned is fore-armed. Might as well let people know Alex is at risk."

Rory and I glanced at one another at the same moment, a flicker of gratitude running through me. He hadn't offered this stranger everything then. Maybe even nothing, aside from what Nate had sorted out for himself.

"Keep your ear out for us?" Rory asked.

Nate nodded, arms crossing over his chest, finally pushing off the counter and turning for the door. "Of course. Give me a heads-up if it's about to get hairy."

"Deal."

Rory and I were silent, watching one another, as Nate left out the back without another word.

"Is he going to be an issue?" I asked Rory.

"What are you going to do about it if I said yes?" Rory snapped. We stood glaring and simmering the room with smoke and spice for a moment before he huffed out a breath. His hands unclenched from the table and waved between us in the air, trying to brush away our mutual anger. "Wait, wait. No, Nate's good. He's got no motive to sell us out, and he's right. A lot of us in this neighborhood go way back with a lot of colorful history between us. You're not the only one with a contracting background around here."

I chewed over that answer and then nodded and headed for the cupboards, grabbing two glasses for water and searching for snacks. "I would've left with Adam," I said.

Maybe I would've killed Nate first. But I did want Rory and the others to trust me. I wanted to be trustworthy. That probably included not killing their friends.

The chair at the breakfast table squeaked against the floor as Rory rose, his shadow crawling up the cabinet in front of me. I held myself still, my arms raised to rifle through the snacks, and my eyebrows lifted as Rory's hand stroked up the back of my thigh and cupped up around my ass.

"You would've left with all of us," Rory growled, fingers digging in just slightly.

I smirked and pulled out a box of chewy granola bars with dark chocolate chunks. "I suppose you could've caught up. You're not as dumb as you look."

I turned and Rory only stepped closer, fitting me between his larger frame and the counter. "You and I can play a lot of games, but not this one," he said, almost whispered.

He was tense, bracing for my attack. I didn't know if it

was sleeping in the same room with Garrett or trusting Jamie at the garage, but I held my breath and glared up at Rory without having to fight the urge to toss him away from me. When I didn't move, Rory moved in another inch, our hips kissing and his hand sliding between my thighs and up to touch my sex. His fingertips burned against me, and I reached out, grabbing onto a handful of his T-shirt and yanking down.

Rory sank to his knees in front of me at the unspoken order, and I caught a deep breath at last, no longer pinned in.

I'd just satisfied myself with Adam, but the sight of Rory on his knees, face upturned to mine and still scowling, was somewhat tempting. I didn't know if I wanted to fuck him or just understand the full scope of what I could make him do.

"If you want to leave, leave. But if you need to run for your own or Adam's safety, we are coming with you," Rory said.

My lips twitched at how irritated he managed to make the vow sound, as if I'd been twisting his arm to force the words out.

I lifted my heel from the floor, pressing my knee to his chest and then a little higher, propping it on his shoulder and exposing myself to his view. A view he didn't indulge in, his eyes still fastened on mine. He was waiting for permission.

"You get one lick," I said, my pulse pounding in warning, the quiet of the room somehow rushing loudly in my ears.

Rory's hands moved to my hips, pushing up the tails of Jamie's shirt, his gaze finally falling to my core, studying every inch of me.

The clock above the sink ticked every passing second

like a drumbeat; the refrigerator hum turned into a roar. There was only one light on above the stove, leaving us in shadows. Would Adam come down, wondering if I'd vanished? No, he was asleep.

It was just Rory and me, the tug of war between us pulled taut but at a quiet standstill.

I nearly shoved him back as he leaned in, his hands drawing my hips forward to meet his mouth, my body arching.

He made one lick count for many, tongue digging all the way to the crease of my ass, teasing my opening, swirling around every fold, dragging slowly up to my clit. A growl thrummed against me as he paused and rubbed his tongue over my clit in a massage before flicking up and away.

I swallowed my own response, something between a snarl and a whimper, and his eyes raised to mine again.

"Another," he rasped, but it was too much like a demand rather than a plea. Still, he didn't move, didn't try to take it for himself without waiting for me to agree.

"No," I said, sliding my knee off his shoulder, pushing his hands off my hips. I turned back to the counter to grab the water and granola bars, and Rory's erection brushed against my calf, encased in loose cotton sweatpants.

"Go upstairs and don't wash your mouth until you've made yourself come," I said.

Rory grunted as I stepped away, and I took one glance back on my way to the doorway. He was kneeling, back straight and head tipped up, chest heaving and erection tenting the crotch of his sweats. Massive, powerful, and conquered.

I smiled and hurried back upstairs to Adam.

I WOKE up to their whispers and the slight rustle of sheets at my back. Adam's perfume was heavy in the air, powdered sugar whipped into a cloud. Garrett's scent was rising too, juicy and dripping over the edges of the nest.

"She's sleeping," Garrett gasped out.

There was a slurp of sound and then a deep draw of breath from Adam. "She is team Garrett-fucking-Adam just as much as I am."

I grinned at the wall, my eyes still shut, proud of my mouthy little omega. Adam must've helped himself to Garrett again, because there was another wet noise and a strangled groan from Garrett.

I rolled over and rested my cheek on my hands, eyes just open enough to be able to see Adam licking and kissing at Garrett's bare chest. Garrett's eyes were wide on mine, his brow furrowed and his fingers tangled in Adam's hair. I smiled at him and his whole body seemed to unwind, back rising to press himself to Adam's mouth, shoulders sagging into the mattress, throat arching under my gaze.

"Are you really going to let our omega suck you off like you're breakfast?" I asked, keeping my voice soft, not wanting to interrupt them. I liked the view, Adam's back bowed over Garrett, Garrett's shining mane spread out over pillows, just touched by the morning light trickling in from the high window.

"Don't interrupt my plans, alpha," Adam snapped, making both Garrett and me smile.

"She's right," Garrett sighed, twisting his fingers in Adam's hair to make my omega whine and pause.

I sat up with a glance from Garrett, and he rolled Adam into the pit of the nest. Adam was naked, but Garrett was in a pair of thin boxers. He had a darker tan up his arms to his biceps and a smattering of freckles over the expanse of his back, a few winking at me from just above his ass.

Adam was hard and he looked smaller beneath Garrett, still strong and handsome, but prettier too, more like the omega he tried to hide.

"If I'm getting teased without a lock or a knot, I want a refund," Adam said, almost pouting up at us.

"You had your lock last night," I said quickly, not quite ready to play out that scenario of Garrett fucking Adam into me. It would be too much pressure, my body too pinned down.

Garrett leaned down over Adam, careful to throw his hair over his other shoulder so I could watch him kiss Adam, their tongues hungry against one another. Garrett reached between them, tweaking Adam's nipples and then wrapping one large hand around Adam's cock. Tiny, petty jealousy struck me at how much more Garrett was able to hold, but there was appreciation too.

Adam was wild in the bond, almost as desperate for sex as he had been during the heat.

Because he'd chosen Garrett for an alpha but hadn't gotten the chance to enjoy him yet.

"He needs you," I said.

Garrett pulled away suddenly, mouth open and eyes wide on mine, and Adam stroked up Garrett's chest and over his shoulders.

"I really fuckin' do, Gare."

Garrett glanced between us for a moment and then grinned, bending once more to press a smacking kiss to Adam's lips before turning to me with that bright puppyish excitement of his.

"Bottom drawer on my left side table. Lube and a big box. Would you grab both?"

I rose and both men stared eagerly up at me. "Don't do anything too fun without me."

Garrett grinned, and Adam's eyes narrowed, lips smirking slightly. He would try and get the other alpha in trouble, and I found his urgent playfulness infectious.

I kept the bond open between Adam and I as I left the nest for Garrett's room. It was early, not even 7 a.m., and Jamie's door was still closed. I snuck into Garrett's room, pausing for a moment and realizing the heavy layers of scent were already so blended with my omega's that it didn't bother me.

Adam lit up with a sudden burst of arousal so strong, I had to pause and take a breath. I hurried forward and drew open the bottom drawer of Garrett's side table, relieved to find it tidy and clean inside. There was a smaller box cast aside on Garrett's bed, a familiar bulb-and-stem-shaped hollow in the faux velvet. Was he using the plug on Adam now?

I growled to myself, grabbing the lube and box, and then headed back to the nest.

Garrett had cast aside his boxers while I was gone, and he and Adam were fully naked, arms tangled around one another, mouths connected with starving cries, cocks rubbing together between them. Garrett rolled to the side and wrapped one leg around Adam's hips. I paused to appreciate the black round plastic peeking out between Garrett's asscheeks.

The plug wasn't for Adam then.

I glanced at the box with excited suspicion, and then moved down into the nest.

Garrett reared up at my arrival, leaving a gasping Adam beneath him, both their stomachs marked with sticky pre-cum.

"We'll start like this first," Garrett murmured, pressing two fingers into Adam's mouth to stifle Adam's whine.

Adam sucked eagerly, eyes tracking my progress to join them.

"You want him on his stomach or his back?" Garrett asked me.

It should've been up to them, but Adam's delight was warm in the bond, echoing Garrett's interest in my answer.

"His back. I want to watch his face," I said, passing Garrett the lube.

"Have you looked inside yet?" Garrett asked me, nodding at the box in my other hand. I shook my head, and he blushed. "You should. That part's for you."

I would've looked then, but Garrett withdrew his fingers from Adam's mouth at that moment, stretching above him again, balanced on one hand. He lowered himself for another deep kiss, and this time I reached out, brushing his hair to one side and then stroking down his back slowly. It'd been a while since I had multiple sex partners at the same time, and even longer since I was in the mood to watch them interact, and I'd forgotten how much there was to see.

Garrett's hand slid under Adam's thigh, just circling his hole as Garrett swallowed Adam's hiccups of sounds. My own touch continued down Garrett's back, narrowing to two fingertips running down the seam of his ass, right to the black round of plastic. I pressed into the plastic, and Garrett's head lifted from the kiss with a loud moan, his finger at Adam's ass forcing its way inside. Adam gasped and yelped, and I saw the catch of the digit at his entrance.

"More lube," Garrett and I said at the same moment, sparing a quick smile before I helped him drip the fluid onto his finger. I sat back to let Garrett focus. This time, his index finger pumped smoothly in and out of a squirming Adam.

I turned to the box at last, curious about what Garrett would have hidden away for me. The first thing I found were leather straps, and I frowned. Restraint wasn't really one of my interests. Certainly not subjecting myself to it. But as soon as I lifted the straps away and saw what was underneath, I realized what I was looking at.

"Ungh, fuck yes, another," Adam gasped out.

I glanced over and found Adam fucking himself onto two of Garrett's fingers. Garrett was watching me, and I reached into the box, pulling out the modest but delightful, intricately-textured blue dildo. It was just a bit flexible and thicker than the outline of the plug now resting in Garrett's ass. He grinned at me, and Adam gaped at the synthetic cock in my hand.

"You want this in your ass?" I asked Garrett, a rich purr rising up my throat.

He swallowed the sound and shrugged lightly. "I mean…wouldn't be the first time. But no one's ever, you know, been wearing it before."

"Goddamn," Adam laughed, still bracing his feet to the floor, idly riding Garrett's fingers. "Shit, you are so, so—Fuck!" He yelped as a third finger squirmed inside of him. Garrett's cock was comfortably large, but as much stretching as he could offer Adam would make the knot easier to take. "So fucking perfect for us," Adam whined.

My breath caught in my chest. Not because I was surprised, but because my head had been traveling the same line of thought. Garrett was such a submissive alpha. I saw what he could offer Adam—spoiling and care and emotional openness—but he offered me control just as readily. He didn't want me riding his cock, proving he could tame me. Quite the opposite.

"Give me the lube, pretty boy," I purred. "You don't get an inch until you've got your knot in our omega."

Garrett gasped at that, sitting up and passing me the lube. He reached out to squeeze Adam's neglected cock, and Adam howled and bucked into Garrett's fist, fucking into the grip until he came with a high-pitched cry. I poured fluid into my palm and reached between them, Garrett's rich and sweet pheromone surrounding me, his breath brushing against my cheek as I took his own cock in my slippery hand. He joined me with his hand covered in Adam's release, and together we coated his length in the mess, taking special care over the start of the knot's swell.

I leaned in and kissed Garrett's stubbly cheek and then whispered in his ear, "Be good to him and I'll make you come so hard you can't form full sentences."

Garrett purred and nuzzled his cheek to mine tentatively before drawing back and searching my face. "Kiss?" he asked.

I hesitated, but it seemed like an awfully small request from a man who'd just asked me to fuck his ass with a pretty blue dildo.

My mouth slid over his, pleased by the taste of Adam on his lips, chasing for more. I dug my fingers into the hair at the nape of his neck and tugged roughly, holding him in place as I stroked my tongue against his. I pulled away slowly and then twisted and bent to give Adam the same treatment. Adam arched into the kiss, one hand reaching up to cup my cheek and beg for more, when suddenly he pulled away with a shout.

I sat back and grinned at the tip of Garrett's cock disappearing between Adam's asscheeks.

"Does it hurt?" I asked Adam.

"It's fuckin' fire."

"Relax, babe," Garrett said, holding still and giving a

cursory pump of his slippery fist around Adam's cock. "You're doing so good. Such a perfect treat on my—Fuck, that's it!"

It did the trick, Adam immediately beginning to bounce between Garrett's hand and his length. Garrett reached under Adam's back, scooting him closer and letting gravity and Adam's own excitement do the work. Adam's cheeks were flushed, his hands gripping pillows above his head, his cock weeping arousal down into Garrett's grip.

"We should get him a toy lock," Garrett murmured to me.

I raised an eyebrow. "He has a real one. I plan on treating him to it once I'm done with you."

Garrett flushed and groaned at that, or at Adam's whining and fitting himself down another two inches of Garrett's cock. "Fair enough," Garrett rasped, starting to slowly rock in and out of Adam. "Jesus, Adam, baby, you feel fucking incredible. So fucking tight."

I remembered what Jamie had said it felt like, like not being allowed to finish, and wondered if that was something Garrett might like. I even wondered what it would do to his knot. Would it hurt too much to enjoy, or would it provide a new and powerful high?

"Fuck," Adam gasped at the first nudge of Garrett's knot. "No, no, can't!"

Garrett retreated immediately, and I leaned forward, batting at his hand around Adam's cock. "Move, he can take it."

"But—"

I pulled Garrett's hand off of Adam's cock and leaned forward to suck on the tip. Adam gasped and bucked into my lips, nudging against my tongue and then deeper. I could take him to the base if I wanted, but instead I focused on the pressure of suction.

"Eve, I need—" Garrett hissed.

I swatted his chest, and he let out a chuckle. He could wait. Adam wanted this knot, I knew as much, he just needed to be coaxed. Adam was whining and chasing my mouth, sighing as I rested my hand on his hip, pushing him down and following, twirling my tongue around the head of him before swallowing deeply. He groaned and then Garrett joined him.

I pulled back to the tip of Adam, licking at the treat of fluid I found there, before repeating myself, swallowing Adam down at the same time as I pushed him against Garrett's cock.

I sat up at the perfect time, the knot lodging inside and Adam coming with a sudden bellowing shout, painting Garrett's chest in his release. Their eyes locked together, and I slid away to leave them to it as I stripped and went about fastening myself into the strap-on. Garrett rocked slowly, petting at Adam's chest, purring heavily.

"You're perfect," Garrett moaned. "God, do you feel good, baby?"

"Yes, yes, yes! Hnnnng, I'ma come again, holy fuck!"

I grinned and peeked over Garrett's shoulder to see Adam, dewy with sweat and trembling with the grind of Garrett's knot in his ass. I slipped my finger into the ring of the plug in Garrett's ass, grabbing the lube and applying it as I worked the plug in and out, reopening him for my use. Garrett hissed, eyes slamming shut and head tossing back.

"Fuck, I might—"

"It won't stop me," I warned him. "You asked to get fucked, and it's happening either way."

Garrett held his breath, grabbing onto Adam's hips to keep him from moving, and I pulled the plug out. Probably better to move quickly than make good on the threat. It would be more fun to overstimulate Garrett before he'd already gotten off.

I glanced down to admire the view of a cock jutting forward from my hips as I coated the length in lube, the bright blue comical but exciting too. I liked my body, liked being a woman, but it was fun to have a dick every now and again, the knowledge that the person I was about to use it on was gladly surrendering themself to my strength. Trusting me with the strenuous pleasure of a good fuck up the ass.

"Lean forward," I said to Garrett.

It took a little maneuvering, and Adam whined and started to rock again as the head of his cock bumped into Garrett's chest. Garrett had to lift Adam's hips even higher to give me room to fit myself behind him, but Adam was too far gone to care, using the new leverage to grind himself on Garrett's knot. I petted down Adam's dangling leg with one hand as I lined myself up at Garrett's ass.

The drive in was smooth—Garrett hadn't been lying about being familiar with this cock—and his gasp was full of relief.

"Fast?" I asked.

"And hard, I can never get it rough the way I want," Garrett gasped out.

I took a moment, admiring the wedge of the blue cock head stretching the ring of muscle, the full haunches of Garrett's muscular ass, the freckles smattering up his ribs to those broad shoulders. Beautiful. His and Adam's scents blended seamlessly to the point where I could almost imagine Garrett was another omega.

Mine.

Pretty and big and desperate for me to make him shatter.

My first stroke was slow, stretching him with a few steady and rocking thrusts until my hips kissed his ass. After that, I followed his pleading, drawing out in an even fluid motion before driving in with a snap. The pound of my hips meeting his ass rubbed the base of the dildo against my clit, dull but delicious enough to crave repeating the act over and over again.

"Fuck!" Garrett shouted, and Adam moaned loudly beneath him. "Again, again. Fuck, yes."

I hadn't even noticed my own arousal, but it was slippery between my thighs as I started slamming into Garrett, wrapping my hands around his shoulders to brace him to take me. Adam and Garrett cried out together, twisting and contorting themselves to kiss sloppily, their teeth audibly bumping under the force of my fucking.

"Oh my goooood," Garrett cried out, his head dropping to Adam's shoulder, ass raised and just barely bouncing with every strike of my hips.

There wasn't enough friction against my sex, but something about the steady *thump thump thump* of our bodies together made me warm and breathless, my cunt clenching and eager for Adam's perfect cock.

Adam was arching under Garrett, baring his throat, and while Garrett was gently licking the spot, he was more focused on rocking between Adam and me. Stupid noble bastard wouldn't bite Adam the first time he got his knot in. Of course not. He'd make them talk first, decide the same thing all over again.

Adam was ours. Garrett was…

"Please," Adam whined, stretching his throat for Garrett's bite.

"Fuck, I—Shit, yes," Garrett gasped.

I was a shit person. A terrible example of an alpha. But

I was *Adam's* alpha, and I knew what he wanted, and how I could offer it to him.

Garrett pushed up on shaking arms, crying out. "Fuck, I'm coming! Come on, baby."

And when Garrett's hand wrapped around Adam's cock, squeezing roughly, I reached up and grabbed on to the tangle of his hair, drawing him back into a pretty and taut arch.

Adam gasped, painting his own stomach, and Garrett groaned, bucking roughly.

And I tugged again on Garrett's hair, drawing Garrett's throat to my mouth.

"Eve, wait!" Adam gasped, eyes growing wide.

But it was too late. I was already sinking my teeth in.

Garrett was *mine*.

THIRTY-ONE

Garrett

Arms banded around my chest as I thrashed and shouted, scorching, blinding pain in my throat.

A whine below me set me freezing, remembering that I still had Adam trapped on my knot. And fuck. That dildo was still lodged in my ass.

Eve had fucking bit me.

Of course she had, I thought. And what was worse, there was a tiny little piece of me that was delighted. Maybe more than tiny. A respectably sized nugget of relief and pride that she'd chosen me, claimed me.

I settled, shifting Adam on my lap so my knot rested more comfortably inside him, and then reaching for his hand, squeezing my fingers around his. Eve's bite drew out slowly, and there was an answering tug at the base of my cock that made eyes fall shut and my dick stiffen. When her tongue swiped over the mark, my knot throbbed and my purr thrummed.

"What the fuck?" I growled out, trying to keep a balance between my anger and the part of me wanting to reassure Adam.

Eve just licked my bite again, and I shuddered.

"Eve, you can't just—" Adam started.

But then something shifted, *opened*, inside of me, and suddenly there was a direct line between—

Not Eve. No, this giddy, nervous sweetness wasn't the alpha. It was Adam. Eve had created a bond between me and Adam. He was as secretly, anxiously pleased as I was, and a little terrified. I put away my own irritation immediately and reached to him. The empty space between us filled up like a wave rushing in, bright and needy and sweet.

"You wanted my commitment and time to develop things with Adam," Eve said, and I realized that she was missing in this new connection between Adam and I.

"Don't lie, that's not why you did it," Adam said to her.

I was too busy studying the bond. Adam was like a breeze, just constantly slipping by and caressing me. Eve drew back, dildo slipping out, and I groaned, suddenly hollow, but it gave me room to settle down. I sat back and wrapped my arms around Adam, drawing him up on top of my lap so we could kiss. He hummed into my lips, his own arms twining around my shoulders, our bodies hunched oddly. Next time I knotted him, I'd do it from behind so we could cuddle better afterwards.

There was a shift in the bond, an interruption to the back and forth between Adam and I, almost a shy spying sensation. Eve was cool, reserved, still bound up and guarded, but even Adam pulled away from the kiss, eyes wide and searching for her. She was unstrapping herself, her head down and her lips red with my blood.

"Eve?" Adam called, as if she weren't aware that she'd joined us in the bond and he was afraid to alert her.

She tossed the harness aside and looked up at me at last. "I want to keep you. For Adam…and for me."

It wasn't an apology for biting me without asking. It wasn't even an attempt at an excuse. As a justification, it was actually pretty shit. But it made my heart clench in my chest, a proud glow of warmth rushing through me. And I didn't even care that she could feel the answer in the bond. She moved to us, pausing briefly at my side to kiss me, not nearly as long as I would've liked, before curling up at Adam's back, our arms folding him between us.

"Will you keep the bond open for a while?" Adam asked, tilting his head back and nudging his cheek to hers. His throat was bared, and I wondered if it was a good time or a terrible time to mention how close I'd been to biting him.

Eve nodded. "As much as I'm able. Sometimes I need the space to…to handle my own head," she admitted through gritted teeth. "But yes, I will try and keep it open for you both."

"I won't just spin my wheels waiting to bond you," I said to Adam. "But this won't rush us either," I warned Eve.

She shrugged, a hint of a smug smirk on her lips proving that it was more or less moot now. Adam and I were bound, just through her. It was only a matter of time, anyway.

I wanted to be angry, to give her another lecture, but there was a playfulness now from her where a minute ago, there'd only been her watching us interact, and I wanted to hold onto the moment. Eve kissed one of Adam's marks and then grinned at me, eyes glancing to my throat.

"I need to nurse that."

Adam laughed. "God, we're all gonna end up fucking again, aren't we?"

"Wha—?" I started, but then Eve moved, her mouth latching hungrily onto the wound, and my flagging knot grew swollen and tight all over again, my hips bucking up into Adam and making him whine.

"It's the best worst trick she pulls," Adam said, breath hitching, body bouncing on my lap eagerly. "Mine next, Eve. Please."

I gasped as Eve pulled away with another lick, and then she was nibbling on one of her many marks on Adam and he moaned, clenching around my knot.

Oh. We *were* all going to end up fucking again.

I grinned and started to thrust.

———

I DIDN'T MEAN to stare at Adam while he slept, it was just that I woke up before him and he was…all soft against my side, lips barely parted and eyes twitching under his lids. The angles of his face were so sharp and clear, and it was rare to see all the muscles of his expression perfectly relaxed. I was just observing the brief furrow of his brow, the lock of his jaw, the flick of his tongue, and then suddenly green eyes were blinking drowsily back at me.

I scrambled for something to say as his gaze focused, and only the stupidest result came out. "How's your ass?"

Adam snorted and curled in closer, my arms wrapping around him automatically as he laughed against my shoulder. "S'okay. How's yours?"

"Not bad," I said, nodding, my own chuckles rising in my chest.

"Where's Eve?"

"Down in the gym with Jamie, I think."

Adam's forearms pushed against my chest so he could prop himself up, frowning briefly at my throat. "And how's the bite?"

I stretched my throat, a twinge and ache answering, but

a little amused thread of sympathy reaching me from Adam too. Sympathy and worry.

"She did a good job of nursing it," I said.

"Well, she's had plenty of practice," Adam said, a little too sharply.

I rubbed my hands up and down his bare back, but he remained stiff, eyes on the bite, and I realized for the first time that Adam might be upset for his own sake and not just mine.

"Does it bother you that your alpha bit someone else?" I asked gently.

Adam startled and blinked, but his gaze drifted over my head to stare at the wall, fingertips drumming over my collarbone.

"She did it for you," I said slowly. "I mean, I hope she did it for herself too. But she wanted you to—"

Adam nodded and cut me off. "I know, I know." A slow smile spread over his lips. "And it's…it's really nice to not be alone in this bond for once."

I stretched up, and Adam met me halfway for a long kiss. Eve was keeping her distance, but she was here, watching us in the bond, a soft stroke of approval shared with me for soothing Adam. I'd thought she was being unnecessarily cold, but now I understood a little better. She was keeping parts of herself from Adam, yes, but only because she had to keep them from herself too. There was a clean quality to this connection with her that made it easy to forget I'd just been bonded by another alpha. She was present, but not intrusive.

I used the path she'd created for us to send Adam a burst of affection and stability. He hummed and then threw a leg over my hip, collapsing down onto my chest and burrowing his face into my throat, right over the bite.

He huffed. "Smells like her here," he murmured.

A tentative tongue flicked over the mark, and I hissed, arching for more, making Adam chuckle.

"It's not as good as when it's her, right?" Adam asked, before licking the mark again.

"It's…it's pretty fuckin' good," I groaned.

It might not have been a direct line down to my cock like it was with Eve, but it was still *Adam's* mouth on me, on a bite, almost as if he'd been the one to claim me rather than the other way around.

"You know I want you, right?" I asked, my breaths coming in heavy and fast, my hips starting to roll against Adam's thigh over my lap.

"Mhm."

"As my omega."

Bright waves of joy from Adam at that, approval from Eve again too. "Mhm."

"Will you—ungh." I grunted as Adam climbed on top of me, lying almost flat and simply rocking our cocks together. It was playful and simple and somehow filthy too, just based on the basic urge to scratch the best itch and get off. "Will you tell me when you're ready?"

Adam's mouth popped off Eve's bite, and he licked his lips, pushing up on his palms to stare down at me. The green in his gaze was vivid, his dark hair hanging into his eyes. I reached between us, stroking his chest and then flicking his nipples. We'd been naked in bed all day and it seemed kind of ridiculous to still be wanting more, but there was no denying the direction we were headed, rubbing our whole bodies together.

"What if I was ready now?" Adam asked, but there was just the faintest flicker of doubt in the bond.

I arched an eyebrow and smoothed my hands around his ribs, down to his ass, pressing him closer and reveling in his groan as I forced him into the rhythm of my choosing.

"Say so."

Adam swallowed, his cheeks flushed, mouth working without a sound coming out.

"Or don't, because we're in no rush now, right?" I reminded him.

No rush but the one to come together, release all over ourselves into a complete mess. I'd take him to shower and clean up with me after.

"No rush," Adam agreed, sighing and then digging his toes into the mattress and rutting desperately on top of me.

———

"WHAT THE FUCK IS THAT?"

I winced, my shoulders temporarily rising to my ears at the bark in Rory's voice before I forced them down again. Eve was upstairs with Adam, and Jamie was at the sink, washing potatoes and staring at me over his shoulder. He didn't look surprised at the bite on my throat, and I wondered if Eve had already mentioned it to him.

"It's a bite," I said, keeping my voice even.

Rory gaped at the mark, lines digging into his forehead, then smoothing out, then digging in again. "She bit you?" There was no growl this time, just a genuine tip of his voice, pure confusion.

I nodded slowly.

"Were you fighting?" Rory asked, stepping closer, squinting at the mark as if he were trying to see if it was fake.

"We were fucking," I said, my eyes widening at Jamie for support. Not that he would likely know what to do.

"You fucked Eve?" I'd expected Rory to be mad, although I didn't know why. He'd been in support of her being pack in his own way.

"She…fucked me?"

"Is that a question?"

"Do you want a play-by-play?"

Rory glared at me, but there was color rising up his throat. Huh. Maybe he did want the play-by-play.

"Adam and I will bond, when we both feel the timing is right. In the meantime…this allows us to have a connection too," I said, intentionally leaving out the bit where not a word of this had been discussed *before* Eve set her teeth in me.

"You're letting the bacon burn," Jamie said gently.

Rory glared at him but turned back to the sizzling skillet. "You're not… You don't have questions about this?"

Jamie shrugged. "You good?" he asked me.

I nodded, and he did the same. Rory huffed at us.

"Does it hurt?" Rory asked.

"The biting does, but the bond is surprisingly chill. And the bite nursing is *very* rewarding," I answered.

Rory's hands were tight fists, but his scent in the air was warm and surprisingly smooth. "I meant the lock."

"Oh, I dunno," I said, shrugging.

"Yeah, but it's a good hurt," Jamie said, grinning at me as my jaw dropped.

Rory spun around, his red face whipping in both our directions, back and forth, and he looked about ready to explode.

Oh, I realized too late. *He's jealous.*

"We're out of beer," Rory snapped. "I'm making a run."

Jamie's hand covered his grin, eyes rolling slightly as Rory stomped for the backdoor, grabbing the car keys off the counter. The door slammed shut behind him, and I raised my eyebrows.

"Whoops."

Jamie waved, "Don't worry about it. I give them a week. Max, two. She checks out his ass every time he walks by. You really good with that bite?"

With Rory out of the house, it was less of a risk to fess up to how it happened, but the answer to the question was simple enough.

"I am, yeah. She's pack. She's working on the bond for Adam's sake. This feels like good progress. Like you and I said before, I wanted a bondmate, and when I met her and Adam…" I wanted two.

Jamie nodded and smiled, pulling a colander of freshly scrubbed potatoes out of the sink. "Help me with dinner. We've still got the chicken to put in the oven."

"Tell me about the lock?" I asked.

Jamie's lips flattened briefly, and he was quiet, going about wrapping up the potatoes to bake. Jamie had never really been much of a kiss-and-tell guy, and it occurred to me that pack or not, his time with Eve might be off-limits to me.

"Or not," I offered him.

He hummed and shrugged. "I like her. I don't know if what happened was a one-off. Hopefully not. I'm glad you guys have a bond."

It was a more intimate admission than any sexual details, and I let the subject drop, pulling the dressed chicken out of the fridge and getting it ready to go in the oven. Eve perked up in the bond, checking on me, and I found myself smiling as Adam joined her, more direct and warm. I had a bondmate.

She was prickly, seductive, manipulative, protective, aggressive, and observant. The best and worst of an alpha. Soon I would have Adam too.

Which meant the stakes were higher than ever to keep us all safe.

THIRTY-TWO

Rory

Eve, *you're healed and you're going around biting my pack, and I think it's time for us to have that fight because—* I growled and shook my head.

Eve, we have unfinished business.

No.

Time to see which alpha has the bigger bark.

I groaned and rolled my head on my neck, glaring at the stoplight in front of me.

Eve, I would really like it if you could give me brain damage with some serious headboard banging, snap my dick off with your lock, and then take a good chunk out of me with your bite.

I snorted and turned left into the neighborhood. *Yeah, that one is definitely the winner.*

It had taken me forty minutes of meticulous grocery store browsing to sort my head out after the discussion with Garrett and Jamie. I wasn't mad at Eve; I was jealous of my packmates. I'd grabbed one good lick of her the night before—enough to know I wouldn't be satisfied until I'd choked myself on the taste of her—and then she'd gone and fucked and bonded Garrett.

And locked Jamie.

I growled again and stifled the sound. Not angry. Jealous. Not angry. Jealous.

Jealous and horny.

My phone rang, and I reached for it blindly, turning onto our street.

"Hey, I'm almost back. Went a little crazy at the store, but I'm good."

"Rory? It's Nate."

I grimaced at my phone screen, wishing I'd checked the caller ID to start with. After last night, I wasn't sure if it could be good news to hear from him so soon.

"Look, we all know I'm kind of paranoid," Nate said without waiting for me to speak. "I've had some security set up for the neighborhood for a long time. Just listening in for my own sake. There's some chatter coming our way."

"Chatter?" I repeated.

"Pretty sure they mentioned your new alpha."

My teeth gritted in my jaw, and I pulled into our driveway, stopping before the garage. "Okay, what are you hearing?"

"Think we've got incoming. Tonight, coming from the south."

South of our suburbs was just farmland. "You're sure?"

"Ninety percent."

"Can you narrow it down for us?"

"Already working on it."

"Thanks. We'll cut it off before it reaches the neighborhood," I said.

"Can I make a recommendation?" Nate asked, but again, he didn't bother waiting. "You've got backup in here, friends. Use us. Better to give due warning anyway."

The automatic refusal was on my tongue, but Nate was

right—if we weren't successful at keeping trouble out of the neighborhood, it would be better for everyone to have the heads-up. Most of the families who lived around us could take care of themselves. And if anyone did want to lend a hand…well, it wouldn't hurt. We had Nate to thank for even knowing what was coming.

"You're right. Mind sending out a flare? I've got to let the pack know what's going on."

"Can do. Want volunteers headed your way?"

"Yeah, that's good. Thanks again, Nate."

"You got it."

I disconnected the call and let out a long breath, bracing the heels of my hands against the steering wheel and bleeding my tension out in a slow push. "Fuck," I snapped, my bark better released now while I was alone than inside with the pack.

We'd known this was a possibility. Eve had warned us from the start. If we could keep any of Omikron's goons getting into the neighborhood then that was a success, but the fact that they already knew where to look didn't bode well in the long run. Getting help from the locals was great for one night, but sooner or later it would become a strain on the other families, one I didn't want to take advantage of.

I shook myself and got out of the car, grabbing the absurd load of groceries I'd gathered and hauling them inside in one go.

"There you are—thought you were going for beer?" Garrett asked, laughing.

Eve and Adam were downstairs, and our modest kitchen was now crowded. With pack. These were my people, regardless of the unusual way we'd come together. My people at risk tonight.

"What is it?" Eve asked, eyes narrowed on my face.

"Nate picked up signals. He thinks we've got Omikron headed for us tonight, that we might be able to cut them off before they get into town," I said quickly. The plastic bags were digging into my fingers, and I glanced down at them and then back up to Adam. "Oh, I—uh, got you some stuff. Snacks."

I passed him a handful of bags as he stared blankly back at me.

"Ice cream and chocolate and stuff," I added, frowning. Adam and I wouldn't be bondmates, but I wanted to be friends, to be a good pack alpha to him.

All the more reason to make sure Omikron doesn't touch him again.

Garrett waved his hands, but then took more of the groceries out of my grip. "Wait, wait, Omikron is coming *here?* But we're going to—"

"Nate's giving folks warning. He thinks some of the others might be willing to help too," I said.

"Do we have weapons?" Eve asked me.

"Some, but we'll have to be smart with them," I answered.

She nodded. "Surprising them will be a good start. They won't pick just one access road. We'll have to spread out. Or I can be visible, try and make sure they pick a location."

My heart leapt into my throat, and my head shook. "No. You should—you should stay here. With Adam. We can deal with this."

"Rory, don't be ridiculous," Eve said with a flippant wave of her hand.

"You hired us for protection."

"I hired you to force you to be Adam's alphas so I could take off," Eve snapped, but she rested a hand lightly on

Adam's shoulder, soothing the remark. "And you insisted on dragging me back, and now we are pack, and this is all *my* doing anyways."

"If you're what they're aiming for, we don't just set you up as a target for them to shoot at!" I shouted.

"Your chances of success against anyone coming drop considerably without me in the picture!" Eve snarled back. "I'm not staying home like some—"

"Time out!"

I startled and blinked, turning my head to see Jamie leaning back against the counter, arms crossed over his chest and a deep frown on his face. He'd barked, and I wondered if I'd ever heard Jamie's full bark before. Either way, it got both Eve and I to shut up.

"I think Rory is right about not presenting you as a target. You are not bulletproof, and we don't have Kevlar," Jamie said to Eve, holding a hand up in my direction to keep me from interrupting. He turned to me next and continued, "And I think Eve is right that she needs to be on the ground with you. She's healed and she's fucking amazing in combat," Jamie said with a shrug.

I glared at him, but Eve spoke up first. "Would you stay with Adam for me?"

Jamie pushed off the counter. "You don't want me on the ground with you?"

Eve's smile was gentle, her head tipping and her arm wrapping around Adam's shoulder. "I do, but Adam is more important to me."

Adam's eyes bugged wide as Garrett and I glanced at one another in surprise, Garrett's smile slightly smug. Jamie just nodded back at Eve solemnly.

"I suppose no one's going to let me help—?" Adam started.

All four of us alphas answered "No," in near barks, and Adam jumped in place and then nodded.

"Garrett, it's up to you. Here with Adam or out with us?" I offered.

Garrett glanced between all of us, frowning and thinking. "You and Jamie are the best of us. Adam's safe here with him. But what if I run to Nate? Bet I can hack clearer signals than the one's he's getting."

Eve and I both nodded. "Smart, go ahead."

But it left just me and Eve. If Omikron sent a small group, we would be okay, but I didn't want the aftermath of Eve taking on another fifty mercenaries by herself.

She can't fuck me if she's bleeding, I thought.

"Don't look so scared, big guy. I won't let them hurt you," Eve purred.

Her teasing was welcome, but it did raise concerns. She and I would be constantly jockeying to push the other one out of harm's way.

My mouth opened, a terrible impulse to demand again that she stay here about to escape my lips, when the doorbell rang.

Without a second's hesitation, Eve grabbed a knife out of the block and headed for the door.

"Wait," I barked, but it was useless and I grabbed the wooden bat out of the closet on my way, chasing her to the door.

"I'm just checking."

"It's definitely going to be the—" The doorbell rang again, and Eve peered out the hole before swinging open the door to reveal, "Neighbors."

Oscar filled up most of the frame, but behind him I could see Dan and Mikey and Pete and… and all the guys from the old unit. Some of the others too, friends of friends, vets I'd gotten to know in our military retirement.

"Neighborhood watch," Oscar greeted cheerfully, his sweatshirt suspiciously lumpy with hidden weapons.

Eve brandished the knife in her fist with a bright grin. "Hey, boys. Who's staying for dinner?"

I grit my teeth and propped the bat against the wall. "Come on in. We'll talk."

"Let's make it quick, though. Nate says we're short on time," Oscar said.

I only led them as far as the living room where the pack was gathered together on the couch.

"I think the first thing we need to address is whether or not you guys want us to stay, or to run," Jamie said, moving to stand next to Eve. He took her hand in a supportive gesture, but I hid my smirk as he pulled the knife from her fingers.

"Stay," Mikey said immediately. "You leave now, we're down men with these fuckers showing up, and who knows what kind of message they'll try and leave for you."

I nodded my head slowly. Leaving now, if we managed to avoid Omikron on our way out, wouldn't stop them from reaching the neighborhood.

"There's safety in numbers," Oscar said to me. "We're here to support you, just like you have been with us in our pasts."

"They won't even reach the edge of the neighborhood," Eve said, uncommonly solemn as she met the gazes of the men standing before her.

She meant the words. She meant them even if she had to take on every Omikron hire herself.

Which she didn't, not now. Now she had us, her pack.

———

"YOU KNOW, I thought you and Eve had a funny energy about you," Oscar whispered. We were perched up in a tree together, long-range rifles in hand, keeping our eye on the road Garrett had pinned for one of Omikron's routes.

I grunted, and Oscar grinned at me, adding, "Assumed you were just banging a lot."

I bit down on my tongue to keep myself from telling the truth—I was miserably un-laid.

"I should've talked to you guys the second we brought A-Alex back," I said. I wasn't sure if it was worth keeping his name a secret anymore, but I didn't want to do anything without consulting with the others.

"I don't think any of us would blame you for your priorities," Oscar said with a shrug. "If I was gonna pick a time, it would've been when you dragged the contract killer back."

My lips flattened, and I lifted the scope of the gun up, double-checking the horizon of the road. Nothing.

"Not saying I object to her now. But it's usually the kinda thing we keep each other updated on."

I nodded. "I'm sorry," I said automatically.

All in all, everyone had been forgiving about the situation. Eve had Dan and Pete with her on the other likely route, and Mikey had stayed back with a few of the others to keep an eye on the neighborhood.

"Maybe, but you'd do it again," Oscar said softly, shrugging at my glance. "That's pack life. Anything for the packmates. The rest of the world second."

I'd always prided myself on putting 'the rest of the world' pretty high on my priority list, actually. That was part of what worked about Garrett and Jamie as my pack. We were all self-sufficient. Independent. Garrett and I frequently had to leave Jamie out of the loop in our work, but he didn't need us to do otherwise.

But Oscar was right, and it wasn't even about my attraction to Eve. Adam needed me as his alpha more than any job had ever needed me as security. Eve needed us as her pack—regardless of how she felt on the matter. She might not have *wanted* us, but she did need us.

The rest of the world second, I decided. I would be selfish on my pack's behalf from now on. And surprisingly, no regret came along with that.

"If it becomes an issue, we'll move on," I said to Oscar.

He huffed. "If it becomes an issue, I'll load the moving truck. Anything for my pack too, man. But tonight, that includes dealing with these fuckers. I've got no complaints."

The burner phone in my pocket vibrated, and I drew it out with a glance at Oscar.

"About two minutes out on your route," Garrett greeted. "I'm on my way north with Hans. Nate's taking over base."

"North?" I set the rifle back on my shoulder, ready to watch the road through the scope again.

"Yeah, looks like they've got just one car coming from there, bit of a backup sweeper."

"What've we got?"

"Two cars on your route, four on Eve's, but she's got the better vantages. You and Oscar need to be ready to jump and run if they spot you."

"We're ready," I said.

"Headlights," Oscar muttered.

"Good luck. Keep it quiet," I said to Garrett before hanging up the call. Hans was pretty tidy, from what I remembered of his reputation. Garrett would be with him more as support than anything else.

"How long you want to wait?" Oscar asked, voice low.

I settled into my seat, watching the approach of the

two SUVs on the road. "Till you're absolutely positive you're going to hit a tire."

Given the speed of their driving, the distance, the road, our angle... I ran through the mental math in my head.

"I'll get back left," Oscar whispered.

"Right front," I answered, focusing there and following, breathing slowly in and out. If we hit the tires at the same time, we could cause a collision from the cars following so closely behind.

"I'm ready."

"Ready on two. One. Two."

I squeezed the trigger, heard Oscar's slow breath out in my ear, and then a moment later, twin pops and the scream of metal on the road.

"I've got the gas tank on the second vehicle," Oscar said.

"Take it." There were decent odds the cars were armored, but I focused on the third visible tire as it limped over asphalt.

Exhale, squeeze. *Pop!* It was out.

The sun was almost set on the horizon, turning the black SUVs into ribbons of reflective color. I watched the backdoors, waiting for mercenaries to appear, giving part of my attention to Oscar's progress.

"Armored. Back left tire out."

"Three points out, no sign of life inside," I answered.

"Do you want to be on the ground?" Oscar asked me.

The truth was, no, I didn't want to be combating hand-to-hand, but it was probably our only option to finish the job.

"Cover me," I said to Oscar, setting the safety of my rifle with my thumb before jumping down from the branch of the tree we've been perched in.

As soon as I was on the ground, a car door slammed.

Omikron had its sights on me. I ducked and Oscar fired at the first sign of life from the SUVs. My position had the advantage of being backlit by the sunset, but the light would only last us a few more minutes. I crouched in the high wheat field, waited until a window rolled down, and then fired carefully into the gap, shattering a little corner of the glass.

Another man jumped out of the second SUV, gun pointed up at Oscar in the tree, and I took him out with a carefully aimed headshot before flattening myself on the ground against the rapid fire of a gun. My phone vibrated in my pocket again and I ignored it, my pulse heavy and loud in my ears, my eyes drawing back their focus to take in the whole scene.

If we gave Omikron's men time to get out of the SUVs on the side where they had cover, we'd be in an extended standstill. I pulled a handgun out of the holster on my side and took three deep breaths, waiting for the pause, watching the road, the cars, the sink of the sun. The sniper rifle wasn't ideal for closer action, but it wouldn't hurt either.

I rose suddenly, charging for the other side of the road, Oscar immediately covering me with a rain of gunfire that kept the agents inside the vehicles.

There were two men already out on the right side of the cars, and I shot quickly before flattening myself back into the high weeds, rolling carefully down into the calf-high water of the ditch. One of the car doors was thrown open, giving me a view inside of two agents hunched down in the backseat, turned to face away from one another. If I could get inside, Oscar and I would have safe cover.

I flinched as a bullet sped by me, too close for comfort, and then returned fire more accurately. We had maybe ten minutes before interruption, and that was just wishful thinking. My pulse struck hard in my throat, my jaw ticking.

"Could use some progress!" Oscar called, now taking cover behind the tree we'd been perched in.

I set aside the rifle and took my chances on the open SUV, jumping back out of the ditch and diving for the agent facing me. He met me halfway, teeth bared, both our hands reaching out to block our guns and sending our shots wild. His partner in the car turned to deal with me, and I used my body weight to throw the man in my grip into the path of a bullet aimed for me. I crouched and then caught my opponent by the ribs, firing back at the second—a spray of blood on the inside of the windows—before tossing the man on my shoulder back on the ground, barely making it into the car, with the doors shut before the car behind me was shooting back.

My phone vibrated in my pocket again, and I gritted my teeth. No one should be calling us, not now. Something was going wrong, possibly even back in the neighborhood. But I couldn't get back there if Oscar and I were dead. I climbed into the front seat, ignoring the thunder of bullets surrounding the car.

The key was still in the ignition, the E-brake yanked up. I shoved it down and put the car in reverse, slamming on the gas, ignoring the twist and scream of the ruined tires, the metal grinding against asphalt, the feel of the car colliding with the second SUV, with the mercs on the road. I yanked the wheel to the left, and threw the car forward in drive.

Thump, thump, thump.

Oscar ran out from behind the tree, and I double-checked the locks, trying to ignore the hammer of Omikron shooting at the driver's side.

"Why'd you pick the car with the most fucked tires?"

Oscar snarled, throwing himself into the front passenger seat.

He had some blood on his arm, but it didn't look too serious.

"Why'd you hide behind a fuckin' tree?" I answered back, fighting an insane smile. Just adrenaline—I wasn't that trigger-happy, right? Except I'd always found combat just a little *too* much fun. It was one of the reasons I'd left the work behind.

"Had to take a shit," Oscar joked, and I snorted.

"Can you get back there and answer some of this?" I asked, my left ear starting to feel deaf with the sound of being shot at.

"Do I look like I can fit between these seats?" Oscar griped, but he threw the seat back until it was nearly flat and grunted as he climbed over.

"Watch your ass, I shot that window and it's not perfect cover," I warned him.

"Yeah, how great of you," Oscar snarled, his ass high in the air as he squirmed his way to the backseat.

The burner phone vibrated, and this time I ducked low, sparing a moment to answer and letting Oscar deal with the mercenaries ruining the paint job of the SUV.

"Eve," Garrett snapped on the phone. "She's got trouble. She's tugging on the bond."

"She's hurt?" My entire body tensed at the thought, hackles raising.

"I dunno, I don't feel pain. Hans and I just finished up here, but you're closer."

"I'm closer but with zero tires," I snapped, as the fourth popped.

"Hang on, I'm almost done with these rats. Way to leave them that present of your rifle, dickhead," Oscar muttered at me. I glanced at him in the rearview mirror and found him making use of the short hole I'd made in the window, firing out of it.

The driver's side mirror revealed another man trying to sneak up on Oscar from behind the car, and I growled and sat up, aiming and firing at him as soon as he threw the trunk open.

"Okay, I forgive you," Oscar said to me, grinning and then taking the last shot. "I think we're good."

"Garrett, I think I've got another car I can grab," I said into the phone, not entirely sure he was listening.

"Meet you there," Garrett answered, solemn and quiet.

"I'll clear the car and head over to where they need backup. You call in cleanup here?" I asked Oscar.

"Sure, leave me with the shitty boring job," Oscar said. "Hey! Be careful. Good luck."

I twisted in the seat of the SUV and met Oscar's eyes. "Thank you."

He nodded, and I was relieved that the two words would suffice at covering the many reasons they needed to be said.

I pushed out of the car, equal parts impressed and disturbed by the scene on the road. It hadn't been that long. And who knew how much time Oscar had before being interrupted.

"Don't worry about it, big man. Help is already on the way. I'll fill this up and steer it into the fields until they get here," Oscar assured me.

I nodded and kept my eyes up and my gun high as I headed for the SUV. Sure enough, it was empty, still running, set in park. And with three tires rather than none.

I jumped into the front seat and tried to keep the tasks ordered in my mind, rather than Garrett's panicked tone. Drive to Eve, finish off managing the Omikron attack, clean up, go home. It was a grocery list of a mission, not an emergency.

Still, I turned the SUV onto one of the field roads and drove through the cornstalks as fast as the car could stand to go.

THIRTY-THREE

Eve

Dan and Pete weren't incompetent, but they weren't Jamie either.

"Stay back," I barked at Pete, shouldering him to the ground before he nearly got himself shot in the face.

The problems had started almost straight away. Dan had rushed for the first SUV almost as soon as I'd blown out the tires, and before giving me a chance to finish the others. He'd ended up trapped between all three SUVs, and while his hand-to-hand was impressive, it was still twelve to one with Pete in my ear shouting useless instructions.

The fact that I'd bothered saving either man was concrete proof of how much of an effort I was making for the pack.

"Incoming from behind!" Dan shouted.

I glanced briefly over my shoulder before returning my focus to the goons surrounding us. "Don't shoot. Could be friendly."

The vehicle was an exact match for the ones we were

facing off with, but I thought the figure through the windshield looked familiar and Garrett was determined and rushing in the bond. Help was on the way. Thank fuck.

Sure enough, the new SUV made no effort to slow, but simply swerved around us, driving itself directly into one of the other vehicles providing cover for Omikron's men. It backed up, only to ram itself forward again. A moment later the driver's door opened and Rory's broad, tall frame appeared.

"Stay here, hold any fire well away from us," I shouted to Dan, not sparing a glance at Pete still on the ground.

I'd managed to claim one vehicle for our own cover, and Rory was quickly securing the next.

He's not bad at all, is he? I realized, admiring the efficient single shots it took Rory to incapacitate each agent. I hurried out to meet him on the road, jogging up to his back to use him as a shield against the gunfire, before dodging to his left to help cover his weaker angle.

"G's on his way," Rory said without glancing at me.

"We're almost done here." Or we would be, now that Rory was on hand.

"You hurt?"

"No, just at the disadvantage of having to babysit while I work," I answered.

I grabbed Rory by his shirt and tugged him toward me, swinging around his back. I grabbed the mercenary charging at us with the knife in his hand, hooking my ankle around his knee as I dodged a stab, unbalancing him and taking him down to the ground. Rory stood over me as I wrestled the man, firing shots above my head.

"Here comes Garrett," Rory warned, just before an enormous screech and crash.

"How many left?" I grunted out. A hand grasped around my throat, squeezing, as I twisted the forearm holding the knife until there was a snap and a scream from the man below me. I finished him off with a shot, and Rory pulled me up from the ground and then retreated, dragging me back behind the second SUV.

"Just three, let me see," Rory said.

He pinned me between his own body and the glossy, dented back end of the vehicle, red tail lights still shining, turning us both vivid and bloody. He ducked, staring at my throat. Behind us shots were still firing, but I could hear the call and response between Dan, Pete, and Garrett.

"M'fine," I said, shrugging Rory's hands off my shoulders. He stood straight, glared down at me, and then he was swooping forward again. His mouth was hard and hot, nose bruising against mine, hands grasping my jaw just above where I'd been choked.

He groaned into the kiss, licked into my mouth, and I held myself frozen at the assault. No, not an assault. A kiss. A good kiss, actually, frantic but confident too. One he needed and I could offer, even if I couldn't bring myself to participate. His teeth bit gently at my upper lip, tongue swiping, and then he pulled back with a gasp of air, eyes growing wide.

"You're bleeding," he said, his thumb swiping up to brush just below my left nostril.

"I got punched in the face," I explained.

Rory relaxed and glanced over my shoulder. "Just one left. They're finishing up."

"You didn't have any trouble?"

"Lots," Rory answered, a rare grin on his lips. "But Oscar's cleaning up."

There was still some of Rory's taste on my tongue, creamy and nutty and dark, surprisingly flavorful and pleasant, not too sweet. I nodded at his answer and then hooked two fingers into the collar of his black T-shirt, yanking him closer.

His eyes hooded, lips parting in invitation. *Not an alpha, Rory*, I tried to tell myself, but it was impossible to see Rory as anything else. He was massive, temperamental, and protective, and while his scent was growing on me, it was undeniably heavy.

"If we had time, I'd beg you to throw me into the back-seat and fuck me stupid," Rory rasped, pupils blacking out the color in his eyes, lips ruby red with a little of my blood and the glow of the tail light.

A surprised laugh bubbled up from my throat and I leaned in, tilting my head and biting at his pulse. Not to mark him, but just to claim my dominance. Rory leaned in heavily, pinning me to the back of the SUV, but it wasn't a trap, just proof of my power over him as he started to rut against my hip and pant into my shoulder, my teeth pinching his skin.

"*Eve!*" Garrett's call was even more desperate in the bond than it was tearing out of his lips, and I pushed Rory back, the nip snagging briefly on his throat, his feet stumbling under him as I shoved him away.

I stepped out from around the corner, into the squared pit of asphalt we'd been fighting in, and found Garrett standing across from me. His face whipped in my direction and his shoulders sagged, relief like a massive wave beating down into our bond. Adam's immediately echoed in a second, lesser tide. He marched forward, Pete and Dan already busy loading Omikron goons into vehicles. Rory stepped out from behind the SUV, and Garrett spared him another relieved glance and a nod before stopping short just in front of me, brow furrowed and gaze pleading.

I reached up and stroked a clean finger down his nose

before lifting to my toes and kissing him briefly. One eyebrow raised at my taste, still rich with Rory.

"Time to clean up, then home," I said.

Garrett sighed and nodded, but his face lowered to mine for another kiss, brief and gentle, before he stepped back again.

"Let's be quick then," he said. "The semis are almost here."

———

GARRETT'S HEAD was on my lap, his body taking up most of the backseat, and I left my fingers loosely tangled in his hair. His eyes were closed, but I didn't think he was really sleeping more than processing the night, his brow occasionally tangling and then smoothing out again.

Even with the extra hands, removing evidence from the scene was still quite a job. I knew of cleaners who might've been called, but they were already on Omikron's books and I wasn't sure what we'd get instead. Better to handle the matter ourselves. Two semi trucks had arrived with supplies for us to haul away the SUVs and bodies. We'd washed the road, scanned the surrounding area for any evidence, all while having to duck away anytime someone spotted a car. The roads were quiet and primarily vacant, but the work was tense.

I looked up from Garrett to the rearview mirror, gaze immediately clashing with Rory's until he looked away again. His taste had faded from my lips, and there was too much already spinning in my head to dissect our kiss from earlier. I understood we were on some kind of strange sexual path with each other, but our kiss had been both more intimate and more reassuring than I'd expected.

The clock on the dash of the car was blinking some

narrow and impossibly late number as we pulled into our driveway. I was dirty, sore, tired, and hungry, and it was all beating down on me in a way I would've generally packed and hidden from my own mind. But the bond was open. For Garrett and Adam, for my own connections with them.

I was left *feeling*, toiling with both my own muted emotions and their louder ones. The difference was exhausting.

Then the door from the garage opened, a second after Rory had parked the car, and Adam and Jamie appeared, Adam bursting with a new and more immediate cascade of relief and pride, and some of those problems seemed to be buried under his excitement at having us home again. I slid out of the backseat with a gentle nudge to Garrett, who sat up.

Adam met me at the car door, tense but not throwing himself at me. I lifted one arm and then he was there, pressed to my side, cheek to cheek, arms tangling around my waist. I draped my own arms over Adam's shoulders and stroked his back.

"Nothing interesting happened here, right?"

Adam shook his head. "Jamie and I watched *Jeopardy* reruns and toasted marshmallows."

"The new neighbors, Hannah and Marc, stopped on a walk when they saw us over the gate, but I blew them off by saying the rest of you were out," Jamie said.

I glanced at Rory over Adam's head, but he seemed nonplussed by the mention.

"You kept the bond open," Adam murmured to me.

"I tried," I said, nodding, stepping back and making room for Garrett to step out too.

He and Adam immediately wrapped around one another, Garrett's head bowing to whisper in Adam's ear. I left them to it, perfectly aware of how they still seemed to be clawing for one another in the connection I'd made. It might've been poorly planned, but I was right that giving them a taste of a bond would only make them crave the real thing.

"Tired?" Jamie murmured as I hauled myself up the steps to the kitchen door after Rory.

I nodded, my hand reaching out of its own accord to find Jamie's arm, searching for his bare skin as if it were an anchor. "I want to give them a little space tonight," I said softly, glancing back at where Garrett and Adam were still embracing.

"Do *you* want a little space tonight?" Jamie asked.

"Some. Not a lot," I admitted.

Rory was pulling a beer out of the fridge, tipping it in my direction, and I shook my head.

"Shower and come to my room if you want," Jamie said, voice soft.

Rory's back was to us, his head tilted slightly to listen as we moved slowly through the kitchen. I considered what had started between Rory and me, last night in the kitchen, tonight at the end of the fight. I recalled the creamy dark flavor of his mouth on mine, but also the way my shoulders had tightened as he crowded me, the way he'd automatically responded to my teeth on him.

I didn't want to fight tonight, for fun or otherwise. Garrett and Adam were soft and tender with one another, my body was aching without me having the advantage of turning the volume down. I needed rest and ease.

I squeezed Jamie's wrist in my hand and nodded. "Meet you there."

It was almost a shame to know that left Rory as odd man out.

GARRETT AND ADAM had both put up a little privacy barrier in the bond while I showered, allowing me to duck out as well. They were holed up in the nest, and I suspected I would be welcome to join them, but not missed if I bowed out. I needed the break after the work of the evening, and I thought they deserved the room to forge the bond on their own.

Jamie was sitting up in his bed, cradling a guitar in his arms, strumming aimlessly and occasionally off-key.

"That's not the one you're working on," I said.

Jamie paused in his playing and shook his head, setting the guitar down in its stand by the bed. "That's a long work in progress between finishing up the rest of my jobs."

I stepped inside the bedroom, my hand on the door-knob, wordlessly asking Jamie whether to leave it open or closed.

"Up to you."

I shut the door behind me and padded over to the enormous bed, climbing up onto the mattress but facing the headboard. "Still think you're willing to give up your work if it comes down to it?" I asked.

Jamie smiled back at me and nodded. "I said finishing jobs. I'm not taking any new ones on for a while. Till we know how things might shake out."

I scooted closer on the bed, and he twisted toward me, rolling onto his side, one hand reaching out to graze a knuckle over my bare knee. I was wearing a night dress Rory had brought home, silk and short, with brief slits up the side for ease of movement. It was wonderfully soft and in a dark shade of rust red I thought looked nice against the warm tone of my skin. Rory had good taste.

"I had fun with you in the city, weird as it is to say," Jamie said, interrupting my train of thought.

I blinked, and my lips quirked up. "I had fun too."

"How was tonight?"

I grimaced. "Better after Rory met up with me. The three of you really are…preferably competent."

Jamie let out a bright belly laugh and grinned at me. "High praise, Eve. Thanks. I meant…how's the organization?"

His hand on my knee drew away to tap at his own head.

"Not ideal," I admitted. I studied him. He was in sweats and a T-shirt. Did he sleep in all those clothes or was he modest for my sake? How much effort would it take to convince him to strip?

"What are the least heavy burdens?" Jamie asked.

"The technical consequences of the act," I answered immediately. "Will there be legal repercussions? Blowback on the three of you from the neighborhood? What comes next from Omikron? Also, the…toll of keeping the bond open for Adam and Garrett. Rory kissed me."

The rest, the morality and the guilt and the *questions* about who the men and women on the other end of my gun were, those issues were better left packed, or I risked unpacking the entire history of my work as a contract killer.

"Did you knee him in the balls for it?" Jamie asked.

"You had to latch onto the last concern?"

Jamie shrugged. "It's the most interesting to me."

"I didn't. How would you feel about having sex?"

"A fan of the concept. How was the kiss?"

I glared at Jamie, and he grinned back at me. "The technical consequences do concern me too, but I trust that Omikron wants things as quiet as we do. And there's been no mention of you or Adam in connection with any crime, which means they don't pull law enforcement strings," Jamie said, rolling onto his back, his hands propping up his head and his ankles crossed. "As for the neighborhood, they may ask us to leave, and we will do it if we need to. We'll adapt. We've already talked about that. We can't predict Omikron at this point, but Garrett says there's already discussion about avoiding their jobs. Too high a risk."

I preened at that. We'd done what we could to warn other contractors away from Omikron, at least ones who had any interest in their own humanity over their paycheck. But where ethics might fail, self-preservation would surely win. My track record of putting their hires in the ground was a persuasive argument for others to stay away.

"I can't answer the question of the bond, I guess," Jamie admitted, frowning up at his ceiling before looking back to me. "But I think they'll have their own soon, and you can adapt when and how much you share with them. How was the kiss?"

I frowned and glanced at the closed bedroom door.

"Pretty sure he'd let you see him tonight, if you wanted," Jamie said, more carefully.

I was pretty sure that was true. "Can't we just fuck rather than talk?"

Jamie's smile was calm, but his eyes narrowed slightly. "As a coping mechanism or for fun?"

I bit off my groan and sat up on my knees. For all of Jamie's roundabout conversation, he was stretched out in the middle of the bed like an invitation. I knew he liked direct and explicit agreement on the matter, but surely a little enticing was allowed. I lifted one knee and settled myself straddling over his hips, the slits of the night dress riding up to the tops of my thighs.

"I like you. I am mentally wound up and physically exhausted. I need some dopamine and some sleep, but also you…" I trailed off, reaching out and sliding my hands under Jamie's T-shirt to rest them against his stomach, staring down at the spot where the cotton gathered against my wrists. "I relax around you. You aren't threatening." *You make me feel safe* was another version of the confession, but it carried too much weight.

Jamie's hands circled my wrists, dragging them farther up his chest, taking the shirt along as he sat up.

"You're pleasant company when you're not asking too many questions," I added, flicking my eyes up to his, trying to tease but finding his own dark gaze intent and powerful.

"Thank you. That was all important for me to know," Jamie said, raising his arms for me to drag the T-shirt off over his head. "Tell me what else makes you feel secure?"

I frowned at that. "Adam's nest. The Charger, when I'm driving. Having a gun in my hand. Good running shoes—"

Jamie laughed and shook his head, his hands stroking up and down my thighs. "Sorry, no, that's all good information too, but I meant during sex. With me. You were tense at the garage."

Oh.

"Breathing room. Being on top, like this," I said, rocking slightly on Jamie's lap. My arms were around his neck, our faces close but not touching. "I do like tying the other person up too."

Jamie nodded and glanced at the door. "Maybe save that for Rory, but sure, makes sense. What about clothes?"

"I'd rather be naked."

His hands scooped up from my hips, dragging up the silk and rubbing it against me, over my breasts on the path. I shrugged out of the night dress and rose up on my knees.

"You too," I said, reaching back to the hips of his sweatpants. "What do you like?"

Jamie laughed, shimmying out of his pants and then kicking them down to the foot of the bed. "Talking. Thought that was obvious."

"Dirty talking? Do you want to be a wicked, filthy alpha? Fuck my pussy with your rock-hard—"

"Eve!" Jamie laughed, jerking underneath me, falling back onto the bed. "Jesus, stop!"

I found myself grinning. Adam liked dirty talk; I would save it for him and Garrett instead.

"I like *connecting* with the person I'm with," Jamie said, raising his eyebrows up at me, all collapsed in his sheets and pillows, dark and angelic. He shrugged. "Kinda boring, huh?"

"It's downright deviant to me," I said, smiling. "Well out of my wheelhouse."

"It takes practice."

"I do love to acquire new skills."

"Kissing is a good start," he said.

I wrinkled my nose and spread my knees farther apart, settling my sex onto his cock and rubbing myself over the spot, stimulating my clit with his tip. "Kissing here."

Jamie's lips parted, and he looked down thoughtfully to where we were touching. "Not what I—what I had in mind, but it's a good interpretation, actually."

I was beginning to understand the appeal of his idea of talking, playful and calm, taking all the window dressing out of sex—the seduction and the aggression, the frantic needful energy—and making it into something friendly and honest.

"Sit up," I said, reaching down to spread the lips of my sex, the path a little smoother now as I was growing more aroused and slippery.

Jamie pushed up on the heels of his hands, and I leaned down, cupping his face in my hands and bending my head to his, nibbling on his lips, breathing in his sigh and going back for more.

"Let me know if I get too close," Jamie breathed, wrapping his arms loosely around me, one hand stroking over my chest and down between us to bump against my clit.

The air of the room was cool at my back, Jamie warm against me, his cock growing stiff and hard, trying to rise and find its way into me. The lamp by the bed was on, our shadows high on the wall to my right. I looked there now, at the strange twist of us, the sliver of light bleeding through between our chests. I leaned into Jamie, watching us blend together on the wall, and he purred against me, dressing wet kisses over my shoulders and collarbone.

Maybe I made an exception to Jamie's closeness because the warmth of him against my breasts and stomach was wonderfully comforting. I rose to my knees, and Jamie immediately notched himself against my opening. I left the shadows on the wall and turned back to him, tilting his face back and covering his mouth with mine, swallowing his groan as I sank down with shallow thrusts and dives of my hips. He was hot and hard and thick inside of me, distracting the pressure with soft touches up my sides.

"Lie back," I murmured to Jamie.

He fell back into the pillows with a sigh, hands on my waist as I leaned over him, riding his lovely length, rubbing myself into that knot. I wondered if I *could* take it, if it would be any different because of how relaxed I was with him.

"I like eye contact too," Jamie said, smiling up at me, his chest heaving and his heels bracing against the bed to join my rhythm.

I'd had my own gaze pointed down at where we were joined, studying his knot, but I turned it up to his now. My chest grew painfully tight, my breath short, but with the ache came a sweet pound in my core.

"I like you too, by the way," Jamie said, drawing a surprising heat up into my cheeks. "You feel like a thunderstorm coming." He arched up to kiss at my answering frown and whispered against my lips. "I just want to stand out in the field, wait for lightning to strike, make me electric for that moment too."

A pretty and dangerous thought, implying I had the power to destroy him. I slanted my mouth over his, wrapped my arms around his shoulders, and clutched at every inch of skin I could claim. Jamie's answer to my kiss was as languid as I was starving, like he was offering himself up as a feast to me. A sacrifice on the altar.

I growled at the thought and pulled away, the now familiar urge to *bite* rising again as I stared back at him, our bodies colliding and crashing.

"If you bite me, I'll bite back," Jamie rasped out a teasing warning, grinning up at me as I licked my bottom lip.

I swallowed hard and nodded. I didn't want to claim Jamie on a stray impulse, and I wasn't sure I wanted to be claimed.

"Can you breathe?" he asked, and I realized I'd been holding my breath.

I sucked in a gasp and let out a moan as the drumbeat in my core grew erratic, threatening to throw me over the edge. "Barely," I admitted, but I held onto him even more tightly before he could offer to pull away.

His mouth brushed over my pulse, and I shuddered, my lock starting to close around him. He licked the spot, kissed it, moving up and down my throat as I stopped bouncing on his length and switched to simply grinding myself into his knot.

"Fuck, fuck, Eve, I'm—"

I didn't need the warning, I was with him, arching my throat and clasping him inside of me, falling over the edge in a slow repetition, like a moment suspended in a constant rewind and repeat. Jamie's sweat was under my hands, my shoulder in his mouth—not biting, just burying his groan —and for a moment, designation and pack and Omikron all left my head. All the boxes and all the hidden compartments and a long, secret, lonely history, gone.

Lightning had struck, and Jamie and I were electric.

THIRTY-FOUR

Garrett

Adam whined and squeezed around my knot, and I groaned into his shoulder, trying and failing to resist the instinct to rock into him. We were on our sides in the dark nest, the bathroom light still on after our shower, the glow stretching out over Adam to let me admire my handiwork of fucking him into a sweaty, begging mess.

"What's better? Knot or Lock?" I teased.

Male omegas were really built for the lock, but luckily for Adam and I, he also had a prostate that couldn't avoid the pressure of my knot.

Adam panted, rubbing himself harder against me, searching for another orgasm. "Shut up. Both."

I hadn't meant the question to be a Me versus Eve thing, but Adam's answer was satisfying in both cases. I reached around his hip, wrapping my hand loosely around his cock, waiting for a hiss of irritation. Instead, Adam rattled with a relieved moan. I squeezed my fingers tighter, delighted by the excess of his release on his length, making the motion of my hand slick and easy.

"Oh god, Garrett, it's five in the morning," Adam whined, but it was him doing all the work now, thrusting into my hand, pressing onto my knot.

"Tired?" I asked, chuckling. I was a bit, but I couldn't get over how much Adam *wanted* me. He hadn't stopped touching me since we'd made it back to the house, even during a somewhat gory shower together. To be fair, I hadn't stopped touching him either. Heats were going to be fun.

"Uh-huh," Adam said, just working even harder against me, huffing as I continued to refuse to move. "I think Eve's asleep. I can't feel you."

I kissed his shoulder, tightened the loop of my fingers. "You can feel me here."

"I—I want a bond, Garrett. I thought I wanted to wait, but I don't," Adam murmured, head turning to bump against mine, searching for my mouth.

I stretched to kiss him, and he whined into the kiss, shuddering and coming, forcing me to do the same by the vise of his ass around my knot as he finished. We collapsed into stillness, panting, my hand painted with his release. I lifted it up to Adam's lips, forcing him to clean one finger before sucking on the rest myself.

Pure sugar. Like a can of frosting. Suddenly, I wanted him thrusting into my mouth. I would have to wait for my knot to deflate.

"I meant what I said," Adam whispered, just a little hint of anxiety.

I'd been distracted by the sudden whip of an orgasm, and I had to go back and search my memory.

Oh.

I nudged my nose against his cheek, kissed his jaw. "Are you sure? Could be tomorrow. Next week."

Adam was quiet for a long moment, soft in my arms,

but there was a sharper scent rising up around him. "Are *you* sure?"

I blinked.

"We can wait," Adam said. There was nowhere for him to go, not until my knot deflated, but he managed to draw away all the same.

"Hey, wait, I'm just..." I shifted slightly, propping myself up on my forearm, spooning my knees tighter behind his as I gazed down at him. "I'm just trying to make sure I'm not taking advantage."

Adam nodded. "And I don't want to rope another alpha into a bond they're not—"

Ah, fuck! "Adam," I groaned, dropping my head into his throat and shaking it, scent marking him all over again. "Okay, hold up. I honestly...I forgot about that. You're not roping me into anything, and I was just worried about doing the same."

Adam's cheek bumped against my forehead, and I sat up again. Wide gray-green eyes stared up at me, studied me. "I like this sort of proxy bond we have going on, but it just makes me want the real thing. Especially in a situation like tonight. Eve did her best, but sometimes it was just shut, and I never knew if one or both of you was in trouble."

I nodded. I'd been half distracted all night by the same problem.

"It's not just about the danger, though," Adam said, trying to twist and hissing as the position pulled the wrong way. "I didn't really believe that alphas like you existed. And now that I've found one...I would bite you myself if I could."

I purred so hard, my chest vibrated at the suggestion. Eve had done the job for him. For herself too, I wanted to believe.

"But I *am* a bit of a…not ideal omega," Adam said slowly, frowning. "I mean, the Omikron thing. And not wanting kids. And being…just, me, I guess."

My heart thudded painfully, throat tightening. I'd really fucked this up if Adam was spiraling so far. I'd been trying to be the opposite of Eve, but I'd forgotten that for all her faults, she and Adam *worked* together. He needed me to be myself, but he needed me to be his alpha too.

"Omikron isn't your fault, and the fact that this is something you took on, on your own, is just another reason you have my respect," I said quickly. "And I've been thinking about kids, waiting to feel disappointed, and honestly, I'm not. I picture my future and I picture…well, a lot of trouble. And the five us together, facing it. And that's a weirdly and unexpectedly exciting vision. I like that you're cunning and that you didn't settle for a pack before now because that's what the world told you were supposed to find."

"I'm not settling now," Adam pointed out. "You guys are kind of fascinating. You know, for three alphas living in the suburbs."

I laughed, and Adam smiled up at me. Suddenly, a nervous worry popped up in my head.

"We're—I'm—we're falling in love, right?" I asked gracelessly, gaping down at Adam.

I mean, I was. With him. With our impossible bond-mate. But if I was the emotional support proxy to his connection with Eve—

Adam's eyes lit up, cheeks flushing all over again, and a brilliant crooked grin stretching over his face. "I sure as fuck hope so."

The air went whooshing out of me in a relieved gust, and my arms circled around Adam, drawing him up with me as I knelt in the nest with him on my lap.

"Holy fuck, that's deep!" Adam yelped, arching against me. He had sunk even farther onto my knot, and the sudden squeeze of his ass on my length brought my arousal back online again. "Oh *shit*."

"Good position?" I teased, my own voice a little strangled.

"Don't ask me questions when your cock is reaching all the way to my brain, Garrett," Adam moaned.

Flattered by this optimistic estimation of my size, I nudged my hips against Adam's ass just to hear him shout. "Still want my bite?" I asked, kissing his throat.

"Unnnnghh." I laughed and nipped the spot, startling Adam. "Yes, yes, yes, yes."

The frenzied answer made me want to sober him again, be sure, but we'd already run the conversation through, and I didn't want to confuse him or give him the impression I had any more doubts. Anyway, this high he was in would help soften the burn of the bite until I started nursing.

Shit, we weren't going to get any sleep tonight. *Again.*

My thrusts were shallow, my thighs burning with the effort, but Adam was so beautifully loose and desperate on my lap like this, it was impossible to stop.

"If we had a chair, Eve could lock you at the same time," I mused, a little breathless.

"I would *die*," Adam moaned, and then amended, "We should try it in the heat."

I laughed, and the matter was settled. Adam, perfectly flawed, hilarious and clever and strangely shy, was my omega. I stroked a hand up his chest, bowing him backwards against my shoulder, and his head dropped to the side in offering.

There was just one issue.

Eve had left no fucking room for my bite. Her marks

decorated Adam's throat and shoulder like armor. I had no idea what it would do if I tried to bite over one of her marks, but I suspected mine wouldn't take as well. Luckily, I enjoyed improvisation.

I grabbed Adam's shoulders and pushed him forward, being sure to keep myself fastened as firmly to his ass as he seemed to be enjoying. He fell limply face-first into the nest, his ass high, and long back on display for me.

"Jerk off for me," I said, adding a little bark into the words and grinning as Adam howled and arched, his arm shaking as he followed orders. His head turned, cheek flat against the mattress and mouth open on a steady moan. "You want my bite, Adam?"

"God, yes, Garrett, please."

I leaned in, and Adam gasped as my weight added to the pressure of my knot in his ass. I arched over him, pushing his elbow away from his side and exposing his ribs. With a soft push against his left side, and a twist to the right, I dove down.

My teeth were rough, digging into skin, muscle, my mouth open as wide as I could, wanting to cover as much of Adam's rib with my bite as I was able. My mark wrapped around his side, his blood hot on my tongue, and then came the fever, delirious and desperate. I growled, and my hips kicked urgently against Adam's ass, his need becoming my own, his arousal overwhelming in its power, consuming. And deeper, below just the sexual impulse, was something tentative and excited, greeting me warily, bite shy.

The bond. I reached out and grabbed on, sharing my confidence with Adam. The bond rose up around us both, warm and pleasantly suffocating, the rest of the world blocked out to leave only us, tangled and teasing and craving one another.

Adam came with a buried bellow, clamping down on my knot, and I resurfaced from the bond with a gasp of air, blood on my lips. My tongue stroked over the wound, and Adam and I sighed, our threads spinning together.

———

THERE WAS no sunlight in the nest until later afternoon, so all I knew when I woke was that it was sometime before 3 p.m., Adam and I were a mess, and Eve was stretched out on Adam's other side, her scent strangely sweetened, almost airy.

"It's pretty," she whispered, touching lightly on the marks on Adam's side. "Next time, bite him here," she added, pointing down to the inside of Adam's thigh near his cock.

I opened my mouth to say there wouldn't be a next time; I'd already done the job. But then one of her marks seemed to wink at me, and a possessiveness spiked in my chest. She'd claimed Adam a dozen times at least. Surely one more bite from me wouldn't hurt.

"How was your night?" I asked, trying not to smirk. Adam and I had been busy, but not so much as to avoid noticing the distinctly *amorous* vibes coming from Eve before she'd gone quiet.

"Fine," she said without a hint.

"Any new holes in our packmates?" I asked.

"Only Adam's," she said, pointing out my mark on his ribs. "I put Tabs on the hunt for Faith," Eve added, sitting up.

I rolled away from Adam before sitting up. It was time to do a basic laundry on the nest—not too much to ruin all the scenting Adam had done, but enough for sanitary purposes.

"We should wait for Adam to wake up," I said.

"It isn't good news," Eve whispered, frowning down at Adam.

Worry doubled between us in the bond, and then she shut me out. Fair enough, that probably wasn't an emotion she wanted to deal with in stereo.

"We should still wait for him," I said.

"Does he have to know?" Eve asked, looking up at me.

I opened my mouth and then shut it again. She wasn't being coy or deceptive, she meant the question honestly. The news would hurt Adam, and as his bondmate, she didn't want to share it if she didn't have to.

"Yes," I said, keeping the answer simple. I had no doubt Eve would earn a lecture from me again someday, but she was trying to learn, and that was enough right now.

Eve's lips pressed flat, but she nodded. I assumed she would let that be it, but instead she reached out and petted over Adam's new mark before leaning in and kissing him awake.

"Mmm, good morning, alpha," Adam mumbled, reaching out for Eve.

"Adam—"

"Eve, wait!" I cried, realizing her goal.

"—Faith was auctioned."

I groaned and covered my face with my hands as Adam sat up like a shot. Maybe a lecture would've been in order after all.

"Wait, *what?!* How do you know? Who to? When?" Adam's fingers went diving into his hair, yanking hard on the strands, gaze frantic on Eve.

"I don't know who did the bidding, but I'm looking into it," Eve said, pulling his fingers loose and pressing his hands between hers. "Last week. A yacht in international waters off the west coast. We've been looking for something like this, but they kept it almost entirely silent. It was hearsay that reached Tabs, and we're only seventy-five percent sure it was Faith."

"That's an important margin," I bit out.

"But if it was her, she was auctioned as pre-estrus," Eve said, finally gentling her tone.

My eyebrows kicked up at that. Faith was only a few years younger than Adam, so for her to still not have had her first heat was rare.

"I don't—" Adam's eyes watered, and I scooted in to wrap myself around his back, glaring over his shoulder at Eve, who blinked back at me, impassive as usual. "I don't know if that's a good or bad thing."

"I think they held onto her until the auction because they couldn't find a buyer," Eve said. "There's no rut without the heat; she wouldn't have the same draw."

"Less blunt!" I snapped at her.

"No," Adam breathed, patting my arm weakly. "No, straightforward is better, actually. Can we be sure it was her?"

"We're following the trail," Eve said. "I don't know what it will take to be positive, aside from finding a way to get eyes on her, but if that's what needs to be done, it will happen."

My anger burned away as Adam sagged in my arms. "You think she could still be in the country?"

Eve winced at that. "I can't say."

"I know, but tell me what you *think*," Adam pushed.

"No. We're a thorn in Omikron's side. They know we're looking for her. If we found her, it could cause major issues for them. We're lucky to believe she's still alive."

I glared at Eve, but Adam nodded. "You're right. I'd sort of…been reassuring myself that it wasn't likely. Fuck."

"We will find her. I can reach out to some clients, ones that don't fit Omikron's profile," Eve said. "See if they can dig into the event, find out more."

"Is this something we can ask around about in the server?" I asked Adam.

He sucked in a breath, straightening in my arms and nodding. "Yeah. Yeah, that's a good idea."

"I'm not sure they'd know anything, we barely found out about it *after* the fact," Eve said, frowning.

"Maybe that's the alarm we need then. If someone in the server is ready to feed us info about the auction, about Faith—"

"Then they might be the plant in the server who got us caught in the first place," Adam said, scrambling out of my arms and heading for the dresser where he'd started stashing his small collection of clothes.

"I can rip the arrow out when you're here to stem the wound," Eve murmured to me.

I stared at her briefly and shook my head. "Rip the *band-aid* off. Band-aid. Jesus, a whole arrow? No one *rips* an arrow out, Eve."

"Knife," she tried.

"No! What about *arteries*?!"

"Ice-pick?"

My mouth hung open, and Eve's lips curled up at the corners. She leaned in and pressed a kiss to her mark on my throat as I tried to bury the purr that rose in response.

"I'm saying we balance each other for him," she said, pulling away.

I reached out and grabbed her elbow, drawing her back to me, ignoring the growl as I kissed her firmly. "I am not your excuse to be an asshole," I ground out at her.

She glared back, but in the bond there was hunger.

"Be more careful," I warned her, mostly to test my theory.

She was growling, eyes narrowed back at me, but the bond told a very different story, and her scent grew heavy but not as harsh as it used to be.

"Are you two going to keep eye fucking each other or help me oust a spy?" Adam called from the door.

"We don't have time for me to put you in your place right now," Eve snarled, rising from the mattress. "But just know that I'll savor the moment later."

Shit. Now *I* was the one aroused. Not fair.

Fun. But not fair.

THIRTY-FIVE

Adam

Garrett woke early most days, but not after Eve wore him out. Which, fair enough, same. We'd all been winners, including me as I watched her wrestle him onto his stomach and spank him until his ass was hot to the touch, before sucking him off for over an hour as I played with his knot.

I admired the red handprints still marking up his bare ass. It was early, Eve had left the nest, and I was antsy.

Faith had been auctioned. Maybe. She still hadn't gone into her first heat, and she was missing. Alive. *Maybe.*

I slipped out of the nest in a pair of sweatpants and one of Garrett's hoodies and went looking for a distraction.

Rory was in the kitchen, eating cereal while standing, and he stiffened as I walked in. "Morning."

"Can I go for a walk?"

"Not by yourself."

I bristled at the answer and then shook it off. "I know. I get that. Omikron knows where I am. And I know you guys think I'm safer here, and I trust you all and I'll do what I need to to make it easier on you all. But…I'm going a little crazy in here."

"Oh." Rory stood up straighter, brow drawing together. "Yeah, we can…I can walk with you. I wanna grab a gun first. Do you know how to shoot?"

"Roughly, yeah."

"Good enough at close range," Rory said with a shrug, and I stifled a laugh.

He passed me the bowl of cereal, and I stared blankly back at him.

"I mean, I know it's just a walk, but…eat some breakfast," Rory said, firm and frowning, before stomping out of the kitchen.

I stared down at the bowl in my hands and then crossed to the counter, adding more cereal and following the growly alpha's orders. As far as domineering commands went, breakfast wasn't so bad.

Rory came back a few minutes later, a harness on under his hoodie and another in his hand for me. "It's Jamie's. I, uh, let him and Eve know you'd be out," Rory muttered, brow tense.

Garrett had clued me in on Rory's outburst after hearing who Eve had been having sex with, and I was endlessly curious and amused about his feelings for my dangerous alpha.

"He's like a…cool cucumber, huh?" I asked, tentatively poking the bear in front of me.

Rory blinked and frowned and then nodded. "Yeah. I guess so."

"And Garrett's just a big ol' ball of flirt," I added. Rory's frown grew more serious. "And I'm kind of a neurotic con man turned needy omega. And you're…"

"A crusty cinnamon roll," Rory finished for me, lips twitching.

"Eve really doesn't have a type, does she?" I suggested.

Rory blinked at me and then shrugged. "Hoodie off so we can get the harness on."

Fine, play it cool, big guy, I thought, smiling and setting my borrowed breakfast aside. Rory's crush on Eve was getting more evident by the day, and it was making him… weirdly charming. If nothing else, I could relate to being kept at arm's length by Eve.

"She'll crack sooner or later. She always does," I said to him.

Rory grunted and fitted me up with the harness. I put my hoodie back on and grabbed a few more bites of cereal, assuming that Rory was going to ignore the topic of conversation I'd tried. It wasn't until we were heading out the front door that he finally spoke up.

"She's interested. She just needs to trust that I don't really want to win a challenge," Rory said.

I nodded and squinted at him. "Do you think you could, if you wanted to?"

He shrugged. "That's not the point. Maybe. Probably not. She's too smart to relax around a threat, so she just needs to know I'm not one. Same as you and the others."

I hummed, stretching as Rory followed me out of the house and down to the sidewalk. "Omega biology doesn't even give you that much. We respond to threats with sexual need."

"No, omegas respond to threats with adrenaline just like everybody else. It's pheromones that create arousal. Adrenaline just adds to the mix. You can learn to differentiate," Rory said matter-of-factly.

"How?"

"Learning other ways of meeting adrenaline, keeping your body relaxed and your mind energized. It's part of combat training," Rory said, raising a hand and waving at a familiar face across the street, one of the guys who'd come to the pack house to help out a couple nights before with Omikron. "There was a military cell overseas that used omegas and their perfumes as a way to disarm enemy soldiers. They trained alphas how to ignore the hindbrain response to the perfume."

"Were you one of them?" I asked.

Rory shook his head. "I heard about it, but I didn't know any omegas to attempt practicing. Your perfume, though…it's hard to explain. There's the hindbrain response, but also you kind of smell like home? So I have an alpha reaction, but not to *you* specifically."

Rory had moved his walking up to my side, staying between me and the road, occasionally checking over his shoulder. He and I had never spoken so much before, and I found him surprisingly relaxing to be around, given how aggressive I'd assumed he was from the start. His scent was also more mellow this morning than it was when he and Eve were bickering.

"Do you have any combat training?"

I blinked and turned to stare up at Rory. His eyes were focused out, watching the neighborhood around us.

"Uh, no, definitely not," I laughed. "I got into some fights growing up, and I try and stay in shape——"

Rory shrugged. "Being willing to throw a punch is fine, but knowing *how* to is something else. We should cover some basics. Evasive maneuvers, defensive tactics, just in case the rest of us aren't ever fast enough."

He's my alpha, I thought, surprised and unexpectedly pleased. Not in a knot me, bite me, bond me way, like Garrett and Eve. Not in the way I'd assumed alphas took claim of an omega. Rory said I smelled like home and then offered to teach me how to defend myself. He brought me clothes and told me to eat breakfast. He was protecting me, and he'd been the first one to declare that having children wasn't a determining factor in being family, pack.

"You don't have to, we'll keep you safe," Rory added, words rolling out faster, maybe even nervous.

"No, sorry! I want to, yes. I appreciate that—you. I appreciate the offer, and I accept," I said.

Rory nodded, still glaring and frowning out at the rest of the world, daring it to make a move in my direction.

———

"ADAM, LEFT! DUCK. OKAY, NOW—NO!"

I huffed and stumbled back, sweeping sweaty strands of hair back off my face again. Across from me, Jamie rose up from the crouch, shaking himself loose. He didn't look half as worn out as me, but Eve had mentioned he was in impressively good form, which meant a lot coming from her.

"Sorry, Jamie, if you'd finished that, you might've sprained something. Adam, you need to focus," Rory said, hands on his waist.

He was in a pair of gym shorts, hands and forearms bound with athletic tape after giving me a 'warm-up' on a punching bag that had left my whole body as loose and formless as jello. He was shirtless, showing off a rather beautiful collection of sacred geometry designs tattooed over his arms and chest, an unexpectedly thoughtful adornment on the alpha.

Fingers snapped in front of my eyes, and I shook my head, clearing my mind.

"I need a break," I whined.

Rory rolled his eyes, and I cleared my throat, embarrassed I'd let the sound out in front of him. "You said you kept in shape," he reminded me.

"I mean, I did! For a while. And then, you know, I was running for my life, and then I was locked in an apartment, and now I'm…here."

"Meh, meh, meh," Jamie teased, dodging out of the way as I lunged at him. "I'm kidding! Rory, he's probably right. Your warm-ups are killer."

Rory looked dubious, but he was also six-foot-five and built like a brick wall. He probably ate barbells for breakfast with his cereal. He opened his mouth to argue the point, and the door to the basement opened.

"Are you torturing my omega?" Eve called out, announcing herself as she moved lightly down the stairs.

Whatever point Rory had been prepared to make seemed to dry in his throat. Eve's hair was piled high on her head, and she was dressed in deadly spandex, every muscle and curve visible, those arms I loved to pin me down bare and elegant, loose at her sides.

"He asked me to train him," Rory said, just a touch defensive.

"He offered and I agreed, but I didn't know his version of training was attempted *murder*," I corrected.

Eve approached me, and I leaned into her. I'd found her scent overwhelming and harsh once. I didn't know if it had changed, or if the bond just altered my sense of smell. Maybe she had some addictive ingredient, like alpha nicotine.

"You're a mess, sugar," Eve murmured, wrinkling her nose at me.

I was really sweaty, but no more so than when she was having her fun with me during sex. "Make the mean alpha leave me alone," I said, faking a pout.

Rory growled, but the sound was more familiar now—

annoyed and maybe even a little amused. "I'm *trying* to make sure he knows how to defend himself. If he has to."

Eve hummed and dug her fingers into my aching shoulders, drawing out a moan from my chest. "Good of you, but I want him still standing tomorrow too. Come on, big guy, time to pick on someone your own size," Eve said.

I expected Rory to laugh. Eve was probably about half his weight. Instead, his stare became keen and focused on her, hungry. Jamie stepped out from between them and waved me over to the far wall of the basement gym.

"This could get rowdy—let's watch from a safe distance," he suggested.

Eve kissed my cheek and then patted my ass, directing me after Jamie. "Hydrate and stretch."

Considering Rory was looking at Eve like she'd just proposed some elaborate foreplay, I was surprised we were invited to stay and watch, but then again, I wasn't going to say no. These two were fascinating, and kind of ridiculous.

"Should we text Garrett?" I asked Jamie.

He laughed and shook his head, passing me my water bottle. "Garrett'll make Rory self-conscious. Better just keep it to ourselves and hope he doesn't realize he has an audience."

"I was running evasive maneuvers with him," Rory said to Eve.

"Fine."

"Do you want—"

"We don't need choreography. Just see what you can get away with," Eve challenged.

She looked so much smaller from this distance, but she was standing relaxed and open, where Rory was crunching in on himself. Then he tensed, his knees bending slightly, and dove for her.

Eve sidestepped him, grabbed him around his back,

and then propelled herself backwards, making Rory somersault and land heavily on his back. Eve rolled and sprang back up, catching one breath and then returning to almost the exact same position she started in.

"You can do better," she said.

"She makes that look annoyingly easy," Jamie murmured with a shake of his head.

"Is she finished healing?"

Rory stood, his back to Eve, and I thought there was a soft curve on his otherwise grim lips, but I couldn't be certain.

"I don't think so, but she's able to compensate," Jamie said. "Mostly healed."

I nodded and watched as Rory spun and started another attack, this time using his height as the advantage, grabbing Eve from behind, trapping her arms and holding his ground as she tried to unbalance him again.

Jamie sat forward, eyes narrowed as Eve struggled. His mouth opened, but he shut it just as quickly. At that same moment, Eve kicked out at the inside of one of Rory's knees, and he grunted, losing stability and allowing her to throw them both to the mat. He was still holding her tight in his arms though.

"You're worried?" I whispered to Jamie.

"Only that he'll get competitive and forget—"

Eve's heels braced against the floor, kicking her up and backwards, forcing Rory's arms loose. She rose quickly, but Rory was ready, rolling and grabbing one of Eve's ankles, yanking her back to the floor. I gasped as she hit the ground, but she barely made a sound, her feet bracing and her calves locking Rory's head between them, squeezing fiercely. There was a tense silence, Rory's hand still grasping onto her ankle, and then suddenly it released, slapping at the floor. Eve held him tight, Rory's face red and pointed down at the mat, and Jamie and I both tensed.

Rory let out a strangled grunt, and Eve released him. He sagged against the floor, gasping for air as she skirted away and stood, glaring down at him, hesitating. He let out another grunt, a huff, and then I realized he was laughing, his back shaking. He pushed up onto his knees, staring up at Eve with something like reverence.

Jamie snorted, glanced at me, and then nodded to Rory's lap, where there was an obvious bulge tenting the thin material of his gym shorts.

"Jesus," I whispered.

"Yeah. Those two need him," Jamie agreed, grinning.

"Again," Eve taunted.

Rory rose from the floor, his shoulders broad and knees slightly bent, throat red from being strangled. "Again," he nodded.

THERE WAS a side effect to all the training and sparring of the last few days.

Fighting was an aphrodisiac to an alpha.

Garrett was thrashing in the pit of the nest, his hands stretched back behind his head with a pretty bow of silk tying his wrists together. Eve's nails were digging into his chest as she rode his cock, her breaths harsh and uneven, brow furrowed. Garrett howled and Eve paused, grinding against his knot before finding me in the corner, her head tipping playfully as Garrett tried to buck up into her.

"Not joining us?" Eve purred, the muscles of her thighs tensing as she held Garrett down below her.

I grinned and shook my head, my own hand wrapped

loosely around my bare cock, only squeezing every few seconds to stimulate myself as I watched my alphas.

"You know you want to," Eve growled, rocking on Garrett and drawing out a long and whimpering moan from his lips.

Her lock must've tightened around his cock; he always went completely limp at that point.

"What I know is that every night we train with Rory, you end up dragging me and Garrett up to bed and fucking us until we can't so much as twitch. So I'll just wait for my turn when you've worn Garrett out, please and thank you."

"Eve," Garrett rasped, arms straining, eyes wide.

My alpha was glaring at me, her eyes narrowed. She pricked at me in the bond, and I arched an eyebrow back at her.

"You could just fuck him, you know," I said, but my voice wobbled, aware that I was treading on slightly dangerous ground now.

"Sugar," Eve said, except the word was laced with bark, and my hand clenched around my cock, making me gasp. "Come here."

I let out a soft whine, and Garrett started trying to thrust up again. I rose compulsively from the corner I'd tucked myself into and shuffled on my knees over to my alphas.

"Untie him," Eve said, her voice dark.

She'd been playing sweet for days now, and I'd forgotten what it was like when I drew out the side of her that possessed me completely, even my own will. Maybe I'd been egging her on *on purpose*.

I hurried to untie Garrett's wrists above his head, not sure what was coming next. Garrett's hands flashed to Eve's hips, his eyes wide and a little wild, and I gasped as he rolled them so that Eve was on her back. But she must've known what was coming because she was still glaring at me as Garrett started to fuck her wildly, pushing her knees back toward her chest, his own head thrown back.

"Fuck his ass," Eve said to me.

My cock throbbed at the order, and Garrett shuddered. I wasn't even sure if he was aware of his own position or if he was just chasing his own relief. Apparently, Eve's lock worked something like a cock ring on him if it tightened early enough, refusing him his orgasm and making him a little crazed.

"Are you—?"

Eve reached around Garrett's hips and spread his ass for me. "Do as I say," she said softly.

Arousal was running down my length and I hurried to obey. Not that it was some kind of *hardship* to fuck my alpha, even if what I really wanted was to be between them.

I pulled the plug free from Garrett's ass, distracting him briefly and making him moan as I pressed my cock to his hole, pumping my length and lubricating him with my excessive pre-cum.

"Now," Eve barked, not loud, but sharp all the same.

My hips bucked, following the order, and Garrett and I groaned in unison.

"Good boys," Eve purred, the praise a little rough as Garrett and I started to thrust in unison. "Fuck your alpha the way she likes."

I wrapped my arms around Garrett's chest to anchor myself, pressed my lips to his shoulder, and stared down at Eve as he and I rocked together. She was sweaty, breathless, eyes hooded and glinting with hunger back at me. A warning in her stare, but also delighted amusement.

She was going to break and take Rory sooner or later, I was sure of it. But it was in my best interest to enjoy this almost obsessive desire of hers in the meantime.

I gasped as Garrett started to clench on my length, not quite a lock but close, and did as my alpha bade me.

THIRTY-SIX

Eve

"Hey. We're going up to help with dinner."

I grunted in answer, my feet slipping against the mat as I grappled with Rory, half tempted to nip at his bicep just to shock him into letting me go.

"Have fun, you two," Adam chimed in, following Jamie up the stairs.

I *was* having fun, actually, in spite of Adam's recent taunting. I had been for the past few days of sparring with Rory after he finished training Adam. Not that the same could be said for all of us.

"What's got your panties in a bunch?" I rasped at Rory as soon as the basement door shut behind the others. I tried to hook my foot behind his ankle, but he shifted a step. "You know, I take issue with you growling at my omega like that."

Adam had been improving in his training, but every so often he used his ability to read people as a second weapon. He'd made a stray comment, one I hadn't been able to hear, under his breath as he tried to slip free of a hold from Rory, and got a full alpha growl in response before Rory cleared his throat and called their session done.

Rory's hands flexed and tightened against me, and then his arms wrapped around my waist, lifting me off my feet and tossing me back. I gasped, catching my balance with a few bounces and glaring at Rory as he drew back, turning away from me toward the mirrors. I gave him a snarl in warning and then launched myself at his back, wrapping my arms around his shoulders, my foot braced at the base of his back.

And with a quick bark of a growl, Rory reached back with one arm and swung me around his shoulder, throwing me aside again. There was no chance of getting my feet under me this time, and I landed on my left hip and shoulder, rolling away, laughing.

"Has someone been holding back?" I asked, pushing up off the floor, spinning to face Rory again.

His eyes were already fastened to me, wide and worried, but they narrowed in anger at my question. "Holding back?" he spat, an eyebrow arching. He was braced to fight but not charging at me, and there was a harsh, almost chemical note to his scent. His mouth opened and then he blinked, pausing and looking away. He sighed, body slowly relaxing, visibly forcing the tension out of himself.

Rory shook his head and stepped forward, aiming to move past me. "I'm not in the mood for this. I'm going—"

"Upstairs?" I asked, stepping in front of him.

He blinked at me, and the glance seemed to touch every inch of me before darting away again. Rory grunted and stepped to the right. "Yeah."

I mirrored him and grinned as that glance returned, annoyed and narrowing. "To shower?"

Rory's jaw clenched. "Eve—"

"Be honest. You jump in the shower and jerk off after every training," I said.

I knew what I was doing, goading Rory like this, but I wasn't sure he did. He tensed and his cheeks flushed, but his hands were in fists and his stare was over my head, on the stairs, like he was trying to teleport away from me. I stepped forward and watched his chest, bare and beautifully decorated in his intricate tattoos, flex and brace.

"Are you hard now?" I asked.

"Are you wet?" Rory snarled, teeth suddenly bared as he lunged forward, eyes blazing on mine. Just as quickly, the color rinsed from his expression and he sucked in a breath, a shaking hand reaching up to cover his eyes. "Fuck, I—I'm trying to—"

"Why don't you find out."

Rory went quiet, face still covered. That harsh note was still in the air between us. He straightened and dropped his hand slowly, and I was frustrated at how unreadable he suddenly was. I reached out between us, my hand hovering just in front of his hips, heat kissing my palm. It might've been an accident or unconscious, but Rory swayed in front of me, pressing himself gently against my touch. He was only just starting to grow stiff, and his cock jumped against my hand, his frown deep and tortured even as an anxious purr trembled up from his chest.

His own hand reached out, just barely grazing against the waistband of my workout leggings, when I pulled away.

"If you can," I challenged.

His expression shuttered again, and I realized with an unexpected pang of disappointment that at some point in the past week, or month, I might've played with Rory a little *too* long. Cat and mouse was all well and good until the mouse was dead, and I wasn't sure if I'd let Rory's simmering arousal cool rather than bring it to a boil.

It's not a loss, I tried to tell myself, but the voice in my head was unconvincing.

And then Rory snarled and dove for me, managing to scoop me up from the floor with one arm around my waist. My growl was instinct, but there was a grin stretching my lips, and Rory threw us to the floor, knocking the air out of me. One of his legs wedged between mine, and I arched, grinding against the muscle of his thigh, his cock rubbing against my hip. Rory's eyes fell shut, his lips parted, and then I twisted, pinching his thigh between mine and shoving him roughly over. His arm around my waist dragged me with him, and I straddled his hips, seated directly over his rapidly thickening cock.

I rocked on the spot, and Rory's face went slack, mouth open in a moan.

"Eve, I—" he gasped out, but I interrupted him by reaching back to take his arm around my waist and twist it just roughly enough for him to lose his grip on me. He arched beneath me with a howl that cracked open into laughter. "Fuck!"

I rose up above him, releasing his wrist before I could do more than bruise it. Rory sat up and reached for the back of my thighs, fingers digging into muscle, holding me in place. I could shake him off easily enough, but I waited to see what he would do. He shuffled onto his knees, immediately pressing his face between my legs, purring into the fabric of my leggings.

"You smell wet," he growled.

I grabbed the short strands of his hair on top of his head and pulled until his eyes flew up to meet mine. He opened his mouth, teeth bared, and wrapped a gentle bite around my sex through the leggings, dragging and nipping right over my clit. I was so surprised by the clench of my cunt that I almost missed the slow glide of Rory's hands up the back of my thighs, but then his fingers hooked into the waistband of my leggings and I remembered my challenge.

With a grip on Rory's shoulders, I yanked myself away and threw him to the floor, a satisfying *smack!* of his face against the mat and an annoyed grunt from him in answer. I jumped around to his back, hooking my arm around his throat and squeezing as he sat up. Rory's purr thundered in his chest as he rose, the sound vibrating against my bicep along with the pound of his pulse.

We were reflected in the mirror, me clinging to his back, our skin glowing and sweaty. Rory's face was growing red, and I was just about to release him when he rose up to his knees, holding my gaze in the mirror as he reached into the loose waistband of his gym shorts to fist at his hard cock.

"Push them down," I hissed, nipping at his ear.

He wrestled his shorts down with his free hand, revealing the angry length of his cock in his fist, as dark as his face. I flexed and released, and Rory shuddered against me. He was pumping himself roughly, covering his fingers over his head and then spreading his pre-cum around his thick shaft.

He's going to get himself off like this, I realized, squeezing and releasing again, allowing Rory to gasp for one breath before I tightened my hold again, his purr now a roar echoing off of every surface.

Except, of course, that wasn't what I'd ordered Rory to do.

His free hand reached up to my shoulder, and he threw himself forward. I released his throat as he vaulted me over him and then flat onto my back with a harsh slam of the mat against my shoulders. I groaned, and Rory arched over me, grinning, face still red and sweating.

His shorts were still inched down his hips and his cock was hard, just a foot or so away as he bent and bit at my left breast through the sports bra. One of his hands reached in at the collar, gripping the flesh and pinching at the nipple. It was too much torture and relief all at once not to let him continue.

"Take it off," I said, and his hands were quick, yanking the elastic band up over my breasts, his mouth immediately latching onto a nipple as I was left to wrestle the bra the rest of the way off.

"Fuck, you taste good," Rory growled.

Which was such a rare thing to hear that I rewarded him with an arch of my back, my hands reaching up to stroke his shoulders. Normally my scent, my taste, was found to be an irritant. Rory was all depth and richness and sweetness now, and I was still rough smoke compared to him, but he was lapping and sucking on every inch of my breasts like I was dessert.

One of his hands smoothed down my stomach and I considered throwing him off of me, but the promise of being touched was better than the game I'd issued. His fingers found their way into my leggings, and I wiggled closer to his cock, reaching back above my head to wrap my hands around him. He was as thick as Adam, but without any of the softness.

You like a challenge, I reminded myself.

Rory's hand cupped possessively around my sex, fingers rubbing and gathering the generous arousal pooling against my folds.

"Fuck. Fuck. *Eve*."

The ache in my name was too much. I threw my legs

up in the air and back, latching them around Rory's shoulders, and rolling us again.

Rory snarled up at me from the floor as I stood. "If you walk out of here—"

I paused. He was sprawled out on the floor beneath me, face staring up at me from directly between my legs. "You'll what?" I asked, mostly just curious.

He looked puzzled for a moment, annoyed, and then he sighed and went lax. "Go upstairs to shower and jerk off, I guess," he admitted lowly. "You know I'm not really going to force—"

I hooked my fingers into my leggings and yanked them down to my knees, cutting off Rory's confession.

Yes, I knew Rory wouldn't force me, or hold my unwillingness to fuck him against me, or try and threaten me into finishing what we'd started here. It was why I hadn't left yet. It was why, in spite of his being massive and snarling and bossy, I still wanted to sit on that fat cock until I could feel it up in my throat.

Rory was torn between watching the leggings on their path down my legs and just staring up at my cunt.

"Don't tell me it was that easy to break you," I said, kicking off one leg.

Rory huffed, shook his head, and then sat up. I was still stepping out of the other leg by the time he jumped up from the floor, and I'd barely glanced at him before he had me up in his arms and then thrown against the mirror, pinned there between it and him. His hips were nestled against mine, dark eyes glaring down at me, and he rocked in place, rubbing his cock through the lips of my sex.

"Don't tell me it's this easy to catch you," he said, that cocky little eyebrow arching again.

Generally, no. But the truth was that Rory was hot and

hard and huge against me, and while that wasn't usually my *type*, he was holding a momentary appeal.

Okay, maybe more than momentary. I stretched in his arms, his eyes widening in surprise as I rubbed my cheek to his once, and then tilted my head to slant my mouth over his in a kiss. He groaned into the kiss, our tongues stroking in time with the gentle thrust of his cock up and down against my sex. Our chests were plastered together, my nipples hard and vibrating with the force of my purr.

I wanted to crush Rory. I suspected that someday, I might want him to crush *me*. I wanted to prove to us both that I was the dominant alpha, that he would be conquered the way I once was. The fact that we both enjoyed the battle made him that much more appealing.

I wanted to bite him. Fuck him.

Lock him.

It would be brutal and rough and possibly painful, but…but we liked that, the pair of us.

I scratched my nails deep into his back, and Rory's mouth yanked away to howl in pain. I reached up and tightened my other hand around his throat. His hips kicked against mine, trying to notch his cock inside of me. I shoved him roughly, and Rory stumbled back, mouth open on a question.

I kicked my foot against the back of his legs and he dropped hard onto the mat with a breathless grunt.

"Stay down," I barked, full alpha, and Rory's fisted hands flattened against the mat in their effort to obey my command.

I hooked my heel into his drooping shorts and finished dragging them the rest of the way off. We were both fully naked now, equally and separately powerful. But I'd told him ages ago that I was the alpha, and I'd meant the claim. We both knew it was true. Rory *wanted* it to be true, a weight of strength off his shoulders when he was with me, just like I shed my own when I was with Jamie.

"Do *not* challenge me," I warned Rory.

He was licking his lips, full and surprisingly gentle in a kiss, and I considered using them now. He'd been so thorough with that tongue of his the other night in the kitchen. But his cock was weeping and begging in its stretch toward me.

"Yes, alpha," Rory whispered.

I resisted the call to shiver at the word. Maybe another time, I would show Rory what his surrender did to me, but I wanted to hold the reins tightly now.

I knelt over his lap, just rubbing the very tip of his cock with my sex for a moment, watching his fingers clench at the mat.

"Put yourself inside of me," I said, pressing one hand to his stomach to keep him from surging up.

"Let me touch you first," Rory rasped out, eyebrows drawn almost completely together. "Lick you, taste you."

"No."

Rory moaned briefly, wrapping his hand around his cock and holding it still just at my opening, his fingertips sliding up to press into me briefly. He wasn't even an inch inside of me, his chest heaving with breath, gaze pleading.

"I said, *inside* of me."

Rory's growl was bit off, his hips lifting from the floor, cock pressing into me with a slight burn from the stretch, but dense relief at the pressure of him too. He was halfway in when I slammed myself down, both of us shouting wordlessly up at the ceiling.

"Oh god, yes, Eve. Alpha, please."

The word was different on his lips than Adam's. A constant reminder of my dominance, both won and *offered*. I'd expected that to leave a bitter taste in my mouth, but all

I could taste now was Rory's need on the air, creamy and dark and desperate.

"*Eve*," he choked out.

My lock was tightening already. "You like it?" I asked, laughing.

Rory let out an animal groan, his eyes rolling up slightly and his hips starting to bounce. Ahhhh, he wanted me to move. I leaned forward and pinned him down, one hand on his chest and the other on his throat, careful but stern.

"Did I tell you to fuck me?"

"No, alpha," Rory rasped, relaxing beneath me.

"I asked you a question before," I reminded him.

"Yes, I fucking like it, it feels like you're about to snap my dick off. I want it around my knot, but I think it might fucking kill me," Rory snarled, glaring at me.

I tweaked his nipple, and his hips snapped up and then hit the mat again immediately, his cheeks flushing.

"Sorry," he said, almost sounding as though he really meant it.

I purred, and Rory shuddered as I rose slowly up his length and then slid gently back down again. Which was nice. He was thick and hard as a fucking rock and his knot wasn't as pronounced as Jamie's, but it still felt good against my opening now that I was used to the sensation. But slow and steady wasn't really our speed.

"Hands on my hips," I whispered.

Rory's hands were tight on my hips, but he didn't do anything else.

"Good boy," I purred, and Rory glared at me, but his own purr grew even louder.

I rose up again and then slammed immediately down. I held Rory to the floor and fucked myself onto his length like I was trying to kill us both. He scrambled and thrashed beneath me, throat flexing under my palm, and his cock throbbed inside of me.

"You tell me before you're about to come or you never get this cunt again," I snapped to him.

He nodded eagerly, his whole body tensed in one long line of strain. Holding himself back, I realized.

"Are you going to help or not?" I asked, grinning and panting as I kept the rough, hard pace.

Rory let out a bellow of relief, ass drumming against the floor with his own thrusts and rough fucking. His knot stretched and tugged at my cunt, but he was careful not to bury it in me. His thumb stretched over my hip to rub and press against my clit, and he howled as my lock started to tighten.

Any closer to coming, and I wouldn't be able to take Rory's knot. He would be too swollen and I would be too tight.

What would it feel like if it were inside me now, grinding and digging against my lock?

Find out, a voice whispered in my head.

And I'd always been a creature of impulse when it came to these men.

"Eve, fuck, I'm too close, we have to—"

It took more than just the idea though. Strictly speaking, Rory and I weren't meant to be compatible. He didn't understand at first the sudden force of me trying to bear down on his knot, and he drew back.

I squeezed my fingers around his throat until his gaze snapped to mine, his eyes widening.

"You're mine," I gasped out.

I hadn't learned how to do things in half-measures. If I was keeping Adam, keeping this pack, then I was going to *possess* them entirely. Even Rory.

Especially Rory, who spent too much time worrying about the others to really enjoy being part of the pack.

Rory pushed his hips up and there was a popping sensation, painful, but in that low and aching way that just pulsed with the blood pounding in my veins, and then neither of us could draw away from one another. I yelped, immediately twisting my hips, and it only took one nudge of his knot against my front walls for me to be coming, a violent crash of sensation that was more explosive than pleasurable.

Rory howled, and I released his throat, allowing him to shake and buck below me. He was hot and flooding me, his fingers digging in roughly to my hips, grounding me from the torment of where we were joined. I yanked on one of his shoulders and he sat up, arms twisting around my waist to pull me flush against his hips.

"You're mine," I breathed, and Rory nodded loosely.

His head fell back and his eyes were blown black with arousal. He shivered, and the press of the knot left us both gasping. I hadn't come down from the first rush and there wasn't anywhere left to go, but the crushing force of knot to lock just suspended the moment.

"Eve," Rory hissed, tilting his head, exposing his throat.

There was only one natural conclusion.

"Yours," he moaned.

I growled and dove down, biting him so deep it hurt my jaw, snarling into the echo of his pain flooding the bond. The relief too. The old hints of jealousy he'd been bearing against the others. The satisfaction of this tenderly destructive physical relief.

Rory groaned and came again, making the clasp of us together a little less sharp. I rocked and stars burst behind my eyes, my purr embedded in Rory's throat.

Rory sighed, and the flex of muscle strained against my

teeth. I'd bitten too deep. It was time to start cleaning and healing him, but I stayed in place, my jaw aching.

"I was afraid you'd regret it," Rory murmured.

I licked around the wound, slowly disengaging. "This won't make me sweet," I said, and he snorted. "But no, I don't regret it."

"I don't know when I'll be calm enough for us to pull loose. Hurts like hell."

"And you love it."

Rory leaned back and met my eyes. He was surprisingly calm in the bond, centered and relaxed and…easy to sit alongside. "I do, yeah."

I swallowed and ducked my head, licking at my mark and feeling Rory throb inside of me. It had hurt like hell. Now it was starting to feel dangerously good. Painful, but powerful. I shifted and Rory groaned, moving gently beneath me.

"Adam is laughing at us," Rory whispered.

That was true, but Adam was pleased too. A lovely, warm, supportive beam of sunshine in the bond.

"Mm, I'll spank him later for it." Rory's arousal answered in the bond, and I smirked. "Oh. Do you want to watch, or—"

"We'd better get you a paddle or your hand is going to get sore," Rory rasped in my ear.

THIRTY-SEVEN

Eve

Rory had transformed overnight from an enormous growling bear into a ridiculous pussy cat, complete with rubbing up against me as he passed on the way to pour himself a cup of coffee in the morning and lying on the couch with his head in my lap, purring. I would've been annoyed if I weren't being bombarded with contentment by my new outrageously satisfied bondmate.

Adam and Garrett, on the other hand, were providing me with plenty of anxiety as Adam paced in front of the couch, Garrett watching him with a worried furrow on his brow.

"I keep getting *distracted*," Adam hissed, hands clenching at his side. "I went to a fucking barbecue while Faith's out there—"

"Where?" I asked, cutting off Adam's tirade.

He blinked at me, the steady drum of his footsteps stalling against the floorboards. "What? I don't know! That's the problem!"

"It is," I said, nodding. "One we are doing our best to solve, but—"

"She's my *sister*!"

"And she has been in danger for weeks," I said bluntly, interrupting Rory's hum of comfort. One of his eyes opened up to glare at me, a prick of irritation coming from him in the bond.

Adam gaped at me, face red and eyes filling up, while Garrett battered me with frustration.

"It was not your fault, Adam," I said, and Rory huffed and went back to purring. "And it's not your fault that you can't pry information out of the other omegas on that server."

"She's right," Garrett chimed in quickly, frustration melting away into gratitude. "Either they don't know anything or they're refusing to tell you. We just have to keep trying."

Adam's arms flapped at his side. "But—"

"But what? What do you want to do? Get in the Charger and start driving around, knocking on the door of every dubiously moral alpha in the world to see if they have your sister hidden away?" I asked. Garrett growled at me, and I rolled my eyes. "He's a grown man, quit coddling him."

"He's *upset*," Garrett hissed back.

"Of course he is, but he'll be in much worse shape if we tiptoe around him and he gets it in his head to take off looking for Faith," I answered.

Garrett gaped at me for a moment before turning to Adam. "You wouldn't?"

Adam glared at me, those sharp cheekbones even more prominent with the tension in his expression. I tilted my head, waiting for him to crack, ignoring the twinge in my chest as one of those tears that had been filling up his pretty eyes spilled over.

He huffed and sagged, falling onto the large footstool in a heap. "I just can't believe I haven't *done* anything."

I sighed and nudged Rory's shoulder. "Move," I murmured to him. He turned his head and rubbed his cheek against my thigh before sitting up, allowing me to cross to Adam. I sank down on my knees in front of Adam so I was able to see his face, wrapping my hands around his calves. "You have provided incredible amounts of information against Omikron. You found me, this pack. You've been *searching* for information on Faith's whereabouts. So have I," I reminded him. I'd just found the information too late.

"But—"

"Adam, if I had the remotest idea of where she was, we would be on our way," I said.

Adam's chin lifted, his eyes narrowed at me, and I was surprised by the note of suspicion coming from him. "Would we? Or would you be more concerned about keeping me safe because I'm your—"

I sat up, grabbing his face in my hands and pulling him in for a rough and deep kiss, his whine almost strangled against my tongue. I released him when he struggled against me and gripped his chin in a firm pinch, holding his blazing stare. "You matter to me, you little shit." Adam's eyes went wide and he hiccuped, lips parting but no sound coming out. "You are hurting, and so am I because of this…not entirely awful bond we have," I said through gritted teeth.

Adam's smile wobbled. "Is this you being romantic?"

"*When* we receive information about Faith's whereabouts, it will be my first priority to retrieve—"

"Rescue," Adam corrected.

"—her and bring her back to you. But we may need to have a discussion about where you'd be most safe, depending on how suspect the information is."

Adam swallowed and stared back at me for a long stretch of quiet before nodding, face still pinched in my hand. "I trust you. But you have to be nice to her and not growl at her, and if there's *any* issue—"

"I promise," I said, nodding.

Adam held his breath and then swooped in, wrapping his arms around me and groaning against my shoulder. I tuned into the others for the first time since I'd moved to Adam and then wrinkled my nose.

"Oh, calm down. This is nothing to get excited over," I snapped at a beaming Garrett.

He laughed and shook his head, hands raising at his side. "I can't help it. But sure, I'll just pretend not to notice that you can be sweet when you want."

"I won't," Rory said lowly.

I rolled my eyes, but my hands were already stroking up and down Adam's back. Fine. I cared about my omega…and my pack. It wasn't worth this level of elation they were bombing me with.

I stiffened as the kitchen door opened and then realized Jamie was coming in from his shop. He was the only member of the pack I hadn't bonded with, and I was startled to realize I actually *wanted* yet another connection. Now that I was growing used to sensing my packmates around me, their emotions and their presence, it was unexpectedly irritating to be missing out on Jamie.

"Hey—Oh, hey, this is cute, but we've got a car pulling into the drive."

Adam sat back, and I stood at the same time as the others, Rory hurrying to the window.

"Shit," he barked.

"Omikron," I guessed, heading for the fireplace where I'd hidden a few weapons.

"No," Rory said quickly, a sort of guarded resignation rising up after the initial shock. "No, it's our boss."

It took me a moment before the information really sank in, my shoulders sagging as I stood and glanced out the window. Oh, Wes Pike. Well that wasn't nearly concerning enough to warrant Rory's guilt and Garrett's new nerves.

"*Oh*," I said, smirking as it hit me. "You never told him."

"Maybe they should go upstairs?" Garrett suggested to Rory, nodding his head in mine and Adam's direction.

"Pretty sure he'll still know we're here," I teased. "I fucked Adam on the couch while none of you were around."

"Eve," Adam hissed.

"Trust me, we already knew," Jamie tossed to me, his crooked smile casual as Garrett and Rory shared a tense, unspoken conversation.

Rory seemed to grow taller, watching out the window, and shook his head lightly. "Why lie? It's going to change everything anyway."

Garrett sighed and nodded. "His disappointed dad face just kills me."

Rory and Garrett moved to meet Wes at the door, and I drew Adam to the couch with me, Jamie on his other side. Adam curved into me, hands fidgeting in his lap, and my arm migrated around his shoulders to draw him in closer as the front door opened.

"What the fuck, guys?" Wes Pike greeted my pack-mates. "When was anybody going to tell me you weren't even using the safe house? And what the hell do you think —Jesus Christ, Stevens, is that a *bite mark*?!"

Adam's elbow nudged my side. "Don't look so pleased with yourself," he whispered at me. "What if they get fired?"

"They won't," I answered, as behind me I heard Garrett urge Wes inside the house.

"She's probably right," Jamie whispered to Adam. "Wes is kind of a softie."

Not that Wes Pike looked remotely soft, stomping through the house after Garrett, moving to stand in front of me and glare down with blue eyes on fire and that absurdly square jaw ticking.

"You needed *security*, huh?" Wes growled at me.

Adam stiffened at my side, and I opened my mouth to snarl back, but didn't get the chance.

"Don't bark at my pack," Rory said. Not a bark from him either, or a growl, but the words were firm and his heat appeared behind me, his hands framing my shoulders on the back of the couch, not touching but making it clear where his support was.

I would ride him until he couldn't walk later as a sign of my appreciation. Maybe not the knot, though; I was still surprisingly sore from that experience.

"Rory, Garrett, this is—"

"I approached you in order to find alphas for Adam," I said to Wes. "I trusted you to know some that would actually keep Adam safe and not make him miserable. I had a good feeling about these two."

Wes' jaw hung loose at that declaration, his eyes darting over my head between his employees.

"It wasn't my intention to stay," I added with a shrug.

"We made that choice," Rory said to Wes. "The bites are—"

"Fresh," Wes said, squinting at Rory's.

"We'd already made the decision to bring Eve and

Adam into the pack," Garrett said. "Look, we should've told you about the safe house ages ago, you're right. And maybe about our pack decision too, but…but that's not strictly your business."

Wes looked back to me, glaring again, and Rory's hands slid to cover my shoulders. Part of me wanted to shrug the touch off, but I knew he only meant it as a sign to Wes that he was serious about me being pack. I wanted to bare my teeth at the other alpha, but I understood that his respect meant something to Garrett and Rory. *And theirs means something to me*, I grudgingly admitted to myself.

"If there's anyone you should be bothered about, it's me," Adam said to Wes. "I'm the one who put a target on the pack's back. On Eve's too."

"Just don't be bothered," Garrett rushed out, hurrying around the couch to stand in front of Adam. "It's done. We're bonded. The safe house is available."

Wes arched an eyebrow at Garrett, but his shoulders softened and he released a slow breath, helping himself to the footstool in front of us, which creaked in warning. "I went to the safe house to give you guys some good news, actually."

Adam sat up at that, and I squeezed his shoulder gently as Garrett stepped aside. I very much doubted Wes had heard anything about Faith when we still hadn't, but any progress in the case against Omikron would be good in the long run.

"Our lead in the FBI just got us word that they have proof of criminal activity against five of Omikron's top investors," Wes said.

"In relation to Omikron?" Garrett asked.

Wes shook his head, palms open to us. "No, but the hope is they will broker a deal on information against Omikron's higher-ups."

"And if there is no information for them to give?" Adam asked, voice raising, obviously disappointed in what Wes was offering.

"Someone will know something," Garrett assured Adam.

"They'll just replace those men," Adam snapped back.

Wes and I shared a long look, and I spoke up, "It may be the moment of chaos we need to break it up further, to learn more. It's a crack in the wall, and that might be all it takes."

"It might also be enough of a disruption to take the attention off of us for a bit," Garrett said to Adam.

"You've had trouble? Here?" Wes asked, frowning. "Jesus, why didn't you guys say anything? You're my best employees—didn't you consider there might be some company perks?"

"Weapons?" I asked, perking up.

Wes huffed and glared at Rory, ignoring me. "What do you need?"

"We've got a local friend on surveillance, but he could use some backup, and extra hands for the neighborhood would help," Rory said. I tugged on our bond, and he let out a soft laugh. "And weapons."

As much fun as hard-ass Rory was to tease and wrestle, I didn't mind soft, indulgent Rory so much. Especially since it only seemed to take a good rough fuck to draw him out. I was more than happy to indulge him.

"I will pay for any resources," I said.

Wes started to growl and then quickly stifled the sound as Garrett and Jamie both shifted forward in my defense. "That's not necessary, these are my—"

"They are my pack, and there's only so far you should involve yourself, for the sake of your own pack," I said.

Wes' stare dropped and his jaw ground, but he

nodded after a moment. "Fine. I can get you a contact on untraceable weapons. We've got easy jobs in the office this month, so I can make sure you have familiar, trustworthy faces around the neighborhood. I'll keep on the FBI's ass too."

"Thank you, Wes," Garrett said.

Wes nodded again, rising up from the stool. "Look, you guys can come to me when shit goes belly-up, all right? Even when you're being dumbasses," he added, with a glance at me. "But don't lie to me. I'm around to help you."

"I know it might not make sense to you, but Eve and Adam aren't our pack now because of Omikron or the danger they're in," Jamie said, speaking up for the first time.

"We're pack because we fit together better with them," Rory said, his hand cupping gently over my shoulder, thumb stroking at my collarbone.

Wes' lips twitched at the declarations, and my eyes slid to Adam, who was as surprised and flattered by our pack-mates' statements as I was.

"Bonds don't happen lightly," Garrett said, catching my eye and grinning.

Maybe I hadn't given him fair warning, but he was right—I was deeply possessive of these men now that I was in their pack. I'd expected them to slow me down or get in my way, and it was a surprising revelation to find that even if they weren't *as* strong as me, they didn't subtract from my own strength. They added to it, actually, not that I would outright tell them so unless I had to.

"No, they don't," Wes agreed. Now that his temper had faded, I realized he had a surprisingly sweet and fresh scent to him, a little too sticky and syrupy for me, but not as sour as I'd gotten from him before. "All right. Sounds like I need to get to work."

"I'll walk you out," I said, rising and ignoring the pointed stares from my pack.

I kept thinking those words. *My pack.* It was feeling almost normal now.

Wes grunted and followed behind me to the front hall, Rory following us halfway before I turned to shake my head at him. Wes waited until we reached the door to say his piece, as I knew he would.

"You hurt a single one of them, I'll hire another contractor to kill you," Wes warned in a low alpha growl.

Easier said than done, I thought, but since that would only rile him up and I now appreciated his almost fatherly protective instincts for my men, I said, "Fair enough."

He blinked at me, head cocking and eyes narrowing. "And don't fucking sneak into our house again. Lola told me about that."

I smiled. It had taken her long enough. That was well over a year ago now. "I won't."

He squinted. I could reassure him further, but I'd more or less used up my niceties for the day. Hopefully, Rory or Garrett would be in the mood to get pounded in one way or another once Wes left.

"Fine," Wes muttered, shaking his head. I opened the door for him, and he stepped out before pausing just over the threshold. "I hope they're good to you too."

It was well and truly the last thing I expected to hear from him, so instead I only watched as he walked back to his car.

They are, I thought, closing the door as the engine outside started up.

THIRTY-EIGHT

Adam

Jabroni has logged off.

I groaned and pressed my hands over my face, breathing hard into my palms and rubbing at my tired eyes. Soft footsteps padded over the floorboards behind me, and my shoulders tensed.

"I'm pushing too hard," I moaned into my hands.

Eve said nothing, just slid over the arm of the chair and wrapped herself around my back, one leg draping over my lap as she drew me into her arms. I sighed and let her push my hands away from my face, my head falling back on her shoulder. She purred for me, the sound still charmingly broken and yet impossible to resist relaxing into.

"They may not know anything," Eve reminded me. I grunted, and she grazed a kiss against my temple.

I leaned into the mark of her lips on my skin, expecting her to draw away again, but her nose just nuzzled into my hair. "You're so…" I trailed off, suddenly afraid of speaking the words.

"Hm?"

I hesitated. Eve's remark the other day, that I *mattered* to her, hadn't been a surprise, but the fact that she'd said as much had caught me off guard.

"It's not that you're different now," I said slowly, waiting for that moment of tension, watching the bond between us and expecting the wall to go back up again.

"Aren't I?" Eve asked softly.

"No, but I guess… I just feel like now I get to…have more of you?"

Eve's hands soothed up and down my chest. I wanted to be angry with her for how easily she calmed me. I sometimes wondered if I weren't so busy falling in love with Eve and Garrett, I would've already found Faith. But the truth —as much as I hated to admit to myself—was that I'd been too busy spinning my wheels and running away from Omikron to turn and face them and find Faith. Until that night in the casino. Until Eve.

"You do have more of me now," Eve said, twisting so we could look at one another. Her eyes narrowed briefly. "You'd better like it."

I laughed at that and nodded. "I do."

Eve's smile was smooth and calm, no feral teasing, no guarded secrets. She leaned in, and I sighed as her mouth met mine. Eve might always be the alpha who would bite me again, who would call me a little shit and tell me she *liked* me. But she was mine, and for once I didn't doubt that fact. I sank into the kiss, our bodies twisting in the oversized armchair to fit closer together. Garrett and Rory were out briefing the new recruits from their boss, and Jamie was finishing up one of his last commissions, so Eve and I had the house to ourselves.

In less than two minutes, I was thrusting my hips against hers in time with her tongue licking against mine, wondering if she would strip me completely or just enough for us to fuck.

This is why Faith is missing—you're too busy being a hopeless omega, a sharp voice snarled in my head.

Eve pulled away first, strong fingers combing back my hair as she stared down at me. "Adam, you're not—"

A chime from the computer caught our attention, Eve sitting up and dragging me with her.

Private message from SubnBreed69.

"Do you trust them?" Eve asked me as I lurched forward, snatching up the laptop from the side table.

"Not... I don't know, really," I admitted, glancing between her and the screen.

She nodded. "All right. Let's see what they have to say. It's something, right?"

Maybe, I thought. But it was the first private message I'd received from anyone on the server since I'd started digging for information.

SubnBreed69: You know everyone just thinks Omikron has you now, right?

I huffed and typed back. *I figured as much. They're trying, but I'm safe.*

SubnBreed69: You get why that's hard to believe.

"You haven't told them about us?" Eve asked, and I shook my head. "Why worry about it now? Obviously, Omikron already knows."

"You're right, actually," I muttered, answering with, *I packed up.*

SubnBreed69: No way.

I'd been shouting on the server for years about how much I hated the idea of bonding a pack. I didn't blame them for their disbelief.

Eve leaned in, setting her lips to the lobe of my ear and making me shiver. "Brag about me."

I snorted and continued typing.

DontGiveADam: Used my wiles to get the alpha they sent to finish me off to bond me instead.

"Clever boy," Eve purred.

SubnBreed69: LMAO! Fucking genius. Where are you guys?

"Suspicious," I said.

"Very," Eve agreed.

DontGiveADam: Not even going there. No offense.

SubnBreed69: Fair enough. Look, I think I have a lead on Faith.

DontGiveADam: How? From where?

SubnBreed69: Not even going there.

I snarled, but Eve's hands covered my shoulders, her fingers slipping into my collar to stroke over a bite mark. "Can you blame them?" she asked.

"Yes. I can," I bit out.

DontGiveADam: Fair enough. And thank you for reaching out, at least. I get why people are suspicious, but this is fucking Faith. She deserves better than everyone covering their ass when she's in trouble.

SubnBreed69: Agreed. So here's the basics. There's a club in Montreal, basic stripper shit, except it caters to alphas only. And there's an "executive" package.

"Say the name, dickhead," Eve snarled, but she was already pulling out a phone and typing rapidly as Subn-Breed69 continued to type.

SubnBreed69: Pretty sure it's a company with trafficked omegas. They just announced a new "True Believers" feature.

"Faith," I gasped.

"Maybe. Remember that you don't even know if you trust this person," Eve said.

"But—"

"I'm verifying the club now. And I promised you, remember," she said. "I'll follow the lead. But just keep your expectations realistic, sugar."

I sucked in a deep breath, but Eve pursed her lips and

we both knew the truth. My hopes were already way too high; this was the only information I'd had in months. I needed to believe it was real. That I hadn't just wasted all this time while my sister was—

"Stop," Eve snapped, gripping my chin. "Don't stall out. Type, keep your head on."

I shook myself and turned back to the conversation.

DontGiveADam: It sounds like a possibility. Name of the club?

SubnBreed69: La Mousure Rouge. Will you go?

"Say yes," Eve said as I'd already started typing no.

"What, why?"

"Because if it's a trap, we want them to be prepared for the wrong thing," Eve said, shrugging.

Of course, she's my sister, I typed out. "But what if that just means Omikron is, like, *extra* prepared?"

"Sugar, I'd rather they all ran up to Montreal for me to deal with, than be here when I left," Eve said.

Which was…sweet. "Kiss," I ordered.

Eve slanted me a challenging look but then leaned in, sucking briefly on my bottom lip. "Get back to work."

I glanced back at the computer to find another message.

SubnBreed69: Isn't it time to stop being so cocky?

I snorted and shook my head.

DontGiveADam: Maybe, but I'm not dead yet. I'm going.

SubnBreed69: Well, shit. Good luck, man.

I banged out a quick thanks before tossing the computer aside, and twisted to face Eve. "Is it legit?"

"The club exists, and it seems like the claims are close. Still looking into the trafficking angle," Eve said.

"You think omegas are volunteering to be pawed at by alphas?"

"Perhaps, ones who don't want a pack or bonds," Eve

said with a shrug, looking up at me with a frown. "You don't think that's possible?"

"Well…okay, yeah, it's possible," I admitted, frowning. I'd heard of rich omegas hiring alpha escorts to get them through heats before they settled down with a pack. Mouthguards kept the alphas from taking an uninvited bite. Presumably, there might be an alternative in reverse. "How are you going to get in?"

Eve huffed. "Like they could keep me out."

Worry tumbled in my chest the longer I thought about the plan. I wasn't stupid, I didn't think I'd be a big help to Eve if the lead was real. And if it was a trap, my being with her would be even worse. I still didn't like the idea of her leaving, going up against a bunch of faceless mercenaries *again*.

"You're healed now, right?"

"Right as rain, sugar."

I chewed on my lip. "And you'll take one of them with you?" I asked, meaning one of our packmates.

Eve's expression hardened, her gaze drifting over my shoulder. "Do you think I could get away with *not* taking one of them?"

A sudden laugh burst out of me as I imagined Rory's face when he heard the news. "No, probably not."

Eve grumbled and continued texting her magic contact, the one I could barely get her to share any info on. Tabby, that was all I knew. "Text the guys," Eve ordered me. "We shouldn't waste any time."

RORY'S EXPRESSION exceeded my expectations, his brow knotted and teeth bared, broad shoulders hunched almost all the way up to his ears, looking taller and broader in the living room than usual. "This is bullshit," he growled.

"I know we said we'd follow any lead, but this one sounds...especially bogus, right?" Jamie asked Eve, frowning with his arms crossed over his chest.

"The club has connections to Omikron in their financials, so I wouldn't say especially," Garrett said slowly, his laptop open in his lap, but he was just as worried as the other alphas obviously were. "It's a risk, but we... I mean, it would be a risk no matter what, right?"

"I'm going, it really isn't up for debate," Eve said with a shrug.

"Eve—" Rory snapped.

"What *is* up for debate is which of you will come with me to help," Eve said. "Adam needs to remain here, it's the best safety we can give him, especially with Wes' reinforcements. But I could use an extra pair of competent hands."

I was curled up on the couch, my arms around my knees, as I stared up at my four alphas squaring off.

"I'd like to go," Garrett said quietly.

My stomach lurched at that, and he and Eve both spun to stare at me. "Sorry, I—" I shut my mouth and then closed it again, shaking my head. "It's fine. I want—I need you guys to bring Faith back if she's there, and that's literally all that—"

Except I couldn't finish the sentence.

Garrett and Eve were my bondmates. I didn't like the idea of Eve going to deal with Omikron, but her role as tarnished knight in a Dodge Charger was already more or less cemented in my head. She left me, she took care of problems, and she came back. She always came back. Garrett was...Garrett was comfort and company and touch; he was the one who was always *with* me. Eve was learning to be those things too now, but—

"Hey," Garrett said, hurrying over to the couch and settling at my side. "I just want to do whatever it is you need me to, you know that."

I sighed and let the words out in a rush, "I don't want both my bondmates gone at the same time. I know! I know I should be telling you *all* to go—"

"Not a chance," Eve and Rory said at the same time.

"—but if something happens and you're both in danger, I'll be a total fucking mess here and…and if—"

"I'm going to be fine," Eve said to me, simple and flat. "But Garrett, I agree with Adam. You should be here with him. Omikron shouldn't be swinging by when they think Adam and I are both heading north, but we know they're aware of our location and it would be better to be cautious, assume they have eyes on us."

"Deal," Garrett said, nodding once and wrapping an arm around my shoulder, pulling me in to press a quick kiss to my temple.

"I'm going with you," Jamie and Rory said to Eve at the same time.

"See, now you and I just get to watch them argue it out," Garrett said low in my ear, drawing out a half-hearted smile from my lips.

"Can't they both go?" I asked Eve.

"You're rusty on the field," Rory said matter-of-factly to Jamie, who glowered back at him.

"He's not," Eve said with a wave of her hand.

"I am compared to Rory," Jamie admitted, the words drawn slowly out, like he resented having to confess them. "If you didn't mind working with me…you'll be even more satisfied with him."

"Oh, I wouldn't say *more* satisfied," Eve purred at Jamie, who let out a soft laugh as Rory glared at them both.

"It will look natural around here if I take off for a

while. And protecting Adam needs to be equally important to us as retrieving Faith," Rory said, words sharp and firm. "He's pack. And she's his family. A smaller team going into Montreal might be what we need to sneak up on Omikron and—"

"Listen," Eve said, raising her hand to halt Rory's speech. "All of that may be true, but I'm not going to compromise or follow orders just because you're used to being in charge of a mission. You follow *my* lead, or you stay here."

Rory glared down his nose at Eve, and I thought for sure he was about to refuse.

"Obviously," he snarled out instead.

Eve smiled up at him—the feral and teasing one I was so familiar with—and his cheeks flushed. "Oh, good boy," she purred, rising up onto her toes and licking a kiss over his mouth as he remained stiff, annoyed, and obviously embarrassed.

Jamie turned away, and for the first time I saw a smile on his face that didn't sit quite right, like he was having to force it to stay up. "Well, that'll be an interesting trip," he said to me, shrugging.

"Don't worry. Rory won't let anything happen to her," Garrett said before his eyes widened. "I mean, either of them."

But I knew what he really meant. Finding Faith was a long shot.

Do you really want to send your alphas on a wild-goose chase? I wondered.

"It's something, Adam," Eve said, catching my eye, somehow reading my mind when I only had the barest access to hers. "And anyway, I never mind blowing off some steam by kicking the shit out of mercs. If they're still taking jobs from Omikron at this point, that's on them."

I let out a half-hearted laugh and nodded, trying to ignore the new queasy turn of my stomach. It would be fine. If Eve could take on dozens by herself, having Rory along certainly wouldn't hurt.

"I'll book your flight," Garrett said. "And you'll probably want to drive a car back, just in case."

Just in case they found Faith. Faith was worth the risk, at least that much I was certain of.

THIRTY-NINE

Jamie

I set the last plate on the shelf in the kitchen as the first whiff of smoke and curious sweetness reached my nose.

"Couldn't have shown up when I needed someone to dry, huh?" I asked. I was trying to tease, to be easy and charming, but a sharp bitterness broke through in the words. I grimaced at my own reflection in the glass cabinet.

"Why are you down here polishing the silver in the middle of the night?" Eve asked, jumping lightly up onto the counter. Her hair was braided back, loose and thick, and she was wearing the button-down I'd lent her weeks ago.

"Shouldn't you be upstairs with your omega?" I countered, but that was just as bitter as my first question and I dropped my gaze to the floor, fingertips tight around the edge of the counter.

It didn't matter, Eve's stare was a tangible tease, pleasantly scratching and trying to guide my eyes back up again.

"Adam's feeling sentimental and anxious. Garrett was

getting annoyed with my…bluntness. They're calming down together," Eve said.

"I'm feeling a little sentimental and anxious myself. Maybe you better go find Rory," I suggested, turning away from the counter.

Not fast enough, though. Eve's legs snapped around my hips, grabbing onto me and yanking me back to where she sat, tightening around my waist, the loveliest trap I'd ever found myself in. And yet my only response was a lump growing thicker in my throat.

"Don't tell me you're jealous," Eve murmured, bumping her forehead against mine.

I smiled at that, studying the faint freckles that always seemed like a surprise every time I studied her face. "No, I'm not. Well, maybe a bit. I'm jealous that it makes more sense for Rory to go with you to Montreal. I'm worried about you."

"Oh, you know me, I'm—"

"Don't," I rushed out, glaring at her. "Just… You don't have to reassure me. I know what you're capable of. I'm going to be worried anyway. I'd be worried if I was with you too."

"Maybe it's better that I'm taking Rory, in that case," Eve murmured, her arms sliding over my shoulders.

"Oh, Rory is going to be *so* worried," I said, grinning, finally able to swallow down that lump. "The worriedest."

"Worriedest?"

"Mhm, worried-worst."

"Oh dear, Jamie, you're delirious," Eve teased, squeezing her thighs around my hips.

I leaned in and she met me in the kiss, twining closer, her lips parting and a soft hum singing against my tongue. I reached around her hips, lifting her easily off the counter and turning us toward the door.

"Are you sneaking back in with Adam and Garrett tonight?" I asked.

"Not if you plan on keeping me busy," Eve said, tracing kisses up my jaw and then biting playfully at the corner.

Maybe I should've encouraged her to spend time with her bondmates, her omega, but I was feeling greedy. And yeah, jealous too. I wanted to be the one going to Montreal with her because without the bond, I'd be relying on Garrett and Adam to tell me how she was, whether or not she was safe.

Or you could bite her, my hindbrain chimed in. But I'd told her weeks ago if she claimed me, I'd claim her right back, and she hadn't taken me up on it. And I wanted that, my mark on her, as much as I wanted the bond. I didn't think I'd be able to resist if she bit me.

I tried to ignore her distracting kisses as I carried her through the house, upstairs to my bedroom. Eve and Adam had settled into the nest together, apparently permanently, and it seemed like the guest room was going to be left just that, unless Eve decided to grab a space for herself. I preferred her floating between our rooms, occupying space with whoever suited her for the moment. She and Rory had nearly broken a hole through his wall into my bedroom the other night.

"Do you think you'd ever be up for two alphas at the same time?" I asked absently.

Eve stiffened and then relaxed almost immediately, her face thoughtful. "I'm not sure. It sounds crowded. But maybe someday. Garrett—"

"I was thinking Rory, I guess," I said, laughing at her wrinkled nose. "What?"

"I just... Rory and I are still more fight than anything. It's fun, but I...like the way things are between you and me," she said, lowering her voice like she didn't want the others to hear. The warm tone sank into me, easing the remaining tension in my muscles.

"It's not how you are with Adam and Garrett?" I asked.

Eve's lips curved, thick black eyelashes batting at me as she shook her head. "Not really. I'm the alpha with them. With Rory too. I *generally* prefer that."

I wanted to watch her with them all, just to understand the difference, but I liked that she came to me as an equal rather than a challenger. Not that I would've had a problem surrendering.

Eve's foot nudged my bedroom door, and then she wiggled and slid her way out of my arms, stepping back. Her hands went to the buttons of the shirt she was wearing, plucking them free at the collar down to her breasts.

"Does it still smell like me?" I asked, pulling my own shirt off over my head.

Eve paused to lift the collar to her nose, shaking her head and frowning. "Not anymore."

"Leave it on," I said.

Eve smiled at me, watching me out of the corner of her eye. "For you or for me?"

"Either," I said with a shrug. If she left it here while she was gone…well, yeah, I would do the embarrassingly needy thing by keeping it nearby for her scent mark. And if she took it with her, I'd have the possessive alpha pleasure of knowing my mark was on her in some way.

I kicked off my jeans and underwear, moving to the bed as Eve toyed with the buttons of the shirt, flicking one after another open. Her eyes tracked me as I lay back and reached down to stroke my cock, watching her until there was only one button left still fastened below her breasts.

She shifted onto the bed with one knee, the fabric sliding open to reveal her bare pussy. My tongue flicked out over my lip, and Eve chuckled, her knees straddling my calves. One of her feet planted on the bed, her leg tipping out for me to admire her openly.

"You going to come closer?" I asked, my purr already thickening the words.

"Mm, I'm thinking about it," Eve said, rising up to standing, balancing carefully on the mattress with every light step forward.

I shuffled farther down on the bed, my feet hanging over the edge as she paused at my hips, stroking my cock with the soft inside of her foot briefly.

"You don't need to worry about me, Jamie," Eve said.

I hummed and tried to focus on the picture of Eve's dark sex moving closer to hovering over my face. "Part of the package, I'm afraid. Would you worry about me if the positions were reversed?"

Eve growled and cut the sound off. I suspected we both knew the answer was that if the roles were reversed, Eve would *not* be staying home and waiting for me to get back. Which made me a bit sick about the idea all over again.

And then she was kneeling down, and all I could breathe was the rough scent of her. I wanted to burn my tongue on her taste. I reached up, cupping my hands around her warm thighs and guiding her down to my mouth, flicking my gaze up the length of her to find her dark eyes on mine.

I held her stare as I opened my lips against her, stroked her from hole to clit with my tongue. Her breasts rose with a deep breath before she rolled softly against my mouth, eyelashes fluttering with satisfaction. I drew one hand away from her hip, catching her own in my grip, pressing our palms tightly together, and purred against her sex, thrusting my tongue inside of her as she moaned and rocked against me.

She could smother me, for all I cared. I'd die happy, drowning in smoke and spice and pussy.

"I would worry about you, yes," Eve whispered, the words dissolving into a groan and a rough kick of her hips, my nose nudging at her clit accidentally and then more intentionally. "I'll still worry about you."

I wanted to turn my head and sink my teeth into the flesh of her thigh, force a bond that would allow me some reassurance of her safety while she was gone. Or drive me insane every time there was a flinch of pain. It would serve Eve right to have bond claimed without asking, but I suspected she'd take it with less grace than Garrett had.

I lapped at her, suddenly desperate to have my cock inside of her, to hold her in the one way I could, buried inside of her with that look of shocked surrender on her face as she held her breath and rode my length.

"Oh fuck, Jamie," Eve gasped, her thighs tensing around my ears. I nuzzled at her clit, fucking her with my tongue, sucking up every little taste of her before shifting up with a gasp and latching my lips around her clit.

Her fingers clamped around mine, my hand holding her hip tightly, even as she tried to pull away. I lashed at her clit with the tip of my tongue, worried at it with my lips, and purred against her until she was crying out, arching above me, the tail of her long braid swishing softly against my stomach. She shuddered as she came, my chin growing slick with her release.

I wrapped my arm around Eve's waist and sat up, grinning against her at the garbled little yelp of surprise. Her legs latched around my shoulders, her free hand holding onto the back of my head.

"What are you—Oof!" Eve landed back on the bed with a quick twist from me, snarling and laughing at the same time as I cleaned her with an eager tongue, her flavor scorching my throat, heating my blood and stiffening my cock.

I swirled my tongue once more over her clit, smiling at the sound of her grunt of approval, and then pulled away. Her head was at the foot of my bed, one hand still clinging to mine, cheeks pinked from pleasure. Eve was undeniably beautiful, sexual and pristine, but rarely soft.

"Have I mentioned that you're beautiful?" I asked, blinking down at her.

"You've been very neglectful with your compliments," Eve said, smirking, but her gaze was warm.

I turned my head and kissed the knee by my ear, stroking the soft underside with my thumb, trying to think of the words that wouldn't make her eyes roll at me.

"If you bite, I'll bite back."

My thumb stopped, and my eyes grew wide. Eve's hand in mine squeezed once, drawing my attention back to her face. She was relaxed, smiling, and she slid her leg off my shoulder, pinching her knees around my ribs to draw me forward. Her other hand reached for mine, and she guided them over her head to rest against the edge of the mattress as I stretched out above her, cradled in her thighs, our stomachs pressed together.

I was stretched out on top of her, my knot nestled against her opening and cock pressed to her folds, and Eve was breathing easily beneath me.

"You're sure?" I asked, dipping my head to kiss her jaw, throat, and collarbone, hunching my back and nuzzling into the slouched fabric of the shirt she was still wearing so I could mouth at her breast.

"Mhm. Better have the hat trick of alphas around here," she said.

I sat up to glare at her, and she laughed, pulling one

hand free and drawing my face down to hers. "I'm sure, Jamie. Mmm, I taste good on you."

"You do," I agreed, sighing as her purr thrummed into the kiss.

Her hand left my face to reach between us, guiding the head of my cock to her sex. I sank in immediately, watching the subtle change of her face, her lips falling lax and eyes widening.

"Too much like this?" I asked, rolling my hips slowly forward, trying to focus on her rather than the burning grip of her cunt around my cock, the urge to buck and ride the itch in the base of my spine.

Eve opened the last button on her shirt and then arched, pressing her skin into mine, our purrs filling the room. "Not too much," she said, stretching up for another kiss.

I kept waiting for her to tense, but the only thing tense between us was the grind and plunge of my cock inside of her. Her legs wound around my hips, urging me on, and her hand found mine again. I wasn't holding her down, more like she was holding me on top of her, and it made my teeth ache, my body fighting against the frantic need to piston inside of her.

"I was going to make you wait. Make you so annoyed and impatient that you'd just run up and bite me one day," I said, grinning down at her.

Eve laughed. "It wouldn't have taken long," she admitted, lifting her back and moaning as her breasts rubbed against my chest. "Jamie, I—I won't beg."

Maybe not, but she turned her head and arched her throat under my gaze. Part of me wanted to share this vision with my packmates, and the other part of me knew it was too precious. Still, they would see the mark on her. That was mine and only mine. I had a feeling this version of her, splayed out and surrendering, was just mine too. She and Rory would take out their aggression on each other—reminding Rory that he didn't have to be the strongest person in the room, reminding Eve that she *was*. She and Garrett would take care of Adam together, be two halves of what would make him safe and satisfied and happy in our pack.

And I would have this, this part of Eve that didn't *need* to be alpha, that trusted another person completely.

I ducked my head and licked a stripe up her shoulder. She tensed, but only for a moment, sighing and nudging her head against mine. I sucked over her pulse, my thrusts inside of her slow and deep, all the way out and then in as far as I could push without knotting her. I wanted the friction of fucking rather than the cock-pulverizing agony Rory had described knotting Eve as.

"Jamie," Eve hissed, stretching even farther under me.

I grinned, nibbling up the muscle of her throat to her jaw, where her resulting growl vibrated.

"For fuck's sake, Jamie." Eve arched again as I sucked on her earlobe. "Just bite—Ah!"

It was just harder than a nip, tender and careful. I only needed to break the skin, not tear a piece off. Eve's blood was sharp and metallic on my tongue, my bite just barely penetrating the lobe captured between my teeth. But it was enough. Surprise and humor and…and an unexpected depth of affection and trust trickled into the bond, blending perfectly with my own emotions.

Oh, and there was her annoyance. I chuckled and went back to sucking on the tiny bondmark. Eve let out a rare whimper and rocked up to meet my hips with sharp and quick motions, my knot pressing against her clit. Her hands were tight against mine, like she was holding on to me to keep from falling from a great height. I wanted to hold her in place and push her there all at once. I pulled away to kiss her throat briefly before returning to my mark.

Eve gasped with the connection, and hunger rose in the bond.

"Come for me, and I'm yours," I whispered into her ear.

She huffed, irritated at the order, but her lock was tightening the harder I drew on my mark—her cunt swelling and claiming me, fastening me firmly inside of her. There was very little blood, which was good considering she'd be leaving with Rory first thing in the morning.

As Eve's gasps grew steady with every thrust and her lock started to clamp around my cock, she drew our hands close to her face. She kissed the back of my fist, and I purred against my mark, holding myself deep inside of her and rubbing my knot into her clit to finish her off.

The lock squeezed tight around me, like someone had wrapped a string around my cock and then pulled at both ends, strangling and wonderful all at once. Eve let out one bright cry, and then my wrist was at her mouth. She bit down, teeth striking into the inside of my left wrist, the sensation akin to a bullet running through me, but the shock and pound running directly to my cock.

The bond amplified, lovely smug satisfaction from Eve, her orgasm exploding in my head, setting off one of my own that met her lock with a clash of thunderous friction. I bellowed into Eve's throat, her thighs around my hips squeezing and holding me inside of her, our hips both bucking closer.

"How am I supposed to wear fucking earrings, Jamie?" Eve growled against my wrist before licking on her bite and making me shudder with what had to have been a second release, one that would've been clearer if I hadn't still been crashing from the first. "Next time, I'll bite your fucking finger off."

I laughed, shaking on top of her. "I'll bite your tit."

"I'll bite your balls."

I must've been made for this woman, because all I could think of was the intriguing prospect of Eve's mouth on my balls.

"No, I won't," she corrected with a sigh, softening and pulling her hands free of mine to wrap her arms around my back. "Your nose, maybe. I'd bite Rory's balls."

"He'd probably like that."

She snorted, turning her face to mine, her lips red and stretched in a smile. The bond was warm, little threads of the others watchful and pleased behind the haze of Eve, a content and satisfied fog surrounding me.

"You're going to miss me," she said.

I blinked and nodded once. "Yeah, I am," I said, trying not to sound so weary about it. I shifted us onto our sides, and Eve's lock dragged like a bite down my length, drawing out a groan from my lips.

She leaned in to kiss me. "Not for long. I'll be safe."

"You better," I said.

We were on the wrong end of the bed, but Eve was wrapped up in my arms, her leg thrown over my hip and her bite throbbing on my wrist. I didn't plan on moving until the morning came and it was time for her to leave.

"You be safe too," Eve whispered, and she was wrestling her own worry back in the bond, trying to hide it from me.

I brushed a kiss over her nose and down to her mouth. "I promise."

She purred and brought my wrist back to her lips. I rolled us again so she was draped over me and attended to the mark on her lobe, grinning at the tiny red marks I'd left.

"I'll bite you on your foot so you can't walk," Eve muttered.

I laughed and bucked up to hold myself deep inside of her, wondering how long it would take for her to be ready for me again.

FORTY

Eve

It was in moments like this that I wished I could shut the bond down again. Rory was nervous and impatient, and all three of my other bondmates—*Four fucking bondmates, Eve? Really?*—were simmering with poorly-contained worry in the garage of the pack house.

Jamie's eyes were fixed to his mark on my ear, a furrow on his brow and a slight smile on his lips. He'd tended it thoroughly through the night until I'd fallen asleep with his chest against my back and his lips still clasped around the lobe. No one had been surprised or bothered to see the mark this morning as we'd packed the SUV with our small bags. I had a fresh passport for use, and I'd already arranged for an old cohort to meet me and Rory with gear at the airport, so all we needed was enough to not look suspicious.

"Do you think you'll have to stay hidden after?" Adam asked, tiptoeing closer.

"Our best plan will be to come back here as quickly as possible," I told him, reaching out and pulling him against me. He sagged and sighed as I kissed a handful of my marks on his throat.

"I keep thinking this is a mistake," he whispered. "The chance of Faith being there—"

"It's a chance," I said simply, "and that makes it worth the trip."

I let my eyes fall shut at the thick, sweet wave that rose in Adam. Gratitude and affection, warm and tender and enveloping. And a deeper, heavier emotion I suspected was love but hadn't taken the time to address yet. I leaned into it for a moment, found it surprisingly gentle and not at all the grip and pull I'd been expecting to resist.

"Thank you," Adam whispered.

I kissed him, brief and firm, and then stiffened at the sound of footsteps slapping outside of the garage. It wasn't even six in the morning. I pulled away from Adam and all of us turned to watch the neighbor, Hannah, jogging down the sidewalk. She raised a hand and smiled at us, but continued her workout.

"She's an omega," Adam whispered, curiosity in the bond.

"What?" Garrett asked, eyebrows rising.

Adam nodded and shrugged. "She's on suppressants. I noticed at the barbecue. Sometime, when it settles down, I'd like to meet her."

I pursed my lips at that. Adam had also been an omega on suppressants before I'd met him, and I suspected he related to the older woman. I would look into her before I let Adam meet her alone.

"We need to get going," Rory reminded us.

Adam stepped back, and I slid over to Garrett, taking his face in my hands and pulling it down to meet mine. "Be good," I purred, and Garrett grinned.

"Always," he answered, glancing at Rory over my

shoulder. "Please don't leave Rory in Canada, no matter how irritating he is."

I sighed and nodded. "I'll do my best. Keep my omega satisfied."

Garrett growled in response to that, but his amusement filled the bond. I turned, and Jamie took my hand, walking around the vehicle to open my door for me.

"Be careful," he said, keeping his words low and private.

"I will be incredible," I said, smiling at him. "Keep them safe."

He nodded solemnly, and I met him halfway for a slow and thorough kiss. The bond thrummed, Garrett and Adam twined together to soothe away their own worries, Rory steady and striving for patience, Jamie wrapping around me as if it could keep me with him. Jamie's lips were greedy, and I eased the kiss with little nibbles, raising his hand between us to give my mark on his wrist a last lick before sliding into the front seat.

Jamie walked around the SUV to join the others as Rory backed out of the garage, an edgy and sharp note in the bond in contrast to the others' little waves of worry.

"You're excited," I realized.

Rory's frown was deep, but it didn't disguise what was in the bond, something like the playful crackle of static on skin.

"Is it time alone with me?" I purred.

His eyes flicked toward me as his hands clenched around the wheel, and I laughed.

"It isn't," I said, just a little tartly.

"I mean…that's an obvious plus," Rory said, his expression easing slightly. "I…I missed being in the field."

"You enjoyed the fight with Omikron." It wasn't a question. Rory had been buzzed that night, excited and powerful, and he had every right to be.

"I did," he said softly, one shoulder shrugging.

"I did too."

Rory looked over briefly and then back to the road, and whatever he was thinking was too quick and subtle for me to translate in the bond. "I didn't want to believe we were the right pack for you and Adam. Now I just hope we are. But I know you're the right alpha for us."

It was too unexpected to hear those words out of Rory's mouth, so I reached over and set my hand over his crotch, squeezing roughly and then laughing as the car swerved and nearly took out a mailbox.

"Eve!" Rory barked.

Balance restored, I leaned over to his seat and kissed my mark on his throat before settling back and buckling my seatbelt.

———

OLD MONTREAL WAS wet and glittering, cobblestones shimmering with warm lights glowing at every door.

"This doesn't look like the kind of place where you'd want your seedy nightclub," Rory said under his breath.

His arm was draped over my shoulder, providing light protection from the cold night, and every so often his hand would reach up to touch the corner of my blonde bobbed wig. He had a wide-brimmed black felt hat on, shadowing his face from passing eyes, and I'd brushed a little dark temporary dye into the notable gray streak on his chin. He was still enormous and undeniably alpha, and I'd worked the majority of our disguise on myself with the wig, blue contacts, and a heavy coating of makeup to tweak my features and pale my skin.

"It's wealthy, old money, some of the best hotels in the city," I pointed out. "It's exactly where powerful alphas would come to stay on business. Which means it's the kind of place where this business would be protected."

Rory tensed around me but nodded slightly, glancing down again and smirking. "How can you walk in those? On cobblestones too."

Stilettos weren't my preferred footwear, especially on a night like this where there was work to be done, but they were a necessary evil and a last-minute weapon in a pinch.

"Practice," I answered smoothly. "We're almost there. Don't walk in looking around like you're waiting to witness a crime. We check our coats—"

"Where did you manage to hide your weapons?" Rory asked, his large hand sliding down my bare arm to cup my hip, stroking over the holster strap briefly.

"—we order ourselves drinks, don't you dare embarrass me with a beer in this place," I said as Rory huffed. "We admire the girls. Let me put down the money. And—"

Rory ducked his head to growl against my ear. "Eve, I *know* the plan. I'll even let you pick the girl. You're in charge. I'm backup."

"Are you *flirting* with me?" I purred, glancing to the side to see Rory's smirk.

"A bit. I can do a cuckolding thing, right? Just watch the two of you together?"

I rolled my eyes. The plan was to choose one of the women for a private dance as a way to get off the main floor without tipping off security too early.

"I'm not going to make her dance for us, Rory," I grumbled. "Save it for Garrett."

Rory's grin flashed. "Not really the same appeal, if I'm honest. But you're probably right—Adam would get very jealous if I let you seduce another omega."

"I don't think Faith will be here," I said quietly.

"Neither do I," Rory agreed. "But Adam is our omega, which means it's worth checking."

And since that kind of statement was the reason why Rory was an alpha worth my bite, I stopped in the middle of the street, allowing the locals and tourists to pass us as I slid my hands into Rory's back pockets—noting the waistband holster where a switchblade was carefully tucked away—and pulled his hips to mine. In my heels I was just a few inches shy of being his height, and we fit pleasantly together as I tipped my head and his lips met mine eagerly. Rory's hands cupped at my back, sliding under the thin threads of straps that crossed over my bare skin, tracing carefully over old scars, making sure not to smear the makeup that hid them.

"How quiet do you want to leave this place?" I whispered against his lips. "It has Omikron connections, but if she isn't here—"

"If she isn't here, this place is a trap," Rory murmured back. "It doesn't matter. Let's burn it down."

Our teeth bumped gently as we both grinned. I'd worried I would bring a storm of trouble and violence to a pack unprepared to weather the disruption in their lives. Now I was wondering—at least with Rory, and I suspected Jamie—if I wasn't rescuing them from boredom.

"Come on, big guy. Let's go to work."

Rory huffed in annoyance at the endearment, but he followed me into the little alleyway dressed with strands of red lights. "You're sure about the security?"

I shook my head and shrugged my shoulders beneath his arm. "No, but if I'm wrong and they catch us, the shit hits the fan early."

Rory's smile flattened, and he glared at me, gaze just

visible beneath the shadow of his hat, eyes glinting red, but I sensed his amusement in the bond.

I knew La Moursure Rouge would have an alpha placed at the door, and while he was sizably impressive and had a beautifully intimidating stare, he didn't really stand up to Rory or me, passing his hands over us in a cursory sweep that seemed almost lazy. The club's entrance was filled with luscious greenery, casting sensual shapes in shadows on the black walls. There was a beautiful red-headed woman with an almost vacant stare at the glossy counter inside who took our cash and Rory's coat. I watched both her and the doorman out of the corner of my eye, but neither moved to make any alert at our presence.

The security cameras were discreetly tucked behind mirrors and plants and ivory statues of women in the arms of beasts, their throats bared and bitten. Music and lights drummed in time with one another from around a dark corner, and an intentionally angled mirror revealed a glimpse of the stage, where an elegant body twined around a golden pole under a hazy spotlight.

Rory's hand on my back guided me to the hall, a long bulb of pale blue neon guiding the way to the main floor. The bar was just ahead of us, a small party of men gathered together at the far end, with a few more scattered down the length.

"Mamont on ice," I told Rory.

He nodded and stepped to the corner of the bar. I leaned into his back, smiling at the first man who glanced at me, who smirked back. He was older, with a pale and predatory gaze that studied me avidly—not handsome, but muscular beneath his dress jacket.

Mercenary, I decided. The party at the end of the bar who were only half watching the incredible dancer on stage fit the profile too. I counted the blurry shadows of more men out of the corners of my eyes. Rory's excitement and anxiety were rising in the bond, and I thought he must've come to the same conclusion as me.

Everyone in La Mousure Rouge was here for us. I wasn't surprised the night was a trap, and there was only one way to be certain Faith hadn't been set as legitimate bait.

I watched the dancer on stage, holding my breath against the rising bitter edge of the grapefruit peel scent of the man still staring at me. She was small, thighs thick with muscle, but also softened with rich foods, stomach beautifully rounded. She had a heart-shaped face and danced on bare feet. She also had an intriguingly miserable expression on her face, somewhat empty, as if she was daydreaming of being elsewhere and even that fantasy was dissatisfying.

There was no way to tell from this far away, but I suspected she was an omega, as the bar advertised. There were a few tables of solitary or small groups of men around the stage, although not as close as they could be. They looked as little interested by her performance as she did, and I was more certain than ever that the audience tonight was made up entirely of professionals who'd answered the bid for our deaths. I doubted everyone was fooled by mine and Rory's disguise, which meant it was more likely they were all waiting for a cue.

We weren't going to make it backstage without shots being fired.

Rory turned away from the bar slowly, a drink in each hand, and I took mine immediately so he could reach for a weapon if he needed. I glanced up at him, and he nodded once. He trusted that the drinks were safe. Considering everyone else at the bar looked like they had seltzer water or untouched liquor, perhaps they planned on us being tipsy before the fight? They were in for a surprise, because I fought better when slightly relaxed.

"I want a table by the stage," I said to Rory.

"Of course you do," he purred, following as I led him by the elbow through the thin crowd on the floor. A place like this should've been packed any night of the week. "Her?" he asked, nodding at the girl whose thighs held the pole firmly between them as she remained suspended and in the semblance of surrender, spinning slowly as the song wound down, pert and unmarked breasts on display.

I shook my head. "No, let's watch another first."

There were a few girls on the floor, in shadowy corner booths near the doors backstage, easily shuffled or hidden away when bullets started to fly.

Rory pulled out a chair for me at a metallic brass table, and I sat down, smoothing my tight skirt as I went. I kept my drink in my hand, eyeing the warped reflection at the far end of the stage, where a dim mirror reflected the finale of the omega's dance. Figures stood on the balcony behind our heads, perfectly in place for a headshot. From our new seats, I could smell the scent of wilted freesia from the stage, the omega's tragic perfume.

The lights on the stage dimmed as she stepped down delicately from the pole, and not one member of the audience moved a muscle. I rose, Rory watching me with a fixed stare as I reached into the low collar of my dress and pulled out a pinch of money I'd tucked away.

The girl's eyes were wide, almost the same shade as Adam's green, and she tiptoed in a rush to me, reaching out to take the money before scurrying away to the back of the stage.

"What was that?" Rory asked me with a forced smile as I returned to my seat.

Thirty-eight men around the room, and a few were

already eyeing the door, rethinking their chances. "Plan B," I whispered to Rory, and then blinked and shrugged as I sat back down. "Or D or F or whatever."

I traced the number of men I'd counted in Rory's upturned palm as the music paused.

"Together or split-up?" he asked.

If we stuck together, I would have Rory at my back but I would also have the responsibility of protecting his. If we split up, it would be like the office building again, just carving my path through enemies, protecting myself and knowing with confidence that Rory was capable of doing the same.

Which he was; I knew that now about the men I'd chosen for Adam and then for myself.

Rory and I would be fine, taking on every man in the club one by one, on our own.

"Together," I said, surprising myself.

We would be fine together too. And maybe slightly less prone to getting shot.

Rory's lips twitched, but his eyes flicked to the left, behind us, and hardened. "Down."

I slid off my seat, grabbing the back of it and pulling it with me to use as a shield from the gunfire above. Rory picked the table up by two legs and did the same, and I slid over the slick lacquered floor to rise behind him, turning and pulling the gun that had pressed between my thighs, firing immediately at the party I'd spotted first at the end of the bar.

"We putting all of them down?" Rory shouted at me, as I pulled him backwards.

"Might as well," I answered, providing us with cover— a rapid squeeze-squeeze-squeeze of the trigger. "Grab whatever weapons you can."

Rory swung the table hard into the nearest man

running at him before jumping into a hand-to-hand grapple as I fired carefully over the bar, watching the splatter against the glass cabinets with grim satisfaction every time I hit my mark. I pulled the knife strapped to my ribs out from the side of my dress and then ran forward, using a barstool for leverage, then the bar top, diving down behind the bar. There was still one man there, reloading his gun, and I ducked out of the way of his shot before grabbing his head and using my knee to help me snap his neck. Rory followed me a moment later as I dug through the men I'd taken out for their guns, mine freshly emptied.

"Five just left out of the front of the building," Rory said, his pupils blown black, head flinching to the side and then grabbing me and tucking me beneath him as someone fired at the bottles of liquor behind us, glass and alcohol exploding and raining down over our heads.

"Left?"

"Yeah, ran."

I'd rather no one who'd signed up with Omikron made it out of here tonight, especially not if they posed a chance of coming to find us later, but at least it helped our odds.

"Halfway," Rory said, pulling back and tipping my chin up for a hard kiss. "You can see their reflections in the bar mirror."

"I've got balcony, you take floor," I said, and he nodded.

"I'll give you a boost."

Jamie had been an amazing partner, and we'd worked independently. Rory and I found a synchronistic rhythm together, not unlike the push and pull of our fucking. He knelt, and I climbed onto his shoulders, the pair of us balancing as he rose up from the floor, firing ahead to cover me as I reached up for the balcony ledge. I grabbed onto a bar and swung myself up, just in time to shoot first at the man running in my direction.

Most of the others were on the other side of the room, where they'd been aiming at us behind the bar, and I took them down one at a time, dodging into the alcove of an upstairs restroom briefly.

"Still having fun?" I called down to Rory, dragging the ankle of a dead body closer so I could rummage for weapons.

For a moment, there was only the uneven drumbeat of gunshots, a brief grunt and scream from below. I should've been worried, but the bond was full of an almost giddy excitement, Rory's handling of the men on the floor brutally efficient. I jumped out from the alcove and fired quickly at the men rushing me from around the balcony, grinning at the sound of Rory's voice calling back to me.

"I am, and you know it. Come on, let's finish them off and see what else they have for us."

FORTY-ONE

Rory

"We're locked up," I called, jogging back down the stairs, double-checking one of the SWAT-geared men we'd taken out on our way downstairs. "Receptionist left right after we arrived."

"Rory, look at this."

I stopped in the doorway, admiring the sensual shape of Eve bent over the desk in the security room of the club, the slit at the back of her dress riding high as she examined the screens in front of her. There was a scratch bleeding down one of her calves and a bruise growing dark along her jaw, but she was every bit as vivid and alive in the bond as I was.

Her head turned, and an eyebrow arched at me, drawing out a sheepish grin on my lips. "Sorry, what is it?" I asked, crossing to the desk, my hands itching to reach out to her. I paused, and it took me a moment of staring before I shook off the fog of victory and understood what was on the screens. Room after room, bed after bed, and girl after girl huddled on the mattresses. "Jesus. Think they're all omegas?"

The screens were marked as basement level, and they were exactly what La Mousure Rouge was rumored for—a series of private rooms, each containing a girl handcuffed to a small bed. There were a dozen rooms.

Eve shook her head slowly. "If they are, that's a gold-mine. Here, this is the owner in his office," she said, pointing to the last screen, where an older man sat in a large chair behind an ornate desk. And there at the owner's feet was the girl we'd watched dancing, her head bobbing over his lap.

"Jesus, he's—he's still *here*? Are any of them Faith?" I asked.

There were a few girls whose faces I couldn't see—most of the girls looked bored or as though they were trying to sleep—but there wasn't any of them that was a match for Adam's sister.

"We should check," Eve said, straightening and then glancing down to her side.

I nodded, and then realized I had my arm around her, hand on her hip. Her lips twitched, and before I could pull away she leaned into my side, twisting and wrapping her arms around me. Our reflections on the security screens looked like a couple out on a date together, embracing.

Vigilante courting ritual, I thought. *Taking out a pack of mercenaries in a disgusting omega trafficking strip club.*

"I only know a few languages," I said, studying the rooms with the young women again.

"I can take care of getting the girls out of the cuffs, but someone needs to occupy him," Eve said, pointing to the owner.

I frowned and shrugged. "That's easy enough. You'll let them out?"

"Wouldn't you?" she asked, smiling up at me. "I just want to make sure he won't come running if I accidentally spook one. Then we come back here and erase all this footage of us."

My smile flashed again at that, and I reached out, wiping away a spray of blood on her cheek. "I saved a bottle of the Mamont for you."

"Ooo, someone's looking to get laid," Eve teased.

"After all this excitement? I mean, I was thinking about a bath, but sure, we can arm wrestle for who's on top," I answered, darting away as she glared at me. I followed her to the door. "You'll cheat, but I'll like it."

Eve shook her head, turning it away from me, but I still caught the swell of her cheeks as she headed for the staircase waiting behind the stack of scorched mercenaries we'd left in the hall. I jogged down ahead of her, heading right for the door at the end where the owner was lurking.

"Be careful," Eve called softly.

I paused, turning back and finding a strange, soft smile on my lips, need and comfort all twisted together in the bond. "I will."

I pulled to a stop outside the office door, pressing my ear to the ledge. There was already an aggressive eucalyptus-like scent emanating, and I heard a few choice grunts from inside. I checked the ammunition in the gun I'd grabbed and then grabbed the handle of the door. Locked, of course.

I stepped back, aimed between the handle and the doorjamb, and fired.

There was a yelp from inside as the bullet broke through the lock, and I shoved hard on the door with my shoulder. The walls of the office were incredibly thick, probably soundproof, which explained why the owner was still in here getting his dick sucked.

Emile Levesque was sixty-eight years old and had owned a number of dubiously-intentioned businesses in his lifetime, several of which ended after costly sexual harassment lawsuits. Apparently, he'd decided to abandon legitimate employee relations and instead transition to purchasing the women he wanted dancing in his clubs.

The girl who had taken Eve's tip scrambled out from behind the desk and into the corner, huddling there as Emile shouted and rose up from his seat, stuffing his only half-hard cock back into his trousers and shouting for security over my shoulder.

"Security is gone," I informed him as his red face gaped at me. I didn't speak French or Quebecois, but he understood the threat of a gun pointed at him with none of his men running in to stop me.

"What do you want?" he stuttered out instead, in a thick and halting accent. "Take the girl."

The girl was still dressed in only a decorative pair of underwear, and she looked more threatened by my presence in the room than Emile did. I pulled my phone out of my pocket and flipped quickly open to the first photo, stepping forward.

"Have you seen *this* girl?" Faith had some of Adam's bone structure, slightly softened but still sharp, and her hair was the same shade of brown as his. I could see him in her face, the resemblance, and it made her feel more like family than ever.

"*Non, non, mais*—but you can have any girl you want!" he shouted.

My lips curved slightly at that. "I have a girl. She's busy setting all those women you had trapped free."

I turned the phone to the girl cowering in the corner, and she scooted forward slightly, head shaking and then her eyes looking up to me. "You did it. She said you would. I kept him here." Her accent was different—German, by my guess—and she held a wadded-up piece of paper in her fist, Eve's handwriting just barely visible.

Plan B, D, or F, indeed.

"Go on, get out of here," I said to her, jerking my head back toward the door.

"What is it you want?" Emile gasped, starting to stand from his seat before freezing at the audible click of the safety going off on the gun. "Money? Take what you want. The safe is just over—"

I glared at him, and the words died on his tongue, the girl scurrying quickly out of the room behind me. The truth was, I didn't know what I wanted. I wanted a man like Emile Levesque to not be sitting in an office like this, thriving on money and power, mistreating those weaker than him.

"The girls are organizing," Eve said as the door behind me opened again. "I took care of the footage. We can leave whenever."

My gaze remained fixed where Emile sat, sweating behind his desk, pants unfastened and eyes darting between me and Eve.

"What do we do with him?" I asked.

"What do you want to do?" Eve answered, stepping to my side, her hand on my back, her own gun pointed at him too.

Emile took it as an opening, a rapid run of pleading Quebecois pouring out of his mouth at Eve, as if of the two of us, she might be more sympathetic. *It's the opposite*, I thought, and then I wondered if that weren't really true either.

I did know what I wanted to do with this man.

I blinked and turned to glance at Eve, whose expression was passive and calm. Either she knew what I would do next, or she really was willing to let me choose his fate.

In the army, the choice of whether or not to shoot was simplified by the terms of war. It wasn't even kill or be killed, not on a battlefield. It was that we'd all come to that moment in time *aware* of where our choices might lead us.

Emile Levesque certainly hadn't come to the club tonight expecting to die. He hadn't decided to purchase vulnerable omegas and allow alphas to abuse them with the intention of meeting his death in retaliation. He was here for money.

I squeezed the trigger and turned my face toward Eve's as the bullet met its target, a hard but not cruel resolution in my chest at the sound of the collision.

"Did you do it for them?" Eve asked, nodding her head back to the hall, where the young women were trailing slowly out of the hell they'd been trapped in for who knew how long.

I was fairly sure that yes, I had killed Emile for those women and future women like them. But I remembered the night Eve had returned from killing Hugh Redmond. She'd done it in defiance of Omikron, maybe, or maybe because she hated men who abused their strength every bit as much as I did.

"Does it matter?" I asked.

Eve's lips curled up slightly. "Not to me."

We left the office together, my hand reaching for Eve's, ridiculously pleased when she squeezed around my fingers.

In the hall, girls were dragging scraps of clothing out of their basic rooms, sharing with one another, chattering in a mix of languages. The girl from the pole and the office, the one holding a small wad of cash from Eve, stepped forward and glanced between us.

"What will you do about the woman?" the girl asked.

Eve and I exchanged a quick look, and then Eve stepped forward. "What woman?"

Another young woman—older than the others, from what I could tell—was tugging on a mesh top over a bra, balancing on a gravity-defying heel, and she stopped to join our conversation. "The one who sold us. She come here two weeks before. She plan for you."

"Would she be on the security footage?" I asked, my tone too sharp and making some of the younger girls flinch. All together in the hall, the omegas were starting to fill the space with an uncomfortable mix of their perfumes, tinged with panic.

The oldest of the omegas shrugged at us.

"Get out of here," Eve said. "Find an Omega Center, they'll call anyone you want and keep you safe. Rory, come on."

I was already following Eve back to the security room, somewhat helpless to do anything but watch as she grabbed a seat and started typing furiously.

"Two weeks," she muttered.

"Their timing probably isn't perfect either," I agreed.

"Women will stand out. Here, you look at these, and I'll do the others. Just hold this button down to run it backwards."

We had four images up, and I wished Garrett were here with us. He was better at dealing with the rapid-fire view of surveillance footage, but I bounced my eyes between the two screens, one on the front entrance and the other Emile's office. Thankfully, the majority of the office footage didn't include Emile partaking of his wares—although there was enough of that to last me a fucking lifetime. I saw a couple women on the arms of guests, but none that ever appeared in the office or seemed like especially interested guests. I was nearly three weeks back when Eve cursed and backed up her own footage.

"Fuck. *Fuck*, Rory, call the pack," Eve snarled.

I had my phone out, leaning over her shoulder, staring blankly at the screen for a long moment.

"The phone number you have dialed cannot be reached. Please try ag—"

The woman on the screen both was and wasn't familiar, and it took me far longer than Eve to recognize her.

"Garrett's number didn't work," I murmured, watching as she appeared in the office, moving confidently toward Emile's desk, shaking hands with the man. "Shit, she's been right—"

"Rory, Jamie's number isn't working either. They've fucking blocked calls," Eve said, and it was as if I had two heartbeats drumming in my chest, both running twice as fast as they ought to. Eve was tense, her hands in fists. "She's been under our fucking nose."

I stood and left the footage running. "We go back, now."

Eve's eyes were dark, the air around her vibrating with her scent, now almost explosive. "We'll be too—"

I wrapped my hand around the back of her neck and dragged her mouth to mine for a rough and biting kiss, letting her wrestle me away and glare up at me. "We'll get back quicker if we drive. Let's go. It's not too late yet."

Eve let out a growl, but she nodded and her hand slid back into mine. Her grip was almost tight enough to break my fingers, but I held on just as fiercely.

We'd known coming to Montreal was a trap. We just hadn't realized the trap was set back home.

Adam

I frowned at the phone in my hand, waiting for a message to appear, and tried to bury my warring emotions in the bond as if I were Eve. Frustration battled relief, all atop a mountain of guilt. There was urgency from Eve too, keeping me edgy, but she hadn't answered a single text and we hadn't heard from her or Rory since before they left for the club. I knew they were alive, that *something* had happened last night, but not what.

"Hey," Garrett said, appearing on the patio with a steaming cup of coffee, setting it on the table in front of me before leaning over my back and wrapping his arms around my shoulders.

"I'm okay."

"No, you're not," he murmured, kissing the corner of my jaw, the scruff of his beard nuzzling against my cheek. "I'm freaking out too. I get it. But whatever Eve is wound up about, she would let us know if she needed to."

"They probably went for nothing," I said, trying to stamp down the occasional flares of hope that the reason for the way Eve was yanking on the bond was because she was returning with Faith.

"At the very least, they went for you, and that's not nothing," Garrett said, his hand squeezing my shoulder. "And look, if you got bogus information from someone on the server, it means we have someone I can dig into."

I took a deep breath, sitting up in the patio chair and nodding. "You're right. I should check in with the others."

"Want me to grab your laptop? We can work out here."

I nodded and reached back to grab Garrett by the collar before he headed inside, yanking him down and twisting in my seat for a quick, rough kiss. "Thank you."

He flashed me a smile, squeezing my wrist, answering me warmly in our bond.

Jamie joined me at the table as Garrett left, sinking into a chair and frowning at his own cup of coffee. My bonds with the pack were directed mainly by focus and emotion, and the ones formed to Rory and Jamie through Eve weren't as defined as the one she'd made for me and Garrett initially. Still, the shift was enough to make it clear what Jamie's appeal to Eve was. Even in a dark and worried mood, Jamie was grounding to be around, steady.

"They should be back by the end of the day," I offered. The last word we had was from before they'd gone to the club, and they'd sent us an itinerary for a flight home that would leave in a couple hours.

Jamie nodded, but remained frowning. "I wish I understood Omikron's pattern. They come to us to attack, they try and draw Eve out, then come to us again, now draw us out again. They already know where we are."

"Do you think we should've left?" I asked.

Jamie sighed and glanced out at the yard, brow furrowing. "Maybe. I appreciate the support we have here. I get that we can feel safer on our own territory, especially after blocking Omikron's efforts already. But there are advantages to anonymity too."

"Garrett thinks they're running out of resources. Maybe they're trying to do the same with us," I suggested.

Jamie's expression remained frozen. "Maybe."

Garrett returned a moment later, passing my laptop to me and opening his, the three of us gathered around the patio table together. A notification beeped on my laptop as I opened it.

DM from HuntedBiTheWolf.

I frowned, my heart pounding, and scrolled to click the conversation open.

Gaby, or Hunted, had put Faith and me up at her apartment when we were out of money and on the road. She and Faith were friends. I *needed* to trust her, but at this moment I wasn't sure I trusted anyone but my pack. Still… if there was a chance she knew something useful…

HuntedBitheWolf: there's something you need to know

I typed out a reply, my fingers shaking.

DontGiveADam: Hit me.

HuntedBiTheWolf: Beta was digging on you with me last night, trying to figure out if we'd spoken and then trying to twist you into a double agent. I told Sub about it, and they said Beta asked them to give you a lead on Faith on their behalf. That they didn't want it to fall on them if it was bogus.

I let out a whoosh of breath, my shoulders sagging. Garrett looked at me, but I shook my head and bumped my knee against his. I would explain later.

DontGiveADam: it was bogus. Om was there.

HuntedBiTheWolf: then we know

DontGiveADam: watch them, don't boot.

HuntedBiTheWolf: for a bit. we need to clean house soon.

"Adam? Is it news?" Garrett asked, nudging his knee back against mine.

I blinked at him and opened my mouth to relay the jist of the conversation when a knock sounded on our backyard gate. The three of us startled in our seats, Jamie rising up from his chair and standing in front of me like a shield.

The handle of the gate rattled, and Garrett pulled a knife from behind his back, making my eyes widen. *He's just keeping that on him now?*

"Hey, guys, sorry to drop in, but I saw you all out here and Marc got a two-for-one danish deal at the store!"

The knife was tucked away, and Jamie's tense form sagged as Hannah and Marc Graves entered the backyard, a large platter wrapped in cellophane and cheerful grins on both their faces.

"Don't lie, Han. We've been making our rounds with everyone," Marc said, wearing a sheepish grin and reaching up to smooth his thin reddish combover. "We've just never lived in a neighborhood before where everyone really makes a friendly effort."

"Trying to make that good impression," Hannah agreed, beaming.

I let out a slow breath and raised my eyebrows at Garrett. Their timing was way off, of course, but wouldn't it look weirder if we kicked them out of the yard now?

"Let me get you guys some coffee," Jamie said, gathering his manners first out of the three of us.

"I can help carry plates!" Marc offered cheerfully.

"Here, let me grab the other chairs," Garrett said, the both of us closing our laptops as he rose. He rested his hand on my shoulder, soothing me through our connection, and I stayed put.

Eve and Rory wouldn't be back until later today—hopefully—but I had Garrett and Jamie. We could play nice with the neighbors. And anyway, I'd been waiting for a chance to speak to Hannah a little more.

"How are you guys settling in?" I asked.

She had her hair up in a ponytail, and I realized that today the chemical edge of the suppressants wasn't as present, and the subtly sweet berry scent I'd caught before was now warmer and a bit sharp with spice. Her eyes were on mine, body slightly tense as Garrett pulled up a chair for her on his other side, that instinctive prey response of freezing at the proximity of an alpha.

"It's a bit strange—quiet," she corrected, laughing. "I've always lived in the city. But I guess I understand the appeal of a real community surrounding you."

I laughed at that, and Garrett smiled at me. "I'm definitely learning the same."

"Oh, of course! You and your pack are newly bonded!" Hannah said, clapping her hands together. Her gaze was sharp on mine. "It must be a dream come true."

I opened my mouth with some kind of standard omega platitude and then shut it again, leaning my knee over to Garrett's to touch. "Actually, I never really wanted a pack."

Garrett huffed out a laugh, and the door from the garage opened behind us.

"All set," Marc said.

Hannah let out a sigh and nodded, still holding my gaze. "Good, then this shouldn't be too hard for you."

I turned my head and found Marc close behind Garrett, no sign of Jamie. And then Marc's hand was thrusting forward, a needle jutting out of his fist. Alarm bells rang sudden and loud inside of me, making Garrett stiffen and turn his head, and the needle sank easily into the jugular of his throat.

And for a moment, it didn't compute at all. Marc and Hannah were older, they were a beta and an omega. They were wearing athleisure.

My alpha grunted as I let out a yelp of helpless shock, Garrett's gray eyes widening. "Run!" he gasped.

Hannah was rising from her own chair as I leapt from mine, heading for the door to the house. There was already something sluggish in my veins, or time was slowing in my panic, but I dodged easily around Marc's grasping arm as Garrett lunged at him, growl stuttering, buying me time.

My footsteps tripped as I looked backwards, my alpha grappling with the beta, already starting to sway from whatever drug he'd been injected with.

Faith's face appeared in my head, shadowed by the night, close behind me, running to the gate. I was supposed to keep going, keep running. I was supposed to find her. That was why I'd begged for Eve's bite. That was why I was here.

The door to the garage hung open, and so did the one to the house. Jamie was slouched in the doorway, passed out, and there were a few splashes of blood on the tile around him, some hint of either his or Marc's injury. Garrett groaned behind me, and my whole body was cold.

I'd left Faith that night, kept running, and it hadn't done me any good, hadn't helped me find my way back to her. I didn't want to run and leave my pack behind too. I couldn't. I couldn't leave Garrett. And Eve was coming, she was there, grasping at me in the bond. Oh. *This* was what she'd been so urgent about.

Why didn't she warn us?

I turned around and reached for the closest patio chair, opening my mouth to bellow, scream for help.

But Marc had finished with Garrett, who was sagged on the patio, fighting and failing against the drug. He tossed the chair away with easy force, wrapping an arm around my throat and clapping a hand over my mouth as I yelled.

I threw my elbow back against his ribs, and he grunted, bending slightly, but didn't let me go.

"Get them all inside before the neighborhood wakes up," Hannah said, stepping forward over Garrett's limp legs and reaching for my arm with a surprisingly firm grip, another needle in her hand. The stab to my inner elbow was quick and brutal, and I snarled and thrashed in Marc's grip. "The others will be here after it gets dark."

Others. More Omikron? Or…

"We haven't been properly introduced, Adam," Hannah said, already starting to blur in front of me. "And yet we're old friends too."

I'd thought it was a funny coincidence before, but it fit together now, almost glaringly obvious. An omega parading as a beta with a husband. The way she'd swung by the night Omikron had come to the neighborhood. Her early morning run as the pack stood together in the garage.

I opened my mouth to yell, and Marc's hand was brutally hard against my face, fingernails digging into my skin. I groaned and tried one last weak shove at the arms around me.

Hannah was swaying side to side, or I was, the dim light in the garage warping everything around us. "You know me as BetaThinkTwice on your little subvert server. More importantly, I'm Jillian Chapman, silent CEO of Omikron Investments."

Either the drugs finally kicked in or that announcement short-circuited my brain, because there was no fight left in me, only a steady rise of black and quiet and one minor shock of information.

Omikron was owned by an omega.

———

I WOKE WITH A POUNDING HEADACHE, my wrists and ankles zip-tied to the legs of one of the dining room chairs. There was a damp gag stuffed between and tied around my lips, the skin at the corners of my mouth screaming from being stretched taut. The room was blurry, but everything from the mixed scents to the cool temperature to the squeak of vinyl as I jerked in my seat told me where we were.

The basement gym, still in the pack house.

As the room focused, I found Garrett and Jamie, bound and duct-taped, heads lolling limply forward, their backs to the wall of mirrors.

"It's a convenient location," a smooth, cool tone announced.

I whipped my head to my left and found Hannah—no, Jillian—leaning against the wall, her eyes fixed on Garrett.

"Soundproofed too," she continued, pushing off the wall and heading in my direction. She was still wearing her cargo pocket leggings and sweatshirt, her hair still in the same ponytail. "I'm going to take the gag out, and you can scream if you want, but it's useless."

This woman didn't look like the figure behind a fucking scumball omega trafficking organization. She looked like a soccer mom.

Her fingers were quick on the fabric of the gag, and I watched Garrett and Jamie out of the corner of my eye. I couldn't even tell if they were breathing from here.

"We dosed them again. They're not waking up to save you," she said, pulling away the fabric.

I took in a deep gasp and then twisted to spit the excess saliva in my mouth at her. "Where's my fucking sister?"

She sneered down at the wet mark on her hip and wiped it away with the gag, tossing the whole bundle aside with a slight shudder. "I'll tell you if you tell me where

Evelyn Fadil is." I gaped at her, and she scoffed. "Oh dear, you didn't even know her real name."

Eve.

Maybe I should've been offended or shocked to be learning her name this late in our relationship, but I only took one thing from what Jillian said and I held it tight in my heart.

This bitch didn't fucking know where my alpha was. Which meant I wasn't dead in the water yet. And we were still *here*, home. Exactly where Eve was no doubt headed.

"Montreal," I rasped. "At least that's where the wild-goose chase you sent her on was located."

Jillian's eyes narrowed, and her head shook slowly. "You don't know. I mean, of course you don't because we blocked your cell phones, but I thought all those bite marks you're sporting must've been good for *something*."

"Where is Faith?" I repeated, trying to hide my relief at the knowledge that there was a *reason* why we hadn't heard from our packmates.

"Well, actually, I have no idea, and I don't care," Jillian said with a light laugh.

"The fuck you don't!" I shouted, thumping the legs of the chair on the mat beneath me, wobbling precariously before falling steady again.

"You think I waste my time with every auction sale? Your sister is purchased, paid for, and shipped. She's probably been knotted six ways from Sunday by now. Bitten, bonded, and bred," Jillian trilled as I let out a snarled scream and tried to tear my wrists out of the zip ties holding them down.

"What the fuck is wrong with you? What do you have against other omegas?" I asked, because at least if I was talking, I was still alive. Eve and Rory hadn't been caught by Omikron, which meant there was still a good chance they were on their way back. I reached in the bond and hardened my expression, my heartbeat thrumming as Eve tugged back.

"Absolutely nothing. I have some working with me, ones who don't let designation loyalty get in the way of good business," Jillian said, shrugging. There was something of the CEO about her, even in those dowdy pants and humble makeup, just the way she held herself, her feet spread and shoulders back. I'd been conned, thoroughly.

"You *sell* people to abusers," I snarled.

Jillian's lips pursed. "Oh, and have you been blissfully happy with your choice of an alpha, Adam? You look like you've been tenderized," she said, nodding at my bite marks. "And how about the Omega Center, hm? Do you think their statistics are purely perfection? You know they aren't run by omegas, don't you? They're not even a nonprofit. There's an alpha at the top of that pyramid rolling in other alphas' money, gained by the sanctioned *sale* of omegas. But you knew that. It's why you didn't want to register."

I'd been planning to register eventually, once Faith was ready, but I didn't bother mentioning as much. The Omega Center might've been a money mill, but it was generally *safe*. The choice was still the omegas'.

"Congratulations," I huffed. "You're the greater of two evils."

"Yes, but like you said, *greater*." Jillian laughed and shrugged slightly. "I would rather be the monster than be what you've let yourself become, Adam. Their hole to fill. Their *soft place to land*," she spat. "I don't hate omegas. I'm just realistic. We are a commodity, and you know as well as I do that *someone* is going to make a profit off of us. Isn't it better that person is an omega?"

I stared blankly back at her before spitting out the obvious. "Fucking *no*, it isn't."

Eve was simmering in my anger with me, like her own rage was beating through my veins and mine through hers.

"Face it, the only way for an omega to find themself on top of the food chain is if we become like them," she said, glancing over at where Jamie and Garrett sat, limp and drugged. "Well, no, not like them. Like Evelyn. Like one of the cruelest, most ruthless, most ambitious of the alphas. I'm honestly surprised you survived her."

I smiled slightly at that. I was surprised too, and then relieved and grateful, and now I was…

I was Eve's omega in the most purely basic and complete and biological way. She was my alpha. We were what the other never wanted or needed, and the only possible perfect fit.

"Ah, I see. She's on her way, isn't she?" Jillian said, studying my face, her own eyes lighting up. "That's good. I have a proposition to make to her."

I huffed at that. "I doubt that'll go over well. She's really not a fan of yours."

Jillian seemed to think on that. "You might be right," she said, reaching behind her back and pulling out a gun I hadn't seen before. "But I think she'll listen. She and I have a great deal in common, actually. And at the very least, I have collateral."

FORTY-THREE

Eve

"I shouldn't have let you drive," I hissed.

"You would've gotten us arrested five times by now," Rory snarled back.

"And *still* already home."

His hands clenched around the wheel, but we remained steady on the road. "We're nearly there," he said, low and gentle.

I opened my mouth with a growl and then shut it again. Omikron was not Rory's fault. Basic traffic laws like speeding and observing stop lights were also not his fault, although I would've preferred if he'd chosen not to observe them. We'd been on the road for eight hours, which was good time out of Montreal and south of the city, but it was still eight hours where we were out of touch with our pack. We'd only just made it over the border from Canada when that bitch Hannah had obviously made her move, the gut-wrenching anger and panic coming from my bondmates nearly sending me flying out of the car.

"I want you to get anyone from the neighborhood together—"

"Eve, no," Rory snapped.

"—and bring them to our house. I'm not saying this because I don't need you, Rory," I said as he opened his mouth to argue. That made him pause, at least. "I'm saying this because *we* need backup. She's been *right here* the whole time. If she's still here, this is our chance."

Rory sucked in a deep breath and glared at me out of the corner of his eye, turning the corner on the road into our neighborhood. It looked quiet, mundane, manicured lawns and flowerbeds and seasonal flags hanging from the front doors. Not at all like there was a hostage situation taking place in one of the pretty classic houses lining the streets.

We'd been able to alert Wes' men and our friends in the neighborhood, but neither Rory or I felt safe leaving the matter of rescuing our pack to anyone but us. The bonds were there, quiet. The others were alive. It was all I'd held onto for the entire drive.

"I know you don't need me, though," Rory said finally, releasing a sigh.

Our hands reached out at the same moment, grasping tightly onto one another.

"I mean, you certainly wouldn't be *in the way*," I said, a hollow attempt at teasing that only gained a grim smile from Rory.

"Do you see that?" he asked, nodding his head out my passenger window as he pulled to a stop at the corner of our street.

I turned my head and narrowed my eyes until I counted down to our driveway. "That's not our SUV."

"You should get out here if I'm going to sound the alarm without them noticing. Considering we've got the neighborhood and some of Wes' help monitoring, I think they've got to be working with a skeleton crew. We would've seen them shipping in a bunch of mercs," Rory said. I reached for the door handle, and he lunged forward, catching it in his hand. "Hey, wait."

I sat back, Rory trapping me to the seat, his face close and tangled. "You don't save this pack if you don't come out of this alive."

I forced myself to relax and leaned in, rubbing my cheek over his, neither of us able to purr when we were so tense, but our bond humming in rare harmony. "I'm having too much fun to die today, big guy."

Rory huffed, breath hot on my throat, but his hand released the door. "Quit calling me that, for the love of god."

"Never," I said easily, sliding out of the front seat and shutting the door behind me.

Rory turned left instead of right as I jogged down the street. "Hannah," or whoever she was, hadn't been spotted leaving our house, so presumably she was still there with the pack. She wouldn't be alone, surely she'd brought *some* reinforcements in by now, so it was just a matter of getting into the house, dealing with them, getting to wherever Adam was—

I swallowed hard, surprised to find my body tensing anxiously.

Did I want Rory with me? Would I be able to reach the others before Omikron took them out? Adam was still alive, calling to me, *believing in me* in that firm and shining way of his, a bright beacon, but both Garrett and Jamie had been silent for hours after their initial panic. I was relying on alpha instinct at this point to tell me they were still alive, and it didn't feel nearly reassuring enough.

I kept my eyes moving, searching for a sniper on any roof or in any window and coming up empty. Rory was right—they couldn't have brought in more guns without one of our team noticing.

The front door of the pack house opened, and my body tensed as a tall man stepped out. He was dressed in a black suit, holding out a shining tablet, and looked slightly nervous at the threshold of the door, like he was waiting for me to start shooting at him. Smart man. If only I had one of the guns Rory made me leave on the other side of the border.

"Where's the other one?" he asked.

Which meant they hadn't spotted Rory. "Montreal."

He had army-short brown hair and a jagged scar down one cheek. He was built bulky for a beta, and he flinched every time I stepped forward up our driveway. I caught a whiff of stress and chlorine off him as I reached the front steps.

There on the tablet facing me, was what looked like a security camera streaming from the basement. A growl rose up involuntarily from my chest at the sight of Garrett and Jamie bound and lolling to the side in chairs on either side of an alert Adam. He was staring at the camera, with the woman called Hannah behind him, the mouth of a gun pointed to his temple.

"You shouldn't have shown that to me," I snarled.

The beta stepped back, but words rushed out. "Come in quiet and you won't hear gunshots on your way down to find them."

"I can be very quiet while I kill you," I warned, but there was another man at the end of the hall behind this one, and he was holding a walkie-talkie. No, I wouldn't make it to the basement without my bondmates being shot.

The beta in front of me whipped his stare back to the man at the end of the hall and then to me again, and I gritted my teeth in a terrifying semblance of a smile. "Lead the way," I bit out.

He stumbled back with a heave of breath and hurried ahead of me, obviously trying to stay out of my reach.

There were two more men standing in the living room and another one on the staircase. A small party, definitely not one that would've stood a chance against me under other circumstances, especially considering the state of the one now opening the door to the basement, using the door as a shield he cowered behind.

"Rawr," I growled, jumping forward and snapping my teeth.

To his credit, he pulled his gun on me, even if it did shake in his hands.

"Enough," said the one behind him, who I now recognized as our dear neighbor *Marc*.

She's an omega, I remembered Adam saying. Of course the men with her would be betas. She wouldn't trust having alphas around her regularly, not when she was too busy running a massive omega trafficking ring. Alphas wouldn't be able to resist the temptation of wresting the control from her grip, if they didn't try and take a bite out of her first.

I stepped down the stairs, watching the slow reveal of first Jamie's feet, bound to the legs of our dining room chairs, then Adam's, finally Garrett's. Jamie and Garrett were still passed out, but I could almost feel their heartbeats in my chest, or at least I wanted to believe that, a wishful pulse of connection in the bond.

Adam's gaze met mine, the green vivid in his fear, even as he burst and exploded brightly inside of me. Relief, trust, confidence.

"Sugar," I greeted, ignoring the men who had their guns pointed on my packmates. "Hannah."

"Jillian, actually," the woman corrected with a faint smile.

Adam had been right, of course. I caught her perfume now, something like a too-strong bath wash and still bitter with chemicals, leaving a sudsy flavor in my mouth I wanted to spit out.

"I appreciate you making this easier," she said. "Where is Rory Stevens?"

"I didn't have time for him to fold his undies. I left him in Montreal when I realized who you were," I said.

Adam was practically clawing at me in the bond, my heart all but bleeding with his need. He wanted me to light the room up, to tear back the gun pointed at his head and turn it on his enemies. I wanted that too, but I wanted us out of this basement alive just a *tiny* bit more.

"I'm not convinced, but it doesn't matter. We don't need him," she said easily. "In fact, I think I like you better without his influence."

I tried to keep my hands loose at my sides, prepared to move, but also so the men holding guns didn't get any funny ideas about using them.

Wake up, Jamie, Garrett, I pressed. *You're in big trouble for this.*

"Oh, please don't make this boring. I've been looking forward to meeting you," Jillian said with a sigh. "Do you know, we grew up in the same house?"

I startled at that, and Adam gasped.

She smiled again. "Not at the same time, obviously. They'd sold me before you arrived."

"I don't know if Adam mentioned, but I'm not an espe-cially sympathetic person. Is there a point to this?" I asked. So she'd been in the omega house. So what? Lots of girls had, and they hadn't made an empire of exploiting one another out of it.

That smile hardened slightly, and I held myself in place, impatient with the stagnancy, with not being able to *act*.

"They sold me to the previous owner of Omikron," she said. "It wasn't what it is now. They were trafficking out of the orphanage, of course, making little soldiers out of the alpha house, but Emmett wasn't an especially ambitious or clever man until he met me."

"Adam, has she been torturing you this whole time?" I asked, rolling my eyes and studying the room. The camera was on the floor, just in front of me. There were only seven of us in here. No windows. If a gun wasn't fired and the camera wasn't on, the men upstairs might not know what happened.

"Are you acting cavalier, or do you just not love him?" Jillian parried.

"Have you been practicing your monologue for a very long time?"

"Eve," Adam gasped in exasperation as the safety on the gun clicked off. But that confidence of his didn't falter an inch. I remembered it tugging on me when I handed him over to Omikron back at the cabin, the bright bubble of hope that just kept rising up and popping. It was steady now, glaring, the lamp in the lighthouse pointed directly into my eyes.

"I gave Emmett what he needed to make Omikron what I wanted, and then I killed him," Jillian spat out, and for all her goading, at least I'd gotten her to speed it the fuck up. "I loved watching you in the alpha house, by the way. It was inspiring. You were everything I ever wanted to be."

"You should've come and tried it for yourself," I said, and her smile flattened again.

I might've gone through hell as the only female alpha, but an omega would've been eaten alive by the swarm.

"You're making me rethink my offer," she said coolly.

"You must believe it's very tempting to serve yourself up to me on a platter," I answered.

Jillian nodded once. "I do. I would like for us to call a truce. You will walk out of this house, I will walk out of this house, and if you would prefer, we'd never speak again. You would no longer be a number on the Omikron books or an item on my to-do list."

Adam's eyes widened as my heart sank.

"Your terms?" I asked, spreading my fingers flat to keep them from fisting.

"Be honest with yourself. What have you gained since you bonded this omega? What will you be giving up if you keep him?" She was digging the muzzle of the gun into Adam's temple, and if she weren't careful, if she didn't *care*, she might squeeze that trigger without even meaning to.

"Eve," Adam breathed, his brow tangling, breath hitching.

And still the bond glowed in my chest.

"Do you really picture yourself here in this little dot on a map, managing someone else's moods and desires? What will you do all day? Take up knitting?" Jillian laughed. "This is not your life. If you want men, fine, take them, but *these* ones? Law-abiding, helpful citizens. Fucking carpenters? Standing next to you, an alpha so potent and powerful, your bark could bring them to their knees."

"They look very pretty on their knees," I said simply.

"You're giving up everything to be a housewife. The entire world. I don't care if you never want to kill another person in your life, do you really want to be *bored*?"

"What are your fucking terms?" I asked again, even though I could guess.

Jamie and Garrett were stirring, little groggy muted flashes of worry and anger.

"Kill the omega. We'll take care of the others," Jillian said. "Refuse, and you'll die with your so-called pack."

"Eve," Adam sobbed out, his eyes full of tears. "Please."

Jillian was right. Of course I would lose my mind stuck in this house, playing *good alpha* for Adam for the rest of my life. Of course I didn't want to give up traveling, fighting, even killing. I was the animal this woman had watched me become, and there was no going back from that.

Adam let out a gasping cry, as if he could read my thoughts.

But he couldn't, he could only read the bond, and I closed it slowly, his body bowing forward slightly as I watched, his shuddering sobs coming faster.

"Eve, please, don't. Don't, alpha, *please*."

"What about his sister?" I asked.

Jillian shrugged. "I honestly don't know where she is, but I can guarantee she won't be an issue for you."

"Eve, please!"

"I can gag him, if it would make it easier."

Tears coursed down Adam's face, his eyes bright and shining and red with crying. He begged beautifully, as perfect and pretty as he had for my lock that first night.

Garrett stirred, groaning, his head rolling back and eyes glaring briefly against mine.

"A quick decision would be—"

"Yes," I said, holding Adam's gaze, even as he shook and shouted his pleads. "Give me a gun."

There was a pause, Jillian's eyes wide on mine, and then she turned to the man guarding a still limp Jamie. "Give her your gun."

"But—"

"Just take everything but one bullet out, she only needs one," Jillian spat out.

"Eve, please!" Adam screamed. "Please, I love you! I love you, I'll be good, alpha, please!"

Professions of love are a little much, I thought.

The beta moved, quickly popping the bullets out of the magazine until there was only one left. I stepped forward, reaching my hand out, and he hesitated before passing it to me. He scooted back into position behind Jamie, he and the other beta eyeing each other warily.

Garrett groaned behind his gag, thrashing and thumping the feet of the chairs briefly against the mat.

"Alpha," Adam gasped as I pulled on the slide, racking it and loading the bullet into the chamber.

"I've made a lot of kills for Omikron," I mused, double-checking the gun and stepping back slightly.

"You've been magnificent. If you ever decide you want back on our roster, we'd love to have you," Jillian said. She'd stepped to the side of Adam, toward the now unarmed beta.

I nodded slowly and raised the gun, pointing it directly at Adam as I stood between the camera and his chair.

He was sagged in his seat, his knees splayed out, his body soft and surrendered, chest still shaking with quiet crying. My omega, covered in my bites, my claim.

Did I want freedom? *Yes*.

"This next one's for you, sugar," I said.

Adam's chin lifted, his eyes fixed to mine, and I opened the bond.

Pure, unadulterated confidence. Pride too. Love. The glare of the sun right at the edge of the horizon.

It only took a twitch of the gun, up and to the right as I shot, far too fast for the man missing his own gun to react. The bullet struck Jillian in the head.

Garrett roared, slamming himself backwards into the beta guarding him and knocking them both back to the floor as Jamie shot up to life, doing the same to the one behind him. I kicked the camera backward and rushed forward to Garrett as the first shot went wild up at the ceiling. I lunged and grabbed onto the beta's hand, biting at it and tearing the gun free from his fingers.

The unarmed guard hadn't made it to me, and I shot him first, halfway across the room, his body falling immediately to the floor before doing the same with the one beneath me.

For a second we were all quiet, waiting, watching one another. And then Adam let out a little garbled hiccup of relief.

"You are so clever, sugar," I gasped out, sitting up and rifling through the dead guard's pockets until I found a knife. I rushed to Adam, my mouth grazing over his throat before I settled and cut the zip ties clear of his wrists and ankles.

There were footsteps thundering overhead, heading for the stairs.

"Crocodile tears are all part of the trade of a con artist," he huffed, taking the knife from me and moving to cut Garrett free. "But that was a particularly good batch if I do say so myself."

"You knew I wouldn't—"

"Of course I knew," Adam said, beaming at me. I wanted to sink my teeth right into his heart.

I scooted over to where Jamie was on his side, planting myself in front of him until Adam could free him too, pointing the gun up to the stairs.

"You could've kept the bond open!" Garrett barked at me as Adam cut him free.

The door banged open and I stepped forward,

shooting up the stairs. "I needed to focus," I shouted back. "And besides, your panic added to the realism."

"Hey. I knew you wouldn't kill him too," Garrett said, joining me at my side with a bloodied gun in his hand. Jillian's, I realized. "I just hate not feeling you."

"Jamie's still groggy," Adam said from behind us.

"Yeah, I kind of hate it too," I said softly, not sure Garrett could even hear me as he fired up at the stairs.

Suddenly, the footsteps overhead doubled, and the shouting from the stairs grew more urgent.

"Backup," I said.

"Theirs or ours?" Garrett barked.

A gunshot fired, and a man groaned, slumping down the steps.

I grinned, my shoulders easing as a moment later Rory appeared, huffing and puffing, eyes wild. "Ours," I said.

"FBI is on their way. Shit, Eve, I *told* you to try and keep her alive!" Rory snarled, glaring at the bodies over my shoulder.

"Rory, she was *very* annoying," I said, turning away from his glare and sinking down to the floor to help Adam pull Jamie away from the chair and the pooling blood.

"Good work," Jamie said, voice ragged, sitting up and sagging against my side.

I wrapped an arm around his shoulder, breathing him in, even as the air was laced heavily with the metallic tang of gore. I reached my other hand out to Adam, cupping his face.

His smile wavered, another tear spilling over the edge of his eyes.

"We will find her, Adam," I said.

He nodded, and the glow of him never wavered in the bond. Not for a second. "I know."

I pulled him in, and he came easily, lips catching once,

twice, against mine before fitting in firmly for a long kiss. I pulled away again and smirked at him. "Honestly, you omegas are *such* traps. What will you lot come up with next?"

"Fuck off," Adam said, laughing, and then he dove forward, pressing his face into my throat and sighing as I nuzzled the top of his head with my cheek. "I know for a fact you happened to like getting caught by me."

I grinned and nipped at Adam's ear. "Yeah, well, you like my trap too," I teased, waggling my eyebrows.

Rory choked in the background, growling at me. "Seriously, the FBI is coming, you need to *behave*."

"Never," Adam and I said in unison, but our alphas only scoffed and hid their smiles in response.

FORTY-FOUR

Eve

FBI Agent Hernandez was an attractive middle-aged beta, with a low twist of black hair and a slight hint of mascara. She kept us at our dinner table with two other agents for the better part of seven hours, while a team worked on documenting and cleaning the scene in the basement.

"The footage proves the case on its own," Agent Hernandez said, confirming what I'd already known. "And we had already started to point our investigation in her direction. As for the matter of self-defense—"

"We already told you, Jillian pointed her gun at Eve," Adam snapped, his leg jiggling wildly with nerves.

I set my hand on his thigh, and he settled slightly, leaning into my side.

"Yes, which conveniently took place out of view of the camera," Agent Hernandez said with a dip of her head. She glanced at the agent next to her—John Weston, Garrett's acquaintance in the FBI—the pair of them communicating wordlessly as my pack collectively held their breath.

I wasn't worried. Adam, Garrett, and Jamie had all made the statement that I shot Jillian in self-defense. If it was accepted, that certainly made things easier, but if it wasn't…

Jillian had miscalculated in her argument for why I should kill Adam. My pack didn't want to keep me here in this house, didn't want me to pretend to be any kind of alpha but what I was. And if I had to guess, they were a little sick of pretending to be normal too. If I needed to run, they would be at my side.

"I think the emotional duress you were under in the moment would make a powerful enough argument on its own," Agent Hernandez said finally, turning to stare at me with a flatness to her tone that implied she wasn't entirely convinced of my "emotional duress." "But the statements made are…adequate."

Jamie let out a slow sigh on my left, his hand falling from his lap to find mine. I wanted to drag him and the others out of the room, up into the nest. Jamie was still woozy from the drugs, but he'd been a steady rock at my side since I'd helped him step carefully up out of the basement.

"There's going to be a scramble to gain control of Omikron Investments now, and clean up any traces of Jillian's methods," Hernandez said.

"You can't possibly think they'll stop trafficking," I said.

She blinked at me and shook her head once, "No, but they'll reorganize their methods and ruin the evidence we've been working to collect. It would be best for your-selves and our investigation if you all chose to take us up on the offer of Witness Protection."

My pack all glanced at one another, and Rory cleared his throat at the far end of the table. "We aren't interested in endangering our lives any further, but..." His eyes turned to find me.

Witness Protection was a good deal and would most likely guarantee me immunity if the FBI turned up anything about my contract work in their investigation. It would also require us to pick up new and unassuming lives in a place of the FBI's choice. To check in with handlers. To be bound up in the legal matters of dismantling Omikron for the foreseeable future.

"We also aren't interested in hiding," I said, finishing Rory's thought. My pack answered gently in the bond, support and pride.

Hernandez nodded at that, her shoulders dropping slightly. "With Chapman dead, the focus should be off you for a time. We may call you in for further questioning, and we ask that you now turn over any remaining information on Omikron or their associates that you've neglected to share thus far."

"We've shared everything," Garrett said immediately, sitting forward. "But I can download the file for you."

"I'll get it," John said to Hernandez. She nodded at him, and my packmate and the other man rose to leave the room.

"What about my sister, Faith?" Adam asked.

Hernandez blinked at him and then glanced over to the third agent, who answered for her. "Your sister's missing persons case is being handled by a different team that specializes in tracking. I'm sure the changes coming in Omikron will allow for a great deal of leaked information that will assist in her recovery."

"So basically, you don't know shit about her whereabouts," I said.

Hernandez sat up, her hands tensing on the top of our

dining table. "That's someone else's job, I'm afraid, Miss Fadil. My job is legally dismantling the organization that took her and hundreds more like her. Now, I think it's time we allow the five of you to get some much-needed rest. There will be agents posted outside if you need anything."

What I needed, apparently, was to change my name again, but I ground my jaw and held my tongue as the woman and her partner rose from the table. In the bond, my pack reached out to me, tentative shields to no doubt try and keep me from lashing out. Which was useful, considering I didn't want to goad the FBI into staying in our lives longer than necessary.

"We will find her," I whispered to Adam, squeezing his thigh.

He nodded slightly, but I caught the crestfallen expression he tried to hide behind a thin smile. I couldn't blame him. We'd been saying the same for weeks. Even to my own ears, it was starting to sound like an empty promise.

Rory stood from the table and turned, and I twisted in my own seat as soon as I caught the first hint of surprise cross over his face.

"Wes," he said. "Jesus, how did you get in?"

Wes Pike stood in the frame of our dining room, watching Hernandez and a slow trail of agents head to our door. "They just let me through now that forensics is wrapping up. Where's Garrett? Are you all right?"

"I'm here," Garrett called from the stairs, John Weston following behind him. They shook hands in the hall, and then John followed his boss out of our house. I watched Garrett's hand slide into his back pocket with narrow-eyed interest, but with a slight rebuffing from him I decided to save my questions for later.

"We're…surprisingly okay," Rory said slowly, glancing at Jamie.

Jamie had come out of the drugs slowly, but his heart rate had stabilized a couple of hours ago and he mostly seemed subdued. Garrett had recovered more quickly, and aside from a few bruises and scratches, we were all spectacularly unharmed.

"The guys are checking on everyone in the neighborhood and doing a thorough sweep for any last-second trouble," Wes said.

"Thank you," I said, trying not to take too much pleasure in the way Wes narrowed his eyes at me briefly before shaking his head.

"I know they're leaving agents here, but I'm leaving some security too," Wes said.

"Hernandez seems to think this puts us off Omikron's radar," Rory said, crossing his arms over his chest.

"Maybe, but better safe than…"

"Dead," I supplied to Wes, grinning slightly.

"Be nice," Adam hissed in my ear.

"I know we've left you in the lurch recently," Garrett said.

Wes waved a hand in the air. "Nah, we're overstaffed, even with all the bookings. Don't sweat it."

"But…" Garrett glanced at Rory, who nodded once. "We have some unfinished business with Adam's sister, Faith, still missing. How would you feel about us taking a leave of absence?"

"No PTO," Rory added quickly. "We're all set on money. But maybe, if—"

"Keep your benefits," Wes said, nodding. "I get it. Take all the time you need. And resources too. Just call if we can help."

"Thank you," Adam said, sincere and sweet.

"You're proving more useful than the suits, Pike," I chimed in.

Wes' jaw ticked, but he offered us both a tight smile. "This is something I'm glad I can help with. And thank you for protecting—"

"They're *my* pack," I said, stifling my growl. "It's not a complicated choice. Oh, everyone calm down, I'm not even being that nice." I huffed as a tide of warm-fuzzies rose up in me from every direction.

"A little bit of nice goes a long way," Adam said, leaning in to kiss my shoulder and then frowning as he noticed the speckles of blood still on my skin. "We need to clean up."

"I've got cleaners on call ready to come in, but I thought you might prefer tomorrow," Wes said, and then glanced at his watch and amended, "Well, later today."

The pack exchanged a quick look before nodding in near unison. "Definitely later," Jamie said softly.

"I'll get out of your hair then, make sure everyone has headed out," Wes said with a nod, pausing as he turned. "If the FBI doesn't fuck this up, Omikron might actually fall to pieces. A lot of those girls could end up recovered. Good work."

Someone else will rise up, I thought, glancing at Adam and knowing he was thinking the same. *But not tonight*, I decided, patting Adam's leg and tipping my head.

Adam led the way to the stairs with the rest of us following. It was close to midnight, and the last few days had been exhausting, even for me. The house was falling quiet as Garrett and Rory said their goodbyes to Wes at the door and the last of the forensics team trickled out of the house. There would be a mountain of irritating technicalities to deal with in the morning, but tonight, there was only ourselves to worry about.

Our trip up the stairs was slow and weary. I smelled

like stress and blood, and I wasn't the only one. Showers were in order, and then…

And then a lot of sleep, or as much as I could manage.

Adam paused in the hall, frowning, and I ran my hand up and down his back, waiting for him to speak.

"Do you think…would you all mind staying in the nest together tonight?" Adam asked. "I just want the whole pack together."

No one answered, and it took me a moment to realize the other alphas were waiting on me, staring at me, leaving the decision in my hands.

"Shower and then meet us in the nest," I said to Rory and Jamie, who both nodded.

The adrenaline had burned away after hours of sitting around and repeating the same information over and over to Hernandez. Garrett and I undressed Adam with slow and gentle touches, before stripping ourselves more efficiently.

"Keep your chin up," I said to Adam as we stepped under the spray in the large tiled shower.

I leaned forward and kissed his chin, some of my bite marks, his lips, as Garrett worked shampoo into Adam's hair. Together, we made sure his face was up and he couldn't see the blood washing off of us and down the drain.

"You're all right," Garrett murmured, wrapping his arms around us both as I washed my own hair.

"I knew you would come," Adam said to me. "So I didn't have to keep running. And I didn't want to leave you behind," he added, stretching back to rest his head against Garrett's shoulder.

The water was loud and our words were quiet and the bond was just a gentle flow of information between everyone. Adam's exhausted relief. Garrett's comfort in having us all together and safe. Jamie was rinsing off some of his stress, and Rory was ticking along calmly, hurrying to join us.

"Next time you have to beg me for your life, you can make it a little *less* dramatic," I teased, rubbing my cheek against Adam's, laughing over his shoulder as Garrett swatted my ass.

"Hey, my dramatics worked," Adam said, arching an eyebrow. "You really think she was just going to hand you a gun if I just sat there smiling at you like I knew you'd never kill me?"

"Oh, alpha, please, I *love you*," I whined in a high-pitched imitation of his sobbing.

Adam glared at me, fighting the twitch of his lips. "I do love you, you bi—"

I covered his mouth with mine and answered the words in the bond rather than out loud.

"You two are going to give me gray hairs," Garrett mumbled, washing us both with long strokes of his hands.

"You'll be very handsome with gray," I said, nipping Adam's throat.

Garrett's cheeks pinked, and he beamed back at me. "We'll see."

We finished the shower after a little more petting and reassurance, and Jamie was already down in the nest when we made it out. I paused as Adam and Garrett both settled down into the pit with a blanket to share, leaving a space for me between them and Jamie.

"You gonna be okay with a crowd?" Jamie asked me.

I didn't like to be surrounded. But that was true before I'd found these fools, before they'd carved a space for me in their mix, made it fit me perfectly so I never felt pressed in upon.

"I'll be fine. Tell me what's wrong," I answered.

Jamie's frown was brief but deep. "Marc got the jump on me. I stayed here to protect—"

I leaned in and gripped Jamie's face in my hands, kissing him roughly and thoroughly. "We all made mistakes in this. Mine was thinking it would be better if we weren't all together. Now I know better. And now we all know better than to trust sneaky omegas."

"Eve," Adam groaned as Garrett tried to stifle a laugh.

Jamie's smile was soft in response, and I relaxed as he leaned in, brushing a kiss over one cheekbone and then another across my forehead.

"Next time, together," Jamie murmured.

"*Next* time?" Garrett squawked.

For a brief moment, my own luck struck me, hard and quick. I was not a woman who deserved these men. I was not an alpha who ought to have a claim on an omega. I was not a good person. But I had chosen this pack, not quite for myself, and they were proud to be mine.

I was proud to be theirs too.

I batted the thoughts away before I could say something absurd like, *I love you all.* Especially while Rory wasn't in the room.

I stepped down into the nest and settled myself on my side, Jamie at my back. My hand rested over Adam's chest, tangling with Garrett's fingers. A moment later, the door opened and Rory came stomping in, not even bothering with studying our geometry before helping himself to a spot above our heads, his hand passing briefly over my cheek.

"Coffee timer is set," he said. "I'll make breakfast. Anyone need anything?"

"We're good, big guy," I said, and he let out a quiet

growl before we all settled into comfortable, harmonious, quiet.

———

THE NEXT MORNING, I was wondering if I'd made the right choice.

No, I wasn't, but I was feeling extremely irritated by the absurd domesticity taking place.

"Really?" I asked, my teeth biting around my toothbrush as I glared into the mirror at Rory standing at my back.

His reflection shrugged. "Didn't wanna be left out."

The five of us stood together at the counter in the nest bathroom…brushing our teeth. Garrett nudged my hip, and I grimaced, stepping aside for him to spit.

"I think it's cute," Adam mumbled around his own toothbrush.

It was disgustingly mundane and somewhat charming, which probably qualified as the same thing.

Garrett stepped back, perching himself on the end of the counter, and Jamie took his place.

"There's something I need to tell you guys," Garrett said.

"Anything to do with this?" I asked, lifting up the flash-drive I'd pulled from Garrett's pockets this morning when I'd entered the bathroom.

He just smiled and nodded at me, not remotely surprised by my theft. "Yeah. John gave me that. We…kind of swapped info last night. That's everything the FBI has on Omikron. Lotta names of potential customers."

I stared at Garrett as the pack went quiet around me, little flickers and hints of excitement rising from my bondmates.

"There's no way the FBI is gonna manage to serve time to every one of those names," Jamie said, stepping back and catching my eye.

"Plea deals," Adam muttered.

"Insufficient evidence," Rory added with a nod.

My eyes narrowed. "Weren't we specifically asked to *stay out* of the way?"

"I mean, we certainly shouldn't interfere," Garrett said with a solemn nod.

"But we could…clean up any loose ends," Rory suggested with a shrug.

I huffed and rinsed my mouth, slotting my toothbrush into the little holder and stepping away from the counter to glare at the four men playing innocent as their humor and anticipation wriggled in the bond.

"It's not like Omikron's the only fish in the game," Adam said slowly, pausing to rinse his mouth. "There's other organizations like them overseas too. I bet they even trade, make deals."

"Quit playing coy," I growled out.

Jamie laughed. "We're just saying…we happen to have a very specific skill set—"

"Carpentry?" I quipped.

"Come on," Rory purred, grinning at me in the reflection of the mirror, mouth foamy and eyebrows waggling. "You have money, right?"

Maybe not enough to set us up for life, if the life was vigilante justice against sex traffickers but…yes, I had money.

"You know you think it sounds fun, Eve," Adam said with a roll of his eyes.

"What about your heats?" I asked.

"Jamie, would you drive the Charger while Eve and

Garrett fuck me in the backseat?" Adam asked Jamie, and I tried not to choke on my laugh.

"Can I crack a window?" Jamie asked, pretending to think it over.

"Your house," I pressed. "Your lives."

"It's just a house. What are you going to do if we try and just…live here? I don't trust you with knitting needles. You'd definitely stab me the first time I annoyed you," Garrett teased.

I glared at them, but it ran over and over in my head. We would be in danger. Hunted. We'd be traveling constantly, running missions, taking new names, finding new hiding spots together when we needed to lay low.

It *would* be fun. With them. Much more so than if I were alone.

"Faith is first," I said, turning my head to the side, as if I could hide from the tender softness of Adam's response in the bond.

"Faith is first," Rory agreed.

"I'll consider the rest," I said, fighting my smile.

Disguises, injuries, constantly being stuck together as we ran for our lives, as we destroyed the lives of men and women who tried to buy the bodies of those weaker than them.

It would be a hard, exhausting, potentially ugly life. Maybe even a short one, if we weren't careful.

Rory would make sure we were careful. Garrett would make sure Adam was happy when things grew too dark. Jamie would remind me to be human, to loosen my fists and unclench my jaw.

I would make sure they were safe. They were mine now, and I would keep them.

"Breakfast?" Adam suggested.

"I'm taking requests, within reason," Rory said with a nod.

I hummed and reached out for Adam's hand, squeezing it tightly in my own as he reached back.

"I love you," I whispered in his ear. Adam's breath hitched, and his eyes widened on mine as we walked out of the bathroom and through the nest together. "You knew."

"I hoped," he said, grinning back at me.

Epilogue

ADAM

Two Weeks Later

"Any ideas why she dragged us here?" Garrett asked, leaning on me as he and I slowly circled the roller rink, vintage pop blaring over the speakers in time with the spinning colored lights.

I laughed and shook my head, watching Eve winding spirals around a poorly-coordinated Rory, Jamie tagging along out of their way. "I sort of just assumed she really wanted to go roller-skating."

Garrett grinned at that and shook his head. "She's changed."

Rory's arms flapped out at his side as his feet started to stumble, sliding forward and then up and out from under him. He landed on the polished floor ahead of us with a groan, quickly interrupted by Eve's bright cackle of laughter.

"Not that much," I said, grinning.

Which was true—Eve was still cool and removed now that we'd settled down a little since she'd killed Jillian. I didn't know what she did most of the day, and sometimes she took off in the Charger without warning any of us.

But she always came back. She kissed me and petted at me and purred in that rough almost-growl of hers, and she almost *always* kept the bond open.

"You don't mind not being at home on the server?" Garrett asked me.

"I think I needed a break, actually," I said, my grin faltering.

The server had changed its tune on me since word of Jillian's death started leaking out of the cracks. Suddenly everyone supported me again, even if they still didn't have any useful information. It meant a constant barrage of useless messages, and it was getting distracting from what I actually wanted. My sister.

"It's only a matter of time," Garrett said, and I nodded, even if the promise sounded a little hollow.

Eve twirled as Jamie helped pull Rory back up on his feet, and then she paused suddenly, staring over my shoulder. I slowed to a stop with Garrett and stiffened as Eve sped close to us. Was it more mercenaries? Was Jillian's successor after us?

"I have someone I want you guys to meet," Eve said, smiling over my shoulder and waving.

I turned and looked at the crowd of people milling around the rink, but I had no idea which of the many unfamiliar faces might be the one Eve had waved at. Jamie and Rory followed us as we turned and headed for the cafeteria seating, and I thought I caught Rory's sigh of relief as we reached the carpeting.

There was a massive-looking bear of a man sitting alone at a table, eating a tray of french fries by himself but, nope, Eve passed him. She passed another table with a pair of severe and eerie pale twins. And then another of an older gentleman in a suit…

I frowned as we stopped suddenly, a young woman with a head full of rainbow twined braids and a pair of yellow tinted sunbeam-shaped glasses grinning up at us.

"Hey, danger, got you your fave," she said, sliding a cardboard basket of cheese-coated fries to Eve, and then she tipped her head to look around me and saluted Rory with a cup of neon slushie. "Mr. Tightie Whities."

Rory grunted. "Tabitha."

My eyes widened. This was *Tabby*. Eve had only given me little scraps of information about her, and now we were here, meeting her.

"You must be sugar," she greeted me, before waggling her eyebrows at Eve, "He *is* pretty."

I sank down on the bench seat next to Eve as the others stole chairs from surrounding tables and pulled them up to the sides.

Eve's arm draped over my shoulder, and she leaned in, kissing my cheekbone. "Yes, he is. You said you had news."

"Oh boy, do I," Tabby said, grinning. "It's honestly been a goldmine since you sent Jill tumbling down the hill, but here's the best of it."

Tabby set a folded piece of paper on the table between us, and Eve slid it to me.

I blinked at them both and then opened the piece of paper to find an address scrawled out in pink highlighter.

"Faith was auctioned to a fairly new gang who set up shop near the gulf this past year," Tabby said gently. "I can't get any more information at the moment, they've gone dark, but that's the address where she was shipped to—"

I winced at that and tried to swallow down the sudden strangling sensation in my throat.

"—and it's just a seedy little bar and liquor store with apartments above. Pretty sure it's their base."

I couldn't breathe. I just kept staring at every letter, every number written out on the page.

"This is…this is where Faith is?" I gasped out, staring up at Tabby, and then to Eve.

"I think so," Tabby said gently. She had a nice smile, and I couldn't decide if I wanted to leap across the table to tackle her with a hug or grab my pack and run out the door.

"It's a lead," Eve said, her hand under my collar, rubbing gently over one of her marks.

"From a reliable source," Rory nodded.

"Aw, thanks, big guy," Tabby said, grinning back at him.

"Is this why you packed bags for us?" Jamie asked Eve.

I sat up, my mouth hanging open and Eve grinned slyly back at me. "I thought you might want to head out right away," she said. "Charger is ready to go."

Garrett nudged Eve with his knees, a soft smile on his face. "What a good alpha you're turning out to be."

She scoffed, but I leaned in and grabbed her face in my hands, dragging her in for a sudden smacking messy kiss. "The best," I said, beaming at her and then turning to Tabby. "Thank you! So much! You have no idea."

She waved at me and shrugged. "All in a day's work worth doing. Good luck, you cuties."

"Here," Eve said, sliding the little banana flash drive she'd brought to Garrett back in the old safe house across to Tabby. "See what you can start pulling?"

"You got it, danger."

"We're leaving?" I asked Eve, my hands digging into the fabric of her jumpsuit around her waist.

"We'll drive all night, sugar," Eve said, pinching my

chin in her fingers and drawing me in for a licking kiss. "It'll be faster and safer than worrying about a flight. Plus, I packed weapons in the Charger."

We barely all fit in the Charger, but I liked it cozy. It was like having a second nest full of my pack.

"We've got two weeks before my heat starts," I reminded her.

"Plenty of time," she purred. "I don't plan on *asking* them to give her up. We'll be in and out with her in no time."

"Okay, but give the keys to Jamie," I said.

Jamie laughed, but he pulled the keys out of Eve's pocket and rose from the table. "I'll go get her started."

"What does my pretty little omega need?" Eve purred, rising from the table and taking me with her like a fish on her hook.

"You," I said, grinning. "Backseat."

"This is going to be torture," Rory said to Garrett.

"You'll get your turn," Garrett laughed. "Anyway, Jamie is the one who has to drive."

"We'll scandalize the whole expressway," Eve purred in my ear.

"Or at the very least, Rory," I agreed. "I love you, alpha."

Eve tossed her hair over her shoulder and flashed me a feral smile. "Of course you do. What's not to love?"

The End

DON'T WORRY!

Faith and the Dead End Devils is now available for pre-order!

Be sure to check out the first book in the Sweetverse:

Baby + the Late Night Howlers
By Kathryn Moon

Baby's heat is coming...
After years of assuming she was a beta, discovering her omega designation in a biker bar surrounded by alphas isn't exactly fulfilling any fantasies for Baby. She only wanted to have a fun night, not get knotted, bitten, and bonded. Now Baby's entire life is about to turn upside down.

With her heat on its way, she needs to find a pack, a nest, and alphas she can trust.

The Late Night Howlers have given up hope...
After years of waiting for an omega to choose them, this motorcycle club of alphas is ready to move on with their lives. Until one sweet woman takes a chance on them.

A rundown bar and apartment building is no place to spoil a new omega but the Howlers are determined to do right by Baby when she needs them. All they have to do is keep her satisfied while resisting the mouthwatering temptation to bite and bond her, permanently.

When a rival MC comes sniffing after Baby, her safety is put at risk and the Howlers may be torn apart forever.

Lola & the Millionaires duet
By Kathryn Moon

Lola Barnes only wants one thing, to get her life under control. No more chasing alphas who abuse and toss away betas like her. No more hiding in her cousin's apartment licking wounds that won't heal. Armed with her dream job and her less than dreamy apartment, Lola is ready to start a new chapter of her life without alphas.

But that's easier said than done when one stumbling incident after another leads Lola closer to an alluring pack of captivating men. These alphas are everything Lola dreamed of, but they already have an omega—a playful male model who won't stop flirting with her. And Lola is only a beta, one who comes with deep scars and an unshakeable aversion to alphas and their powerful presences. If only she could resist their perfect beta, Leo, whose patience and determination to see her heal breaks down one wall after another.

When the alpha who all but destroyed Lola tries to start a game of cat and mouse that's all claws, the safest place for Lola may be the one she's most terrified of, in the arms of an alpha pack.

As well as author Lana Kole's books:

Lyric & the Heartbeats

A stubborn omega...
After years of wishing, Lyric's dream is finally coming true. She's landed her first tour, when all her life she's been told to settle and find herself a pack. Now she can prove that she's more than her omega designation, more than the perfect mold her mother tried to force her to fit in. All she needs is a band.

Bruised hearts from broken pasts...
After collecting a talented team of musicians, Lyric's dreams can come true. Living on the road with a band is a lot like having a pack, and fighting her own nature is hard enough without worrying about why these alphas watch her like circling hawks.

A pack of misfits...
Between four alphas and a beta who are as sweet as they are sinful focusing all of their attention on Lyric, her independent will weakens every day.
By the end of tour, can she break down her prejudices and open up to the five men who would do anything for her?

Fighting Instincts
by Lana Kole

As an omega, Stellan is supposed to want a pack. Instead, he wanted Elise, another omega.

She followed her instincts. Stellan fought his.
Left behind, Stellan tries to move on with a heart as broken and bruised as his opponents after a fight in the ring. Fighting is all he has, and as an omega, he breaks all the odds. When a bid goes bitter, he's forced to pay it back with his own blood. At least until he's rescued by a handsome alpha and taken home to his pack.

A pack that already has an omega.
Face to face with the omega who left him, Stellan will have to fight his own instincts to find happiness.
Fate brought them back together, and this time, Stellan isn't letting Elise go, no matter what opponents they have to face.

And coming soon...
All Packed Up by Lana Kole

Also by Kathryn Moon

COMPLETE READS

The Librarian's Coven Series

Written - Book 1

Warriors - Book 2

Scrivens - Book 3

Ancients - Book 4

Summerland Series

Summerland Stories, the complete collection plus bonus content

Standalones

Good Deeds

Command The Moon

Say Your Prayers - co-write with Crystal Ash

The Sweetverse

Baby + the Late Night Howlers

Lola & the Millionaires - Part One

Lola & the Millionaires - Part Two

Bad Alpha

Sol & Lune

Book 1

Book 2

Inheritance of Hunger Trilogy

<u>The Queen's Line</u>

<u>The Princess's Chosen</u>

<u>The Kingdom's Crown</u>

<u>SERIES IN PROGRESS</u>

Sweet Pea Mysteries

The Baker's Guide To Risky Rituals

The Knitter's Guide to Banishing Boyfriends

Tempting Monsters

A Lady of Rooksgrave Manor

The Company of Fiends

Acknowledgments

Thank you so much to all the readers who dove in head first to the Sweetverse and fell in love with this interpretation of the rich and wonderfully wide land of omegaverse. You've changed my life and I'm so grateful to you.

And for this book, thank you to:

Moonstruck Cover Design and Photography, whose incredible work perfectly captured the magnificence of Eve.

Meghan Leigh Daigle, my loving and incredibly patient editor who took on extra hats to help with this book. Jess Whetsel for her keen perfectionist eye.

The Beta Babes: Desiree, Chloe, Helen, Jami, Amanda, Ash, Jess, and Elizabeth.

My amazing Moongazers who cheer me on each and every step!

All my writing babes, near and far, who inspire and motivate me. Every month this group of authors and future authors grows larger and I can't tell you how incredibly lucky I feel to know you all.

My Mom, brother, sister-in-law, and nieces for being excited for me without telling everyone they know my pen name. Dad, you see that? No, you don't, because you're not allowed to read my books so QUIT TELLING YOUR FRIENDS ABOUT THEM.

About the Author

Kathryn Moon is a country mouse who started dictating stories to her mother at an early age. The fascination with building new worlds and discovering the lives of the characters who grew in her head never faltered, and she graduated college with a fiction writing degree. She loves writing women were are strong in their vulnerability, romances that are as affectionate as they are challenging, and worlds that a reader sinks into and never wants to leave. When her hands aren't busy typing they're probably knitting sweaters or crimping pie crust in Ohio. She definitely believes in magic.

You can reach her on Facebook and at ohkathrynmoon@gmail.com or you can sign up for her newsletter!